Praise for
If For Any Reason

"Warm and inviting, *If For Any Reason* is a delightful read. I fell in love with these characters and with my time in Nantucket. Don't miss this one!"

Robin Lee Hatcher, award-winning author of *Who I Am With You*

"*If For Any Reason* took me and my romance-loving heart on a poignant journey of hurt, hope, and second chances . . . From tender moments to family drama to plenty of sparks, this is a story to be savored. Plus, that Nantucket setting—I need to plan a trip pronto!"

Melissa Tagg, award-winning author of *Now and Then and Always*

Just Let Go

"Walsh's charming narrative is an enjoyable blend of slice-of-life and small-town Americana that will please Christian readers looking for a sweet story of forgiveness."

Publishers Weekly

"Original, romantic, and emotional. Walsh doesn't just write the typical romance novel. She makes you feel for all the characters, sometimes laughing and sometimes crying along with them."

Romantic Times

"A charming story about discovering joy amid life's disappointments, *Just Let Go* is a delightful treat for Courtney Walsh's growing audience."

Rachel Hauck, *New York Times* bestselling author

"*Just Let Go* matches a winsome heroine with an unlikely hero in a romantic tale where opposites attract. . . . This is a page-turning, charming story about learning when to love and when to let go."

Denise Hunter, bestselling author of *Honeysuckle Dream*

Just Look Up

"Just the kind of story I love! Small town, hunky skier, a woman with a dream, and love that triumphs through hardship. A sweet story of reconciliation and romance by a talented writer."

Susan May Warren, *USA Today* bestselling author

"[A] sweet, well-paced story. . . Likable characters and the strong message of discovering what truly matters carry the story to a satisfying conclusion."

Publishers Weekly

"Just Look Up by Courtney Walsh is a compelling and consistently entertaining romance novel by a master of the genre."

Midwest Book Review

"This novel features a deeply emotional journey, packaged in a sweet romance with a gentle faith thread that adds an organic richness to the story and its characters."

Serena Chase, *USA Today* Happy Ever After blog

"In this beautiful story of disillusionment turned to healing, Walsh brings about a true transformation of restored friendships and love."

Christian Market magazine

Change of Heart

"Walsh has penned another endearing novel set in Loves Park, Colorado. The emotions are occasionally raw but always truly real."

Romantic Times

"*Change of Heart* is a beautifully written, enlightening, and tragic story. . . . This novel is a must-read for lovers of contemporary romance."

Radiant Lit

Paper Hearts

"Walsh pens a quaint, small-town love story . . . [with] enough plot twists to make this enjoyable to the end."

Publishers Weekly

"Be prepared to be swept away by this delightful romance about healing the heart, forgiveness, [and] following your dreams."

Fresh Fiction

"Walsh writes a small-town setting, a sweet, slow-building romance between two likable characters, and a host of eclectic secondary characters."

Romantic Times

"*Paper Hearts* is as much a treat as the delicious coffee the heroine serves in her bookshop. . . A poignant, wry, sweet, and utterly charming read."

Becky Wade, author of Christy-award winning *Falling For You*

ALSO BY COURTNEY WALSH

Harbor Pointe Novels
Just One Kiss
Just Look Up
Just Let Go

Nantucket Love Stories
If for Any Reason
Is it Any Wonder (April 2021)

Loves Park Novels
Change of Heart
Paper Hearts

Women's Fiction
Hometown Girl
Things Left Unsaid

Sweethaven Novels
A Sweethaven Summer
A Sweethaven Homecoming
A Sweethaven Christmas
A Sweethaven Romance (Novella)

COURTNEY WALSH

Visit Courtney Walsh's website at www.courtneywalshwrites.com.

Just Like Home

Copyright © 2020 by Courtney Walsh. All rights reserved.

Sweethaven Press

Designed by Jennifer MacKey of Seedlings Design

Edited by Charlene Patterson

The author is represented by Natasha Kern of Natasha Kern Literary, Inc.

PO Box 1069, White Salmon, WA 98672

Just Like Home is a work of fiction. Where real people, events, establishments, organizations, or locales appear, they are used fictitiously. All other elements of the novel are drawn from the author's imagination.

For information about special discounts for bulk purchases, please contact Courtney Walsh Publishers at courtney@courtneywalsh.com

Library of Congress Cataloging-in-Publication Data

Printed in the United States of America

"I'm still learning to love the parts of myself that no one claps for."
—Rudy Francisco

Dear Charlotte,

It's so boring to start a letter talking about the weather, but I'm going to do it anyway because A. I'm from the Midwest, and B. It's felt like the longest winter of my life here in Harbor Pointe. Finally—finally—I see a glimmer of sunshine, and its warmth is the stuff dreams are made of.

The winter wasn't all bad, of course—my brother Cole led his team to their first ever state title, and while that probably seems like small potatoes to you, it was a huge deal around here. And believe me, after what he's been through, Cole needed the boost.

But now, it's almost summer. And summer in Harbor Pointe, I'm sure I've told you, is like magic. People sometimes ask me why I still live here, in Michigan, in the Midwest, in this ice-cold tourist town, but those people are quiet once they experience a Harbor Pointe summer.

My mornings always start at Hazel's Kitchen, a tiny diner run by my friend Betsy. Even when the tourist crowd shows up, the local crowd rarely thins because we've all become so reliant on Betsy and her baked goods.

Since we're a tourist town, you can imagine all the new people filtering through this place. There are cottages rented months in advance, everyone clamoring for the perfect view of Lake Michigan. And this place delivers. The sunsets would take your breath away.

Then, of course, there are all the festivals. I swear, there's one every weekend in the summer (and even a few in the winter!). There are corn boils and luminary walks and concerts in the park. The downtown comes to life with foot traffic and, for a little while anyway, we convince ourselves that we're in a place where time has stopped.

Because that's how it feels.

I hope you find pockets of this feeling there in the city. I hope it fills you up and inspires you, but I also really hope you're taking care of yourself, Charlotte. I saw a photo of you online last week (I have my Google alerts on for your name so I can keep up with all the beautiful things in your career), and I have to say—you look thin. Are you eating? Does Marcia let you have the occasional carb?

What I wouldn't give to come there and kidnap you, even for a week or two. You could use a week of fun.

Okay, I have to run. Duty calls. I have a bunch of tiny dance costumes to sort through for recital this spring. I'll send photos—all these squishy little ballerinas are going to make even you fall in love.

One of these days I'm going to get back to Chicago to see you dance again. I just know you're even more amazing than you were the last time.

xoxo,
Jules

1

"Death comes unexpectedly."

It was a line from the old Disney movie *Pollyanna*, from a scene Charlotte Page had never forgotten. She'd been terrified by that minister, slamming his fist and yelling such a horrible sentiment—but she understood now. Because death did indeed come unexpectedly.

The thought waged war with her emotions, but she held it together—barely. She wasn't prone to tears, and even though this funeral was only the second she'd attended in her thirty years, she'd decided in the car on the way here not to cry.

Or maybe she simply couldn't because she was still in shock. Maybe losing your best friend only months past her thirtieth birthday was the kind of life event that never made sense, no matter how long you lived.

Nothing about it felt real. From the second she got the phone call, she'd been in a sort of thick fog, and as of this very moment, sitting in the pew of a little church in Harbor Pointe, Michigan, it hadn't lifted.

I'm so sorry.

The words pelted her without permission. She hated that they did. She hated that she'd never said it in person. She hated that Julianna was gone now and she'd lost her chance.

Death comes unexpectedly.

The Harbor Pointe Community Church hummed with conversation, appropriately low and quiet in tone and volume. Charlotte spoke to no one. After all, she knew no one. She wasn't a part of Julianna's community. Their friendship stretched back years, but there was a gap now because their paths had diverged so smartly nearly a decade before.

At the front of the church, on an easel, was an enlarged photo of Julianna, taken just last year, beaming, as she always was, and surrounded by her young children. The frozen image smiled back at Charlotte, a bittersweet reminder of how it felt to be the recipient of her undivided attention. Jules never did anything halfway, including friendship. She was the most genuine soul Charlotte had ever known.

And this—her death—was one of life's great injustices.

That hot, burning lump in the back of her throat flared up, reminding her that she would carry this sadness inside her for a very long time. Maybe for the rest of her life. How would she ever get over this loss? It was too tragic, too sudden, too soon.

Too unfair.

Music signaled the start of the service and Julianna's family entered. Her husband, Connor, walked in with their three beautiful children, bigger than Charlotte remembered.

Connor's lifeless eyes focused straight ahead, like a man in a trance walking a straight line to the gas chamber.

Charlotte looked away, not wanting to stare. Her eyes fell to Julianna's oldest, a daughter named Amelia. A dancer. Julianna's mini-me.

The little girl held her dad's arm as they walked down the aisle, stoic and somber. Alaina, the baby, was in Connor's other arm. A twinge of guilt and sorrow mixed together at the back of Charlotte's throat.

Why did this happen?

She pulled her eyes back to the aisle, thinking it was strange for the family to be on display like this. Wouldn't it have been less conspicuous for them to have been seated first so they could avoid what she had to imagine was unwanted attention?

Her thoughts had run away from her, but the sight of a familiar yet unfamiliar face pulled her back to the present.

Cole.

Julianna's brother had grown up and filled out. He was a man. A solid brick of a man—not the "cute boy" she remembered from all those years ago.

Teenage insecurities pummeled her, renewed like an overdue library book.

Sometimes Julianna's letters had mentioned him, and even seeing his name sent a strange shiver down her spine. Charlotte had always been somewhat sheltered, but she knew a cute boy when she saw one. Cole was cute. More than cute. He was older and cooler and so very good-looking.

And Julianna clearly adored him, even back then.

After she met him when she was a young teen, Charlotte wondered if he'd ever cross her path again. He came for the occasional performance, but mostly he remained a mystery. An unsolved mystery. Which meant her mind could conjure whatever image it wanted to of him, and it did. She didn't know Cole in real life, not really—but that wasn't stopping her heart from racing now.

Her eyes followed him down the aisle where he slid into the pew next to Connor. Gently, Cole took the baby from her father, then motioned for AJ, the middle child, to move closer to him. He might be a solid brick of a man, but he clearly loved those kids.

And she could practically feel the weight of his broken heart.

Julianna's father—a little grayer than she remembered—sat in the pew behind Cole with his "other family," as Jules called them.

The music quieted and a man in a suit stepped onto the stage. He spoke about Julianna like he knew her, said she was a member of this church—not the kind who simply attended, but the kind who got involved. She ran a tutoring club and attended women's events. She served in children's church and—

Charlotte stopped listening, choosing instead to focus on the movie in her mind.

She closed her eyes, a clear picture of herself at age twelve, small-chested and slim and self-conscious, making up for all of her insecurities with a brave, albeit sour, face.

The summer dance intensive was held in Chicago every year, but this was her first year to attend. According to her mother, she'd outgrown her current dance instructor and needed a new challenge. They called it "dance camp" but it was unlike any camp Charlotte knew of.

There were no cabins, no outdoor adventures, no sunshine or swimming. There were only dorm rooms and dance studios.

Charlotte was thrilled with that arrangement. She'd never been good at socializing, so when she found herself standing at the barre, waiting for her first class to begin, she didn't feel the need to say anything to the blond girl standing beside her. The two girls were each dressed in their mandatory black leotard, pink tights, and pink ballet shoes, their hair pulled neatly into a tight bun, looking like clones of each other and every other girl filtering into the room.

Charlotte lifted her hand to the barre and glanced at her own reflection in the mirror. Her eyes darted to a pair of big, bright eyes trained on her.

"You're Charlotte Page, right?" the blonde asked, her smile wide.

Charlotte nodded but didn't speak. Her mother had warned her about making friends in ballet class.

"You're not here for socialization," Marcia had said. "You're here to tighten your technique, to get a competitive edge. You're here to be the best."

"But then the other girls won't like me," Charlotte had said.

"Good," her mother said. "You don't want to be liked, Charlotte. You want to be respected. You want them to fear you."

No, I don't. I want them to like me.

But Charlotte had only nodded.

"I've heard about you," Julianna said with a smile. "What's it feel like to be the best dancer in our form?"

Julianna didn't seem to be flattering her—the expectant look on her face suggested she genuinely wanted an answer to her question. Charlotte had been taught to believe she was the best, and though she knew about humility now, she certainly didn't then.

"My mother says I'm the best dancer in the entire camp," she'd said.

Julianna blinked twice, her big eyes trained on Charlotte. "My mother told me to have fun."

Charlotte looked away, her gaze catching those of two girls on the other side of the room. They whispered to each other, looked Charlotte up and down, then giggled.

"Don't pay attention to them," Julianna said. "They're just jealous."

Charlotte looked at her. "I know they are."

That Julianna wasn't deterred by twelve-year-old Charlotte's attitude was still something of a miracle to her. They'd joked about it many times, but in truth, Charlotte had Jules to thank for teaching her what it meant to be modest and humble. Lord knew her mother wasn't going to teach her either of those things.

Julianna had shown Charlotte that it was possible to be liked *and* respected, despite what Marcia told her.

And how had Charlotte repaid her? With a stab in the back.

No. I'm not thinking about that now.

Connor hadn't moved a muscle since he sat down. At his side, Cole handled the kids like a pro, like a man clearly involved in their lives. She knew nothing about Julianna's brother anymore, only that he was the Harbor Pointe High School football coach, but seeing him with those kids told her he was kind and tender, in spite of how he must be feeling at the moment.

Would he remember her?

What a ridiculous thought. Of course he wouldn't. They weren't friends, after all. In Charlotte's life, only Julianna seemed to wear that title.

What did you do when your only friend died? How did a person recover from that?

The pastor was still talking, regaling the crowd (and it was a crowd) with tales of Julianna Ford, a light in their community, a woman known for her infectious joy, her zest for life, her passion for teaching her young students. Charlotte tried to listen, but it was hard. Her own memories were coming quickly now, as if a projector had been switched on and now played through her and Julianna's greatest hits.

Auditions, rejections, victories, good reviews, bad reviews, professional tours, and finally—after a lot of hard work—both of them becoming part of the company of the Chicago City Ballet. When they were apart, they wrote letters, and when they were together, Charlotte felt an ease in her loneliness.

It was the kind of friendship that couldn't be replaced, no matter how many years passed. Charlotte knew in that moment there would never be another Julianna.

She'd never known a truer friend or had a bigger cheerleader. To Jules, they were never competitors. It shamed Charlotte to think that she had never been able to offer that in return.

Alaina, Julianna's youngest, let out a squeal. Cole shifted her on his lap and the baby quieted. She was only ten months old. She wouldn't have a single memory of her mother.

How did this young family have a hope of moving forward without Julianna? She was the kind of mom Charlotte wished she'd had. Kind. Attentive. Involved. Fun. The kind who held families together like glue.

By contrast, Charlotte's mother was controlling and manipulative and, in all ways, *not* fun. Once a prima ballerina in her own right, Marcia Page had been sidelined by an injury, and Charlotte was pretty sure she still carried a grudge against the world over what she viewed as one of life's greatest injustices.

Marcia had turned all of her attention to Charlotte when she was just a child, pouring every professional hope and dream she'd had into the daughter she said wasn't naturally talented but who, with her help and a lot of hard work, could learn to be great.

How cliché.

As it was, Marcia Page was now a renowned dance instructor. One of the greats, if Charlotte was honest, and she had turned her daughter into a superior, enviable dancer.

But as a mother, the woman left much to be desired. Charlotte's relationship with Marcia had always felt a lot like a business arrangement, which was probably why Marcia deemed it her place to try and convince Charlotte that leaving to attend the funeral was a huge mistake, one that would open the door for up-and-coming dancer Irena Duryea to step in and steal all her solos.

"You're not the hottest new thing anymore, Charlotte. Don't give them a reason to realize it."

By now, Charlotte recognized that her mother's greatest manipulative tactic was fear. Still, she struggled to make decisions for herself. How pathetic was that? She was almost thirty, and she was still checking with her mother before doing just about anything. Still allowing herself to question whether or not taking a few days off to mourn the loss of her only real friend was a good idea.

The thought of it made Charlotte's stomach turn. Julianna had forged her own path. She'd made her own choices, even ones that seemed crazy, like leaving the ballet. Like marrying Connor. Like having kids and opening a dance studio in this tiny tourist town.

She was fearless, and Charlotte was a coward.

The organist began playing a hymn Charlotte recognized, not because of her stellar church attendance but because somewhere along the way, Julianna had introduced her to it. People around her stood and sang along as the pallbearers moved into place beside the casket.

The casket that would be her best friend's final resting place.

The crowd began to sing "It Is Well with My Soul" and Charlotte wanted to scream because nothing was well with her soul. Realization settled on her shoulders. She and Julianna no longer occupied the same world.

And that left her feeling horribly, terribly alone.

2

ONE MONTH LATER

"Get over here, twenty-two!"

Cole Turner, or "Coach" as he was usually called, watched as a lanky kid with a crazy arm ran toward him.

"What are you doing out there, West?"

Asher West tugged his helmet off and spit on the ground. "Doing my best, Coach."

"Well, if that's your best, we might as well pack it up now," Cole shouted. "Don't give me that—that wasn't your best. That wasn't even close to your best. If I'm going to make you my quarterback this season, you need to prove to me you can handle it."

Asher looked away, and for a split second, Cole thought maybe whatever was going on with the kid wasn't about football at all. But he needed Ash focused on the game. "Well?" he barked.

"I got it, Coach." Asher shoved the helmet back on his head and took off in the other direction as Matt Bilby, Cole's assistant coach, fell in to line at his side.

"Maybe go a little easy on him today, Coach," Bilby said.

Cole pulled his baseball cap down lower over his eyes. "Why would I do that? He's got big shoes to fill."

"He's going through some stuff," Bilby said.

"What kind of stuff?"

"Family stuff. You know his situation."

Cole did know his situation. Everyone knew, though Asher didn't like talking about it. They ran the play again, and this time, Asher threw a perfect spiral, right into the hands of the wide receiver.

Cole shot Bilby a look, as if the spiral was justification for Cole's brand of tough love. What was he supposed to do? Treat Asher with kid gloves while he kicked everyone else's butts into gear?

There was a lot riding on this next season, and his team was young. Asher was only a junior, and he was their top prospect for a quarterback to replace last season's star senior, Jared Brown. More than half of last year's team graduated, so the way Cole saw it, he had three months to get these boys into shape, to turn his young team into a strong team, and even he knew three months wasn't long enough.

"Summer practices usually start a little later, Coach," Bilby said. "Maybe give them a little bit of a break since they're all volunteering to be here."

"They're volunteering to be here because they want to win." Cole tucked his clipboard under his arm and faced Matt. "Do you?"

He walked away, aware that his mood was foul and he shouldn't be allowed to talk to anyone in his current state. But he'd been in a foul mood for months—why stop now?

He blew his whistle and the team circled up at the center of the field. Cole looked at the faces of these young boys, boys he'd known, in some cases, for a few years, and in others, a lifetime. They watched him now, most likely expecting an inspirational speech about how they had a state title to defend, about how they weren't seeded to win anything notable this year, about how it didn't matter because they could defy odds and exceed expectations.

But Cole didn't have those words in him. Not today.

Not after seeing Gemma earlier that morning for the first time since the divorce was final. Couldn't she have found a new place to vacation after everything she'd put him through? Sure, Harbor Pointe had been her summer home for years before they got married, but was it too much for Cole to expect a sliver of consideration?

He thought back on the circumstances surrounding their divorce and had his answer. Definitely too much to expect.

"Good practice, guys. We'll meet out here tomorrow morning, same time."

"But tomorrow's Saturday."

Cole looked at the redheaded Teddy Phillips. "And?"

The kid's jaw snapped shut. "And nothing, Coach."

"Look, I don't have to tell you we aren't exactly favored to repeat last year's success," Cole said. "But we're gonna train and we're gonna play like we are. Got it?"

There was a collective muttering.

"I'm sorry, what?" Cole raised his voice.

"Yes, Coach!" the boys yelled in unison.

"Bring it in." He thrust his fist into the circle and the boys piled their hands on top of his.

"Hawks on three," Cole shouted. "One, two, three—"

"Hawks!" the boys shouted and took off toward the school, where they'd shower, change, then head in to one of the first days of summer like they didn't have a care in the world.

Cole envied them that freedom.

Well, most of them.

"Twenty-two!" Cole called out.

Asher stopped and turned around to face him. "Coach?"

Cole waved him over.

When the kid reached him, helmetless and sweaty, he looked up at Cole in anticipation. Cole wished he was the kind of guy who could say everything he was thinking or feeling—the kind of guy who could speak to this kid in such a way that it gave him hope that his future was going to get easier.

But he wasn't. Words didn't come easily to him, and even less so lately. Still, this kid mattered—regardless of his potential as a quarterback.

"You okay?"

Asher looked away, and for a split second Cole thought the kid might cry. He wasn't great with words, but he was even worse with tears. Men shouldn't cry, especially not in front of each other, unless there was an athletic victory involved.

"Fine, Coach. I'm fine."

But it was obvious Asher was not fine. And how could he be? Child Protective Services had showed up at the dumpy apartment where Asher lived with his mom and two brothers, only to discover that this almost-junior in high school had been taking care of the family on his own.

His job at the Dairy Depot couldn't have been enough, yet somehow, the landlord hadn't evicted them yet and nobody had starved. Asher was doing better than a lot of adults Cole knew.

Still, the weight of CPS showing up had to be a heavy one. He'd been working to keep that family together for months, and now, in one day, he could lose it all. They were threatening to take the kids from their mom, and who in their right mind would foster three boys?

Cole slapped a hand on Asher's shoulder. "You need anything, you call me. Day or night."

Asher slowly met his eyes.

"You got that?"

The boy nodded.

"Yeah?"

"Yeah, Coach," he said. "Thanks."

"All right. I'll see you tomorrow."

Asher ran off toward the school, leaving Cole standing on the field, aware that he could've said more. After all, the two of them had a lot more in common than the kid knew. But he'd kept that information for himself, choosing instead to make a point to check in on Asher and his brothers, daily if he had to.

If he'd known how bad things were last year—he stopped himself from completing the thought because he knew it was a lie.

Even if he had known about Asher's situation last year, he wouldn't have stepped in. How could he? He was barely holding it together himself at the time. He thought he'd finally put all that behind him after the divorce, but now he wasn't so sure.

Not after that morning.

Not after *Gemma*.

But he wasn't going to waste another second thinking about his ex-wife. He'd wasted too many already. A year's worth and more. Enough was enough.

He walked into his office and flipped on the light. With practice over, Cole had the rest of the day open. It used to be the thing he loved best about his job—summers off. Summers with Gemma, reliving days that weren't unlike the days when they first fell in love.

Now, though, his open calendar taunted him like a bully demanding his lunch money.

He packed up his things, then walked out the side entrance of the nearly empty high school. His stomach growled. Right on cue.

He made a quick phone call to Hazel's Kitchen and ordered breakfast to go. He'd pick up his food, go home, and get started on his next renovation project.

When he bought the run-down lakeside cottage, he hadn't expected to love renovating it as much as he did. He'd bought it on a whim, planning to fix it up and sell it, but when Gemma left, he sold the house they'd shared and moved in to the old cottage. It had a great view of the lake and no trace of his ex-wife.

His next project was the master bathroom, and he welcomed the distraction.

He pulled up in front of the diner and groaned at the sight of the crowd of people inside. People who knew him and who knew Gemma. People who likely knew she was back in town. Heck, for all he knew, Gemma could be in there right now.

He considered abandoning his order and driving away, but it wouldn't be fair to Betsy. The owner of the small diner relied on regulars like him, and despite how it appeared, he did care about the people in this community.

He'd hit a rough patch—eventually he'd get back to normal. Right?

He turned the ignition of his vintage Chevy truck and went inside. He'd been thankful only days before when he'd realized that after a year, the rumble of voices didn't quiet every time he walked in the room anymore. It was as if people had begun to accept the fact that he'd moved on. That Gemma was gone. That there was nothing else to talk about.

But someone had undoubtedly spotted her in town over the last two days. He sure had, draping herself all over

Maxwell Juniper, pretending she didn't see Cole as they walked across the street in the crosswalk right in front of his truck.

It took everything he had not to take his foot off the brake.

Okay, that wasn't true, but the thought had occurred to him, which should probably concern him a little more than it did.

"Look at you, Coach," Betsy said from behind the counter. "Saw you out there early, whipping those boys into shape."

"We've got a long way to go," Cole said.

"You'll get there," Betsy said, her vote of confidence oddly reassuring. "You always do."

He didn't bother to tell her all the reasons he wouldn't get this particular team "there." He didn't want to sound like he was making excuses, though he did hope this town understood that some years, you simply didn't have the juice to go all the way, no matter how much potential the boys had.

The community was still riding high after last fall's state title. *Go Hawks* signs peppered storefront windows throughout town, even now, months after they'd won the championship. He didn't want to let anyone down, but it would take a miracle for this particular team to even have a winning season.

"I've got your order," Betsy said. "Be right back."

He leaned against the counter, doing his best not to make eye contact with anyone else in the restaurant, when the front door opened and Gemma walked in. She hadn't spotted him yet, so he took a second to look at her, wishing she'd lost her looks or suddenly turned unappealing to him.

Shouldn't it work that way?

Sadly, it didn't. His ex was every bit as beautiful as she ever had been.

Maybe he'd been wrong about chatter quieting. He swore the room had gone silent. Or was he imagining that?

Gemma found a booth against the far wall and led Max over to it, and before she looked up, Cole turned his back to her, facing the register where Betsy would—God willing—soon return with his order.

It had been too much to expect Gemma to find another place to spend her summer, and apparently too much to give up their favorite breakfast spot. Sensitivity had never been her strong suit. He could only pray that she drew the line at talking to him in public.

Finally, after what felt like an eternity, Betsy returned. "Sorry," she said. "I threw a few extras in there for you."

"You didn't have to do that." He kept his voice low, as if it might give him away, even from across the room.

"I know," she said. "But I wanted to. I know it's going to get super crowded in here the next few months, and I'm trying to entice my regulars to brave the tourist crowds and keep coming in. The locals are always much nicer than the tourists." She winked at him and pushed the brown paper bag across the counter. "I'm sure you agree."

Gemma had been a tourist once upon a time, a summer resident only until she married Cole. Was that what Betsy was getting at? If so, yeah, he definitely agreed. "Thanks," he said. He handed over his cash, told her to keep the change, then turned for his quick getaway.

He beelined for the front door, head down and pretending not to notice Gemma and dumb Max sitting in that booth against the wall. He focused instead on the scene outside the front of the diner, where a shiny black Volkswagen Jetta attempted to park in the spot directly in front of Cole's truck. After a failed attempt to maneuver the car into the parking place, the driver put it into drive and started to pull back out into the street, but an oncoming car honked and the Jetta halted abruptly, then lurched backward.

The scene turned to slow motion as the back end of the car swiped across the front headlight of Cole's vintage Chevy and finally came to a stop.

At the sound of the shattered headlight and crunching metal, a collective gasp sounded from the diner patrons near the windows. All eyes were on him.

He darted out onto the sidewalk and looked at the two vehicles, still pressed together, metal entwined with metal.

Cole tried not to think about all the hours he'd spent restoring that truck. It had been months of constant tinkering, but finally, he had something he was proud to drive around. It wouldn't be easy to replace that headlight, and he couldn't be sure, but it looked like there would be some body work involved too.

He knew it was probably a teenager or a little old lady behind the wheel of that car, and he also knew a small crowd had likely gathered behind him, inside the diner, including—unfortunately—Gemma and dumb Max.

Stay cool, Turner.

The Jetta started moving again, broken glass crunching underneath the tires. Once it was clear, he tried to relax a little, but the driver didn't stop the car. Instead, the slow motion started up again and he watched in horror as the Jetta smashed into the truck again, this time wedging the back end even deeper into the front of the old Chevy.

Cole rushed out to the curb.

"Stop!" He shouted at the driver and pounded on the trunk of the car. The brake lights flickered as the car stopped moving.

"Are you blind?" He shouted again.

Seconds later, the driver's side door opened, and Cole waited to see the face of the person who shouldn't have gotten out of the DMV with a license. A wide-eyed woman whose cheeks were stained with tears emerged from the car.

"I am so sorry," she said, clearly fighting to regain her composure. "I am so, so sorry."

He watched as she wiped her face dry with the sleeves of her thin black sweater. The woman's dark hair was pulled up into a high bun—and not the messy kind of bun so many of his students sported every day. This bun was perfect, tight, not a hair out of place.

Her face, with nearly translucent pale skin, was accented by the slightest bit of color on her lips and cheeks, though the pink seemed to be increasing the longer she stood there, undoubtedly embarrassed.

The tears softened him slightly, but that didn't change the fact that she'd plowed into his pride and joy. Twice.

"Is this your truck?" She closed the door of the Jetta and rushed around the opposite side of the car.

"Just give me your insurance information," Cole said sharply.

"Um, it's a rental," she said. "But I can pay for your repairs."

He glared at her. Where had he seen her before?

"Obviously I'm at fault here." She looked at the kissing cars and sighed. "What a mess." Then back at him. "I don't drive very often."

"Really," he said dryly.

Under different circumstances—namely, if Gemma hadn't just returned to town, dredging up a world of hurts he'd yet to sort through or deal with—this whole mess might've played out another way. He might've laughed it off, told this beautiful stranger he'd forgive the accident if she let him take her to dinner. He might even find a way to be charming—he'd been charming before.

But the circumstances weren't different. He was moody and angry and she'd busted up the truck he'd been restoring for years.

"I live in the city, and I walk a lot." She ran a hand over her hair. "Well, I did. I did live in the city. Now, I guess I live here since I recently quit my job and everything." Her laugh seemed nervous. She met his eyes. "Sorry. I talk when I get nervous," then under her breath: "Marcia says it's a terrible habit."

"Great, whatever," he said, inwardly grimacing at his own tone. "Can I just get your information so I can go?"

Her one raised eyebrow told him he was being a jerk. What else was new?

She drew in a slow breath, staring at him, then exhaled, looking slightly perturbed. As if she had the right.

"You're—" Her gaze lingered.

"I'm...?"

She shook her head. "Let me see if I have something to write on." She walked back to the car and pulled a giant bag out of the front seat. She started taking its contents out and putting them on the hood of the car.

He tried not to pay attention as she unloaded deodorant, two different tubes of lotion, hair ties, what appeared to be a scarf, a pair of socks, a wallet, and not a single piece of scratch paper onto the Jetta.

She reached back into the bag and pulled out a Sharpie. "Here!"

He frowned.

She walked back toward him with seemingly no awareness for personal space, then scribbled on the outside of his food bag. She leaned in so close, he could smell her shampoo.

It smelled good.

"That's my name and number," she said.

He glanced down at the bag. She'd written *Charlotte Page* in bold, black letters, along with her ten digits. He looked at her. Why was that name familiar?

Charlotte. It suited her. It had a sort of old-world elegance about it, and so did she.

"I guess just call me when you figure out how much it's going to cost to fix this mess." She looked back at the cars and her face fell. "I'm honestly not sure how to get my car out now."

Her brow furrowed, and Cole studied her profile. He knew it was old-fashioned, but he'd been taught to help women out of situations like this—Charlotte Page didn't likely need a knight in shining armor, but if she did, he was the only one standing close enough to step up and volunteer.

Something stopped him. Why was it so hard to be kind?

"I don't want to make it worse." She held her key toward him and shook it. "Do you mind?"

He studied her face. Wide eyes. Full lips. Perfect skin. Most men would ask her for her number. As it was, he had her number and had absolutely no use for it.

Didn't matter that she was beautiful. Didn't matter that he'd found her rambling kind of adorable. Things weren't different, and he didn't know when they ever would be again.

He set his food inside the cab of his truck, snatched her keys out of her hand, and opened the door of the Jetta. He tried to sit in the driver's seat, but it was so far forward it almost folded him in half. Annoyed, he found the lever to move the seat back, started the engine, and inched the car out of the parking space, and out of his truck's front end.

Once the car was free, he slammed it into park, got out, and started toward his truck.

"I'm really so sorry," she called out.

"Maybe next time you should find a parking lot," he said. It was rude. He knew it was rude. It was as if his anger had taken hold and he had no control over it.

Then, like a jerk, he got into the truck, started the engine, and pulled away from the curb, looking back just in time to see Gemma standing in the window of the diner, watching the entire exchange.

3

Charlotte stood on the street, mortified by the crowd of people that had assembled inside the diner to witness her stupidity.

What was she thinking trying to parallel park? She'd nearly failed her driver's test because of this unlearned skill, and she'd never attempted it since. Her mother thought it was important that she learn in case of emergencies, which, it turned out, Charlotte was thankful for or she wouldn't have had any idea how to run away from Chicago in the first place. But while she had her license, Charlotte almost never used it. Marcia always sent drivers or Charlotte walked.

The theatre was only a few blocks away from her apartment, as was the gym and her favorite coffee shop. Charlotte didn't go anywhere else.

She looked at the rented Jetta and sighed. "Now what?"

"Now you come in for a cup of coffee and a plate of pancakes," a voice from behind her said.

"Oh, I can't eat pancakes." Charlotte turned toward the voice.

The wild-haired girl smiled at her. "Everyone can eat pancakes."

"Not me." Charlotte heard the disappointment in her own voice. Did she want pancakes? She'd never minded not eating them before. Did she even like pancakes?

"Coffee, then," the girl said. "You look like you could use it."

"I think he was really mad at me," Charlotte said, turning toward the girl. "Not the way I wanted to make my Harbor Pointe entrance."

Once she recognized the man whose truck she'd crashed into, her mortification intensified. At some point, Cole Turner would realize that his sister's friend was the twit who'd ruined what she thought might've been a precious vehicle.

She'd wondered if he might recognize her name, which was foolish and egotistical of her given that in all the years she and Julianna had danced together, she'd only met Cole twice, and neither time did he seem overjoyed to be attending a ballet. Both times, however, he'd made an impression on Charlotte.

In those days, boys like Cole didn't come along very often. Julianna talked about him sometimes, and Charlotte never let on, but she thought her friend's older brother was beautiful. She used to imagine what it would be like to go on a date with someone like that—tall, sturdy, good-looking, athletic. Cole Turner had been the subject of many a teenage fantasy.

Perhaps she'd built him up to be something he wasn't. He'd certainly set her straight today.

"Coach? He'll be fine. He's just kind of moody lately. He's been dealing with a lot. Now, come on in and have something to eat."

Charlotte turned to follow the girl, who quickly stopped.

"You should probably turn your car off."

Charlotte felt her eyes widen. "Oh my gosh." She raced back to the Jetta, turned off the engine, locked the doors, and met the girl back on the sidewalk. "It's been a tough few weeks."

"Well, you can relax now," the girl said, pulling open the door of the diner. "You're in Harbor Pointe. That's what people do here."

"I've heard that," Charlotte said, thinking of Julianna's letters. While her only friend in the world seemed to live in an alternate reality, there was something intriguing about this town she'd written so much about.

It had been a month since the funeral, but that was the day everything had changed. Charlotte had slipped away from the cemetery and driven around Harbor Pointe, finally seeing the place Julianna had described so beautifully in her letters.

She understood why her friend was so charmed by this town, and for the first time, Charlotte imagined what it might be like to live a different kind of life.

Of course, it wasn't practical. She was a ballerina—what did a ballerina do in a tiny tourist town? So, she returned to Chicago, to Marcia, to the ballet—but everything felt different.

It was almost as if for one glorious day, Julianna opened the door to her world and allowed Charlotte a peek inside.

That peek had been enough to spark something inside of her. So often, ballerinas are striving to make it in the big city—but Charlotte wondered if she could make it in a small town. She expected the feeling to go away, this pull toward something other than the only life she'd known, but a month had passed and here she was—crashing into the trucks of moody, handsome men.

"Come, sit." The girl slipped behind the long, white counter and motioned for Charlotte to take a seat opposite her, on one of the stools.

Julianna had mentioned Hazel's Kitchen in many of her letters. How could she not? It was a regular part of her day.

Hazel's Kitchen is my go-to breakfast spot. Actually, all of the locals tend to frequent this place, and if you visit, you'll know why immediately. The owner, Betsy, is certainly part of the diner's charm, but the food is out of this world. If you ever show up in Harbor Pointe, you'll most likely find me in a booth at the back, having coffee with friends or planning our next season of dance classes for the studio.

Charlotte scanned the restaurant. There was no use looking for Julianna today. The realization turned something inside her and sadness hung around her edges. Had coming here been a mistake?

Charlotte turned back to the wild-haired girl wearing a turquoise shirt and apron. "You're Betsy, aren't you?"

The girl smiled. "I am. Have we met before?"

"No," Charlotte said. "But I kind of feel like I know you already. I'm an old friend of Julianna Ford's. More of a pen pal recently, I guess you'd say." The sadness gave a tug. "I mean, I was an old friend of hers."

"Oh. So you know Coach," Betsy said—a statement, not a question.

"Kind of," Charlotte said. "I mean, not really. I met him once or twice." *Dreamed about him a thousand times more . . .* "He obviously doesn't remember me."

Betsy turned a mug over and poured Charlotte a cup of coffee. "I'm sorry. About Jules."

"Me too," Charlotte said.

Betsy seemed to visibly shake away the sadness, then changed the subject. "A pen pal? They still have those?"

Charlotte had learned to drink her coffee black when her mother made it clear that cream and sugar were not part of a ballerina's diet. She didn't particularly like black coffee, but it was a taste she'd acquired. And right now, she was thankful for the caffeine. She'd gotten up at the crack of dawn to drive to Harbor Pointe before she lost her nerve.

After all, she was giving up a lot. Running away, her mother would say, and maybe she was. Maybe leaving before Marcia could talk her out of it was strategic.

"How'd you know Jules?" Betsy asked.

"We met at dance camp when we were twelve," Charlotte said. "We were instant friends, and we danced together for a while before she met Connor."

"Wow," Betsy said.

"She never mentioned me?"

Betsy shrugged. "Not to me."

Charlotte took a sip. What did she expect? Julianna had no reason to discuss her *pen pal* with her *real-life* friends or her *real-life* brother.

But they were more than pen pals, weren't they? They didn't see each other enough, and the letter writing was a poor substitute for face-to-face conversation, yet Charlotte lived for those letters. She loved those letters. In some ways, as much as she sometimes looked down on Jules for abandoning ballet, she also envied her.

And maybe it was that envy, that curiosity, that wondering what it was Julianna had found that Charlotte never had—that led her here.

"So, why come here now?" Betsy asked, as if she had read her mind.

"It was sort of a spur-of-the-moment decision." Charlotte sighed. "Maybe the wrong one, now that I think about it. I wrecked a very cranky man's truck."

"I think Coach was already cranky before you hit his truck," Betsy said. "Though, I guess that probably didn't help. He's been restoring that thing for a long time."

Charlotte groaned. Even worse. "I didn't want to start out with enemies. I mean, it's my first hour in town. And he's Julianna's brother."

"It's fine," Betsy said. "Tourists do crazy things around here all the time."

"Right," she said.

Betsy crossed her arms over her chest. "What are you going to do while you're here?"

Charlotte took a sip of her coffee. "I was going to see if Connor needed any help, you know, with the dance studio." She downplayed her plan because if the idea of buying Julianna's studio was a crazy one, she wasn't ready to hear it.

If Connor didn't want to sell it to her, she had no idea what she'd do. But that was a problem for another day.

After the funeral, she'd gone back to the ballet, and every night, she put on a great show. She performed maybe better than she ever had—but loneliness carved something hollow out of her insides with every curtain call. She spent those moments off stage weighing her options, considering the pros and cons of this life she'd chosen. She made lists. She talked to herself. She was in a position that every dancer in the world envied—it would be ludicrous to give it up.

But she couldn't shake the idea that there was something more for her.

She'd mentioned it to her mother about a week ago, after that night's performance, and Marcia—in true Marcia fashion—said, "Only you could achieve this level of success and still want more, Charlotte." Then she smiled. "I've taught you well."

But her mother had misunderstood. She felt like there was something *more*, but it had nothing to do with the kinds of goals Marcia would've praised. Maybe what Charlotte really wanted was something less.

So, she tendered her resignation, effective immediately, then quietly packed a bag, rented a car, and drove to the only place she could think of that might bring her some peace.

And now, here she was.

"Do you want me to call Connor for you?" Betsy reached into the pocket of her apron and pulled out her phone.

"Actually, maybe you could call Lucy Fitzgerald instead?"

After all, it had been Lucy who had given Charlotte the idea to come here in the first place, and the guts to follow it through.

"Sure thing," Betsy said.

She wasn't ready to face Connor. Maybe she was afraid he'd tell her the truth—that she was a lousy friend.

And while she'd made it to Julianna's funeral, she'd effectively hid herself in the back and done a poor job of paying her respects. She was pretty sure he had no idea she'd been there. And she wasn't sure how to ever explain that his wife's death had served as a cosmic wake-up call, let alone pitch her idea of buying the dance studio.

Facing Connor would have to wait. She didn't have the courage yet. He could crush her grand plan in a heartbeat, simply by refusing to sell the studio to her.

For all she knew, he'd already sold it or shut it down. That's what she was here to find out.

She owed it to Jules.

Betsy had excused herself to the kitchen to call Lucy, and as Charlotte sat there, alone at the counter with nothing but memories and a mug of hot black coffee, that whirlwind of doubt kicked up inside her.

She recognized the signs. A ball of dread wrapped in a coating of fear lodged in her stomach. Sweaty palms. The buzz of anxiety. Yes, she knew them well.

What she didn't know was how to quell the insecurities that kept her frozen, knee-deep in a pile of indecision and uncertainty.

She hated this about herself—hated that all her choices had been made for her all these years, effectively rendering her own decision-making skills useless. She'd finally found her backbone, and now she sat here in a thick fog of doubt.

Was this crazy? Who did she think she was stepping into this precious town with a grand plan to buy the dance studio and . . . what? Become Julianna's replacement?

If she was smart, she'd get back in the beat-up Jetta and drive straight back to Chicago, where she could beg for her job back and chalk this whole episode up to delusion brought on by exhaustion.

But no.

It wasn't exhaustion that had brought her here. It was the innate feeling that something was missing. Julianna's letters were so full of life, just like she had been. She wrote about things Charlotte knew nothing of—and while Charlotte had always brushed off Julianna's small town musings, something inside her had shifted now that her best friend was gone.

What if bigger wasn't best?

Sure, she'd achieved professional success—she was arguably one of the top ballerinas in the nation. Maybe even the world. An elite athlete. She'd trained her entire life to get where she was, which was why it was a crazy move to walk away.

But it didn't feel crazy. It felt smart. Necessary. It felt like she'd made a decision for herself for the first time in her life.

She wanted to experience just a sliver of what Julianna had. Suddenly, it was Charlotte's world—not her friend's—that held no appeal.

A few minutes later, the front door of the diner swung open and in walked a leggy redhead wearing a navy blue dress with white polka dots on it and a wide red belt.

Lucy Fitzgerald.

Julianna had written to her about her spunky friend who wrote for the local newspaper.

Jules was a great writer, and Lucy was easy to recognize by her descriptions. Charlotte had spotted her at the funeral too, but she hadn't dared introduce herself. Grieving was easier if she remained anonymous. It wasn't hard. Lucy had been surrounded by friends, and while Charlotte was accustomed to standing out when she performed, she was also used to being invisible offstage.

She'd perfected it, really.

Betsy appeared in the doorway of the kitchen in time to see Lucy gasp at the sight of Charlotte. Lucy brought both hands to her mouth and let out a squeal. "Charlotte?!"

Oh, thank goodness, Charlotte thought, thankful Lucy seemed genuinely happy to see her. Charlotte couldn't help but think of the way Julianna had always brought people together. Here she was, doing it even after she was gone.

Lucy pulled Charlotte off the stool and into a tight hug —the tightest hug, in fact, that Charlotte had ever been pulled into. Lucy was one of Jules's closest "real life" friends. Because of that classification, and Charlotte's as a "long-distance" friend, Charlotte had never felt competitive with Lucy.

Now, wrapped in the other woman's arms, she felt the loss of their mutual friend more deeply than she had, even when Lucy had called her with the news. Grieving alone was easier.

And yet, Charlotte felt an odd comfort in the arms of this stranger.

"I can't believe it's you!" Lucy pulled away. "I can't believe you're here!"

Charlotte tried to keep her eyes from watering and her voice from shaking. She tried to rid herself of all the telltale signs she was cracking up, but she had a feeling she wasn't a very good liar.

"Did you not really mean for me to come?" Charlotte asked.

"No." Lucy squeezed Charlotte's arms. "I mean, yes, I just didn't think you would."

Lucy knew about Charlotte because Julianna was chatty, and though the two women had never met, Lucy had thought to call her with news of Julianna's accident. It was the worst phone call Charlotte had ever received.

She'd just finished rehearsal and the office assistant at the ballet found her in the hallway. "You have a phone call in the office," she'd said.

It was strange. Nobody called Charlotte. But it was the only way Lucy could get a hold of her without asking Connor to hand over his wife's phone.

After she explained who she was, Lucy said, "Charlotte, Julianna's gone."

"Gone where?" Charlotte asked—stupidly, she now realized.

"She pulled out into an intersection and a guy plowed

right into her minivan. He was texting and driving." Lucy paused. "She was dead when they found her."

The word hung on the line between them. *Dead*. It was as if it had been translated incorrectly, like whatever had really happened to Julianna wasn't being communicated.

"Charlotte? Are you there?"

A deep dread carved itself a home inside of her as she tried to process what Lucy had told her. *Dead?* Julianna was young—Charlotte's age. She had a husband and kids. How could this have happened?

Death comes unexpectedly.

Before they got off the phone, Charlotte jotted down the details of the funeral and then Lucy said, "Look, if you ever need to get away, you can always come here. Maybe you could help with the dance studio? Julianna has a lot of students who are going to be lost without her."

Charlotte went through the motions of the next few days, expecting to "go back to normal"—whatever that meant, but normal never came, only the haunting knowledge that something was missing. Maybe losing the only person you could genuinely call "friend" was meant to turn you inside out.

"Let's get breakfast, you can tell me everything," Lucy said, swiping Charlotte's bag off the back of the chair. "Betsy, can you bring us two number two's?"

"She doesn't eat pancakes," Betsy called out as Lucy led Charlotte toward a booth near the back of the restaurant.

"She does today!"

Lucy was just like Julianna had described her. She was a little loud, smiled with her whole face, and never met a stranger.

Something about that comforted Charlotte.

"I can't believe you're here," Lucy said, settling in to the booth.

"I can't either," Charlotte said. "Are you sure it's okay? You probably didn't really mean for me to come."

"Are you kidding? Of course I did." Lucy grinned. "I never say anything I don't mean. Are you going to run the dance studio? I heard they canceled their spring recital."

"Maybe?" The idea hadn't stopped nagging her since the day Lucy mentioned it. She could buy Julianna's studio, teach and begin an entirely new life.

Charlotte had never fancied herself a teacher, but she'd held masterclasses and workshops over the years. She'd always enjoyed it, which was unlike her mother, who only taught because she could no longer perform.

"You'd be amazing," Lucy said.

"Well, I'm off to a great start. I crashed into Cole Turner's truck."

Lucy's eyes widened. "You crashed the vintage Chevy?"

Charlotte grimaced. "He was pretty mad. I mean, of all the people I don't want mad at me, Julianna's brother is at the top of the list."

Lucy waggled her eyebrows. "Julianna's very good-looking brother."

So Charlotte wasn't crazy. Cole *was* still beautiful. She'd thought it as soon as she realized who he was, but he'd doused that feeling the second he turned rude.

"Okay." Lucy waved her hand in the air. "We'll deal with that later. Now let's talk about you. Did they finally give you some time off at the ballet?"

"Not exactly," Charlotte said. "I kind of took a leave."

"For how long?"

"Forever?" Charlotte's voice turned up at the end, as if it were a question. "I mean, maybe forever, I don't know." How did she explain what had come over her when even she wasn't sure it made sense? "Julianna's death—" Charlotte's voice betrayed her. "I'm just reevaluating things, is all."

After the funeral, Julianna's choice to leave the ballet all those years ago made sense.

And Charlotte's choice to stay did not.

Lucy nodded soberly. She didn't say so, but Charlotte thought she understood, at least as much as she could. After all, not many people could truly understand what life as a principal dancer in the Chicago City Ballet had really been like. Years of living up to other people's expectations of her—years of striving to be the best, as if being the best was all that mattered—it had taken a toll.

And the truth was, Charlotte hadn't taken a leave. She'd quit. She'd walked out, broke her contract, burned the bridge.

There was no turning back.

"I saw you at the funeral," Charlotte said.

"You were there?" Lucy stilled.

Charlotte straightened. "I stayed at the back. I didn't want to interfere. Everyone knew her so much differently than I did."

Lucy reached across the table and covered Charlotte's hand. "That's not true. We just saw her more often."

Charlotte blinked to keep the tears from falling. "Two days after the funeral, I found this in my mailbox." She pulled out the lavender envelope.

Lucy took it and smiled. "Leave it to Jules to still send snail mail."

"We've always written letters," Charlotte said. "Ever since we were kids."

"I know," Lucy said. "She told me."

Charlotte smiled at that. Somehow, the knowledge of it made her feel seen. Or maybe it made her feel known.

And everything inside of her wanted to be known. Maybe that was part of it—Harbor Pointe was filled with people who knew Jules, people who loved her and still mourned her.

Charlotte had realized somewhere in the passing days that if she died, the conversation would be about who would replace her at the ballet, not about how much they would miss her. Nobody would miss her, especially not now, with Julianna gone.

Something inside her broke at the thought of it.

One of the servers appeared with their food. "Two number two's."

Lucy grinned. "You're about to have the breakfast of your life."

Charlotte looked down at the plate—very different from her usual morning meal. Pancakes. Eggs. Bacon. Hash browns. Orange juice.

"And don't even think about not finishing it all."

"This is more food than I eat in a day," Charlotte said.

"Obviously." Lucy gave Charlotte a once-over and started cutting her pancakes into bite-sized pieces. "So, the letter?" she prodded.

"Right." Charlotte stuck her fork into her scrambled eggs. "It was like her description of this place spoke to my soul," Charlotte said with a sigh. "And believe me, I know how stupid that sounds."

"It doesn't," Lucy said, piling three pieces of pancake onto her fork and dragging them through a puddle of maple syrup. "It makes perfect sense to me. You need rest. And who can blame you? You've been working since you were how old? Like fifteen or something?"

"Eight."

Lucy frowned. "Eight?"

Charlotte nodded. "I got my first professional job when I was eight."

"Good grief."

Charlotte sighed. "I do need a break." But more than that, Charlotte needed to call her own shots for a while. She needed to figure out who Charlotte Page was when she wasn't on that stage.

She pushed her plate of uneaten pancakes away and pulled her mug toward her, warming her hands with it.

Lucy swallowed another bite of her breakfast. "Where are you staying?"

Charlotte shrugged. "I haven't figured that out yet."

Lucy laughed. "This is so spontaneous, Charlotte."

Was that another word for "foolish"?

"I know," Charlotte said with a groan. "And not at all like me."

"You'll stay with me. Case closed."

"I don't want to impose."

"Please, I have a great guest room with its own bathroom and a view of the lake," Lucy said.

As they walked out of the diner twenty minutes later, Lucy slid her arm through Charlotte's, making her feel, for only the second time in her life, like she'd actually made a friend.

When she exhaled, she felt a healthy dose of worry leave her body. And she had the craziest feeling everything was going to be okay.

4

Whatever good feelings Charlotte had had meeting Lucy and getting settled in her adorable lakeside cottage, with a perfect view of the red lighthouse Jules often wrote about in her letters . . . well, they were gone now.

Standing in front of Julianna's house, she was about to get hit with a healthy dose of reality, and just thinking about it had her on edge.

She glanced down at the envelope in her hand to be sure she had the right place. She did. No more putting it off. She was here because Julianna Ford had drawn her here with her descriptions of a beautiful, charmed, laid-back life. Because Charlotte, who'd spent years being envied by little girls and up-and-coming dancers and most likely everyone in her company, found herself envying her friend and this simple life she'd built.

Everything about Julianna's world appealed to her. Sure, it likely came with its own pressures and stress, but what would it feel like to be loved and cherished simply for who you were and not how you performed?

She owed it to her friend to do whatever she could to make sure the people she loved, the business she loved, were all okay. She had so much to atone for.

She knocked on the front door and waited, listening to the commotion inside. Connor Ford was a city planner, but that's about all Charlotte knew about his job. Its title. She'd known Connor only as "Julianna's boyfriend" and later as the man who took her best friend away.

Not that he had been the reason Jules left the ballet. Charlotte knew better than to assign him that blame—that blame she kept for herself.

Over the years, Julianna had been back to the city only once, when she attended a new Cinderella ballet in which Charlotte was playing the title role.

Charlotte was certain, looking back on it now, that she should've reacted differently knowing her friend had come all that way to see her. As it was, she'd been awkward and standoffish, all but blowing them off after the show ended.

She'd been unhappy with her performance, and the fact that Julianna was in the audience made it worse. In truth, she realized later, she'd been acting like a spoiled brat. She'd written Jules the longest letter apologizing and sent her VIP tickets for any future ballet she wanted to attend.

Julianna had never used them. But she did forgive her, that much was obvious, because she had a heart of gold. The kind of heart Charlotte should've been striving to have while she was striving for accolades and professional acclaim.

It shamed her to think about how she'd lost herself.

Or maybe she'd never really known herself in the first place. Had it really taken the death of her only friend to wake her up?

The door opened and a young boy stood on the other side, staring at her through the screen.

"AJ, I told you not to open the door to strangers," a man's voice called out before Connor appeared behind Julianna's middle child.

"Hey, Connor," Charlotte said.

Surprise splashed across his face. "Charlotte? What are you doing here?"

At least he remembered who she was. "May I come in?"

Connor tossed a worried look over his shoulder. She probably should've called first. She didn't know a lot about social etiquette—it wasn't like she spent a lot of time visiting friends in Chicago.

"Amelia, come watch your brother!" Connor called over his shoulder, then shooed AJ away, joining Charlotte on the porch. "Sorry, it's kind of a disaster in there."

She gave him a sad smile. This man that her friend had fallen so head-over-heels in love with looked like a shell of himself. Not that she knew him well, but the guy standing in front of her was a very different version of the guy Jules described in her letters.

A pang of jealousy resounded in her chest.

"What are you doing here?" he asked again, not accusing, but not friendly either.

"I didn't get to say anything at the funeral," she said. "I didn't want to impose."

He frowned. "You were there?"

She nodded quietly. "It was a beautiful service." Was that what people said about funerals? Should she comment on how lovely the luncheon was?

He looked away. "I hardly remember it."

Her heart tightened in sadness. It didn't surprise her. He'd seemed in a daze the entire time. And who could blame him? How did you say goodbye to the person you loved most in the world? "I got a letter from Jules, a few days after—" She couldn't say the words. If she said them out loud, that made them true. And even though she knew they were true, she didn't want them to be.

Connor leaned against the post at the front of the porch, refusing her eyes. His jaw twitched, and she couldn't be sure, but she thought maybe he was working—hard—to keep from crying.

"That's why I'm here," she said quietly. "That and to see if I can help you."

He scoffed. "Help me what?"

Charlotte tried not to let his tone deter her. "Help with whatever—anything you need."

He looked at her then, his eyes glassy. "Where've you been all this time, Charlotte? Her thirtieth birthday, the births of all of our kids, our wedding—" He glared at her now. "Do you know how much it hurt her that you could never be bothered?"

Charlotte deserved this. She hadn't been a good friend. She was always on the receiving end of goodness. Julianna's goodness. And yet, Jules never made her feel badly for it. She understood the demands of the ballet. She understood Marcia. She understood in ways that nobody else did.

"I'm sorry, Connor," she said.

He shook his head. "She always made excuses for you. Said your life was harder than people realized."

Charlotte's gaze dipped to the porch beneath her feet. She wouldn't claim to have a hard life—not to Connor—but the reminders that Julianna understood made her feel all the lonelier now.

"Why are you really here?"

"I was actually wondering what you plan to do with the dance studio."

An accusing thought ran through Charlotte's mind: *You're only doing this to ease your guilty conscience.*

She shoved it aside, willing it false. Sure, maybe a piece

of her wanted to be sure Julianna's life had been good enough—that it didn't pale in comparison to the life she would've had in the ballet—if Charlotte had not intervened.

But that's not why she was here.

"I know you have no reason to trust me," she heard herself saying. "I wasn't nearly the friend to Jules that she was to me. But I want to change that. She made me want to be better."

He blew out a heavy sigh. "Me too." His voice quavered, and she hated that her presence on his porch was causing him pain.

"I'd like to buy the studio," she said. "Take it off your hands. Make it a priority to take care of the students Julianna loved so much."

"Isn't that a little beneath you?" He dragged his gaze to hers.

She smiled sadly, knowing that her elitist attitude had not gone unnoticed. "Like I said, I want to change."

He looked away. "I haven't figured out what to do with the studio yet, but I guess you're right—I probably need to sell it or shut it down."

"Don't shut it down," Charlotte said. "It's part of her legacy."

From somewhere in the house, a baby started crying. Connor swore under his breath and looked at Charlotte.

"Julianna's assistant is there now. Ask her if you want to help with the studio. I have to deal with the kids." He pulled the door open and stopped, as if he had more to say. He must've thought better of it, though, because he snapped his jaw shut and walked inside, closing the door behind him, but not before she caught a glimpse of the mess in the living room.

She didn't know Connor well, and admittedly, what she

did know of him was mostly from his wife's letters, but even she could see he wasn't coping well.

She stood on the porch for a long moment, and a wave of grief thick and strong nearly knocked her over. It had come from nowhere, and now it lingered, leaving Charlotte unsteady on her feet.

Charlotte pulled out her phone and searched the address for Julianna's dance studio. She plugged it in to her GPS, but as she pulled away from the curb, she glanced back at the quaint house situated in the middle of the Harbor Pointe neighborhood. In the second-story window, she spotted the face of a little girl, watching her.

Caught, Amelia dropped the curtain and disappeared, doing nothing to calm Charlotte's overworked nerves. She wanted to help. For once, she wanted to do something for someone other than herself.

Slowly, she pulled out into the street and drove across town toward what she discovered was an adorable little studio situated on Mulberry Street.

She peered down the block at the rows of brightly colored buildings, the colors of the sky in the midst of a summer sunset. Pinks and yellows and teals all winked back at her, as if the town itself had a personality that deserved to be recognized.

Jules had described Mulberry Street in her letters, and while she was an excellent pen pal, even her beautiful words didn't do this place justice.

Charlotte locked the doors of the beat-up Jetta, reminded herself to call the rental company, and made her way to the brick building that Jules had converted into a dance studio.

The lobby was much more spacious than she would've expected, with a reception area and the school's logo neatly positioned on a brick wall behind it. The entire vibe was very Chicago, very upscale. Very Julianna. Her friend had always had impeccable taste.

"Can I help you?" A voice caught Charlotte's attention. A girl, probably in her early twenties, stood in the lobby, looking disheveled.

"Hi, I'm—"

"Charlotte Page." The girl said it with considerable awe in her voice.

"That's right."

"I've seen you dance," she said. "I have season tickets to the Chicago City Ballet."

"Oh." Charlotte wasn't sure how to respond. Typically, ballet dancers didn't have the same kinds of fans as celebrities. She'd signed programs for many young girls, and stopped to chat with the gray-haired crowd, many of whom had a "lovely grandson I'd love to introduce you to"—but it wasn't often Charlotte was recognized, in street clothes no less.

It made her feel self-conscious.

"What are you doing in Harbor Pointe?" the girl asked.

"I was a friend of Julianna's," Charlotte said.

"She told me. But I never would've thought you'd actually come here."

Charlotte smiled. "I wanted to see if there was anything I could do to help out."

"Here?" The girl sounded as shocked as she looked.

Charlotte laughed. "Yes, here."

"Oh, wow. What did you have in mind? I'm Brinley Watson, by the way, Jules's assistant."

Charlotte shook the girl's hand. "It's good to meet you." She looked around the space. "Show me around?"

Brinley grinned. "Happy to." She led her down the hall where Julianna had everything she needed for the perfect dance studio. Two large spaces with windows for parental viewing and ample seating throughout.

"During the week, this space is full and loud. This is the only dance studio in Harbor Pointe, so Julianna has all the kids." She faltered. "*Had* all the kids." Her face fell.

The pang of sorrow returned. Charlotte quickly replaced it with thoughts of Julianna in this space. She'd never seen her friend teach, but she didn't have to to know she was amazing at it.

Brinley turned on the light in one of the dance studios. "This is Studio A. It's a smidge bigger than the back studio."

"How many teachers are there?"

"Julianna and two others. Jules taught most of the classes. I teach a few of the little kids' classes, but I'm a novice and really more of an administrator. I shouldn't even really be talking to you."

Charlotte's mind started spinning. "Do you have a copy of the schedule?"

"We're kind of frozen, actually. We didn't get to do the spring recital. Without Julianna, everything just kind of stopped. She just handled so much of it herself. The kids were devastated."

Charlotte saw the disappointment in Brinley's face.

"I mean, they were devasted about Jules most of all," she quickly added. "We all were."

"Where is the recital held?"

"In this great theatre outside of town," Brinley said. "There's an old campground with a lodge and cabins and a surprisingly cool performance space."

"Sounds different," Charlotte said.

"It is," Brinley said. "It's been getting harder every year to convince the owner, Mr. Kent, to let us rent it, but he had a soft spot for Jules. Said she reminded him of his oldest daughter. She's on Broadway."

"Wow," Charlotte said. "Do they have a lot of events out there?"

Brinley shook her head. "They used to. Mr. Kent and his wife put on the most amazing musicals. Turned that place into a real tourist attraction, but about five years ago, the wife died and Silas practically boarded up the place. I don't think he ever recovered."

Charlotte thought of Connor. Would it be the same for him?

"We were just a few weeks away from the performance, but then Jules—" She looked away. "Well, I don't know how to do it without her."

"That must be hard."

Brinley's face fell. "I feel like I'm letting her down. She loved these kids like they were her own. If she knew we didn't see it through, after all their hard work . . ." Brinley shook her head, leaving the unfinished thought dangling in the air.

Charlotte took a few steps into the studio. "Do you think the students remember their dances?"

Brinley nodded. "Definitely. They worked on them all semester. They're like little sponges."

"What if we went ahead and did it?" Charlotte asked, the idea still forming in her mind as she spoke.

"The recital?"

Charlotte nodded. "As a tribute to Jules. Like, a memorial or a celebration of her life." A wave of excitement rose in her chest.

"You think her family would be okay with that?" A line of worry deepened in Brinley's forehead. "Connor hasn't been doing that great."

Charlotte stilled. That was an understatement. "I think it's worth a shot. Maybe it would even be helpful. And we could announce that we're going to keep the studio going—

if Connor agrees to sell it to me."

Brinley's eyes widened. "You want to buy this place?"

Charlotte felt her cheeks flush. "I was hoping to."

The younger woman seemed to be holding in a squeal.

"Don't say anything, though," Charlotte said. "It's not a done deal or anything."

Brinley pressed her lips together and ran her index finger and thumb over them in a straight line like an imaginary zipper. "I won't say a word. It would be a great way to introduce you to the community," Brinley said. "And maybe it would get Amelia dancing again."

Charlotte frowned. "Amelia's not dancing?"

Brinley shook her head. "Not since the accident. It's really sad because that little girl loves to dance."

Charlotte sat with that for a moment. "That's upsetting."

Brinley nodded. "Maybe you're right—maybe this will help."

"And what if we added a few tribute dances for Jules? Just to make it about her—give the kids a chance to say goodbye," Charlotte said. "You know, if we can convince people who were close to her to do it?"

Brinley smiled. "What a great idea."

"Yeah?" Charlotte couldn't help it—the compliment encouraged her.

"Definitely." Out of nowhere, Brinley gasped. "And oh, my goodness, Charlotte! You could perform!" Her voice kicked up to its higher register.

Charlotte laughed. "I'm retired."

Brinley gasped. "What?"

One look at her face and the wave of self-doubt washed over Charlotte again. *You're making a terrible mistake.*

"Long story," Charlotte said lamely.

"Jules always performed a solo to close out the night,"

Brinley said. "And Connor always performed a number with Amelia."

Charlotte's stomach twisted. How were they going to make that happen? "Let's worry about that later—can you reach out to the parents and secure a new date with the theatre?"

"I can do that," Brinley said. "We'll bring the students back in and the other teachers and I will refresh their memories on the recital dances and push the performance date to late July or early August? Would that be enough time?"

Charlotte thought it over. It was barely June. Plenty of time. "I can make it work," Charlotte said.

"And you'll perform?" Brinley appeared to be holding her breath now. "For Jules?"

"I'll think about it," Charlotte said, knowing full well that at this point, she'd do anything for Jules.

Brinley took out a notebook and walked over to the front counter. She opened the pad and began writing furiously.

"What are you doing?" Charlotte asked, peering at the sheet of paper. She tried—failed—to read the scrawled words Brinley was writing.

"Making a list of people to contact. Everyone loved Julianna. I think a lot of people are going to want to be involved. If we get the people here, could you choreograph something for them—maybe three or four numbers? We could have groups or couples."

"I'm not a ballroom dancer," Charlotte said.

"Well, you're a lot better than everyone else in town, so I doubt anyone would care." She tapped her pen on the paper. "I know a lot of people are going to want to be a part of this tribute. The high school football team. Julianna's friends. Hildy and Steve, the people who run Haven House?"

She said it like Charlotte should know what it was.

"Jules told you about it, right? It was pretty special to her."

She hadn't, in fact, told Charlotte about it.

Brinley sighed. "I bet she never in a million years thought her own kids might end up there."

Charlotte frowned. "What do you mean?"

"Haven House is this great transitional home, run by this sweet older couple who've been taking in kids for decades. Basically, it keeps kids out of the system if their parents are going through a hard time. So, say Connor realizes he can't function and isn't able to take care of his kids for a few weeks—he can take them to Haven House and they'll give them everything they need until he's ready."

"And if he's never ready?" What would keep people from dumping their kids at this place and taking off?

"Sometimes that happens, I think, and then the state gets involved. But mostly Haven House just provides a little bit of help when parents hit a rough patch. Julianna volunteered there every week. I'm sure Hildy and Steve will want to be a part of this. They were like family to her."

Charlotte glanced down the hallway, then back at Julianna's assistant. "You really think her kids might end up there?"

Brinley shrugged. "If they do, it will only be temporary. Connor loves those kids, but . . ." Her voice trailed off.

"But . . . ?"

"It's a lot without Jules. Did you ever see them together?"

Charlotte shook her head, not counting the time they came to see her in *Cinderella*. "Not really. She met Connor after she left the ballet, and that's when things started picking up for me, so I didn't really get the chance." *I didn't really make our friendship a priority.*

"As far as Connor was concerned, Jules hung the moon," Brinley said. "I mean, they were so in love it was disgusting. But you know, in the best way."

Charlotte's heart sputtered. She'd never loved anyone like that, and she'd certainly never been loved like that. She couldn't fault Connor for treating her the way he had—she couldn't imagine how painful his loss must be. As it was, her own loss felt heavy enough.

"I'm sure it will all be fine," Brinley said. "I'm betting there will be lots of people reaching out to make sure Connor and the kids are okay."

"Like, her brother?"

Brinley nodded. "Cole loves those kids. And Jules has lots of friends. And like I said, Haven House is there for them if they need it."

Charlotte's mind wandered back to her visit with Connor. He certainly seemed to be struggling. Would this recital help bring some closure to this horrible tragedy?

Would anything do that?

"Why don't we put together a planning meeting with volunteers I know would love to help?" Brinley said, capturing Charlotte's thoughts. "There is a list of regulars who come in to do hair, makeup, help fix costumes, sell refreshments. Jules had a whole team—she never did anything small."

"I bet she didn't." Charlotte smiled.

"Would this week work?"

"My schedule is wide open," Charlotte said. "Count me in."

Brinley handed Charlotte her phone, and she put her number in and handed it back. "I cannot believe I have Charlotte Page's phone number," she said with a sigh.

Charlotte laughed and gave Brinley a wave. "And you're just about the only person in the world who thinks that's something special."

"I know that's not true," she said.

Charlotte flashed her a smile and headed for the door. "Keep me posted!"

"Bye, Charlotte!"

As she walked out, Charlotte heard Brinley say to someone she assumed was on the other end of her phone, "You are not going to believe who just came in to the studio."

5

The next day, after football practice, Cole stared at the broken headlight on his old red truck. He wouldn't admit it out loud, but restoring this Chevy had been like therapy for him in the weeks and months following his split with Gemma. Making sure the truck looked its best had become a therapeutic obsession for him.

When he finished, he moved on to the house renovations. Apparently, this was his way of working through his feelings. Better than sitting on a couch spilling his guts to a stranger, that was for sure.

He'd have to search for replacement parts after the damage done by yesterday's mishap, and he wasn't happy about driving a broken truck around town until it could be fixed.

Practice that morning had been rough. He'd been rough. Bilby didn't even have to say so—Cole knew. He needed to get his head screwed on straight or he'd do more damage to those kids than good. And that was the opposite of his goal as a coach. He loved football, sure, but he started coaching because he wanted to make a difference for the kids, get in

Charlotte shut the car door with her hip and walked to the front of the Jetta, then held the bouquet out in his direction. He could see sprays of color poking out of the top of the brown wrapping.

"You brought me flowers?"

Nobody had ever given him flowers.

Her face fell. Again with that tone. He needed to work on that. Hildy would smack him upside the head if she heard him speak to a woman like that. He reached out and took the bouquet, unsure how to hold it. He sure wasn't going to cradle it the way Gemma would've.

She looked past him and into the garage. "Is it bad?" she asked with a nod toward the truck.

He turned and looked at it as she walked past him and stood in front of the truck, surveying the damage she'd done. "Oh, wow. It is bad."

"It'll be fine," he said. "I just need to order a new headlight." Not entirely true. There was more work to be done to repair the truck, but why go into that now?

"It's a really old truck," she said. "That's probably going to be hard to find, right? I mean, they probably don't keep them in stock at the hardware store." She glanced at him, her eyes wide.

"Um, no," he said, softening his tone. "They don't." There, that was better. Not nearly as rude as he'd been before.

"You'll send me the bill, right?" she asked, turning toward him.

"I've got your number," he said, with no intention of sending her anything. No intention of ever seeing her again, really. She'd just given him flowers, for Pete's sake.

But you did keep her number...

She stood awkwardly in front of him, like she had more

to say but also like she didn't know where to begin. He wasn't one for small talk.

"Was there something else?" he asked.

She swallowed, a surprised look crossing her face. "Just that those probably need water. You know, so they don't die."

He lifted the bouquet and gave it a shake. "Got it."

She nodded. "I'm living here now, at least for a little while, so I just wanted to be sure, you know, there were no hard feelings. It's kind of awful to start your first day in a new town with a fender bender. I guess I just wanted to make sure you weren't upset. I mean, obviously you should be upset, but maybe the flowers will help make you less upset?"

"I'm fine," he said, feeling indifferent.

She nodded again. "Great."

"Great."

She eyed him for a long moment. "They told me you don't like to talk to people, but they didn't tell me you were a grouch." She huffed, walking past him toward her car.

What she'd said should probably upset him, but for some reason he found himself amused. "A grouch?"

"Yeah, a grouch. You know, like the Grinch or Oscar or Scrooge. Someone comes over to your house with a peace offering, you should at least say thank you." All five feet, eight or so inches of her straightened as she squared off in front of him.

"Uh, thank you?" he muttered.

She rolled her eyes and continued toward her car. "Send me the bill, Scrooge."

"Scrooge was a miser, not a grouch," he called out.

She spun around and glared at him. He expected her to roll her eyes again and keep walking, but instead she marched back to him, and for a second he was mildly afraid. She yanked the bouquet out of his hand, rifled around in it, then produced a small white envelope. "You can keep the flowers, but I'm taking this back."

He frowned as she shoved the flowers back toward him. "What is it?"

She steeled her jaw. "You'll never know."

And with that, she trudged back to her car, got in, started the engine, and drove away.

Cole watched the car disappear around the corner, looked at the disheveled bouquet in his hands, and he couldn't help it—he smiled.

6

What an idiot!

Charlotte sped down the unfamiliar street as fast as she could without going over the speed limit. So far, her trip to Harbor Pointe was going swimmingly. Julianna's husband had made it very clear what he thought of her and Julianna's meathead brother seemed intent on putting her in her place.

How many times could she apologize?

She glanced at the small envelope she'd snatched out of the bouquet—at least he'd never read her heartfelt apology or the line she'd almost not written: *Maybe one day we'll actually become friends and this will be a funny memory that makes us laugh. Julianna would get a kick out of that, don't you think?*

How desperate was she to make friends that she extended such a vulnerable olive branch to someone who'd just snapped it in half?

Idiot!

From now on, she'd concentrate only on the people who were nice to her. Like Lucy and her friends from the diner, who'd somehow taken her in as if she'd been a part of their group all along. Charlotte had expected to feel like an outsider, but somehow, that morning, she'd found herself enjoying conversation and an egg white omelet at the diner.

This was Julianna's everyday life, filled with friends and brunches and people who loved her. Charlotte thought she could get used to it, even if a part of her did feel like she was pretending. Even if she'd spent the last two days dodging calls from her irate mother.

These simple moments brought her so much peace.

"Is that all you're going to eat?" Lucy's friend Haley had asked with a glance at Charlotte's plate. "Fruit and an egg white omelet? Do you *know* how good the cinnamon rolls here are?"

Charlotte's eyes meandered to Haley's plate, where one giant, frosted cinnamon roll waited to be eaten. She could smell it from across the table.

But that was not breakfast. Breakfast was about fuel. Eggs were fuel. Cinnamon rolls were not.

"So you and Julianna were pen pals?" Quinn Collins asked. Quinn's Forget-Me-Not flower shop was just a few doors down from the diner. Jules sometimes wrote about her too. Apparently, Quinn had a hunky Olympian husband, and Julianna had shared all the details of that saga with Charlotte last year.

It was sort of surreal sitting here at the same table with people she'd imagined through Jules's letters.

"Julianna and I met at a summer dance intensive when we were kids," Charlotte said. "We were roommates. I remember being so annoyed they stuck me with this girl who was obviously not serious about ballet. She was there to make friends."

The others laughed.

"Sounds like Jules," Lucy said.

"I think Julianna enrolled in the intensive thinking it would be like a sleepaway camp. Not intense training for up-and-coming prima ballerinas." Charlotte smiled at the memory. While thirteen-year-old Charlotte was passing up the dinner rolls, Julianna was sneaking Twix bars after lights-out.

"I didn't know everything was going to be so intense," Jules had said on their third day there.

"Then why did you come?" Charlotte had asked.

Jules swallowed her bite of chocolate and caramel with a shrug. "I came to have fun. To make friends. To do something different for a change. And, honestly, to get out of my house. My parents fight all the time."

"So you don't even want to be a professional dancer?" Charlotte asked, thinking that it was best if she didn't—the less competition, the better. And while Julianna may not be serious about it—she was good. Really good.

"I love dancing," Jules said. "But not with people hollering at me all day. Takes all the fun out of it."

Charlotte rolled over in her bed, annoyed that she'd been paired with someone who so obviously didn't belong there. But in the end, it had been the biggest blessing of her life.

And also in the end, Julianna's mindset changed. While Charlotte was driven by regimen and order, Julianna was driven by passion. And the passion ended up taking her pretty far. She became a beautiful, accomplished dancer.

There really was no telling how far Jules would've gone if she'd chosen to pursue ballet instead of the life she ended up with. If fate—or Charlotte—hadn't intervened.

"Charlotte is the youngest principal dancer in the Chicago City Ballet," Lucy said.

Oohs and aahs circled the table.

"Well, I was," Charlotte said, her laugh nervous and awkward. "I quit."

"You quit and moved to Harbor Pointe?" Haley said in disbelief. "You had the life girls everywhere dream of and you gave it up to move *here?*"

A tickle of concern scurried down Charlotte's back, kicking up that familiar self-doubt she'd been trying to ignore. Leaving the ballet hadn't been a completely rash decision. She'd taken a good four weeks of entertaining the idea before handing in her notice.

The artistic director, Martin DuBois, never one to show emotion, said she'd be missed, thanked her for her years in the ballet, and then basically dismissed her with a flick of his wrist. Charlotte had never felt more irrelevant in her life.

Of course, that was his way. He had an ego to protect, and he certainly wasn't going to beg her to stay. He would send the message that she was replaceable, that she was nothing special, confirming all of her insecurities.

Without dance, she was nothing.

Lucy eyed her. "You gave up a lot, Charlotte. It's normal if you're having regrets." Then, after a pause, "Are you having regrets?"

"Not exactly." Charlotte turned her mug of lukewarm coffee around in her hands. "I feel okay. I mean, it was the first real decision I ever made for myself, so I suppose it's natural to doubt it was the right one."

They all reassured her it was, in fact, natural.

"I just hope you aren't disappointed," Quinn said. "Life in Harbor Pointe is very different from life in Chicago."

"And so far, I'm not making a great impression," Charlotte said.

"She crashed into Cole Turner's truck," Lucy said with a knowing glance across the table.

Collective eye-widening happened around the table.

"You crashed the vintage Chevy?" Haley asked.

"Not a crash, exactly," Charlotte said. "But he seemed pretty mad."

"Cole is kind of—" Quinn started.

"Cranky," Haley interrupted.

"Moody," Lucy added.

"Terrifying," Quinn said.

All three of them laughed.

"Should I be worried? I mean, I smashed the headlight, tried to correct my mistake, and smashed into it again." She grimaced. "I heard metal crunching."

"I'm sure it's fine," Haley said. "He just doesn't like to talk to people, is all."

"He's had a few hard years," Quinn said. "I mean, it's not like his crankiness isn't justified, especially after Jules."

Betsy walked over and tapped the table. "Need you behind the counter, Haley."

Haley gave her boss a mock salute. "Hear you loud and clear, boss."

Betsy smiled, shook her head, and walked away.

"Duty calls," Haley said.

And then the conversation shifted back to Charlotte's plans for the recital and the dance studio, and she didn't get any of the dirt on the man whose truck she'd crashed into the day before.

Getting the flowers had been a sort of spur-of-the-moment idea, and one, it turned out, that seemed to have flopped. Ballet boys were always getting flowers, but she had a feeling it was different in the real world.

She drove across town now toward Lucy's cottage, wishing she'd had the good sense to stay away from Cole Turner the Super Grouch in the first place.

7

Sunday morning, Charlotte woke up early because Lucy Fitzgerald didn't seem to know how to get ready quietly.

Music blared from the bathroom while a slightly tone deaf Lucy sang along at the top of her lungs. Charlotte rolled over with a groan, but then, seconds later, the door to her bedroom opened.

"Sorry, Cee, I wouldn't be a good friend if I didn't invite you to church this morning."

"Cee?" Charlotte opened her eyes, but her hair was covering the one that wasn't covered by the pillow.

"Should I not call you that? I'm big into nicknames."

"It's fine," Charlotte said.

"Good," Lucy said. "So . . . do you want to come?"

"To church?" She rolled onto her back.

"Stupid idea? Forget I asked. Go back to sleep." She started to close the bedroom door.

Charlotte sat up. "I've never been to church."

Lucy stopped and stared at her. "Never?"

Charlotte didn't want to think about all the things she'd

never done. She wanted to try them all. Everything she'd missed out on, though she knew a senior prom was probably out of the question. She shook her head. "Marcia isn't religious."

"Marcia?"

"My mother."

Lucy frowned. "You call your mother by her first name."

Charlotte looked away. "She's a very different kind of mother."

"Well," Lucy said, "you don't have to be religious to go to church. Do you want to come?"

Charlotte shrugged. "I don't really know."

"That's right. You haven't been in the decision-making business long."

"What's it like?" Charlotte asked.

Lucy smiled. "I guess there's only one way to find out."

Charlotte gave her a nod. "Church. Okay. Let's see if I'm a person who likes church."

Lucy's expression seemed to say "Okay, weirdo" but she quickly turned that face into a smile. "Bathroom's all yours." She started off down the hall but popped her head back in. "Oh, and Cee?"

Charlotte met her eyes.

"No ballerina bun today, okay?"

Charlotte's jaw opened slightly, as if to respond, but she quickly snapped it shut.

Lucy smiled. "Great. See you downstairs. We have to leave by eight forty-five."

Charlotte hurried to get herself ready, aware that there was nothing in her luggage that would suffice for church clothes.

About five minutes before they were supposed to leave, Lucy appeared in the doorway. "Ready?"

Charlotte sat on the bed in her bra and underwear.

"Oh, sorry." Embarrassment skittered across Lucy's face. Charlotte gave her body a quick glance and shrugged. "I'm a dancer, Lucy. I'm used to changing clothes in front of a whole company of people."

"Why are you just sitting there?" the redhead asked. "We need to leave."

Charlotte shrugged. "I don't have anything to wear to church."

"You must have something." Lucy walked over to the small guest room closet and opened the door. Inside, she'd find yoga pants, leggings, dance tights, a couple of leotards, two pairs of cut-off jean shorts, cotton shorts, and a wide array of tank tops. "What is all this?"

Charlotte stood and faced her. "Those are my clothes."

"These are, like, gym clothes." Lucy dropped two handfuls of clothing onto the closet floor. "Don't you have any real clothes?"

"I have several cocktail dresses," Charlotte said. "But I left those all in Chicago." She met Lucy's dumbfounded expression. "What? I'm a dancer. I pretty much only needed dance clothes."

"Okay, but dancers still, you know, have lives," Lucy said. "What did you wear when you went out with your friends? Or on dates? Or to the movies or the opera or the museum?"

Charlotte turned away, the view of the lighthouse catching her eye out the window that overlooked the lake. "I didn't do a lot of that."

She could practically hear Lucy's jaw drop. "You can't tell me dancers don't go out."

"Dancers do all those things." She faced Lucy. "But I didn't."

Lucy tossed the pair of jean shorts she was holding. "But you had dates and friends and fun parties to go to, right? I mean, I can remember Julianna telling me more than once about some of the amazing things you were doing in the city."

"I might've exaggerated a little in my letters," Charlotte cut in. "To make myself sound less pathetic."

If Lucy was mad at this admission, she didn't let on. Instead, a look of empathy washed over her face and Charlotte suddenly felt like she was twelve years old and Lucy was her all-knowing big sister.

"Come on, let's find you something to wear," Lucy said.

Charlotte took Lucy's extended hand, and Lucy gave her a little tug, then led her into her room, where there was a less-beautiful view but a substantially larger closet.

Charlotte would've chosen the view every time.

"Here," Lucy said, holding up a cute turquoise sundress. "It'll be too big for you, but we can cinch it with a belt." She thrust the dress toward Charlotte and then went back to her closet, emerging seconds later with a thick red belt. "Don't just stand there, we're going to be late."

"Are you sure I shouldn't have a less-flashy belt?" Charlotte asked, tossing her wavy hair behind her shoulder. She rarely wore her hair down, out of habit mostly, so it made sense that after only a few minutes, she was ready to throw it up into her trademark bun.

"It's church, not a convent," Lucy said.

Charlotte frowned. She took the belt from her friend, wrapped it around her waist, moved it to the very last hole, and suddenly the dress fit like a dream.

"You really need to eat more carbs," Lucy said with an eye roll.

"I eat carbs," Charlotte said. "I have an app that measures exactly how many I can have every day."

Lucy groaned. "Charlotte, you've got to loosen up." She

pulled a pair of red sandals from her closet. "These are going to be too big for you too."

Charlotte slipped them on. "Probably only a half size too big. I can manage."

"Perfect. Let's go."

"I don't have a Bible or anything," Charlotte said as they walked out the back door toward Lucy's car.

"You don't have to have a Bible," she said with a laugh. "Just show up. That's good enough. And for the record, nobody would've kicked you out for wearing yoga pants either."

Charlotte liked the way that sounded but doubted it was true. Religion reminded her of ballet. All or nothing. Rigid rules. Consequences for your actions.

What were the consequences for living a completely selfish life?

They drove through town, the cotton-candy-colored buildings grabbing her attention again. Funny those colors didn't turn Harbor Pointe into something tacky. Somehow, the place maintained its individuality and its charm.

"I still can't believe you're here," Lucy said, tapping the steering wheel as they waited for the light to turn green. "Julianna would be so excited."

"I didn't intend to put you out," Charlotte said. "You've already been so nice to me."

"Are you kidding? You're the most exciting thing that's happened to me in months."

Charlotte laughed. "And I thought my life was boring."

There was a pause as the light changed and Lucy stepped on the gas. "Are you okay, though, Charlotte?"

Charlotte looked at her, and for a brief moment Lucy met her eyes, then went straight back to watching the road. "What do you mean?"

"It was a rash decision is all I'm saying," Lucy said.

"Julianna bragged about you a lot. I think I have a handle on how unique your situation is. Quitting something you've worked so hard for is a big deal."

Charlotte turned and looked out her window just in time to see a powder-puff-blue building with a giant neon-pink ice cream cone sign out front. "I'm okay." She thought she was anyway. Last night, she'd dreamt of her final curtain call. She'd made her exit without anyone knowing. She didn't have a party or flowers or any kind of celebration—she'd simply walked away.

She hadn't even said goodbye. Jameson had probably been hurt by that. He'd been her partner for a long time now. Leaving like that hadn't been fair to him, but Charlotte was so afraid of losing her nerve.

Part of her missed it. At times, her body still moved, almost instinctively, like when she was waiting for her tea to steep the night before and found herself up on her tiptoes, assuming the position the way she had in countless classes over the years.

But she wasn't willing—at least not yet—to say she'd made a mistake.

"Jules always said you were something special," Lucy said. "Said everyone knew it except you."

Charlotte's mind raced back over a decade when her first critical review released. She was so relieved when she read it, thankful this notoriously hard-to-please critic had mostly positive things to say about her performance. She'd been so proud until Marcia pointed out that he'd called Charlotte "beautifully graceful if somewhat delicate." It was a tiny criticism sandwiched between several compliments, but it was the only thing Marcia seemed to take away from that article.

"You wouldn't understand, Lucy," Charlotte said. "You have amazing friends and a job you love and people to share your happiness with. You've gone on dates and had boyfriends and you've got a closet full of the kind of clothes you actually leave the house in. I don't have any of that."

"No, but you had countless adoring fans applauding your every move."

Charlotte stilled. "I guess maybe I want someone to love the parts of me that no one's cheering for." She'd only realized it just now. "And I kind of want to be around people who want to know me as a person—not only as a dancer."

Lucy pulled into a parking place in the lot of a gorgeous white church, put the car in park, and looked at her. "I hope you find what you're looking for."

Charlotte nodded but found herself unable to respond thanks to the obtrusive lump in her throat.

Keep it together.

They emerged from the car, walked toward the front of the church, and instantly Charlotte was overcome with anxiety. What if she stood up at the wrong time or people stared at her? What if they made her say her name out loud in front of everyone or kicked her out for wearing a semi-gaudy red belt and shoes?

She followed Lucy through the front door and into the lobby, where they were greeted by a sweet woman named Beverly, who Lucy told her was related to Quinn somehow —stepmom or something? Beverly had a genuinely motherly way about her, though she was nothing like Charlotte's mother. Probably more like the kind of mother Jules was.

"Charlotte was a friend of Julianna's," Lucy said.

Beverly took Charlotte's hands. "We're all so sad about what happened."

"Me too."

"Well, I'm glad you're here today," Beverly said with a warm smile. She handed them each a program and sent them on their way.

As they walked toward the sanctuary, Lucy stopped to talk to nearly every person they passed, dragging Charlotte along like she was a bird with a broken wing. Charlotte smiled as Lucy introduced her to everyone, *she was Julianna's friend*, and it wasn't until Lucy stopped in the middle of the aisle to chat with a Sunday school teacher named Delia that Charlotte took a second to look around.

Her eyes circled the sanctuary, which was surprisingly spacious given that the church didn't appear to be all that large from the outside. Rows of pews lined the room with a long aisle down the center. The planked wood floor had a rustic look to it, and the walls were painted white.

People milled around like it was social hour, and though Lucy had done a good job of informing many of them who her *not from around here* guest was, there was still a curiosity on most of the faces that looked her way.

Self-consciousness washed over her. Charlotte wasn't used to attention like this. She was used to the kind of attention she couldn't really see. She'd always been grateful for the stage lights because they blinded her to the individual faces watching her perform. Out there, it was just her and the music.

In here, though, she felt like she was standing naked on a stage with all the lights on.

She glanced back at Lucy, who was still chatting away, and wished she could plop down on the pew and hide.

Did they all know she didn't belong here? She didn't exactly look like the rest of them. She'd spent her life believing God was this strange celestial being that liked to toy with the emotions of the people scurrying around on the earth, and blaming Him for saddling her with a mother as controlling and awful as Marcia Page. That's on the rare occasion she thought of Him at all.

But now that she stood here, supposedly to worship

Him, she wasn't sure she could ever reconcile her anger with Him for taking Julianna.

These were the things she was thinking when she happened to glance toward the very back corner of the church where a familiar, sturdy form sat, eyes fixed squarely on her.

She didn't dare look away.

Cranky Cole Turner at church—who would've imagined? Had he come to get washed clean after behaving poorly toward her?

Who was she kidding? No way he was even giving her a second thought. And yet, if that was true, then why was he still watching her?

"Lucy, can we sit?" Charlotte whispered as the music started and the milling seemed to lessen.

"Oh my goodness, of course. So sorry." Lucy moved into the pew where they'd been standing the last five minutes, making sure there was room enough for both of them before taking her seat.

Charlotte sat next to her and let out a deep sigh, keenly aware that throughout this entire church service, Cole Turner could watch her from behind and she would never know.

Also keenly aware that she wished it was the other way around.

8

Cole sat in the very last pew in the back of Harbor Pointe Community Church, trying to focus on the service, but he found himself terribly distracted.

Amelia and AJ sat beside him, both unusually quiet. He'd picked them up that morning and found them sitting on the steps, dressed for church. He put the truck in park and watched them for a brief moment, wishing he could take away their pain.

Wishing someone would take away his.

Connor wasn't ready to face the church crowd—or any crowd—and while he hadn't said so, Cole had connected the dots and determined that his brother-in-law might be wrestling with some anger toward the good Lord above.

He knew a little something about that. After all, he hadn't been back here that long himself.

His eyes darted from the stage to Charlotte then back to the stage.

Then back to Charlotte.

He'd seen her twice before, and both times, he'd been struck by her beauty. But seeing her now, in that dress, with her dark hair in long waves that hung past her shoulders, well, it stirred something in him he thought died the day Gemma left.

But it wasn't just her beauty, was it? As he walked out the door that morning, cup of coffee in hand, he stopped at the vase of flowers sitting on the kitchen counter.

He still couldn't get over the fact that she'd given him flowers.

It was a strange thing to give someone like Cole, but she'd been so earnest when she pulled that bouquet out of the car—there was something sort of innocent about her that had him thinking about her wide blue eyes for the rest of the day. He'd been so distracted, he'd given up on making any progress on his truck or the bathrooms in his old cottage, and ended up crashing on the couch watching ESPN with a TV dinner.

A wasted day, all because of this waifish person who'd come crashing (literally) into his life.

Watching her now, he noticed she seemed out of place. She kept fiddling with her belt and pushing her hair back over her perfect, angular shoulders.

But her eyes never left the stage. It was like she was filled with wonder at the service unfolding in front of her.

He had to hand it to Pastor Newton and his team. It was the first official summer service. They always seemed to kick it up a notch when the tourists arrived, as if it was important to lure the summer crowd in, and maybe it was.

The message (what he'd caught of it) had been designed to entice people to come back next week. It was a feel-good message about God knowing you, your innermost thoughts, and loving you for who you are. What you did didn't matter as much as the condition of the heart.

It wasn't lost on Cole that the condition of his own heart left much to be desired. Truth be told, he didn't want to be here, but family dinner at Haven House was a Sunday tradition, and Hildy's only rule was "If you want me to feed your belly, first you let the pastor feed your soul."

So, he came. Because he wasn't going to turn down Hildy's pot roast.

Not that Cole was a stranger to church. He'd been coming for years, since Hildy and Steve first got up in his business. For a long time, Cole bought everything they were selling—but after Gemma, he wasn't sure what he believed about God anymore.

Maybe he'd had the wrong expectations when he signed up for all this faith stuff in the first place. As it was, he wasn't sure he wanted anything to do with any of it. More to the point, after the way he'd failed, God probably wanted little to do with him either.

That was fine with Cole, so long as he got pot roast and freshly baked homemade dinner rolls.

Julianna bought all of it, but it had been easy for her. She wasn't here when Mom left—she was off in some dance program. She didn't have to pick up the pieces. She didn't have to watch their father try to recover.

And her marriage hadn't epically failed. She had a successful business, a beautiful family, and plenty of people who loved her.

What was God thinking taking her so soon?

It would've made more sense to take Cole—after all, his life wasn't nearly as promising.

Beside him, AJ played with a hymnal from the back of the pew in front of him. His pudgy little hands flipped through the pages. Cole was about to quiet him down when a small, folded program from Julianna's funeral fell out onto the boy's lap.

AJ picked it up and flipped it over, the image of his smiling mother staring back at him. Before Cole could snatch it away, the little boy let out an ear-piercing scream in the otherwise quiet sanctuary.

Heads turned toward them, and heat rushed straight up Cole's back, as he felt himself shrinking under dozens of watchful stares. AJ's scream disintegrated into a sob as the little boy called out one heartbreaking word—"Mom-my!"

"Uncle Cole, do something," Amelia said insistently.

Cole scooped AJ into his arms and moved to the end of the pew, lifting a hand as an apology to the rest of the congregation. What had he been thinking bringing his niece and nephew back here? And whose idea was it to hold funerals in churches anyway? Now, every time they sat in that sanctuary, all they would think about was the fact that Jules was gone.

In the lobby outside the sanctuary, Cole set AJ down, then knelt in front of him and leveled the boy's gaze. "Hey, buddy."

AJ's bottom lip quivered, his cheeks wet with tears that showed no signs of stopping.

"I'm sorry you had to see that," Cole said. "And I'm sorry about your mom."

More crying. "I miss her."

"I know, kiddo. Me too." He hated this. Hated that he couldn't fix it. Hated that he couldn't make the pain go away. Hated that AJ and his siblings would only have a handful of memories of Julianna when they deserved a lifetime.

The service was ending, and Cole glanced back toward the pew where he'd left Amelia, surprised to find Charlotte and Lucy Fitzgerald sitting on either side of his niece. An usher opened the doors that separated the two spaces and people began to filter out. Cole picked AJ up and avoided the many looks of concern.

Through the glass, he watched as Charlotte and Lucy

talked over Amelia's head. Charlotte draped a long, toned arm across the back of the pew, nodded, and then smiled down at Julianna's oldest daughter. Lucy turned just in time to catch him staring at her pretty friend through a Red Sea part in the crowd that now assembled in the lobby.

He quickly washed away whatever stalker-ish expression was on his face and turned his attention back to his nephew, who now stood at Cole's side, finally calmed down.

Most people kept their distance from him these days, but Lucy Fitzgerald wasn't "most people," and she was walking straight toward him. When she arrived in the lobby, she hitched her bag up on her shoulder and squeezed AJ's arm. The boy's eyes found the floor.

Lucy knelt down in front of him, reached into her purse, and pulled out a stick of gum. "Gum?"

AJ nodded, took the gum, unwrapped it, and shoved the whole stick in his mouth.

"That works?" Cole asked.

"Gum and candy," Lucy said. "Works like a charm."

"Good to know."

She stood now, eyeing him with a raised brow and a half-grin. "She's something, huh?" She nodded toward Charlotte.

He was a few years older than the redheaded reporter, but they'd both lived in Harbor Pointe their entire lives, so he knew she had a reputation for saying what she thought, for being far too perky, and for writing articles people actually enjoyed reading.

Once she filled in for a sick sports reporter and Cole had to help her muddle her way through coverage of the high school football playoff game. It was the last kind thing he'd done, he was pretty sure.

Amazing how circumstances could turn you into

someone you hardly recognized when you looked in the mirror.

Before she left that meeting, she'd said to him, "You put on this front of being this super tough, super angry football guy, Cole Turner, but deep down, you're just a big teddy bear with a big old heart."

He didn't respond to her question now. Instead, he brushed past her and back into the sanctuary to retrieve Amelia, feeling like an idiot that Lucy had caught him staring.

"You should talk to her." Lucy followed him toward the front door.

"That's all right," Cole said over his shoulder. *I'm the last person in the world she'd want to talk to after the way I behaved yesterday.*

Lucy shrugged. "Your loss, then."

Cole half laughed. "See ya, Lucy."

"See ya, Teddy Bear."

9
---

*C*harlotte sat in silence at the back of the empty church. Amelia sat beside her, hands folded in her lap, not saying a word.

She'd been stunned to see the look of desperation on Cole's face as she turned toward the heartbreaking scream at the back of the room. He'd picked AJ up like he weighed nothing, then carried him out with a kind of care that reminded her of the way he'd been the day of the funeral.

Her heart wrenched. *I wish I could help.*

That's when she noticed Amelia, left alone in the pew. That's when she decided if she could do nothing else, she could make sure the little girl was okay.

"Thanks."

She turned toward the voice to find Cole standing in the aisle, holding AJ's hand. She stood. "Sure." She looked at AJ, then back to Cole. "Is he okay?"

Cole nodded, but he looked slightly overwhelmed. "He will be." He looked past her to the little girl, still sitting quietly where he'd left her. "Bug, you ready to go see Miss Hildy? She made you an apple pie for dessert."

Bug.

The nickname endeared her to him against her better judgment. This big, strong man wasn't the kind of uncle who only saw his nieces and nephew on holidays. He was familiar with them. Involved in their lives. She felt the subtle shift in her opinion of him, but her face remained indifferent.

Amelia said nothing. She stood, slipped past Charlotte and into the aisle beside Cole. His eyes found Charlotte's—after all, she was staring. "Thanks again."

"Sure," she said.

He turned to go, holding a small hand in each of his own, and as they passed through the doors, Amelia glanced back, blinked, then disappeared into the lobby.

And Charlotte felt more helpless than ever.

Monday morning practice was a disaster. The kids weren't communicating. Cole wasn't communicating. There was an all-around feeling of *I don't want to be here.*

By the end, most of the boys were dragging, so Cole called the practice early, and he didn't hide his frustration. He didn't even call them in the middle of the field for their post-practice pep talk—he just sent them off to the locker room with a grunt.

"You okay?" Bilby wore a disapproving look.

Cole turned toward his assistant coach. "Fine."

"You don't seem fine," Bilby said. "You were pretty hard on them today."

"They need it," Cole said. "They're not working hard enough." They trudged toward the school, Bilby working double time to keep up with Cole's pace.

"They don't have to be state champs, Cole," Bilby said. "But we can make them better men."

Cole stopped. "Are you going to be the one to tell that to the athletic director? The boosters? They're on a high from last season, yeah, but they expect the same thing this year."

"Well, that's not how this works." Matt squared off in front of him. "You're the best coach I've ever worked with, but not because of your winning record. Because you care about the kids. You seem to have forgotten that the last few months."

Cole resumed marching toward the school, Bilby hot on his heels.

"I know it's been a hellish few years for you, Coach," he said to the back of Cole's head. "But these boys look up to you. They could use a leader."

"I got it, Bilby." Cole pulled the door open and stormed into the school building. He walked down the hall to his office and closed the door behind him, hoping the light slam punctuated his sentence—and told his assistant coach he was done talking about it.

He turned and found Asher sitting on the couch.

"Ash. What's up?"

The kid looked up at him. "Hey, Coach. Can I talk to you for a minute?"

"We can make them better men."

Matt's words hung over him like vines from a tree.

He could've talked to Asher yesterday at Hildy's Sunday dinner. Cole ate Sunday dinner at Haven House fairly regularly, but this was the first time he'd been there with Asher and his brothers. Trouble was, he was so preoccupied with his niece and nephew, he'd barely spoken to Asher, even though he could tell something was bugging him.

Asher had barely looked up from his plate, and whatever

was on his mind, it hadn't gone away overnight. He'd been completely distracted all morning.

"'Course." Cole stepped farther inside the office, dropped his clipboard and a football onto the desk, and sat down across from his quarterback. "What's going on?"

Asher leaned forward, elbows on his knees. He was a wiry kid, but strong, fast, and able to see the field and adjust on the fly. That was rare. In truth, Asher West had even more potential than his predecessor, and Jared had gotten a full ride to Michigan State. It might take another year before Cole helped Asher realize that potential, but it was there—he knew it was.

Think of how a scholarship like that could change Asher's life. If the kid was willing to put in the time, he'd be—

"I have to quit the team," Asher blurted, interrupting Cole's thoughts.

"Say again?" Cole tapped on the desk with his fingers. He hadn't pegged Asher as the kind of kid who was afraid of a little hard work.

"I'm sorry, Coach. I know you put in a lot of time with me, and you don't really have a backup, but I can't make the practices anymore."

"You going on vacation or something?" Cole heard his rough tone and made a mental note to soften it.

Asher looked at him. "Yeah, Coach, like I've ever been on vacation." It wasn't like the high school junior to mouth off, but his words dripped with sarcasm. And they should. What a stupid thing for Cole to say.

Haven House kids didn't get vacations. They were all in survival mode.

"Well, what is it, then? You afraid to follow in Brown's footsteps? Afraid of a little hard work?"

"I'm not afraid of anything." Asher's jaw tightened. "And you wouldn't understand."

"I understand you've got one heck of an arm, kid," Cole said. "I understand this is about your best chance at having a life outside of Harbor Pointe."

"Oh, really? You think some college is going to come snatch me up?"

"Why not? Worked for Jared."

"I'm not Jared," Asher said. "MSU isn't gonna give me a full ride."

"Don't be so sure," Cole said.

"Coach, you're just getting my hopes up talking like that," he said.

"You've got what it takes to play college ball, Ash." Cole looked at him. Was he just getting his hopes up? His mind scrolled through all the moments Asher had impressed him. It was like a highlight reel of potential. It would take work, and it wouldn't happen overnight. Might not even happen this season, but he believed in Asher. Cole knew he could turn him into a stellar quarterback by his senior year.

Asher shook his head, as if he was mentally tossing the idea around. "It's a pipe dream, and you're just trying to get me to stay."

Cole drew in a breath and studied the kid. In all these months of coaching him, Asher had always remained quiet and withdrawn.

His conversation with Bilby rushed back. Cole might've blown it on the field that morning, but here was a chance to do better. This kid didn't need tough love right now, and Cole knew it.

"What's going on, son? Really?"

Asher shook his head, and Cole could see in just seconds, the boy had shut down. He didn't trust Cole enough to tell him anything. And that was Cole's fault.

"You wouldn't get it," Asher said. "But I have to quit, so you'll have to find another quarterback."

And with that, Cole's only hope at a winning season walked out the door.

He let out a sigh—a heavy one—and rubbed his temples. The knock on his door was followed by Matt's "Hey."

Cole leaned back in his chair, motioning for his assistant coach to sit down.

"What was that about?"

"He just quit," Cole said.

"He quit?"

"Yep. Didn't give a reason, but he's done."

"He can't quit. If that kid quits, he can kiss college goodbye. No way he'll be able to afford it without a scholarship."

"I can't force him to stay."

"What did you say to him?"

"Asked him why. Asked him if it was because he was scared. Asked him if he didn't want to do the work." Cole sighed. He shouldn't have said that, he knew it wasn't true. What did he think—he could bully the kid into staying? He glanced over and found Matt's look of disapproval waiting for him.

"I know," Cole said. "I could've handled it better."

After a long pause, Matt cleared his throat. "I'm not supposed to know this, but I think Asher was out looking for a second job yesterday. I saw him downtown."

"So?"

"So, I think he got one at the donut shop and they open at four in the morning. His shift probably doesn't end until at least ten. I don't think this is him wanting to quit. I think he just needs the money."

Cole shook his head. "Well, why didn't he say that, then?"

"Maybe you didn't give him the chance."

He tapped his fingers on the desk again.

Cole felt like a first-class jerk. Asher had to know that Haven House wasn't a long-term solution. It hadn't been designed that way. So, if their time there ran out, and parents weren't a viable option, Asher and his siblings would go into the system.

This kid was trying to make money so he could keep his family together. He wasn't out selling drugs or stealing cars—he quit to work in a donut shop.

And Cole had practically accused him of being afraid of a little hard work.

Way to go, Turner.

"Do you know how much longer they can stay at Haven House?" Bilby asked.

Cole shook his head. "No, but I can find out."

He racked his brain trying to think of anyone who could help. The urgent look on Asher's face—the constant line of concern knit across his brow—that sixteen-year-old kid's entire life was a disaster and not because of anything he'd done. He wanted to keep his family together, and football was a casualty of that. Of course it was. Football meant nothing if he and his siblings were split up.

Cole had an opportunity here—a real chance to help a kid who had been put in his care. It had been a long time since he'd really made a difference in anyone else's life, and he vowed in that moment to step up and be the coach these boys needed.

And if they won games in the process, great. And if they didn't, Cole would make sure they walked away with something much more important.

"Let me see if there's something I can do," Cole said.

"Like what?"

"I'll let you know as soon as I get it figured out." Cole picked his keys up off the desk. "I'll call you later."

10

Monday morning, Charlotte woke to find four new text messages. All from Marcia.

Okay, you've had your little break. Time to come back to the real world!

You only have so many years left, Charlotte. Now is not the time to have a mental breakdown!

Martin isn't going to wait around for you, Charlotte. He will find a replacement!

And Charlotte's personal favorite:

You're making a huge mistake!

It wasn't like her mother to use so many exclamation points. She must mean business. But for the first time in her nearly thirty years, Charlotte didn't care. It was as if it had finally hit her that she was responsible for her own life. She had no one to blame for the emptiness but herself. She'd bought everything Marcia sold, and the result had been a life of loneliness.

She'd achieved every professional goal she'd set for herself (with Marcia's influence). And only now did she realize it had all left her feeling a little empty. Living for applause, for "atta girls," for the approval of others had left her cold. She was ready for something new.

Ready for her work to mean something.

She'd woken up early and gone for a run. It cleared her head and gave her a chance to explore Harbor Pointe.

She rounded the corner, easily getting lost in her thoughts as she ran through the quaint neighborhoods that were about as different from the Chicago landscape as a person could imagine. It was odd how Lake Michigan views could be so different depending on their surroundings.

Cottages with neatly manicured lawns lined the brick road, most accented by sprays of purple and pink flowers. Children rode their bikes, laughing and playing. Across the street, two girls were jumping rope. It was like something out of a movie.

Two women pushed strollers in the opposite direction, and Charlotte moved out of their way as they passed, both of them smiling and giving her a polite "Hello."

So this was what a small-town life was really like.

She reached an intersection and recognized the street to her right. Julianna's street. The stark realization that things were not always as they seemed smacked Charlotte—hard. Behind the walls of these idyllic homes, at the heart of desirable neighborhoods, there was pain. Real, unbearable, up-ending pain.

She turned down the street. She knew Connor probably didn't want to see her, but she'd told him she was going to be a better friend, and she meant it. And maybe a part of her wanted to tell him about the rescheduled recital.

Maybe she wanted his approval.

She slowed her pace, eyeing the front porch when she noticed a little girl was sitting on the swing, writing in a notebook.

Amelia.

Charlotte stopped in front of the gray cottage. The thick white trim perfectly accented the windows and door, but unlike the other houses she'd just been admiring, the Ford yard wasn't so neatly manicured. Dandelions covered the green grass like a blanket, and the flowerbeds were overgrown. She knew nothing about tending to a yard, but even she saw the difference between theirs and the others on the street.

I just want to help.

"Hey, Amelia." Charlotte stood at the bottom of the porch steps.

The little girl looked up but didn't respond.

She'd briefly introduced herself at church the day before, but as she stood in front of Julianna's oldest child now, she found herself tongue-tied. So many things she wanted to say. Stories she wanted to share. Apologies she wanted to offer.

The sound of a vehicle approaching drew the girl's eyes. Charlotte followed her gaze toward the street just in time to see a familiar truck ambling toward her.

Cole.

Her stomach twisted.

He parked along the curb and exited the truck while Charlotte did her best to focus on his trademark scowl and not how attractive he was.

So far, she was failing.

But honestly, any woman with a pulse would've struggled in her situation. Yes, he was grumpy and rude, but he obviously had a soft spot for his family, and that was maybe even more attractive that his muscular torso and eyes as dark as hot fudge.

Today he wore jeans, a navy blue T-shirt, and a baseball cap, topped off with a pair of aviators that made him look like a male model.

Oddly, Charlotte had the feeling Cole had no idea just how attractive he was. He could've easily been the kind of guy who brought a new girl home every night, but she also got the feeling he had no interest in that.

Of course, that only made him more appealing.

He walked around to the other side of the truck and took off his sunglasses. He glanced at Amelia, then back at Charlotte.

"Hey," she said.

"Hey."

She stood, awkwardly, for several seconds, feeling every bit the imposition she was.

"What are you doing here?" he asked with another glance at Amelia.

That she hadn't divulged her connection to his sister by now was probably not ideal, and yet all of their interactions until now had been less than friendly. He couldn't blame her for not working it into a conversation they weren't having.

"I stopped by to talk to Connor," she said.

"You know Connor?" Cole looked confused.

"Not really," she said. "I knew Jules."

The frown line etched in his forehead deepened. "You did?"

"We danced together," Charlotte said. "Before"—she waved her hands toward the house—"before all this."

His eyes caught her and seemed to have no intention of

letting go.

Thankfully (or maybe not?) the door opened and Connor appeared. He held Alaina and looked even more exhausted than the last time she'd seen him.

He spotted Charlotte and frowned. "What are you doing here?"

People seemed to ask her that a lot, and it certainly didn't make her feel welcome.

"I came by to talk to you about the dance studio," Charlotte said.

"Amelia, will you take your sister inside?" Connor asked.

The little girl stood, and then, in a way that a much older person would've done, she slipped the baby into her hands, positioned her on her tiny hip, and walked into the house, closing the door behind her.

"Is she okay?" Charlotte asked, haunted by the sadness behind her eyes.

"She's fine," Connor said. He pushed his hands through his hair and let out a sigh. "The sitter will be here soon."

"I told your sitter not to come." Cole took a step closer and Charlotte's skin tingled at his nearness, as if every nerve-ending in her body stood at attention.

She had very little experience around men, and frankly, she wasn't sure how to keep her cool when her body responded without her permission.

"I've got to get to work," Connor said.

Connor didn't even look like he'd showered—and it was almost nine in the morning.

"I called Hildy," Cole said.

"Why?" Connor's face flushed red.

Cole shrugged. "You need a break, man. I'm going to work out here in the yard, and she's coming to get the kids for a few days."

"No," Connor said. "I'm fine. I don't want my kids at Haven House."

Charlotte didn't miss the change in Cole's expression, but she couldn't place it.

"Sorry, man," Connor said.

"She offered," Cole said. "They could come to my house, but I only have the one extra room. Steve and Hildy will make it feel like vacation for them."

Charlotte felt heat rush to her cheeks. She wished she'd kept on running. As it was, she felt like she was standing in the middle of a family conversation, a family she was very much not a part of.

Connor's full attention landed on Charlotte, as if he'd just remembered she was there. "What did you need to talk to me about?"

"It can wait," she said.

"No, I need something else to think about." He tossed Cole a side-eye, which even Charlotte could see was meant to make a point, and gave her a look that said *I'm waiting.*

Her eyes darted to Cole, who wore the same expression, and now she wished she could hide in a corner.

She hadn't intended to discuss any of this with Julianna's cranky older brother, but it didn't seem like she had much choice.

"I told Brinley I'd like to head up the recital," Charlotte said. "But we wanted to make sure it was okay with you. We'd like to do a little more with it than your typical dance recital."

Connor crossed his arms and now wore a look that seemed to say he couldn't be bothered. "What does that mean?"

She pressed her lips together, aware that her question about wanting his approval had been answered. She desperately wanted it. She longed for someone else to tell her she was good enough to do the thing she wanted to do, which in this case wasn't performing. It was organizing and executing a dance recital that would serve as a tribute to this man's late wife.

And convince him to let her buy the dance studio.

She felt wholly unprepared for this epic task. And yet, there was also a deep sense of purpose like she hadn't felt in years. She needed to do this. For Jules, yes, but for herself too. She needed to prove she was more than what she'd always been. What if Connor took away that chance?

"We want the recital to be a tribute to Julianna," Charlotte said. "A celebration of her life."

Connor's face twisted in a way she hadn't expected.

"Knowing Jules, I think she would've wanted her students to have their recital."

"She would've," Cole said quietly. "It was her favorite part of the year."

Charlotte glanced at him and a collective sorrow fell on the three of them. For a moment, however fleeting, they all had one thing in common—grief.

"It's fine," Connor said, avoiding her eyes. "Go ahead with the recital. It's a good idea."

"I'll handle everything," she said. "But there was one other thing—" It was a big ask, and she knew it. How did she even broach the subject?

He dragged his gaze to hers. "What?"

"Brinley said you and Amelia always did a dance," Charlotte said.

Connor's lip twitched. "We did."

"No pressure at all, but I'd love to help you with that if you want."

"I'll think about it," Connor said.

"I think it would be good for Amelia, and—"

"I said I'd think about it," Connor interrupted.

Charlotte snapped her jaw shut.

The silence turned awkward again, and Cole's eyes darted to hers.

"We're also going to have a few tribute dances." Charlotte struggled to find something to say to fill the space. "People who loved her can do fun numbers in her honor, and—"

Connor cut her off again. "It's good, Charlotte," he said. "Jules would be so happy." His voice broke and he looked away. "Maybe you're right, Cole. Maybe I do need to take the day off."

Cole clapped a hand on the other man's shoulder. "Let me handle things here, all right?"

"Thanks, man," Connor said. He turned toward the door, then stopped and turned back. "I'm sorry I was so rude to you the other day, Charlotte. You meant the world to Jules, you know that, right?"

The words burrowed down inside her, and all she could do was nod in reply. Anything else, and Charlotte might've felt the depth of the loss they'd all suffered, and that was too raw, too real, for her to manage right now.

11

Connor went inside, leaving Cole standing on the steps with a woman who was apparently not who he thought.

"Do you think he'll be okay?" she asked.

He stuffed his hands in his pockets. Coming here after practice had been a rash idea, a plan meant to distract him from things he didn't want to think about. Or maybe sort out what he needed to do to get his coaching back on track.

He planned to mow Connor's overgrown grass, pull some weeds, check on the kids, make sure the guy was eating and then, with any luck, he'd go home and crash.

That plan had gone awry.

"I do," he said. "But it's gonna be a while." He started off toward the garage and realized she was following him.

"I wish there was something I could do," she said.

He stuck his head inside the garage and pressed the button to open the door. "You didn't say you knew Jules."

"You didn't bother to ask."

He deserved that. He didn't acknowledge it, but he knew he deserved it.

"Sorry," she said. "That was rude."

"I can take it." He spotted the lawn mower buried in the corner.

"I met Jules when we were just kids," she said from the doorway. "She was my only friend."

He glanced at her, but she wasn't looking at him. She seemed to be off in her own little world. When she snapped out of it and made eye contact with him, she shifted.

"She never mentioned me?"

Cole shook his head. "I really didn't keep up with all the dance stuff Jules did back then. I had a lot going on at home." He hoped she didn't ask what—his dysfunctional family was about the last thing he wanted to discuss.

"But it wasn't just back then," she said. "We've always kept in touch, even after Jules left the ballet and got married. We were like pen pals."

"Pen pals?"

"People who write letters to each other," Charlotte said.

"I know what a pen pal is," Cole said. "You're from the city?"

She nodded. "Chicago."

"So, how'd you end up here?"

She leaned against the doorjamb and watched as he gingerly took a step closer to the mower. "I needed a fresh start."

"And you came here?" He would've laughed, but the look on her face stopped him. "It's just really different from Chicago."

"That was kind of the point," she said. Embarrassment skittered across her face. "I wanted a quieter life."

He tugged on the mower, clearing a path to the door. "Well, you'll certainly get that in Harbor Pointe."

"And I want to buy Julianna's dance studio."

He frowned. "Buy it?"

She shrugged. "Someone should keep it going."

He squinted, sizing her up. He didn't know Charlotte—had no memory of her, and Julianna hadn't mentioned her to him, but he had a feeling she could do a lot better than owning a dance studio in a small tourist town. "Why?"

She looked away. "I have my reasons."

"Fair enough." He wasn't one to push for conversation. He freed the mower and now stood at the front of the garage.

Charlotte came around the side to the driveway and crossed her arms over her chest. "Can I help?"

"Help what?"

"In the yard?"

He squinted down at her. "Have you ever done yard work?"

"No," she said. "But how hard can it be?"

He eyed her for a long moment, dressed in her workout clothes (which showed enough skin to require him to lasso his wandering thoughts).

"I'm not as fragile as you think," she said pointedly.

"I never said you were fragile."

"All right, then tell me what to do."

∽

Charlotte ran home to put on more appropriate work clothes, and by the time she came back, Hildy had picked up the kids and Cole had mowed the front yard.

She considered inching her car right up on the bumper of his truck, just to be funny, but decided against it. She didn't know Cole well, but she did know that his sense of humor wasn't likely one of his best qualities.

The fictitious version of him she'd created in her mind all those years ago had been completely wrong.

Besides, he was watching her—probably to make sure she didn't crash into the truck—and that was too unnerving for humor.

She parked the car, got out, and met him on the sidewalk.

"Are you sure you want to volunteer for this?" he asked.

"It's the least I can do," she said.

"Why's that?" He adjusted his ball cap, then turned his attention to her.

She looked away. It didn't feel like the right time to tell him what a lousy friend she'd been to his sister. "Can I just work on the yard?"

He shrugged, then handed over a rake. "It's all yours."

Charlotte had no idea what to do with a rake, which was undoubtedly exactly what her face communicated.

"Here." He took it from her, then gave her a lesson on raking, in which he was slightly condescending. "Think you can do that?"

She took the rake and rolled her eyes, which he likely couldn't see because she was wearing sunglasses. "I got it."

They worked in silence for what felt like ages. It turned out that yard work was a lot more difficult than Charlotte would've ever imagined, and yet it calmed her. Gave her something to focus on, a task she could accomplish without any pressure, which was a welcome change.

Cole finished mowing, then started weeding the opposite end of the yard. If she didn't know better, she'd say he was avoiding her.

Which was why it got a little awkward around noon when her stomach growled. She stood and admired the section she'd just finished weeding, rubbing her right shoulder with her left hand. Kneeling in that position for any length of time was working a number on her body.

"I think I need a break," she said. "Are you hungry?"

He leaned back on his feet and looked at her. For a long moment, it was almost like he was trying to decide if he wanted to let her in on a secret.

"It's really not a hard question," she said.

He stood. "I could eat."

"Okay," she said. And that's when it dawned on her that she'd inadvertently asked him out. Not really, but she felt every bit as self-conscious about it as she would if this were a date. Especially since she'd never been on a real date.

"I'll drive." He tossed her a look that almost translated as amusement.

Almost.

She grabbed her purse from her car, trying to slow her pulse. The fact was, she'd never been alone with a man, not socially anyway. And not a man who turned her insides out the way Cole did.

It stung a little that he didn't remember her, even after learning she'd known Jules for years, but she couldn't blame him. They'd only met a couple times, and though she thought they'd shared a moment, it was quite possible she'd worked it up to be a lot more than it was.

She had an overactive imagination, after all.

The fact was, she'd built an entire daydream around that one encounter, and though it had been a long time since she'd let that dream go, it still kind of disappointed her that reality was so different than her fantasy.

Cole was *not* the man of her dreams after all.

12

Charlotte pulled herself into the cab of the truck, surprised that it was so clean, but then, the exterior should've been a dead giveaway of that. Where this vehicle was concerned, Cole was meticulous.

They drove toward downtown in complete silence, and while he seemed perfectly comfortable with that, her mind wouldn't stop racing for something—anything—to say.

"I met you when we were kids," she blurted, instantly wishing she could retract her statement.

He peered over at her, then back to the road. "You did?"

She watched the houses pass by out the passenger side window. "Yeah, I was about fourteen. You came to talk to Jules."

A stoplight gave him the opportunity to look at her, and she willed it to turn green—and fast. Apparently, her will was not strong enough because this was the longest red light ever. "That was you?"

It was as if he'd just remembered that night.

Julianna and Charlotte were about halfway through their third summer at the ballet intensive, and Charlotte wasn't sure how many more they would have. She danced professionally most of the year, and she knew it might not be long before Marcia forbade the intensive. As it was, the only reason her mother still allowed it was because the past two years had led to some very important connections in the dance world. Training with top-rate teachers had led to legitimate jobs, and that was always Marcia's goal.

And that was fine with Charlotte, because her most important connection was Julianna, whose carefree approach to the whole thing always seemed to leave Charlotte wondering what else might be out in the world, waiting to be discovered.

One night, after their classes ended, Julianna begged Charlotte to go out with a big group of them. Of course, Charlotte had refused—she saw the value in a good night's sleep, and she didn't want Marcia to catch her.

"Charlotte," Jules had said on her way out the door, "I'm worried about you."

She frowned. "Why?"

"All you ever do is dance," Julianna said.

"That's why we're here, Jules." Charlotte pulled a water bottle from the small fridge in the dorm where they were staying. "To dance."

"Right, but we're also here to live," Jules said.

Charlotte opened the bottle and took a drink. "You know my mom is expecting very specific things from this showcase tomorrow." The professionals in the audience could help elevate Charlotte's career—it was what she needed to get to the next level.

Julianna pulled the front door open and tossed a glance over her shoulder. "You sure?"

For the briefest moment, Charlotte imagined what would happen if she did go—even just for a little while. Would she fit in? Would the other dancers accept her?

Would she finally know how it felt to belong? But reality quickly answered for her. "I'm sure."

She'd spent the evening decompressing with a TV movie and drifted off to sleep on the couch, exhausted from a grueling day of dance.

She may've slept there until morning, but a knock at the door jolted her awake.

The blue light of the television flickered in the dark suite, and she squinted to see the clock. It was after midnight—did she dream that knock?

Another knock answered her question.

Julianna had probably forgotten her key. Charlotte pulled herself off the couch and padded toward the door, sleepy and out of sorts. She opened the door.

"Jules—" She stopped short when a boy's face stared back at her. Without thinking, she slammed the door shut and locked it. Not only was she barely clothed, she was alone. And she had no idea who this guy was.

He knocked again. "I'm looking for Julianna," he said through the door.

"She's not here."

"Do you know where she is?"

"She's out with friends."

She heard an audible sigh on the other side of the door.

"Who are you?" Julianna hadn't mentioned a boyfriend.

"I'm her brother. Cole?"

He said it as if it were explanation enough. Charlotte's heart pounded—it was highly unlikely he wasn't who he said he was, but why was he here in the middle of the night?

"Is everything okay?" she asked.

"Not really," he said. "I called but she's not answering."

"Where do you live?" She pressed her ear against the door, then looked out the peephole and watched him answer.

"Harbor Pointe," he said. "It's in Michigan."

"What's the name of Julianna's dance teacher?" she asked.

He groaned. "I think it's CeCe or Cecily or something."

She pulled the door open. "It's Celia. And you should know that—she's only the most important person in Julianna's life."

He stared at her. She stared back.

Finally, he shrugged. "Sorry?"

"You can wait in here."

"Thanks." He held her gaze.

Her heart turned over. So *this* was what it felt like to be attracted to a boy. She'd never quite understood it before. She didn't meet many boys outside of dance, and frankly, none of them had ever made her feel like this.

She stepped out of the way so he could come inside. They had a small common area next to the bedroom, and she motioned for him to take a seat. She watched as he slunk down on the small sofa and raked his hands through his hair.

"Are you okay?" She leaned against the wall.

"Do you know how late she'll be out?" he asked.

Charlotte glanced at the clock. "I think she should be home any minute. She doesn't usually stay out too late."

"You sure you don't care if I wait?" he asked.

She shook her head. "Not at all. The remote for the TV is there." She pointed to it, then started toward the bedroom.

"Why aren't you with her?" he asked.

She stopped, turning back to look at him. If he hadn't been looking right at her, she might've taken a minute to admire him. He looked like someone who would play the football star in a movie, not like a boy who would be sitting on her sofa in the middle of the night.

Her cheeks flushed. "I don't go out much."

"How come?"

"We have a performance tomorrow," she said. It was almost the truth. She also didn't go out because social settings only highlighted all the ways she was different, all the ways she didn't fit in. She couldn't afford to get distracted, not if she was going to join a company and make it as a professional dancer.

"Doesn't Jules have a performance?" he asked.

Charlotte nodded.

He leaned back on the couch, his T-shirt pulling tight over his chest. "What a disaster." He rubbed his face with both hands.

"What's a disaster?" she asked.

He shook his head. "Sorry, I shouldn't have said that."

"It's okay." She lingered a little too long, her insecurity working overtime. Why did she suddenly want to know everything about him? "Do you want something to drink?"

He nodded. "That'd be great."

She opened the refrigerator and pulled out a bottle of water, tossing it to him and closing the door with her foot.

"Thanks for this." He opened the bottle and took a drink, then his phone buzzed in his pocket. He shifted to get it out, flipped it open, looked at the screen, clicked a button, and tossed the phone on the couch beside him. He looked up, found her staring, and quickly looked away. "Sorry. And I'm sorry to barge in on you unannounced."

She studied him. Sandy-colored hair. Long, dark eyelashes covered deep-set, intense brown eyes. Differently developed muscles than the ballet boys she spent most of her time with. Sturdy jaw. Really lovely, manly-looking hands.

She leaned against the wall. She should go to bed. She really did have a big day in the morning.

But something about him kept her from moving. He seemed broken, and she was overcome with the desire to fix him. "Why are you here?" she asked quietly. "Families don't usually come until the final performance."

He scoffed. "Well, our family won't be coming at all."

She frowned. "What do you mean?" Julianna's parents always came. Cole didn't though. He always stayed behind for football practice. Probably couldn't be bothered with his sister's ballet, which was a shame because if that weren't the case, Charlotte would've met him sooner.

And she really wished she'd met him sooner.

"I really need to talk to Jules," he said. "I need to make sure she hears this from me." He sighed. "She's going to be crushed."

"Hears what?" Now Charlotte was worried. Had someone died? Was someone sick? Whatever it was—she could see by the look on his face, it was bad. And he was here out of genuine concern for his sister.

What would it feel like to have someone care about you that much?

The door behind Charlotte opened and Julianna burst in. "Charlotte, you should've come! Nico did the dumbest thing—" At the sight of her brother, Julianna stopped. "Cole. What are you doing here?"

His eyes found Charlotte, and she quickly understood what he was too kind to say.

"I'll leave you guys," she said. She slipped into the bedroom and lay down in her bed, pulling the covers up to her chin and trying not to eavesdrop.

The low timbre of Cole's voice made it difficult to hear what he was saying, but after he spoke for a few minutes, she heard Julianna's quiet sobs.

"That can't be right," Jules said. "Mom would not do that to us."

"Jules," Cole said. "I'm not making it up. Mom's gone."

Sitting here now, in the cab of Cole's truck, Charlotte couldn't help but wonder what had happened to that sweet, kind older brother who'd traveled three hours to the city to track down his sister to make sure he was the one to give her the bad news that their mother had walked out on them.

In his place, there was now a cranky, irritating, angry man with no social skills and zero manners.

A man who gave up an entire day to take care of his brother-in-law's lawn.

Charlotte shook the conflicting thoughts aside. "Yeah," she finally said, answering his question. "That was me."

13

*S*o that was why Charlotte was familiar. They'd met several years ago. Why hadn't she said anything before now? And why did he feel suddenly uncomfortable that she knew more about him than he'd thought?

He remembered that night. He remembered Julianna's roommate—he'd been instinctively drawn to her for no good reason. Maybe he'd simply been in pain, and she was the one to show him kindness.

Whatever it was, Cole wouldn't sort through it with her beside him. To that end, she spent lunch and the rest of the afternoon holding up both ends of the conversation.

And he unintentionally reclaimed his title as "Rudest Man in the World."

Eventually, he noticed, she stopped being nice. Stopped asking him questions. Stopped trying to draw conversation from him. That well had run dry, as she unfortunately discovered.

When they finished the yard work, they stood in silence on the sidewalk, admiring their handiwork.

There. Now Jules's house looked like it belonged on this street. No longer an eyesore of neglect, the cottage wouldn't give away her family's secret pain. Satisfied with their work, Cole strode over to the garage, closed the door, then gave Charlotte a wave.

"Thanks for the help," he said. "I'm going to go check on Connor."

He disappeared into the house, aware that he'd just dismissed her like she was the hired help and not a friend of his sister who'd just spent her entire day doing something simply because she wanted to help.

The next morning, after practice, Cole opened his refrigerator and pulled out a carton of eggs. He closed the door, pausing at the sight of Charlotte's phone number, stuck on by an *I <3 NY* magnet Julianna had given him ages ago.

He pulled his phone from his back pocket and opened a new message. He punched the number into the "To" line and typed:

Thanks for the help yesterday. You gave me a good idea.

He stared at the words, then deleted the second sentence.

Thanks for the help yesterday.

He clicked send.

He waited for a minute to see if she'd reply, then realized he was being stupid and shoved the phone back in his pocket and started making an omelet. Moments later, he felt his phone vibrate. He pulled it out, disappointed to discover a text from Bilby and aware that that disappointment was dangerous.

I was right. Asher's at the donut shop.

Cole stared at the words for a moment, thinking of the idea he'd had yesterday, working with Charlotte on the yard.

He stuck the carton of eggs, along with the bowl he'd scrambled, back into the refrigerator, grabbed his keys, and went outside to his truck. He drove toward downtown, pulling into a spot in front of the donut shop just as Asher was walking out the door.

Cole saw the kid recognize his truck, then turn and walk the other way.

Great.

He got out and started down the sidewalk, a few yards behind Asher. "Hey, twenty-two!"

Asher stopped and slowly turned to face him. "Coach."

They stood for a few seconds, as if having a duel, each one waiting to see who would make the first move. "Heard you got a job here." Cole motioned toward the donut shop with his head.

"So?"

"So, I've got an offer for you," Cole said.

Asher's expression went from indifferent to mildly interesting, but he said nothing.

"I'm renovating my house," he said. "I could use some help."

"So?"

"You want the job?" The idea had come to Cole yesterday when he spent a fair amount of time teaching Charlotte how to do the simplest of tasks. He would've thought that would make him crazy, but he was a teacher after all. It shouldn't surprise him that teaching was rewarding. If he was honest, it was kind of nice to work on something with another person for a change.

Maybe he could teach Asher a few life skills—how to fix

a toilet, how to tile a shower, how to lay hardwood—and the hours would accommodate football practices.

"I'm not a charity case, Coach." Asher turned and started off in the opposite direction.

"I never said you were," Cole called out, following him. "You'd be helping me out."

Asher stopped. "I don't know anything about renovating a house."

"Well," Cole said, "I'd be helping you out too."

The kid frowned.

"Look, I don't think for one second you want to quit football. I've seen you throw. I've seen you practice. I know you love the game more than anything else."

"Not more than my brothers."

"What if you could do both?" Cole asked. "Stay on the team and still make money to help your brothers."

He shrugged. "I don't need a handout."

Cole scoffed. "You don't know me at all if you think this is a handout. I'll work your tail off."

"No thanks," Asher said. "I know what I need to do, and I hate to say it, Coach, but you wouldn't get it."

More proof Asher didn't know him at all.

"Look, I'm not gonna beg," Cole said. "I want you on the team, and I think football is going to give you some great opportunities in the future. I need some help with my house, and learning that kind of work can only help you down the road. That's it. No ulterior motive, no offer of charity." Cole stopped before adding, "And if you're too dumb to realize that, there's not much more I can do"—but it took everything he had to keep his mouth closed.

His father hadn't taught him much in the way of life skills. Everything Cole had learned, he'd learned from Steve. His stint at Haven House hadn't lasted long, but that hadn't mattered to the man. He got in Cole's business when he lived there, and he stayed in it long after he'd gone.

Steve had taught him one important negotiation tactic —"You have to be willing to walk away." If the other party is bluffing, you'll find out fast.

Asher, it turned out, wasn't bluffing. He stormed off down the street without looking back.

Cole got back in his truck and started the engine, watching the kid disappear around a corner. His phone buzzed. He pulled it out and found a text from Charlotte.

I was happy to help.

Cole pulled out onto the street, aware that one little text shouldn't change his entire mood, but also aware that it absolutely had.

14

As promised, Brinley set up a meeting for the volunteers, and also as promised, Charlotte agreed to come.

She hadn't heard a word from Connor about his plans for the dance studio, but the more time she spent in Harbor Pointe, the more she wanted to put down roots. She'd even spotted an adorable little cottage for sale on her run yesterday and had spent the last three miles crunching numbers in her head of what she thought she could afford.

She'd saved enough for a nice down payment and then some. One benefit of not having a social life—she didn't spend much money.

Not that she was in a hurry to move out of Lucy's place. Quite the opposite, if she was honest. She liked having a roommate. She liked having friends.

"This recital is a great idea, Char," Lucy said from behind the steering wheel of her VW bug. "That's not a good nickname. I'll keep working on it."

Charlotte smiled. She'd never had a nickname before.

They were headed toward the meeting at the dance

studio, and Charlotte was thankful for the company. Ever since Cole had sent her that text yesterday, she'd struggled to keep her mind from wandering back into fantasy territory. It was embarrassing how much she thought about him, how she watched for him around town when she was running errands or working out.

That, she would keep to herself, no matter how much she liked her new friend.

"I'm really hoping Connor will sell me the studio," Charlotte said.

"He'd be crazy not to." Lucy pulled into a parking space —without hitting another car, Charlotte noticed—and shut off the engine.

Inside, Charlotte surveyed the group. She recognized Brinley, who was sitting near the front and chatting with two other women, and Lucy's friend Quinn, but nobody else.

At Quinn's side was a very handsome man, and judging by the way he stuck close to her, Charlotte deduced that he must be Quinn's Olympian. Charlotte stared at the way the man watched Quinn while she spoke to a shorter, older woman. He looked completely smitten.

Nobody had ever looked at Charlotte like that. Did Quinn know how lucky she was?

"Cee?" Lucy nudged her with her elbow.

"Huh?"

"You're gawking."

Charlotte looked at Lucy. "Sorry."

"I get it, he's a beautiful man." Lucy waggled her eyebrows.

"No, that's not—"

But before she could explain, Brinley rushed over. "Oh, good, you're here. Are we ready to start?"

Charlotte frowned. "I don't know, are we?"

"It's your meeting," Brinley said.

Charlotte looked around the room of strangers. "My meeting?"

"Yes, you're in charge now, right?"

Oh. Right. Charlotte hadn't thought this through. What did she think, she could take charge of a recital and not actually be in charge?

"Come on." Brinley tugged on her arm, leading her to the front of the room. "I'll get everyone's attention, then turn it over to you. Sound good?"

How hard could it be? "Sure."

Brinley clapped her hands together. "Hi, everyone." The small group began to quiet down. "Good evening. We're really thankful you're here tonight. I know we were all devastated about Julianna's passing, but also disappointed about the recital. And Jules would've wanted it to go on. We are thrilled to have help from one of the country's top dancers."

Brinley looked at Charlotte, who assumed her face had turned pink.

"Ladies and gentlemen, meet Miss Charlotte Page, principal dancer of the Chicago City Ballet."

Charlotte took a step forward as a smattering of applause filled the room.

She smiled. She'd spoken in front of groups before, usually at charity events. She'd taught plenty of masterclasses and workshops. She knew how to carry herself in a crowd.

But somehow, this was different. These were Julianna's people. And Charlotte desperately wanted them to like her.

"Thanks, Brinley," she said. "I came here a couple weeks ago because Julianna spoke so highly of Harbor Pointe and of all of you. When I realized her students didn't have the recital she'd planned, I wanted to see if we could remedy that. A dance recital is a really big deal to a lot of these dancers—and to Jules.

"We want to use this as an opportunity to honor Julianna. A tribute, I suppose."

"A celebration of her life," Brinley added.

"Right," Charlotte said. "So, it won't be just a dance recital, it'll be a little more meaningful this year."

"And it should be," the older woman Quinn had been talking to said. "I'm Martha Trembley, and I've been helping Julianna since the beginning. My granddaughters are teenagers now, and they've grown so much because of dance. So, I mend costumes and help plan and organize where I can. I'm at your disposal."

Charlotte smiled, bolstered by the support. "I appreciate that. One idea we had was to invite people who loved her to get up on stage and be a part of this event."

"Charlotte would choreograph numbers for local couples or groups—just to add a little something special this year," Brinley said.

"There was always something different about Julianna's recitals," a middle-aged woman said. "They always had a more theatrical element. And it was always a family affair."

"She even got her husband involved," another woman said. "He'd do a dance with their daughter every single year since she could walk."

"Who's going to do that this year?" another woman asked.

All eyes returned to Charlotte. She stuttered, then finally said, "I'll talk to him, but if he doesn't want to participate, then we'll do other things to celebrate Jules. Like I said, it'll look a little different this year."

"We really should try to keep them involved," the first woman said. "People look forward to it every season."

"I'm sure they'll understand if Connor isn't up for it this

time," Lucy said. She looked at Charlotte. "I think I can get a group of Julianna's friends to participate." She looked at Quinn. "Right?"

Quinn frowned. "You want me to dance? I thought we were here to help with the set."

Lucy shrugged. "You can pull double duty."

The group began to chatter for a few minutes, throwing around ideas of people who might want to join them in this tribute. So far, the list consisted mostly of people Charlotte didn't know. In fact, the only names she'd recognized were Steve and Hildy from Haven House.

"What about asking the football team to do something?" one of the women suggested. "I'm Patricia Dunbar," she said with a pointed look at Charlotte. "My son plays on the team, and they were state champions last year."

Charlotte froze. They were a single degree away from discussing the one person whose name she didn't want brought up at this meeting. The last thing she needed was for Cole or his team to show up in the dance studio.

"Maybe?" Charlotte's voice sounded unsure. Already it was happening—she was losing her nerve just thinking about—

"What about Cole Turner?" The traitorous suggestion had come from Lucy.

Lucy caught her eye and winked. What was she up to? Cole would kill her if he knew she'd thrown his name in the mix.

"I don't see that happening," Charlotte said.

"You don't think he'd do it for his sister?" Lucy asked, scanning the circle with her eyes. "I know the point isn't to fill the seats, but if we could tell people Coach Turner was going to dance, it would definitely draw a crowd."

"Lucy's right," Patricia said. "State-winning football

coach, big, strong man. Julianna's brother. It's a brilliant idea." She glanced at Brinley. "You should write it down."

"Coach Turner isn't going to go for that," Brinley said.

Lucy grinned. "Let's have Charlotte ask him."

"Me?" Charlotte knew her eyes showed her surprise, but did they also show the *sheer panic* she felt at that suggestion?

"You're Julianna's friend," Lucy said. "And a dancer. You did say you'd do whatever you could to help." Her innocent smile was anything but.

"I think you're forgetting that Cole doesn't actually like me," Charlotte mumbled.

Lucy shrugged. "What's the worst that can happen? He says no. No big deal. We should at least extend the invitation."

She made it sound so easy.

"It's a great idea," Patricia said, as if it were settled. As if she were in charge. "Charlotte will talk to Coach Turner about his involvement as well as the team's. Maybe you could also connect with Steve and Hildy? And you said you'll talk to Connor?"

"I mentioned it to him already."

All eyes were on her.

"I'll follow up."

"Perfect." Patricia smiled, oblivious to the fireworks going off inside Charlotte's head.

"And of course, you'll perform too, Charlotte," Mrs. Trembley said—less of a suggestion, more of a question.

"Of course she will," Lucy said with a grin.

Charlotte started to respond but realized the rest of the room had moved on to a new topic—the set design.

Quinn pulled a sheet of paper from her planner. "Jules and I worked up a great plan for the recital a few months back."

Charlotte half listened as the group carried on,

bouncing from topic to topic. They covered everything from refreshments to hair and makeup to publicity. Everyone already knew their place and had their job. And now, Charlotte did too.

She'd proposed the idea of holding the recital, and she was all for it, but including community members as a way to honor Julianna could prove to be more than she'd bargained for.

After all, the thought of reaching out to the couple who ran Haven House was slightly uncomfortable.

The thought of convincing Cole Turner to be a part of this event?

That was downright terrifying.

15

The next day, after practice, Cole got a text from his high school buddy turned tech mogul, Josh Dixon.

Meet us at Hazel's? I had to get Connor out of that house.

On my way.

Dread twisted in his belly. He didn't want to go to the diner, where the morning crowd would consist of a mix of tourists and locals who made it their daily stop before heading off to the beach for an afternoon of carefree fun.

But Connor was more than his friend now, he was family. And he owed it to Jules to keep an eye on the people she loved, no matter how much he didn't like thinking about the fact that his sister was gone.

Losing her so quickly, without any warning, it was working him over, like salt on an already opened wound. Cole hadn't figured out how to manage the pain of so many disappointments, and talking to Connor only served as an unwanted reminder of what he didn't want to face.

Still, this wasn't about him. Josh and Connor had seen him through the dark days of his divorce—he'd be a lousy friend if he didn't return the favor.

Cole parked in the lot behind Hazel's, got out of the truck, and walked around the building toward the front entrance. Josh and Connor sat at a table right in the center of the busy restaurant.

Cole tried not to groan. Running into people he knew was inevitable here—that's why he usually ordered carryout or came during the off times. He caught a glimpse of Connor's face. Whatever grief Cole felt right now about being out in public, it was a thousand times worse for his brother-in-law.

He needed to grow up and stop being such a baby.

He opened the door and beelined to the table, not bothering to look around at the crowded space. Josh looked up and gave Cole one of those slow head-shakes that said, *He's not doing well.*

Cole sat, trying not to think of the day Julianna and Connor told him they were dating. Connor and Josh were Cole's best friends—and they both knew his sister was off-limits.

But when she'd left the dance company and come home to figure out her next move, she and Connor connected almost instantly.

"We didn't want to keep it a secret from you," Jules said. "But we've been dating for a month now."

Cole looked at Connor, whose expression turned sheepish. "You're dating my sister?"

"She asked me out," Connor said. "Like I was gonna say no."

Cole watched as Julianna slipped her hand in Connor's.

"We aren't asking your permission," she said. "But we'd love your support."

He knew it mattered to her what he thought—Cole was her only real family now that Dad had found a new wife and they had their own kids. He wasn't about to mess that up, and Connor was a good guy. Still, that didn't stop Cole from saying, "You hurt her, and you're a dead man—you understand?"

Connor hadn't hurt her. He'd loved her well until the day she died.

Why would God take her away? Why would He leave such a hole in the fabric of their lives by allowing something so tragic to happen to someone so good?

Cole sat down across from Connor. His brother-in-law looked terrible. Red eyes, pale face, broken spirit. Was it possible he'd gotten worse in the few days since Cole last saw him?

"Hey, man." Cole clapped a hand on Connor's shoulder. "How's it going?"

It was a stupid question. Cole should know better. How many times had he rolled his eyes to that question after Gemma left?

Connor shrugged, then pushed his palms into his eyes. "I shouldn't have come. I need to go get the kids."

"Where are they?"

Connor shook his head. "Still with Hildy."

Cole should've checked in with Hildy after she picked up the kids. It was only supposed to be for the day—what changed?

"My kids are in a transitional home, for goodness' sake."

"Haven House is a great place," Josh said. "You know they'll take good care of them until you're ready."

Connor looked up at Josh, then at Cole. "What if I'm never ready?"

Josh cleared his throat. "Listen, man, there's nothing wrong with asking for help. Hildy and Steve are good people—and they aren't the only ones that will help. Carly and I can take the kids with us sometimes. I'm sure Quinn and Grady would too." He looked at Cole.

"And I'll do whatever I can." Cole would take AJ and Amelia without question, but a baby? He'd be lost as to how to take care of a baby.

"What kind of life is that for them?" Connor's voice broke.

"It's not for forever, man," Josh said. "Just for now."

Connor shook his head. "I don't know when this will ever get easier. You know what Jules was like. She took care of everyone all the time. I can't replace her."

Cole's mind wandered back years, back to a day when his dad likely felt the same way Connor felt right now. He'd faulted him for those feelings—made the man feel guilty for asking for help when he needed it. He'd been so short-sighted, so selfish, but he was a kid. He hadn't understood.

"Listen, I'm heading out to Haven House tomorrow," Cole said. "I'll check on the kids."

"Why are you going to Haven House?"

"Told Steve I'd help him fix a fence," Cole said. They'd made the plan at Sunday dinner. Steve wasn't a spring chicken, and Cole owed the man his life. It was the least he could do.

"You're making the rounds on the yard work," Connor said. "You bringing Charlotte along with you?"

Cole frowned. "I didn't ask her to come help at your house."

"It was a strange sight," Connor said. "Did you have to show her how to pull weeds?"

"Who's Charlotte?" Josh asked.

"One of Julianna's ballet friends," Connor said.

"You did yard work with a ballerina?" Josh waited for Cole's response with a raised brow.

"She just wants to help," Cole said.

"She's a pretty big deal in the ballet, I guess. Like one of the best in the country." Connor looked at Cole. "How do you know her anyway?"

"I don't," Cole said. "Didn't even know she knew Jules till that day."

Connor frowned. "She wants to buy the dance studio."

"So let her," Josh said. "Sounds like she's more than qualified to run it."

Connor turned a mug of coffee around between his hands. "I'm having a hard time giving it up. Jules loved that place."

"Well, you're not gonna run it," Cole said. "Might as well let her."

"Someone else is interested in it." Connor took a drink. "Some franchise dance company based in Chicago. I didn't even know there was such a thing."

Josh closed his menu and set it down. "Could be a nice payday for you."

Cole frowned. "Jules wouldn't want some big Chicago outfit coming in here running her classes. That's the opposite of her vision for the place."

Connor pushed the mug away. "And that's exactly why it sounds like a good deal. It'll become something so different it won't remind me of her anymore."

Cole glanced at Josh, who gave him a slight shrug.

"I just think you should give Charlotte a chance," Cole said.

"You have quite the soft spot for someone who trashed your headlight," Connor said.

"She trashed your headlight?" Josh's brow furrowed.

"We had a fender bender," Cole said. "Right out there, in

fact." Cole pointed to the street in front of the diner, and as he turned, his eyes landed on a table situated next to the large window at the front of the restaurant.

A pair of wide eyes locked on to his.

Gemma.

Cole dropped his arm back in his lap and looked away.

"Well, this is awkward," Josh said.

"It's not awkward," Cole said. But he should've known better. Gemma loved Hazel's as much as everyone else, and she likely spent every morning here, like everyone else.

"No, but it's about to be." Josh gave Cole a nod. "She's coming over here."

Cole stifled a groan. While Connor had been around for the beginning of his relationship with Gemma, Josh had been staying with him the day he finally told her to leave. And everything in between? Well, the whole town had been there for that.

"Hey, Cole." Gemma stood next to him now. Too close. He fisted his hand in his lap. He didn't respond.

"Hey, guys," Gemma said. "Connor, I was so sorry to hear about Jules."

Cole wanted to tell her to mind her own business, to not refer to his sister in such a familiar way. After all, Gemma hadn't sent him any condolences.

"Thanks," Connor said half-heartedly.

"Hey, Cole, can we talk for a minute?"

Cole's eyes traveled up the table to Josh, who was staring at him, eyes wide. Poor guy probably wondered how he got so lucky as to have two of his closest friends broken at the same time.

"I'm kind of busy here," Cole said. Unlike when he was rude to other people, he didn't feel even a hint of remorse for being rude to Gemma.

"Just for a minute. Please?" She put a hand on his shoulder, and Cole quickly shrugged it off. She'd lost the right to touch him when she started having her affair, which actually meant she never had a right to touch him. That realization turned sour at the back of his throat.

"Be right back, guys." Cole pushed his chair away from the table, stood, and walked out onto the sidewalk, around the side of the building so the nosy patrons of Hazel's Kitchen weren't privy to his personal business.

Not that he considered Gemma his personal anything anymore.

"What?" he said, spinning around.

"Whoa," she said. "Why are you so hostile right now?"

He tried not to laugh—not an amused laugh, an ironic *you've got to be kidding me* laugh. "Do I really need to remind you?"

"I told you I was sorry, Cole," she said.

He faced her. "Can we be done now? I've really got nothing else to say to you."

"Look, I just wanted to call a truce. We're both here this summer, so—"

"Yeah, why is that?" Cole asked. "Why are you back here?"

Gemma looked shocked, as if it had never occurred to her that coming back to Harbor Pointe might not be the best idea. "I've spent my summers here since I was a kid."

"And you just couldn't help but come back to flaunt Max in my face?" Cole was beginning to understand the meaning behind the expression about blood boiling. "I live here, Gemma. It's not a vacation spot for me."

She held her hands up as if in surrender, and Cole backed away. He hadn't intended to get that close to her, and he certainly hadn't intended to raise his voice enough to stop an older couple walking on the other side of the street.

"Look, you bring out the absolute worst in me, Gemma." Cole took a step back. "I think you need to just stay away."

"I don't want you to hate me, Cole," she said. "You know I didn't mean to hurt you."

Was she delusional? "What did you think having sex with someone else while we were married was going to do? Make me feel good?"

"We're both adults, Cole," Gemma said. "You need to figure out how to let go of me."

Now Cole did laugh. "You're absolutely insane if you think there is any part of me still pining away for you."

She crossed her arms over her chest. "But you're still angry."

He swore under his breath. "I'm going back inside now, Gemma. And it would be great if you'd find somewhere else to eat when you're here this summer."

"I can eat wherever I want," she said.

"Yeah, you can," Cole said. "But if you have even a shred of decency, you won't eat here."

She straightened.

"But I suppose if you had a shred of decency, you wouldn't have done what you did, now, would you?" Cole stared at her for a long moment, wondering if he'd regret this conversation later.

He started back up the street to the corner, but before he turned, Gemma called out, "Max asked me to marry him."

Cole stopped, but he didn't respond.

Gemma faced him now, he heard her turn. "I just thought you should hear it from me."

He bit back a sarcastic comment and walked away.

16

For days after the meeting at the dance studio, Charlotte busied herself with her morning run, with observing dance classes, with meeting parents—most of whom thanked her profusely for ensuring the kids would have their recital.

She'd managed to stay busy, even without the rigors of a strict dance regimen, and that busyness had allowed her to avoid the thing she really didn't want to do

But unfortunately, the time of procrastination had come to an end.

Which was why she now sat in the parking lot at the high school, watching from a distance as Cole and another guy barked orders at the boys on the field, boys who all complied with whatever the men told them to do.

She opened her phone and saw a missed call from Marcia. Seconds later, her voicemail alert rang.

She couldn't deal with her mother. Not now. Not today. She tucked the phone in her purse just in time to see the boys run to the center of the field and huddle up, all eyes on Cole. She had to wonder what the man was saying, considering that he seemed to find it impossible to 1. Talk and 2. Be nice.

But then maybe high school football coaches didn't have to be nice. Those boys probably all needed a little tough love.

How many dance teachers had she had over the years that subscribed to that tough love method?

What she wouldn't have given for one who actually cared enough to be kind.

Marcia would tell her to stop complaining. It wasn't kindness that got her where she was. As a teacher, her mother certainly subscribed to that theory—and as a mother, even more so.

She drew in a deep breath and pushed open the chain-link fence, making her way out onto the field. It didn't escape her that she'd drawn the attention of at least half of the football players, something she pretended not to notice. She'd almost reached Cole when he glanced up from his clipboard.

Recognition washed over his face. "Charlotte?"

She smiled, but even she knew it probably looked as forced as it felt.

"You know her, Coach?" one of the lingering players said. "Lucky man."

Charlotte felt herself blush, but she quickly looked away.

"Matt, would you take the equipment? I'll be right in."

"Sure thing, Coach." The other adult on the field shooed the boys away, leaving her standing in the middle of a circle that had been painted in the grass. With Cole.

"What are you doing here?"

She felt self-conscious. "Lucy said I could find you here."

His face didn't budge—not even the hint of a change.

"Can we talk for a minute?"

He tucked a clipboard under his arm. "Actually, I'm heading out to Haven House. Fixing a fence, checking on my nieces and nephew."

His curt reply flustered her. She quickly recovered. "I actually need to go there too."

His eyes darted to hers. "Why?"

"Same reason I need to talk to you."

He stared at her but didn't say anything, nothing to indicate he was listening or that she could continue.

She let out a slight scoff. This guy was unbelievable. She shook her head—what was she doing here? And how could someone as sweet and kind as Julianna have a brother who was so incredibly horrible? She was embarrassed to think that she'd thought his thank-you text had signaled some sort of friendship between them. He was just as rude as ever.

"Are you going to tell me what this is about?" He looked at her, eyebrows raised.

"They wanted me to ask you—"

"Who wanted you to ask me?" His eyes narrowed, as if he were suspicious of her.

"Uh, a planning committee," she said, flustered. "For the dance recital."

He shifted the clipboard from one hand to the other and glared at her. "Okay. That's not really my scene."

For some inexplicable reason, she found herself biting back tears. It didn't matter what this *high school football coach* thought of her. Why did his attitude affect her so much? It's not like he was a part of her life.

Did she want him to be? The thought of it sent her insides swirling. That stupid teenage crush she'd had might've actually morphed into something else, something deeper.

She'd need to get a hold of that before it ran wild.

"Charlotte?"

"What?"

"What do you want?"

She lifted her chin, remembering for a moment that some people thought she was something special. Never mind if he was too dense to see it—his opinion didn't have to be the one she believed. "We're doing a few extra dances, tribute dances for your sister, and someone thought you might want to participate, since you were her brother and I guess you had a good team last year or something." She seemed to be raising her voice. "We just want to honor Jules. To celebrate her life. I'm supposed to ask the people who run Haven House too."

He inhaled, an annoyed look on his face. "Okay."

"So, I guess this is me asking if you want to be a part of the recital."

"How would I be a part of it?" he asked.

She wanted to shove him in his big, muscular shoulder, tell him this wasn't how you had a polite conversation, and find out what in the world she'd ever done to warrant his disgust. Instead, she said, "You would dance."

"No," he said. "I don't dance."

"I mean, you wouldn't be alone."

"I said no, okay?" He stared her down. "Now, if you'll excuse me." He brushed past her with all the softness of a Brillo pad.

She stood still for several seconds, wishing she'd never come, wishing she'd never thought he might actually be a tiny bit human under his suit of awfulness. And here she thought they were sort of getting to know each other. Working in the yard the other day, eating lunch together, and him learning who she was to his sister hadn't done a thing to change his attitude.

She hugged her purse to her chest, as if it were some

sort of protection, and then silently turned and started back in the direction of her car.

She'd only made it a few steps when she heard his voice behind her.

"Charlotte, wait."

It would've been wonderfully dramatic to ignore him completely, but she must not have thought of that soon enough because she spun around as soon as he said her name.

He didn't say anything.

"You bellowed?"

He closed his eyes and drew in a deep breath, then let it out, all the while surveying the grass beneath their feet. "I'll take you out to Haven House."

She eyed him for several seconds, wondering if this was how he treated everyone or if she'd won the lottery of disrespect. "That's it?"

"You said you had to ask Hildy and Steve, right?" He looked genuinely confused.

"Yes, I do," she said. "But I think you owe me an apology."

"An apology."

She didn't respond. Instead, she took all emotion off of her face and stared at him, as if to say, *I'm waiting.*

He half-laughed and looked away. "You're serious."

She turned around, fully intending to walk all the way to her car, get in, and drive off. But he stopped her again.

"Fine, I'm sorry," he said.

She faced him. "For what?"

He didn't look amused. "I'm honestly not sure."

Her eyes widened. "You're not sure? Are you so accustomed to talking to people like this that you don't realize it's rude?"

He watched her for a few seconds, and she thought it

was quite possible he was about to call her names or tell her off. But he didn't do that. Instead, he lifted his chin and slowly met her eyes. "I'm sorry," he said. "For snapping at you."

The apology was so unexpected and so honest, she felt a breath catch in her throat.

"Well?"

"Well, what?" Had her knees gone weak? Because a guy was *polite* to her? She had to get control of this foolish little crush.

"Do you accept my apology?"

She held his gaze, despite her trembling nerves. "Yes. Will you do the dance?"

"Not a chance."

She eyed him. "It's for Jules."

He wasn't budging.

"Fine," she said. "I'll tell them I tried, and you said no."

"Good. So, you want to drive with me? I don't trust you behind the wheel."

She tried—failed—to hide her smile. "I'm actually a decent driver. It's just been a long time since I've had any reason to drive."

"Are you ever going to get your car fixed?"

"It's a rental," she said.

His eyebrows shot up. "You probably need to call them."

"I know." Another thing she was avoiding.

He motioned for her to follow him, and she did, adrenaline still rushing through her veins from going toe-to-toe with someone who had no concern for the feelings of his verbal sparring partner.

Not that she was a partner. It wasn't like she'd willingly entered into that role.

As they reached the door to the school, he opened the door and waited for her to walk in.

She glanced at him. "This isn't going to deposit me in the middle of the men's locker room, is it?"

"Uh, no," he said. "This will deposit you in the athletic office."

"I didn't go to high school, so I'm not sure how these things work." She smiled and walked through the open door.

"You didn't go to high school?" The metal door closed behind him with a clang.

"No, I had private tutors mostly. I have the equivalent of a bachelor's degree—just not the actual diploma."

"You were tutored through college?"

She shouldn't have said anything. He probably thought she was a freak. "I don't want to be in the way."

He took the hint and stopped asking questions. "You won't be." He nodded toward a blue plastic chair. "Have a seat."

She did, aware that they were just outside an office with his name on the door.

"I've just got to grab a few things."

"I'll be fine here."

Cole watched her for a few seconds before turning into his office.

She hugged the purse to her chest and prayed she would, in fact, be fine. If those football players started talking to her, she might not know how to handle herself. She found conversing with men incredibly awkward. Men in the real world were different than ballet boys. Ballet boys understood the language she spoke—the language of dance. There was an instant connection that allowed her to communicate. Football boys were like foreigners to her, and she had no idea how to bridge the gap.

She pretended to be busy on her phone, an effort to deter anyone from talking to her, but really, she was stealing glances of her surroundings and eavesdropping on Cole's conversation with whoever was in his office.

They were whispering—sort of—but she could still hear them.

"Who is that?" the other guy hissed.

"That's the one who hit my car," Cole said.

Charlotte's heart sank. They were talking about *her*.

"*That's* her?" the other guy asked. "You didn't say she was hot."

"See ya tomorrow, Bilby." Cole appeared in the doorway and Charlotte found his eyes. "Ready?"

They walked in silence through the hallways, and Charlotte took her time looking in every classroom window. Rows of lockers lined the hallways of the old building, and she could practically hear the sound of teenagers filling the building with chatter.

"You coming?" Cole asked, having moved significantly faster than Charlotte toward the door. "I parked in the back lot."

"I've just never been in a high school before."

He waited for her to catch up, and not impatiently, which she appreciated.

After a pause, he asked, "Do you want to see the rest of it?"

"Like a tour?"

"Yeah, I guess."

"Sure."

They were standing near the main entrance, which he pointed out, then turned his attention to the doors behind them. "This is the main office. If you were coming here on a school day, you'd have to check in here."

"Can we go in?"

He hesitated.

She glanced in the window and caught the eye of a pudgy, plainish woman with dark hair cut into a short bob.

"Did she see you?"

She glanced at Cole and nodded. He groaned. Seconds later, the office door opened.

"I thought I heard voices out here." The middle-aged woman smiled and her eyes nearly disappeared. Her cheeks were plump and pink and her giggle reminded Charlotte of an adorable cartoon character.

"Morning, Joni," Cole said. "Joni, this is Charlotte. She's, uh, new in town."

"Nice to meet you, Charlotte," she said, still wearing her smile. She quickly turned her attention back to Cole. "Been awful quiet around here lately. You should stop in and say hello more often, Coach. Gets kind of lonely in this big old place during the summer."

Was she . . . flirting?

Cole took a step away from the older woman and motioned for Charlotte to follow him. "We'll see ya later, Joni."

Charlotte fell into step beside him, doing her best to stifle a giggle of her own. "Was she . . ."

"Don't say a word."

She snapped her jaw shut. Why she found it amusing that school secretary Joni was flirting with much younger, much less friendly Cole, she didn't know. Maybe it was the way it made him squirm.

Clearly, he did not appreciate being the center of attention.

Toward the end of the hall, he stopped outside an open door. "This is my room."

She looked up at him, but he wasn't looking at her. He was staring into the large classroom. "Can I go in?"

He nodded.

The classroom was sparsely decorated—plain, she'd call it, with a big whiteboard at the front, football plaques and photos plastered to the wall in a row near the ceiling that went all the way around.

"You've been coaching for a while, then?"

"Some of these I inherited," he said.

"State champions?" She stood in front of the fanciest-looking of all the plaques.

"That one's mine."

"That's what they were talking about at the meeting the other night," she said. "You must be good at your job."

Not surprisingly, he didn't respond.

"And you teach history?" She could tell by the other artwork that lined the classroom walls that this was a place to learn where the country came from—images of presidents and a replica of the Declaration of Independence.

He nodded.

"For some reason I thought you were just a coach," she said.

"Most coaches also teach," he told her. "Some teachers also coach."

"What do you like better—coaching or teaching?"

He shoved his hands in his pockets, and for the first time she noticed he still wore a whistle around his neck. "Well, most people see me as a coach."

She frowned. He'd avoided her question. But since he'd stopped being cranky, she decided to let it slide.

A woman poked her head in the door. "I thought I saw you come in here."

Cole gave her a nod, and Charlotte noticed he wasn't any friendlier to this woman than he was to anyone else. It gave her hope that it wasn't Charlotte he despised, though she wasn't sure that should be comforting. Wasn't despising people in general worse than simply not liking her?

She shook the thought away. Trying to figure this guy out was pointless.

"Hi," the woman said, looking at Charlotte.

"Oh, sorry," Cole said. "Rachel Kent, this is Charlotte Page. Rachel's the art teacher."

Charlotte smiled. "Nice to meet you."

"Charlotte Page?" Rachel eyed her. "The dancer?"

Charlotte felt her face flush. "Yes."

"I heard you're helping plan Julianna's recital."

"I am," she said. "Do you want to be a part of it?"

Rachel waved her off. "Oh, my sister is the dancer in our family. I mostly stay behind the scenes."

Charlotte smiled. "I'm working on a few tribute numbers—for Jules. Tried to twist Cole's arm, but—"

"You should do it," Rachel said. "Think of what a kick Julianna would've gotten out of that." Her smile was so genuine, and Cole's was its exact opposite.

"Pass," he said.

"Do you want a tour of the theatre?" Rachel asked. "I mean, I could open it up for you."

"You're—"

"Silas Kent's daughter. He's the owner."

Charlotte glanced at Cole. It wasn't likely he wanted to spend any more time with her than absolutely necessary. To her surprise, he gave her an affirmative shrug. "Do you want to check it out before we head out to Haven House?"

"It's part of a campground, right?" Charlotte asked.

"Sort of a resort?" There was a question in her voice. "I never knew exactly how to describe Wonderland."

"Wonderland?"

"That's what it's called. You'll have to see it to understand, but you'll also have to use your imagination because, unfortunately, my dad's really let it go."

"I'd love a tour," Charlotte said. "It'll be good for me to get my bearings."

The other woman beamed. "Great! I'll meet you over there, but give me a head start to give my dad fair warning."

Cole nodded. "Will do."

Rachel left, and Cole met Charlotte's eyes. "Ready?"

She realized she was about to get into Cole's truck and drive just outside of town with him. Alone. And then out to Haven House. Alone. It felt different than going on a sandwich run.

Maybe it felt different because she was horribly aware of him, of the way he moved—a cool, confident stride—of the way people responded to him, of the way he hardly seemed to notice. He was deliciously masculine in all the best ways, and though Charlotte wanted nothing more than to deny his attractiveness, to do so would be a lie.

Okay, so what? He was good-looking—big deal. That didn't make him her dream guy. That didn't even make him someone worth dating.

And really! Why was she even thinking about it? It's not like she needed to entertain the idea—he was hardly scrambling to ask her out.

Now she'd gone and flustered herself. Shoot. She followed him out to the parking lot, where his red truck was waiting for them.

He stepped in front of her and opened the passenger side door, and Charlotte came to a quick stop. She glanced at him, but he wasn't looking at her, just standing there, holding the door, looking off in the opposite direction.

Cole Turner was holding the door open? For her? A tingle raced up her spine and back down again.

She didn't want to make him feel weird about it, so she quietly slipped into the truck without a word. He checked to make sure she was completely inside, then closed the door, giving her enough time to contemplate the strange irony of the rudest person she knew doing something so oddly chivalrous.

And she couldn't reconcile it in her mind.

Maybe there was more to Cole Turner than met the eye.

17

Not surprisingly, the ride to the theatre was silent. They drove through town and out onto country roads dotted with the occasional farmhouse. After about twenty minutes, they pulled onto a road nearly hidden by full, green trees and made their way back into the woods.

Cole slowed down, carefully navigating the winding roads, and Charlotte marveled at the cabins nestled up into the trees. Not quite camping, but not quite a resort either. It was the perfect mix of nature and luxury.

Or at least it could be. The cabins were fairly run down.

"This place is amazing."

Cole didn't look away from the road. "It used to be. It still could be, I think, but Silas just stopped caring about it."

"People used to come here for shows?"

"Not just shows. For canoeing and relaxing and kayaking." He pointed to a large building with a wide wraparound porch. "That's the lodge. There's a restaurant in there that served nice dinners and yeah, the theatre was always a big draw."

"Kind of like the place in *Dirty Dancing*."

Now he glanced at her, his brow quirked.

"Have you seen it?"

He looked away and appeared to be chewing on the inside of his cheek.

She smiled. "You have, I can tell. There's no shame in loving a good Patrick Swayze movie. About dance, no less."

"I didn't choose that movie," Cole said. "It was forced on me." He parked the truck across from what must've been the theatre building.

She didn't say anything else about the movie or Patrick Swayze, though she did wonder who'd forced him to watch.

"We'll go in there," he said. "The stage door entrance."

Charlotte's gaze lingered over the nondescript black doors at the back of the building. If she stared long enough, they could become the doors of her theatre in Chicago—though nothing about her surroundings was similar. She smiled—how many times had she exited the theatre into the alley to find fans waiting there for her? An unexpected sadness raced through her, but she quickly pushed it away.

The door opened and Rachel appeared. She motioned for them to come in. "Dad's taking a nap," she said as they reached the door. "So, the coast is clear."

Cole took the door from Rachel and motioned for Charlotte to go in ahead of him. She had to give him one thing—he was a gentleman. For a brief moment, she saw a flash of him in a tuxedo at a ballet fundraiser. He'd certainly look the part.

But he'd be bored silly.

What a ridiculous thought. Her imagination was really working overtime today.

She walked into the space and found herself standing in the stage right wing. In front of her stretched a stage, not all that different than the one where she'd spent years performing as a principal in one of the country's most prestigious ballets.

For being in the middle of nowhere, the space was really beautiful.

"This is it," Rachel said. "Our little theatre."

Charlotte drew in a deep breath. Behind them was the scene shop, where sets were built, and even though this place seemed nearly abandoned, she could smell the sawdust and practically taste the memories that had been made right there on that stage.

Names had been painted all over the backstage brick wall, commemorating the actors, the shows, the roles that had come to life right there where they stood.

"Here, I'll get the lights," Cole said. He took off in the direction of what she assumed was the sound booth, typically situated at the back of the theatre. A minute or two later, the stage lights were on and the house went dark. Rachel's phone rang, and she went out into the alley to answer the call, leaving Charlotte alone.

"I think there's a pretty decent sound system," Cole called out from the back of the theatre.

She stepped out onto the stage and into the light, looking out across the darkness that fell over the seats. Even Cole was hidden in the shadows, and for a moment, it was as if she was all alone up there.

A familiar song began, filtering through the speakers overhead. It was a piece from a movie soundtrack, and it stirred something inside her right away. She felt her toes curl inside her shoes, as if her body were made to do this thing she desperately did not want to do anymore.

Was it possible to still love to dance but to not want the life dancing had forced her to have?

The volume increased as Cole tested the speakers, and Charlotte's brain spun with ideas—choreographing a dance in her mind, as if her body was made to move. She was shocked (and a little sad) to realize a part of her missed dancing. How could she not? It was all she'd ever known, all she strived for.

Had she been too hasty in walking away? Why were there no guarantees that she'd made the right decision?

She turned gently, away from the back of the auditorium, trying a move, feet playing out the steps she saw in her mind. She reminded herself Cole was watching—he could see her internal struggle as it surfaced right there on the stage in front of him, but after several seconds of holding it in, the music swelled and Charlotte's shoulders snapped back into position, her arms delicate but strong, outstretched on either side of her.

And it was just her and the music.

She let her body flow with the familiar orchestral piece, the sound of the strings filling her, leading her on a path across the stage. Her muscles tightened as she turned—not full out, but not cautious.

She closed her eyes, marking the steps as they raced through her mind, reminding her how it felt to be sure of herself, to have the confidence that she was excellent, that she was made for this exact thing.

Why would she ever think she could be anything else?

What if this was all she was? What if she really had nothing else to offer?

What if she'd made a terrible mistake?

She snapped back to a standing position and the music stopped. She stared out toward the back of the auditorium, into the sound booth, aware that she'd lost herself and Cole had been the only one to see it.

It was unlikely he'd realized or cared about her internal struggle, but she felt naked and vulnerable all the same.

She turned away, embarrassed. She'd revealed a part of herself she hadn't intended to share.

The house lights came up, though still dim, and she forced herself to pretend. No sense making it even more awkward than it already was. She turned around and drew in the beautiful space. The auditorium was big enough for a good-sized crowd, probably over five hundred people. The floors sloped at the top, looking down on the stage, making every seat a good one, and the theatre managed to have a sort of elegant feel, despite being part of a campground.

"Kind of a shame they don't use this place anymore," she called out to Cole's shadowy figure in the back.

He slipped out from the sound booth and approached the stage, making quick work of the stairs in the center aisle. He surveyed the empty seats.

"They used to put on shows here all year long. Summer was the busiest. Harbor Pointe is a small town, but this place had a reputation, and somehow they drew audiences from miles away." He walked up the stairs and onto the stage.

"Does anyone use it for anything anymore?" she asked.

He shrugged. "Silas always loved Julianna, so he made an exception for her recitals, but honestly, I think it's too painful for him now that he's alone." He stuffed his hands in his pockets. "Not really my scene."

"Yeah, you said that," she said, feigning surprise. "It was a shocking revelation."

He found her eyes and for the first time, something sort of resembling a smile skittered across his lips. It was the faintest spark of amusement, and it almost instantly disappeared. But she'd caught it, and it made her want to see it again. It made her want to be the reason for it.

She gave him a wry smile and a moment passed between

them—the tiniest flicker. And then it was gone, and in its place, the return of his stoic expression.

She quickly looked away.

"It really is a beautiful building," she said. The ceiling was high, with thick wooden beams serving as decoration. And standing on the stage, hearing the music—she couldn't deny it—she wanted to dance.

And that realization made her question everything she thought she'd decided, including her being in Harbor Pointe at all.

18

Cole stood dumbly on the stage while Charlotte continued to look around the dark theatre.

She had such a curiosity about the space, its dressing rooms, its scene shop, how much wing space it had. She ran her hand over the ropes on the side against the wall, muttering something about "fly lines"—and Cole said nothing.

They were in her world now, which had been obvious the second she started moving on the stage. And as the solo member of her audience, the odd notion that he was witnessing something special came over him.

He'd never paid much attention to dance, even though his sister had built her life around it. That was always "Julianna's thing," and it shamed him a little that he hadn't taken more of an interest. Sure, he attended the recitals, and he'd helped her with the construction of the studio, but he could've done better. He could've asked questions or made a point to try and love what she loved so much.

Still, it didn't take an expert to know that Charlotte was in a class all her own—the way she moved, with an odd combination of grace and strength—it had turned something over inside of him, and frankly, he didn't like it.

If his own mother had taught him one thing, it was that women couldn't be trusted. They lied. They manipulated. They didn't stick around. His run-in with Gemma should've served as a stark reminder of that.

He'd be a fool to pretend otherwise.

And yet, there was something different about Charlotte. There was a naïvete about her that had him curious. He'd watched her up on that stage as she spun on her tiptoes, enveloped in light, and he wanted to know more.

But this was how it started, wasn't it? This was how it always started—a faint question that led to a date, then another, and before he knew it, his heart was tied up in a way he couldn't untangle.

Not this time. It didn't matter how intrigued he was by her beauty and her charm—he wasn't about to go down that road again.

He was better off alone.

"Sorry." Rachel walked out onto the stage. "My sister called. You guys good?"

Cole shoved his hands in the pockets of his jeans and nodded. "All good. We'll get out of your hair."

Charlotte turned to the other woman and smiled warmly. "Thank you so much for letting me look around. This is such a beautiful space."

Rachel cast a look of longing over the theatre. "It really is, isn't it? I'm so glad that it's getting at least a little bit of use. And I can't wait to see you dance."

Charlotte smiled, a shyness coming over her. Cole studied her in the lull of the conversation. Connor had said she was one of the best dancers in the country, but her humility seemed genuine.

There he went again—romanticizing his curiosity. He didn't like the way his own mind was betraying him.

"We should go," he said.

Charlotte looked at him, brow furrowed as if he'd said something wrong.

"Right," Rachel said quickly. "And I should go check on my dad."

A wave of loneliness washed over him, thinking about Silas all alone out here at Wonderland, and he wondered if he'd end up like Silas one day.

Would he regret it if he did?

Charlotte thanked Rachel again, and then followed Cole out the door and back to his truck in the parking lot. She stopped in front of the headlight and looked at him.

"You fixed it."

He looked away. His buddy at the autobody shop had come through a lot quicker than Cole had expected. "Yep."

"I didn't notice before," she said. He could feel her eyes on him. It was unnerving. "So, you have a bill for me?"

He pulled her door open and motioned for her to get in the truck, but she didn't move. "It's not a big deal."

"I crashed into your truck," she said.

"Twice."

Her expression turned to amusement. "Twice."

"Did you want to get in or . . . ?"

She seemed to be searching for a reply, but she must've come up empty because she passed by him and got into the truck. He closed the door and walked around the back, trying to calm nerves that had sprung up without his permission.

Women leave. He'd keep repeating it to himself until he stopped this childish infatuation with a woman who was way out of his league.

He slid into the driver's seat, aware that it had been a

long time since he'd had a woman in his truck—and now, in a matter of days, Charlotte had been in it twice. Would she expect conversation on the drive to Haven House?

He preferred the sounds of the road to the sound of his own voice. And it wasn't like the two of them had anything in common. What was a high school football coach supposed to talk about with a ballerina?

And why did he care? He wore silence well. It was his comfort zone.

"I can find out how much that headlight cost." It sounded like a dare.

He tossed her a sideways glance but didn't respond. When he looked back to the road, he had to hide a smile.

Cole didn't understand women, but there was something charming about this one.

"Where is Haven House?" she asked, staring out the window.

"Outside of town in the other direction," he said, thinking of the big farmhouse that had come to feel like a second home to him over the years. "No lake view, but it's still peaceful."

"Peaceful," she repeated. "That's a good way to think of it."

Silence enveloped them, and he wondered if she found it uncomfortable. He was uncharacteristically at ease.

"Usually when I would think of a quaint little cottage town, I'd picture brick pavers on the street, or even cobblestone—Nantucket has cobblestone. I was there once, but not for vacation. It was a work trip, but I wished I'd had time to explore that island. Have you ever been?"

Cole mumbled a quiet, "No,"

She watched the lake out the window like she'd never seen it before. "You see that red lighthouse out there?"

He glanced over at the familiar scene—one he mostly took for granted, now that he thought about it.

She didn't wait for him to respond before continuing. "I can see it from my room in Lucy's cottage. Julianna wrote about it a lot in her letters. I think she was enamored with it too—do you know the history of that lighthouse?"

"No." Something inside him shifted, and he felt himself begin to relax. He did know the history, but he wanted to hear her version.

"It was built in the wrong place. They meant to build it off the coast of Safe Harbor, but somehow the plans were messed up and it ended up here. They talked about moving it, but there were so many reports that the lighthouse was helping sailors that they let it stand and built another one up on Safe Harbor. Isn't that funny? That lighthouse is there because of a mistake—and it's one of my favorite things about this place."

He searched for a reply but came up empty.

"Sorry. Sometimes I talk too much," she said quietly.

"Too much for who?" He glanced at her, then quickly back to the road.

"I'm annoying you, I'm sure. Telling you history of your own town."

"I don't mind."

She looked over at him. "Really?"

He shrugged. "Really." Eyes back to the road, where a large white sign that read *Haven House* was situated.

"Oh, we're here," she said.

His nerves settled at the sight of the property, the sign, the large farmhouse down the gravel driveway.

Haven House.

In many ways, this place was his home. Even now, that's how he saw it.

Outside, two golden retrievers lolled on the front lawn.

"There are dogs," Charlotte said. Her voice was so happy it reminded him of a child's.

"Yeah, the bigger one is Ollie and the other one is Bob," he said.

She laughed. "They named a dog Bob?"

Cole hid his smile. "I named him that. I hate when people name their dogs dumb names like Bandit or Sparky. Just name him something strong and sturdy."

"But Bob?" She peered out the window. "He looks more like a Bandit."

He didn't say anything else. He'd brought the retriever home two years ago, as a gift for Gemma, who quickly said she wasn't a dog person and told him to find the dog a new home. Naturally, he thought of Haven House, which had been taking in all sorts of strays—even human ones—for as long as he'd been alive.

Hildy fell in love with the dog the second Cole put him in her arms. "What's his name?" she'd asked.

"Name him whatever you want," Cole said.

"How about Rocky?" Hildy smiled.

"No, do not name him Rocky," Cole said. "Just call him something simple. Like Bob or Mark or something." He gave the dog's ears a rub, then turned and walked away.

Cole was surprised, weeks later, when he returned to Haven House, to discover that the puppy now wore an engraved nametag that read *Bob*.

The farmhouse had been well cared for—you'd never know it was over a hundred years old by looking at it. With a traditional white exterior, the place had three giant outbuildings, a fenced-in field for horses and, on the opposite side of the house, a big garden where the kids who lived here learned to grow their own food.

Cole spent a lot of time in that garden. It was the main thing he oversaw when he volunteered.

Steve and Hildy were all about life skills. He supposed that's what gave him the idea to offer Asher a job that summer. He'd done similar house projects out here over the years, and it always felt good to be the one to fix something that went wrong in his own house.

He parked next to the house, turned off the engine, and stuck the keys in the ashtray.

"You don't talk much, huh?" She faced him.

He resisted the urge to tell her she'd talked enough for both of them, afraid his tone wouldn't read "playful," but rather "annoyed." And he wasn't annoyed with her at all—that said something because for the most part, people irked him.

But that was more his problem than theirs and he knew it.

Instead of responding, he simply shrugged, aware that he'd barely said two words the whole drive out here.

"I'll try not to take it personally." She opened the door and got out of the truck. "But only because you're related to Jules." She shut the door.

He got out and walked around to the front of the truck, watching her admire the house. "What's Jules got to do with it?"

"If you and Jules have the same blood, then there must be good in you somewhere," she said without looking at him. "Even if you're hiding it from everyone."

She muttered that last part under her breath. He wasn't sure whether to be insulted or amused, but he didn't get a chance to decide before the front door of the old house opened and a little girl appeared on the opposite side of the screen door.

Typically, Haven House was for older kids, but every once in a while, they took in younger children. Like his nieces and nephew. He would bet money Hildy took them home that evening, surveyed Connor's state, and decided to hold on to the kids for a few more days. If he had the room—and any idea how to take care of a baby—he'd take them himself. And maybe he should. They were his family, after all.

Hildy came into view behind the little girl. "Jewel," she said, "we can't open the door to strangers without a grown-up."

The little girl wore a pink sundress, pigtails, and a wide expression. Her eyes darted from Cole to Charlotte and then up to the older woman. "Are they here to adopt me?"

The older woman whispered something in the girl's ear and shooed her away, then she turned her attention to her visitors.

"Well, you're not a stranger at all." She opened the screen door and stepped out onto the porch. "I forgot you were coming today. I would've made your favorite cookies." Hildy squeezed his arm.

Charlotte watched in what he was sure was curiosity, and Cole realized everything he'd wanted to keep hidden about himself was about to come out.

Or at least more of it than he was willing to discuss. Because he was willing to discuss exactly none of it.

"I can leave and come back in an hour," Cole said. "Give you time to whip some up."

She laughed. "If you're lucky I have all the ingredients in the kitchen."

Hildy's dark hair had streaks of gray in it, and she'd stuck a pair of glasses up on top of her head. He'd bet money she had no idea they were there. She still had her signature apron over a pair of jeans and a solid-colored shirt, and she still had her familiar maternal *let me love you forever* expression on her face.

Hildy glanced at Charlotte. "I must say, this is a happy surprise. I'd given up on our Cole ever finding a new girl."

He coughed. "Uh, Hildy, this is Charlotte," he said. "Charlotte, this is Hildy Hawthorne. She and her husband, Steve, run this place."

Charlotte stuck her hand out for what appeared to be a firm handshake, something Hildy didn't do. The older woman opened her arms and pulled Charlotte into a close hug. Charlotte, he noticed, seemed uncomfortable, even standoffish, by the gesture.

Maybe the two of them weren't so different after all.

Hildy glanced at her watch. "It's past breakfast time, but I've got homemade sticky buns inside."

"I always have room for sticky buns," he said.

She smiled. "Come in, let me feed you and you can tell me how you two met."

"Uh, we're not a couple, Hildy," Cole said miserably.

Hildy stopped, narrow eyes darting from Cole to Charlotte and back again. "Huh," she said, as if it were a complete sentence. She motioned for them to follow her inside, and as soon as they crossed the threshold into the farmhouse, a vivid memory returned. It happened every time he came through the door.

In a flash, he was an angry teenager again, standing on the porch of this old place with his sister, watching their dad drive away. On his back, he carried a reluctantly packed bag with nothing inside but a pair of jeans, three T-shirts, socks, underwear, and a hoodie.

And then he heard three words that would forever change his life. "I'm Miss Hildy," followed by five words it had taken him a long time to believe—"It's going to be okay."

He'd spent the night in the dark bedroom, fighting tears and trying not to punch a hole in the wall. It wasn't okay—

his dad had abandoned him only months after his mom had left. Who did that?

In the morning, the smell of cinnamon and sugar lured him from slumber. He'd gone downstairs and learned that things at Haven House weren't like they were at home. There were homecooked meals and chore charts and board games and horseback rides. There was gardening and cleaning and mending and fixing—and those last two were more about hearts than they were about houses and land.

Steve and Hildy took them in when no one else wanted them. They showed Cole how it felt to be loved when his parents were unable to.

Even now, all these years later, it overwhelmed him how much goodness he'd discovered within these four walls. Steve and Hildy made him believe in the goodness of God again. They made him believe in himself. Without them, without Haven House—he had a feeling he would be a very different person.

They followed her into the sun-colored kitchen, where the little girl sat at the table with an open book and an empty plate.

"This is Jewel," Hildy said. "She's new to us this month. We're working on her letters."

Jewel looked at the two of them, a skeptical expression on her face.

"Sounds fun," Charlotte said.

"It's not," Jewel said.

Charlotte walked over to the girl and looked at the book she was writing in. "I had a book just like that when I was your age."

Cole wondered how Charlotte could tell the girl's age. He taught high school, so the little ones all kind of blended together.

"You did?" the girl asked.

Charlotte nodded. "I did all my schoolwork at home."

"Like home-schooled?"

Another nod.

"Why? Didn't you like real school?"

"Well, I was dancing most days when kids were going to school."

"Dancing?" Jewel's eyes lit up. "Like a ballerina?"

Charlotte smiled. "Yes, exactly like that." Her eyes found Cole's, and he realized he was staring. There was that dreaded curiosity again. Was he staring at her like she was an alien? Because she certainly had an other-worldly quality about her.

He wished, and not for the first time that day, that he'd paid more attention to Julianna when she talked about dance. Maybe then Charlotte would be less interesting to him.

All he really remembered was how broken-hearted Jules had been when she left the ballet. He didn't know what had happened, but whatever it was, it convinced her she wasn't good enough to continue as a professional dancer. He hated seeing her like that—depressed and beaten. It wasn't like his sister to be either.

And then the relationship with Connor happened and he helped her find a new dream, sending her life down a completely different path.

"I wanted to take dance, but my mom said there wasn't enough money. I probably wouldn't be good at it anyway."

"I bet you'd be great at it," Charlotte said. "Maybe I could show you a few steps before we leave."

"Really?" The little girl smiled.

"Sure, if it's okay with Miss Hildy."

Hildy dished two sticky buns onto plates and smiled. "I think that's an excellent idea."

"I'm going to go get ready." Jewel ran out of the kitchen, and Charlotte turned back to face them.

"That's about the happiest I've seen her since she's been here," Hildy said. "She's a little young for us, only seven years old, but her mom came through here once upon a time, so when she showed up last week, I couldn't say no."

"Been doing a lot of that lately, have you?" Cole asked.

Hildy gave him a wry look. "You know I wasn't about to turn Connor away." The older woman pushed a plate toward Charlotte, whose hands went up instantly.

"Sorry, I should've told you I already ate this morning."

"What did you have, a piece of spinach and a cup of black coffee?" Hildy gave Charlotte a once-over. "You look like you could use a good homecooked meal."

Judging by the look on Charlotte's face, this wasn't a topic she wanted to discuss.

"How are the kids?" Cole asked, steering the conversation away from Charlotte.

"Quiet," Hildy said. "Amelia especially. AJ's warmed up to the West boys—they're out in the yard with Steve." Hildy's gaze returned to Charlotte. "Now, I would love to know why you brought this beautiful, interesting girl to my door."

Charlotte straightened. The uneaten sticky bun sat in front of her, next to a cup of black coffee, which she picked up and sipped.

She inhaled, glanced at Cole, as if gearing up to pitch a big idea to a perfect stranger required a bolstering of her resolve.

But as she started talking, Cole found it impossible to look away.

And realizing that fact made him very, very nervous.

19

From the moment she walked in the door at Haven House, something inside Charlotte settled. It was almost as if the inside of this house was like a hug from a wise old grandmother, someone who would accept her straightaway, no questions asked.

Maybe it was Hildy and that slightly awkward hug she'd given her as a means of welcome. Maybe it was the little girl working on her letters at the table or the smell of sticky buns or the dogs in the yard. Maybe it was all of those things. All of those things together made this place feel like a home.

And Charlotte had never had one of those.

Now, with a mug of fresh coffee in her hand and a handsome man watching her from the opposite side of the table, Charlotte found herself unable to speak. She wanted Hildy to agree to be a part of this tribute to Julianna, of course, but mostly, she wanted to prove she belonged here —to be accepted without question.

"I'm all ears." Hildy's smile was warm and kind, but she was sneaky. Charlotte noticed that the longer they sat there, the closer the plated sticky bun moved to her.

Charlotte cleared her throat just as the screen door opened and three boys stormed through, followed by an older man and two teenagers.

Cole straightened, and they stopped at the sight of him.

One of the boys, a mop-headed teen, tall and lanky stopped in the doorway. "Hey, Coach."

The other boys grew instantly wide-eyed. They rang out a chorus of "Hey, Coach," making it clear that he was the star in that room. Cole seemed unaffected. She, for one, appreciated the shift in attention.

AJ lifted his hand. "Hi, Uncle Cole." AJ bore a striking resemblance to Julianna's older brother. They shared the same eyes. And the same sad expression.

"Coach is your uncle?" one of the other boys asked, wonder in his voice.

AJ grinned. "Yep."

Cole tousled the boy's hair. "Boys," he said. He extended a hand toward the older man. "Steve."

The older man smiled as he reached out and shook Cole's hand. "Help has arrived."

"Are you here to play football with us?" one of the younger kids asked.

"Uh, no," Cole said.

"Would you?" another boy asked. "Show us a few plays?"

Cole's shoulders drew tight like a knotted rope.

"You should go, Cole," Hildy said. "The boys would love it. I'll get the scoop from your girl, while you guys throw the ball around."

"*Your girl.*" The words hung there, and Charlotte tried them on for size. Just for a fleeting moment.

"What about the fence?" Cole asked.

"Fence isn't going anywhere," Steve said.

Cole looked at Asher, who stood frozen in the doorway.

"Help me teach these guys a play or two, would ya?" Cole glanced at Charlotte. "You'll be okay?"

His unexpected concern for her sent a jolt of warmth through her veins. She nodded.

"You got a ball?" Cole asked as he led the herd back out of the kitchen and through the screen door, leaving Charlotte alone in the farmhouse with Hildy and Steve. Hildy introduced them and then they all settled on stools around the tall kitchen island, a mug of coffee in front of each of them.

"He's a really good man," Hildy said. "You're a lucky girl. And I'm glad to see the two of you together—after all he's been through, I wondered if he'd ever open his heart again."

There it was again. Talk about *all he's been through*. What did that mean? Was she referring to what had happened to Jules, or was there more?

"Like Cole said, we're not together," Charlotte said. "Just friends. I mean, not even really friends. I was friends with Julianna. I think he's mostly tolerating me."

"Oh. Well, maybe I'll pretend I didn't notice him staring at you when you weren't looking." Hildy grinned.

Heat rushed to Charlotte's cheeks.

"Maybe there's hope for him yet." Hildy took a sip of her coffee.

Charlotte needed to change the subject. Fast. "So, I've heard Haven House is a transitional home—is that right?" Charlotte asked.

"Cole didn't tell you what we do here?" Hildy's eyes widened underneath raised brows.

"Like I said, he's tolerating me." Charlotte forced a smile.

"We've been running Haven House for over twenty-five years," Hildy said. "We never had kids of our own, so when the previous caretakers retired, we knew this was exactly what God wanted us to do."

Hildy and Steve wore the same expression—pride—and what Charlotte could only describe as a deep, deep love for something much bigger than themselves.

"Get the book, Hil," Steve said, hitching a thumb over his shoulder.

Hildy rushed out of the kitchen and returned seconds later with a large photo album. "This is an album of photos of every child who has been helped through Haven House over the years." She plunked the book on the counter in front of Charlotte and continued to explain the way the nonprofit worked.

With six different houses in the surrounding areas, the goal had always been for Haven House to continue to expand. Each home housed six kids, ranging in ages from twelve to eighteen, with the occasional exception like Jewel or one of Asher's brothers. These were kids who would otherwise end up in foster care. Some of them stayed for a month or two while their parents went to rehab. Some were there only a few days.

"We're a safe house for kids nobody else wants," Steve said. "Teenagers have an especially hard time in foster care, so we take them in and teach them life skills. We make sure they're getting a good education. They work on the farm and in the garden. They help train the horses, make dinners, all the things they'd do if they were our biological kids. A home doesn't run on its own, it takes everyone doing their fair share."

Charlotte stilled. She didn't know much about that. Her "home," as it were, had been an apartment she shared with Marcia in whatever city she was working in at the time—and she'd hardly call any of those places "home." Marcia used the money Charlotte made to hire a housekeeper who prepared all of their meals, along with a driver and private tutors. Charlotte did nothing for herself.

What a charmed, privileged life she'd lived.

She'd never seen that as a negative thing until now. She wanted to learn how to work in a garden. She wanted to ride the horses and make her own bed.

She wanted to be a better person, to contribute something good and meaningful to the world. She had a feeling just being around people like Hildy and Steve was a good start.

"But most of those kids aren't teenagers," Charlotte said.

Hildy smiled. "Connor's kids are very short-term. I insisted on giving him a break over the weekend, and we'll only have them for a few more days."

Charlotte thought about the last time she'd seen Connor. Would a few more days be enough?

"And we weren't about to split up those brothers. We just go with the flow." They smiled at each other and Charlotte saw their mutual love and respect so clearly it might as well have been a living thing.

A deep sense of longing pulsed through her body. She wanted that, she realized now, more than anything.

"Well, it's wonderful," Charlotte said, gathering herself. "I'm sure you're wondering what in the world I'm doing here."

Steve and Hildy both laughed. "Not at all," Hildy said.

"But if you stick around too long, we'll put you to work," Steve said with a smile. "Just look at Cole."

Charlotte didn't really know what Cole's relationship to Haven House was, but it was clear he was no stranger here. He was a walking box of contradictions. She wouldn't have expected someone like him to volunteer at a place like this.

"I'm told Julianna was a fixture out here," Charlotte said. "So, I thought you might want a chance to be a part of her dance recital."

Hildy frowned. "How?"

"I'm organizing it," Charlotte said.

Hildy gasped. "Charlotte, that's wonderful. It would've made Julianna so sad to think of her students not being able to perform."

Charlotte nodded. "That's exactly what I thought."

"What did you have in mind?" Steve asked. "Did you want me to wear a tutu?"

Charlotte smiled. "Some of her friends and family are going to do tribute dances, in Julianna's honor. I think the teachers are planning to choreograph something to one of her favorite songs, that sort of thing."

Steve took a sip of coffee, then set the empty mug on the counter. "I'm going to go check on the football practice outside. I'm sure Hildy will tell me what I have to do later."

The man walked out the door, and Hildy turned her attention back to Charlotte. "You were saying?"

"I wondered if you and Steve would want to participate," she said. "I know you meant a lot to Jules."

The other woman groaned. "I'm not a dancer, Miss Ballerina."

"Most of these people won't be dancers," Charlotte said, "Everyone will have an instructor, someone to help choreograph their number. We're not going to let you go out there and make fools of yourselves."

"Don't you want to see what a hopeless case I am before you ask me to do this?" Hildy gave her a wry smile.

Charlotte shook her head. "I think you're going to be just fine."

The older woman shook her head. "Well, aren't you the optimist?"

"What do you say?" Charlotte asked. "Are you in?"

"I can't believe I'm agreeing to this, but fine."

Charlotte smiled. "And Steve?"

Hildy leaned closer. "Let me worry about him."

"Thanks for doing this," Charlotte said. "I really want this recital to be special."

"I like you, Charlotte," Hildy said.

"You do?" Charlotte was struck by the words. They were so simple, but so kind. Did anyone in her life actually *like* her? Mostly, other dancers saw her as competition. Some saw her as a person who didn't deserve the good fortune she'd had. There were always jealous comments behind her back, and while she usually pretended not to be bothered, she was always, always bothered.

Hildy picked up her mug of coffee. "I do."

"Thanks," Charlotte said quietly.

Jewel appeared in the doorway, wearing what appeared to be a Princess Elsa dress-up costume.

"Oh my," Hildy said. "Look at you."

"I'm ready to dance," Jewel said with a smile.

Charlotte sat unmoving for several seconds, trying to remember what she was like at Jewel's age. By seven, she was already dancing six hours a day and tutoring when it was convenient for Marcia's schedule. Had she ever simply gotten starry-eyed over the idea of dancing?

"Do you have an open space somewhere?" Charlotte asked. "Doesn't have to be anything fancy."

"Let's clear away a spot in the living room," Hildy said. "Maybe we can get Amelia to join."

Together, they pushed the furniture out of the way and Hildy rolled up the rug to reveal a beautiful hardwood floor.

"Perfect," Charlotte said. "Now, Jewel, let's start with first position." She demonstrated with her heels together, toes turned out, arms curved in front of her.

"I'll leave you two." Hildy excused herself from the room, and Charlotte focused wholly on the little girl at her side. She led Jewel through all the positions, and they were just getting to the plié when she glanced up and found familiar eyes staring at her from the doorway.

"Amelia." Charlotte straightened. "Do you want to join us?"

Amelia's gaze locked on to Charlotte's, but she didn't respond. Moments later, Hildy was back, wearing a kind, knowing smile.

"You haven't danced in a while, Amelia," Hildy said. "Come on out and give it a try."

After a beat, Amelia dashed outside, the screen door slamming behind her like an exclamation point on a sentence she hadn't said aloud.

Hildy sighed. "Time was, you couldn't keep that girl off the dance floor." She shook her head. "Poor thing."

"Should we go after her?"

"Sometimes what they need most is a little time alone," Hildy said. "But only a little time. I'll keep an eye on the clock."

Charlotte turned to the little girl in front of her and smiled. "You did a wonderful job, Jewel."

"Thank you." Jewel grabbed hold of the dress on either side and curtsied.

Charlotte stifled a smile as she curtsied back.

"Will you come back?" Jewel asked.

"I'll try," Charlotte said. "In the meantime, you can practice your positions."

"Okay!" The little girl plunged herself forward, arms wrapped around Charlotte's waist.

Charlotte's hands went up as if someone had just said, *This is a stick-up.*

Jewel, still clinging to Charlotte, looked up and smiled. "You're beautiful, Miss Charlotte." And then she ran off, leaving Charlotte alone in the living room, basking in the glow of the heartfelt compliment.

And wanting more than ever to buy the dance studio and make a life in the little town that had wormed its way into her heart.

20

After the dance lesson, Jewel ran outside to play with the dogs, and Charlotte joined Hildy in the kitchen. She stood at the sink, filling a pitcher with water.

"She's really sweet," Charlotte said. "Maybe we could arrange for her to join a dance class or two?"

Hildy turned off the faucet, stuck a wooden spoon in the pitcher, and stirred. "Are you teaching?"

Charlotte sat on a stool opposite the counter. "I'm hoping to buy the dance studio. I've mentioned it to Connor a few times, but I haven't heard back yet."

"What a great idea," Hildy said. "That would make Julianna so happy."

"I hope so." Charlotte wanted nothing more.

"I know so," Hildy said. "Julianna would love seeing you here."

Charlotte glanced out the window, then back to Hildy, who now leaned against the sink, arms folded across her chest. "Has Cole always volunteered here?"

"Oh, no." Hildy put her glasses on and flipped through the photo album that still sat on the counter. She turned the book around and pushed it toward Charlotte, pointing to a photo of three boys, leaning against a fence, a big black horse behind them. "He lived here, for several months actually. He and those two boys were like brothers."

"He lived here?"

"It's a long story. We all fell in love with Cole. The quiet, troubled ones always steal my heart. The two boys in that photo stayed on the straight and narrow thanks to Cole Turner. Even then, even when everything was falling apart, he still had the biggest heart of anyone I knew."

"Cole." Charlotte studied the photo for several seconds, finding it hard to believe that the man she knew had anything but a heart of stone. He was about as warm and fuzzy as a boulder.

"Don't let his act fool you. He might have a brick wall around him now—and for many good reasons—but if you can get past that, you'll find a pot of gold."

The sound of happy screams from outside caught their attention, and both Charlotte and Hildy moved toward the window overlooking a large lawn at the side of the house. Cole had set up a scrimmage of sorts and even roped Steve in to playing a game of touch football, something that had all the boys shouting and laughing.

Hildy motioned toward one of the boys, the one who appeared to be the youngest. "See that one?"

Charlotte nodded.

"Asher's littlest brother, Henry. Asher is the quarterback on Cole's team."

Charlotte watched as the dark-headed boy tentatively joined the game. Cole knelt down next to him and explained something Charlotte was sure she wouldn't understand. Then, he stood up, slapped Henry five, and set the boy up in line next to him.

The play began, and while Charlotte couldn't understand any of what they were doing, she gathered it was good for Henry because he ended up with the ball, which he promptly ran all the way to the other end of the lawn while Cole and another boy blocked the others.

Henry reached the end, rolled on the ground, then stood up with the ball over his head, a huge smile on his face. Cole raced over to him and picked him up on his shoulders, then took him for a victory lap while the rest of them cheered.

"That's the first time I've seen Henry smile since he's been here," Hildy said quietly.

Charlotte watched as Cole put the boy down and set them up to go again. Maybe Hildy had a point—maybe there was an actual heart hidden underneath that wall Cole had built around himself.

"Does he come around here a lot?" Charlotte asked. "Cole, I mean."

"Every Sunday for dinner," Hildy said. "You're more than welcome to join."

"Oh, no, I don't want to impose," Charlotte said.

"Are you kidding? I'd love the chance to feed you a real meal." Hildy smiled, peering over at her sideways. "You're curious about him."

Charlotte turned her attention back to the yard. When she did, she found Cole standing there, looking in their direction. Hildy raised a hand in a wave, and Charlotte stood there, dumbly, like a statue.

He waved back and one of the kids came out of nowhere, plowed into him, and they were back at it.

After a few more minutes of watching, Charlotte and Hildy moved away from the window, but within seconds, the commotion outdoors brought them back, and this time the screams didn't sound so happy.

Charlotte peered down over the yard and found Cole

locked in what appeared to be a standoff with the one Hildy called Asher. Asher jabbed a pointed finger in Cole's chest, and Cole swatted it away.

Asher yelled something Charlotte couldn't make out, and Hildy groaned.

"What's going on?" Charlotte asked.

"I'm not sure I want to know," Hildy said.

But Charlotte definitely did. She raced outside and into the yard, wondering if whatever was going on might finally give her a peek into the man who had proven to be a mystery.

Cole hadn't expected Asher to take the game from friendly to serious, but maybe the kid had more aggression to work off than he let on.

They'd been in the middle of a play when Asher barreled into Cole out of nowhere, knocking the wind out of him. Cole pushed Asher off of him and stood.

"What was that about?" he asked—and not quietly. "We're not playing rough with the other kids around, Ash."

Asher stood and scrambled off in the other direction, not responding.

"Asher." Cole followed him.

"What's the matter, Coach, you can't handle it?" Asher shoved him square in the chest.

Cole stumbled back but quickly righted himself. "You're forgetting yourself, son."

"What do you want, Coach? Why are you here? You think you can bully me into coming back to the team—I told you I'm done."

Cole frowned. "That's not why I'm here."

"Asher, knock it off." Steve put a hand on Asher's arm, and the kid shook it off.

"Watch it," Cole warned.

"Or what?"

Cole reminded himself that Asher was angry—and not at him—not really. He'd seen this kind of behavior a hundred times. Heck, he'd had the same mad-at-the-world attitude when he was Asher's age.

"What are you doing?" Cole took a step closer to him, and Asher moved away. "What's this really about?"

"I'm sick of you, that's what."

"That's fine," Cole said. "I can go. But if I hear one word of you treating Steve and Hildy like you're treating me right now, you will live to regret it."

Asher scoffed. "You don't scare me."

Cole grabbed him firmly by the front of the shirt. "Well, I should."

Asher pulled away from Cole's grasp, breathing heavy. "What do you care, anyway? I'm off the team. I'm not your problem anymore."

"You think that matters to me?" Cole shouted. "The only thing that matters is that you're doing what's best for you, and right now, this isn't it."

"Yeah, right," Asher said. "The only thing that matters to you is that I come back and play so you have a chance of winning games."

"Wrong," Cole said. "Do I think you should? Yeah. I think you're making a huge mistake. I think you've got potential. I think you're a leader—and I know you could be a great quarterback. But that's not the only thing that matters to me."

"Yeah, so what is?"

Cole's heart worked overtime in his chest. He willed his

breathing to steady. "You, Ash. Look, I get it. I know how hard it is to ask, but sometimes we all need a little help."

"Like you do, Coach?"

"What's that supposed to mean?"

Asher turned away, then shook his head. "Forget it."

"No, speak your mind," Cole demanded.

The kid glared at him. "Fine. You want the truth? You suck, Coach. Yeah, we won games, but look how you got us there. All you did was make sure everyone was scared of you. You were mean—you made us feel like idiots."

The words pummeled Cole like a sucker punch to the gut.

"So forgive me if I don't want to share my problems with you."

Cole watched him for a long moment. "Is that really why you quit?"

Asher ran a hand through his mess of hair. "No. I told you why. But you keep trying to act like we're friends. We're not friends, Coach."

Cole held his gaze for a beat, then looked away. "You're right."

Asher shifted. "I am?"

"I've been asking you to do something I haven't been willing to do," Cole said. "I never let anyone help me either, and the last few years—I could've used it. Same as you."

Asher shrugged. "Yeah, I guess."

"Look, I can't promise you I'm not going to screw up again, but I can promise you that if you need me, I'll be there. On the field or off, no matter what. And I'm gonna do better, all right?"

Asher looked away.

Cole clapped a hand on his shoulder. "The job's still yours if you want it. I'm starting the bathroom demo tomorrow. It'll be hot and sweaty and it doesn't pay well, but you'll learn a skill you can actually use. It's your choice."

Cole stood there for a minute, but the kid didn't respond. "I'm gonna go. I'll see you around."

Cole turned and started back toward the driveway, when his eyes found Charlotte, watching him.

Great.

"Let's go," he said as he passed her, not bothering to make sure she followed. It seemed he was destined for public humiliation, no matter what he did.

He got in the truck and slammed the door, started the engine, and replayed Asher's comment in his mind. *"You suck, Coach."*

And it stung. Because it was true.

And there was no way for him to deny it anymore.

21

*C*ole arrived early to the following day's practice and found members of the team straggling in, looking tired, like boys who were staying up playing video games (or worse) all night long.

He thought about riding them—making them run, or do suicide drills for the duration of practice, but Asher's words were still too fresh in his mind.

A reminder that the man he'd become was not the man he'd ever intended to be.

When Gemma left, he took up offense with life itself, and his boys deserved better.

Once they were out on the field, Cole waited as the boys circled up. He even said a silent prayer for a thunderbolt of an idea on how to unite this team, because so far, nothing was working. Though he had a feeling his approach was all wrong.

"Coach, are we gonna see your lady friend today?" Greg Dunbar asked.

"Yeah, I'd like to get a better look at her." Will Hotchke

slapped Dunbar a high-five and Cole bit the inside of his cheek.

"She looked like she could really work you over, if you know what I mean." Using his face, hips, and hands, Hotchke took his comment from inappropriate to vulgar.

Dunbar's laugh was loud, and the other boys joined in. Cole's face grew hot and his temper flashed. "Take a lap, all of you!"

The boys' groans were followed by a chorus of verbal grievances.

"That's not how we talk about women on my field," Cole shouted.

"Come on, Coach. We were just kidding." Hotchke set his feet and glared at Cole.

"Take a lap, Hotch, or don't bother coming back."

After a pronounced pause, the kid chucked his helmet on the ground at Cole's feet and walked off toward the locker room while the other boys stared. Hotchke was their best running back.

Cole would hear about this later. From the athletic director. From the boosters. From Bilby. He watched the other boys run a half-hearted lap as Matt arrived at the center of the field.

"What'd they do?"

"Disrespected a woman," Cole said. "Don't tell me I'm being hard on them."

Bilby held his hands up in front of him. "I won't. If our job is to make them better men, it starts there."

"We're going to need to make some changes around here, Bilby," Cole said, thinking about how hypocritical it was not to ask for help after telling not one, but two different people there was no shame in it.

"What kind of changes?" Matt asked.

"I need to be a better coach," Cole said. "And I've got to

find a way to unify this team." He didn't bother looking at his assistant coach—he knew the guy was probably staring at him, slack-jawed.

The boys reached the end of their lap. Most were winded, though their run had been anything but fast. They circled back up. Cole stood in front of them, searching his mind for a magic solution to make them a team, but he came up empty.

He had to do better by them. He owed them that. Before he could say a word, he saw the boys' attention drawn in the distance behind him. He turned and saw Asher walking toward them, dressed for practice. Next to him, an annoyed-looking Hotchke.

"Found this in the locker room, Coach," Asher said.

Hotchke didn't make eye contact with Cole. Instead, his gaze focused steadily on the grass between them. Asher pushed Hotchke with his shoulder, and the kid finally looked up.

"Sorry for disrespecting your lady friend, Coach," Hotchke said.

Cole glanced at Asher, then back at Hotchke. "Forgiven," Cole said. "So long as you keep that trash talk out of my locker room and off this field. Better yet, don't talk like that at all."

Hotchke nodded.

Cole took a step toward him, barely a foot between them now. "The world has enough guys treating women like dirt, Hotch. It's so unoriginal. Be a better man."

"Yes, Coach," Hotchke said.

"Now, take a lap."

Hotchke appeared to be trying not to roll his eyes, but Asher grabbed his arm, and the two of them ran off toward the track.

And the sight of their obedience made Cole feel for the

first time in a long time like his team had a shot. He and Bilby split the boys up for drills, and Cole cast a sideways glance at Asher. The kid tossed him a look, then a barely detectable nod, as if to let him know everything was good between them.

They'd been running drills for about forty-five minutes when Bilby made his way over to Cole.

"They look good today," he said. "Asher's got a fire I don't think I've ever seen."

Cole kept his eyes on the field. "He sure does."

"You have something to do with that?"

Cole shot Matt a sideways look, the remnants of their unpleasant conversation playing on repeat in his mind. Cole shook his head. "Doubt it."

But what if it had? What if something he'd said had gotten through to Asher? What if that moment out on the field at Haven House actually made the kid want to turn his life around?

That, not winning games, needed to be his goal. He talked to the boys about being better men—wasn't it time he took those words to heart himself?

"What's this?"

Cole tracked his assistant coach's gaze to the parking lot, where the now-familiar black Jetta had just pulled in. Clearly, Charlotte still hadn't called the rental place about the damage she'd done to the car. Maybe he could have it fixed for her.

Good grief, what was he thinking?

"You're going to need to fill me in on the story here," Bilby said.

He didn't care that Charlotte was there, but he wished she would've waited a few more minutes so the guys would stop razzing him, especially given the way things had exploded that morning over a comment about her.

"No story," Cole said, squinting.

She got out of her car and waved at him like he was a long-lost friend she couldn't wait to hug.

"Oh, yeah. No story."

Cole didn't wave back. Instead, he grunted, then pulled the guys together in a huddle at the center of the field. His plan was to give them a quick pep talk and send them off, hopefully before Charlotte reached them.

Instead, Hotchke and Dunbar noticed her approaching, and they both took off their helmets and stared.

"Gentlemen," Cole said, but it was no use. He glanced at Charlotte, who wore a pair of jean cut-offs and a tank top that was perfectly modest, but that seemed to be having quite the effect on his team. He could never compete with her for these boys' attention.

Truth be told, they wouldn't have been able to keep his attention either when she was around, not that he'd let anyone else ever know that.

He scanned the circle, and for whatever reason, he didn't want them looking at Charlotte the way they were all looking at her now.

For her part, Charlotte seemed completely oblivious to the effect she had on his team.

How was it possible she had no idea how beautiful she was?

Gemma had always liked to be looked at, and she knew when she had a man's attention. It was some kind of game for her—one Cole never had a chance of winning. Charlotte, on the other hand, showed up here looking adorable, wearing a broad smile and an expression that somehow said, *Hey, can we be friends?*

Not that friendship was on these boys' minds.

She was carrying, he now noticed, a box of Dandy's

Donuts, and as soon as she reached them, he got a whiff of the sugary dough.

First flowers, now donuts. What would she give him next? A gift certificate for a pedicure?

She stood on the edge of the circle next to Asher for a beat, smiling at the team.

Cole drew Asher's gaze, then nodded toward Charlotte, hoping the kid had enough sense to be a gentleman.

"Hey, Miss Page," Asher finally said. He turned toward her and took the box. "Let me get that for you."

"Thank you, Asher." She smiled again as her eyes met Cole's. When he didn't smile back, her face fell.

But it wasn't in his nature to smile. What was he supposed to do? Moon over her like these sex-crazed teenagers?

Bilby elbowed him—and not subtly.

Cole dug deep and found a sentence—"We, uh, weren't expecting you"—which probably made her feel even less welcome than his stoic expression.

"But you brought donuts," Bilby cut in, "so you're more than welcome."

Charlotte's smile turned shy. "I thought you'd be wrapping up."

"And you thought right," Bilby said, overcompensating for Cole's crankiness.

"I just had an idea to run by you," Charlotte said. "All of you."

All of them? Like the teenagers who made up his football team?

"I listen better when I'm eating," Dunbar said with a shrug.

A chorus of agreements rang out and Charlotte's face turned a pale shade of pink. "Sorry, maybe I should've asked before I filled you guys up on sugar." Her eyes seemed to ask for Cole's permission to open the box.

At his continued silence (what was *wrong* with him?), Bilby jumped in with quick reassurances. "It's fine. They eat anything and everything, including donuts."

Cole didn't miss Matt's pointed glare.

Asher opened the box and the guys dug in. When they finished, the box looked like it had been ransacked, only a few donuts remaining.

"Want one, Coach?" Asher asked.

"I'm good," Cole said, holding up a hand, and—he was sure—coming across as a first-class jerk. He had no reason, other than unwanted thoughts about Charlotte, to be acting this way. Apparently, his vow to be a better coach ended on the field. He should probably vow to be a better human first.

Asher turned to Charlotte. "Go ahead, Miss Page—we're all ears."

Charlotte smiled. "You can call me Charlotte." She wiped the palms of her hands on her shorts and Cole caught the slightest side glimpse of her triceps. The definition in her arms was impressive. It turned out, there were many impressive things about Charlotte. He knew because he'd gone home after their trip to Haven House and Googled her.

And he'd never admit that out loud in a million years.

He'd heard she was one of the best in her field, and now he'd seen it for himself.

Charlotte had been named the youngest principal dancer at the Chicago City Ballet, which further reading told him was a pretty big deal. The "principal dancer" was the star. Entire ballets had been created just for her.

Artists created with her in mind. One guy even called her his "muse." That was a kind of influence Cole couldn't even imagine. He read about her childhood, her professional career, her strict regimen.

One article chronicled "A Day in the Life of a Professional Ballerina," giving him a peek into her typical schedule. The reporter must've followed her around for an entire day because he outlined her schedule from breakfast (two eggs with a slice of turkey bacon, a small cup of fruit with chia seeds, and some other froofy garbage Cole had never heard of) to training to fitness classes to rehearsals to physical therapy, to hair, makeup, and costumes, and then finally ending with her performance that night. Cole was exhausted just reading about it. No wonder she'd come looking for a quieter, more peaceful life.

Did Charlotte have anything in her life besides ballet?

He understood her a little better after doing a little research. Her life was solitary and regimented. She set goals and then she crushed them. Maybe she'd worn herself out in the process. All of a sudden, her starting over in Harbor Pointe made a lot more sense.

He didn't stop with the one article, he was embarrassed to remember. He read what her critics wrote about her. He clicked links to YouTube videos of her performances and watched them all—one right after the other.

Charlotte in a red tutu number with bright red lips and a wild red headpiece. Charlotte in a white dance costume encircled by a sparkling white tutu. Charlotte in a blue and white dress playing the title role in a ballet production of *Romeo and Juliet*.

She defied gravity. She made it look easy, the way she moved—effortlessly—when he knew it absolutely was not. It was impressive, to say the least. He didn't know anything about ballet, but he did know reaching her elite level took more than talent. It took work and dedication and focus.

And he respected the heck out of that.

Maybe he should have her come and talk to his team. They seemed to lack all of those things.

If anyone had caught him poring over dance videos, he would've not only felt like a stalker, but a fool.

Because he'd gotten more than carried away in his admiration. His sister probably would've used the word "smitten" and she wouldn't have been wrong.

But he was intent on shutting those thoughts down. Charlotte Page might be special, but that didn't matter. Cole wasn't about to make another giant mistake in the romance department. His had been colossal enough to last a lifetime.

So why did he feel like she could read his mind, standing across from him, among his players, preparing to pitch what would most likely end up being a ridiculous idea.

She looked at him.

His mouth went dry. Instead of encouraging her to go ahead and make her speech, he looked at his watch.

Classy.

"Okay," Charlotte said as if she'd made up her mind to continue on in spite of him. "I'm part of a group that's planning a big event to help celebrate the life of Julianna Ford."

Cole's heart sunk.

"Coach's sister," one of the guys said.

"Right." Charlotte's eyes darted to Cole's, and a nervous look washed over her face.

This was about the dance recital? What on earth did she want to talk to his team about a dance recital for? He almost wondered if he should jump in—save her from making an embarrassing mistake. She was, after all, a woman who seemed not to understand men.

Instead, he stayed quiet.

Charlotte looked away, as if trying to figure out how to proceed. There was something about the way she moved—a strange contradiction of sorts. An embodiment of both grace and awkwardness.

At the moment, the awkwardness had the upper hand.

Finally, Charlotte went on. "Well, I had kind of a crazy idea that you guys might want to be a part of it."

What was she suggesting? Cole had already made it clear he wasn't going to get on that stage, so was she here to manipulate him by using his team?

"What do you need from us, Miss Page?" Asher asked.

She smiled. "Well, I'm helping put together some of the numbers featuring people in the community, sort of tribute numbers for Julianna."

"And you want our sick moves?" Hotchke started the hip gyrating he'd perfected earlier and the boys laughed.

"Hotchke." Cole's tone warned.

Hotchke held his hands up in front of him in surrender. "Only jokes."

Charlotte's eyes had widened, her cheeks flushed.

"Sorry," Cole said. "They're like this all the time." Why did he feel like he needed to protect her? She was probably stronger than his entire team put together.

But it wasn't her strength he wanted to protect. It was her innocence. Sure, he'd known there was something different about her, but the article he'd read confirmed it.

When asked about her personal life, Page goes quiet.

"You mean, like my love life?" She asks the question tentatively, as if she's worried she'll have to answer it.

When I tell her, yes, that's exactly what I mean, she shifts in her chair, pulling a long, toned leg up underneath her. "Sometimes we have to make sacrifices for our art," she says. "For me, a personal life is one of those sacrifices."

It's an art worth sacrificing for, but even so, it's difficult not to feel sorry for the beautiful ballerina. Of all the things she has to sacrifice, love seems the unfairest.

He'd wondered what that meant. How much of a sacrifice had she made when it came to love?

Bilby's gaze darted to Cole, a quizzical look in his eye.

Great, Matt would probably prod him even more about "the story" between him and Charlotte if his entire tone changed when he spoke to her.

"What are you suggesting?" Cole asked curtly.

"Well," Charlotte said. "We were hoping you guys might get involved."

A quiet, confused murmur zipped around the circle like electricity.

"You actually want us to dance?" Hotchke asked. "Dude, I was totally kidding." Again with the hip gyration, which warranted groans around the circle. At least the other boys weren't encouraging his borderline inappropriate behavior.

"Well," Charlotte said. "Yes. But maybe not quite like that."

Now the laughter turned mocking and a few of the guys shouted, "Burn!"

Hotchke played it off, and Charlotte looked confused.

She quickly recovered. "We really want to add some fun numbers to the recital—Julianna would've gotten a kick out of you guys strutting your stuff up there."

"We don't have to wear tights, do we?" a kid they called "Whitey" asked.

Charlotte laughed. "I'm thinking football jerseys."

"I don't know, Miss Page," Dunbar said. "No offense, but dancing is kind of for sissies."

Cole folded his arms over his chest. He should probably defend Charlotte's idea, but truthfully, he saw Greg's point.

"I promise you won't look like a sissy," Charlotte said. "Haven't you seen the football players on *Dancing With the Stars?*"

The guys would never own up to watching that show,

though one or two of them muttered something like "My mom watches that."

"Just trust me," Charlotte said. "I think we can keep it fun and cool. Trust me."

"Plus, it's for a great cause," Asher said. "Count us in." He nodded at Cole, who felt a twinge of guilt at the way these boys were so willing to join in this event when he'd so adamantly refused.

Charlotte's face lit up. "Great. I think having big, strong football players dancing is going to be a blast for the audience."

"You think we're big and strong?" Dunbar flexed his bicep.

"Some of us are, *Dumbar*, but not you." Whitey gave Greg a shove.

"Nah, you fools don't hold a candle to what I'm packing over here." Hotchke lifted his shirt to reveal an impressive six-pack but followed it up with an inappropriate gesture.

Cole started to correct Hotchke, but his up-and-coming quarterback jumped in before he could say a word.

"Hotch," Asher said, eyes darting toward Charlotte, as if to say, *Dude, we're not in the locker room.*

Hotchke held his hands out in front of him—an apology of sorts. And Cole took note. Somehow, almost overnight, Asher had become a leader. It was exactly what he'd been hoping would happen.

Asher's actions confirmed Cole's recommitment to the team. They could learn real-life skills out here on the field, and he could be the one to show them.

He *wanted* to be the one to show them.

The conversation turned into a raucous display as the boys threw out ideas for something they knew absolutely nothing about. Cole glanced at Charlotte, who seemed to be enjoying the enthusiasm.

Then, out of nowhere, Teddy Phillips lifted a hand to quiet them all down. "Hold up, hold up," he said. "What about you, Coach?"

Cole felt his eyebrows shoot upward. "What about me?"

"You're dancing with us, right?" Teddy asked.

Cole didn't blush, but he did feel his face heat up. "No."

"No, he should dance with Miss Page!" Asher's eyes lit up like he'd just had the best idea in the world.

Now, Charlotte blushed.

"Come on, Coach," Dunbar said. "You know people would flock out to see the coach of the high school state championship football team dancing a waltz."

The boys grew rowdy again.

"Not happening," Cole said.

"This could be great publicity for the team," Bilby said. "Really bring the guys together."

"The team doesn't need publicity, Bilby," Cole argued. "We won state last year."

Matt lowered his voice. "But do you really see that happening this year? This team needs some unity."

Cole shot him a look.

"I'm just saying, this is the best morale we've seen from these kids yet."

Cole shook his head.

"Come on, Coach, if we have to make fools of ourselves, then so do you," Hotchke said.

Cole bristled at the attention. "Practice is over," he called out. "Hit the showers. And don't stay up all night. I've got big plans for tomorrow."

The guys all groaned, and just like that, Cole threw a wet blanket on the entire mood. So much for that recommitment to being a better coach.

"And there goes the morale," Bilby said under his breath as he followed the guys inside.

Asher picked up the donut box and handed it back to Charlotte. "Mrs. Ford helped out at Haven House. Let me know if there's anything I can do to help you with this."

Charlotte's face brightened. "Thanks, Asher."

Asher gave her a nod, then turned to Cole. He hesitated a moment, then finally said, "Sorry about yesterday. If the offer's still there, I'll take the job."

Cole nodded. "It's there. You start tomorrow."

"I'm gonna do my best for you, Coach."

"That's all I can ask." It occurred to him he should be making Asher the same promise. Why was this so difficult?

"Think about the dance." Asher backed away (probably survival instinct). "You know the guys would go bananas."

Cole waved him off, but not before he caught a toothy grin and a wink in Charlotte's direction.

Once Asher was out of earshot, he turned to his pretty guest. "Don't tell me you put him up to this."

Her eyes widened. "Me? I had nothing to do with any of that. That was all them. I have fully accepted that you are unwilling to participate."

He met her eyes, and got lost for a moment. He was pretty sure she could convince him to do anything.

But not this. He wasn't going to make a fool of himself in front of the whole town—even for Jules. He knew enough about himself to know the "stand and sway" was about his limit when it came to dancing.

"Unless you're reconsidering?" Her tone teased.

"I don't dance," he said.

"It's not that hard," she said lightly.

He found her eyes. "I don't dance." His tone was clipped. Terse. Short.

Her jaw snapped shut, and she looked away. He could see the hurt on her face.

Jerk.

Why was it so hard for him to be kind?

Gemma.

Mom.

He shook the thoughts aside. "Sorry."

The apology sounded about as earnest as everything else he said, which was to say—not earnest at all.

22

The following morning, Cole was relieved they made it through practice without another surprise visit from Charlotte.

It might've been their best practice so far this summer. The guys were focused, and they had a clear leader in Asher. Still, when they finished and hit the locker rooms, Cole overheard something that surprised him—a conversation about their tribute dance. The guys actually seemed excited to go work with Charlotte later on that day.

How could he get them that excited about football again? He knew they all loved the game, but that's not how it seemed when they played. Sure, they were starting to do the work, but something was missing, and he had a feeling if he figured out what it was, it would transform his team.

That afternoon, he showed up at Haven House to finally help Steve with the fence, but when he arrived, Hildy met him outside, that worried look on her face.

He met her near the bottom of the porch stairs. "What's wrong?"

"It's Amelia," Hildy said.

Cole's stomach turned over. He'd barely seen Amelia when they were here Sunday. He'd planned to go in and check on her, but then the fight with Asher turned his mood sour. "What's wrong with her?"

"Is she always this quiet?" Hildy wrung her hands.

Cole shrugged. "How quiet?"

"Silent."

He sighed. "No. She's definitely not always that quiet."

"She's in the treehouse," Hildy said. "She's been up there for over an hour. She ran up there when I told her we were going to go to the dance studio for class later."

Cole frowned. "I'm not sure she'll listen to me."

"Well, it's worth a shot," Hildy said.

Cole ran a hand over his chin. He needed a shave. "I'll do my best." He made quick work of the yard and stopped at the big oak tree with the house built up into it. The house had been there as long as Cole could remember, and even though he'd been a teenager during his tenure at Haven House, he still found solace in that little space.

Somehow, he thought that was why Steve built it in the first place. Kids with trauma needed a safe place that felt like an escape, one where they wouldn't be surrounded by other people.

He climbed the ladder and poked his head up through the hole in the floor of the treehouse. There, sitting in the corner, arms wrapped around her knees, was Julianna's mini-me. Amelia's eyes widened when she recognized him.

"Hey, kiddo," he said.

No response.

He pulled himself up into the treehouse. It had been an easier move back in the day. He looked around. "This place hasn't changed much."

Amelia's brow furrowed.

"Did you know your mom and I lived here for a few

months a long time ago? Hildy and Steve took really good care of us."

She propped her chin up with her arms and studied him.

He situated himself next to her and let the silence turn comfortable between them. "Hildy said you don't want to dance."

Amelia shrugged. At least it was some indication she was listening. He'd take it.

Another few minutes of silence. He didn't want to push her. If she didn't feel like dancing or talking, maybe that was okay. However, it wasn't like the bubbly little girl he knew.

"I get it," he said. "They asked me to dance in this recital thing too."

Amelia's face brightened as she sat up straighter.

He met her eyes and slowly, her lips spread into a smile.

"Are you laughing at me?" he teased.

She covered her mouth with her hands and giggled. "I want to see you dance, Uncle Cole."

"You want to see me make a fool of myself, that's what you're saying." He gave her shoulder a little nudge with his own.

She nodded, still grinning. Probably the first time he'd seen her smile since she found out about her mom. Her smile quickly faded. "I always do a dance with Daddy."

"Yeah, I remember that," he said.

Her eyes turned glassy as she bit back tears.

"Have you asked him to do it this year?" he asked quietly.

She shook her head. "He won't."

Cole knew she was probably right. Connor wasn't in good shape, especially not to do something that would so clearly remind him of Julianna.

And that's when he got the dumbest idea he'd ever had

in his life. "What if you had a stand-in?" He could see out of the corner of his eye that he had her attention. He drew in a breath—he couldn't believe he was about to say what he was about to say. But at some point, his life had to stop being about him and his pain.

It had to be about helping the people he loved.

And if it would make Amelia smile, Cole would make a fool of himself a hundred times over.

"I'll do it if you do it." Cole faced her. Her eyes were lit up like a night sky on a cloudless night. And she almost looked happy.

Cole knew this was what his sister would've wanted. She talked about Amelia's love of dance all the time. If her death stole that love away from her daughter, it would devastate Jules. He couldn't let that happen.

"Really?"

He nodded. "Really."

She looked away, and he could see the moment she changed her mind. "I don't want to dance."

Cole leaned back against the wall of the treehouse. "Yeah, me neither."

Her eyes seemed to scold.

"You love to dance," Cole said, realizing it wasn't the time for jokes. "What's going on?"

She shrugged. He wouldn't make her say it. Dancing reminded her of Julianna. It was the thing they shared—a love, a passion for dance. Of course she didn't want to do it.

If Jules knew, that would break her heart too.

"You know, kiddo," Cole said. "I think watching you dance was one of your mom's favorite things to do."

She was back to hugging her knees.

"She talked about it a lot. I think it made her so happy because she knew it made you happy. And you worked so hard in class all year." Cole reached over and put an arm around her. She leaned in, resting her head on his chest. The seconds ticked by, and she broke the silence with her sniffles. He squeezed her, wishing he could take away this pain from such an innocent little girl.

"I'll tell you what," he said. "The deal is on the table. You can think it over, and I'll get to work, and then you'll let me know later if we're doing it or not."

Her head, under his chin, moved in affirmation.

"Yeah?"

She nodded again, then sat up and looked at him. "I'll try, Uncle Cole. But I don't want to go today."

"No problem," he said. "No pressure."

She hugged him, and his throat tightened. Why had God taken Julianna from them? Didn't He know how much they all still needed her here?

"I love you, kiddo," he said quietly.

She stifled a sob but squeezed him a little harder.

And that sealed the deal. He would make it his goal to get his niece back on the stage, even if that meant getting on the stage himself.

She was worth it.

23

Charlotte had been stewing since her impromptu visit to the football field a few days before.

One of these days she would learn it was a bad idea to show up anywhere Cole Turner was, donuts or no.

She looked at the *Harbor Pointe Gazette*, which she'd laid out on the counter in the kitchen, and ran a hand over the front page. A photo of Julianna stared back at her. Lucy had written an article about the dance recital, and specifically how Charlotte had come on board to celebrate the life of the studio's owner and beloved dance teacher.

Brinley was quoted, singing very high praises of the Chicago City Ballet veteran and "old friend of Mrs. Ford."

"Miss Page is one of the most elite ballerinas in the country, and for her to step foot on our stage at the Harbor Pointe Playhouse is the kind of rare cultural treat we should all make sure to see. I can promise you her performance will be one to remember."

Charlotte had never been a part of something like this. She'd never been a part of something that was so much about someone other than herself. And sure, she wanted to make a good impression on the town because she was hoping to run the dance studio, but that's really not what the recital was about.

It was about Julianna and these young dancers. It was about being rooted in something other than her own praise. It was about finding a place to belong.

Somewhere in the back of her mind, she heard a silent prayer—a plea, really—*Are you proud of me yet?* The thought surprised her. She wasn't intentionally trying to make anyone proud.

And yet, she wanted to be better. She'd been striving to earn her place for as long as she could remember. Was she worthy yet?

Her eyes fell to the image of Julianna. Happiness radiated from her friend's eyes. Julianna had figured something out, a secret of sorts, one that Charlotte wanted to uncover for herself.

Was it this town or the dance studio or her little family? Or was it simply that Jules had decided to live an unselfish life? Charlotte knew nothing about that. And frankly, she had no reason not to be satisfied. But there was this low thrumming down deep in her soul, echoing in a rhythm. *You were made for more than this.*

But without the applause, the approval, who was Charlotte Page?

How did she find out?

And how did she prove herself if performing wasn't in the equation? Without that, what else was she? Charlotte was a performer, even when she wasn't on the stage. It exhausted her to think of all the ways she was putting on a show.

She just wanted to be accepted as *Charlotte*. But she had no idea what that looked like or who that was. And if she couldn't accept herself without striving for an ideal, how could she expect anyone else to?

Day had faded to night, and the house had grown dark without her realizing it. Lucy was covering a city council meeting and had told Charlotte she'd be home late.

"Don't wait up for me," she'd joked on her way out the door. "These meetings get wild. Sometimes they go all night."

Charlotte had grown to love the familiar banter between her and Lucy. Her roommate had become a friend, and she was in desperate need of one of those. Never mind that she held back—a lot. Lucy didn't know her innermost thoughts. Nobody besides Jules ever had.

She walked into the kitchen and turned a circle. This was the first night since she arrived in Harbor Pointe that she'd been on her own for dinner.

She pulled chicken and broccoli out of the refrigerator and closed the door, then a noise outside caught her attention. The front of the house was still dark, so to passersby, it likely looked like no one was home. Except her rented, beat-up Jetta was parked in the driveway.

She crept toward the front room, feeling like a character in a horror movie and telling herself this was a bad idea.

The sound of footsteps outside stopped her breath for a split second.

Was Lucy expecting someone?

Charlotte's heart raced. What if it was Marcia? Her texts had grown angrier the longer Charlotte ignored her. Finally, Charlotte had texted twice to let her know she was fine, just taking some much-needed rest.

Marcia's response?

> *This is not the time to rest. You are destroying everything we've built.*

We. As if Marcia could claim Charlotte's success.

And maybe she could. Maybe Marcia's endless pushing was the reason Charlotte had achieved success.

But why was she thinking about Marcia when there was a would-be prowler outside? It's not like her mother was savvy enough to track Charlotte down, and she'd left no indication of where she'd gone.

Slowly, Charlotte moved back the sheer curtain in the living room, just enough for a view of the dimly lit front porch.

Sure enough, there was someone out there, but it wasn't her mother—it was a man. For a fleeting moment, she wondered why she was relieved by that.

Shouldn't a strange man be more frightening than her own mother? Was it strange she wasn't positive about the answer to that question?

The man didn't seem to be making any attempt to break in to Lucy's cottage, but who was he and what was he doing just standing out there?

Maybe Lucy had a boyfriend she hadn't told Charlotte about?

She squinted, hoping for a better view, but his back was to her. He stood, like a statue, for several seconds, then turned, as if he was going to leave. At the top of the steps, he stopped and stared out into the dark night.

He raked his hand through his hair, angling slightly toward her, enough for her to see that this wasn't a burglar.

It was Cole.

Perhaps a burglar would've been preferable.

Why was Cole Turner on the front porch? Had he come to apologize for general moodiness and jerkery? She decided she wouldn't accept his apology unless it came with flowers or donuts.

And she didn't even eat donuts.

Fearing he might see her, she dropped the curtain and

tiptoed toward the front door, peeking out through the window on the other side. Nobody stood on a porch that didn't belong to them for this long. What was he doing out there?

Her head spun with possibilities, as he turned in a circle, drew in a breath, and seemed to let out a heavy sigh.

Cole faced the door now, standing inches away like he might finally knock or ring the bell. He lifted his fist, then quickly dropped it and darted off the porch.

Charlotte sprung toward the entry and pulled the door open, just as he reached the bottom of the stairs. At the sound of the door, Cole stopped and turned around, and as he faced her, embarrassment washed across his face.

She stood behind the screen door, wondering what the expression on her face looked like to him.

For several seconds, he didn't move. He looked caught, like a child who'd been out throwing toilet paper into the neighbor's trees only to have the lights flipped on.

"Oh," he said. "You're home."

Her eyes shifted over to her rental car in the driveway and then back to him. He stuffed his hands in his pockets and kicked at something on the ground.

"What are you doing here?" Her tone reminded her of the one he liked to use. She didn't care to be polite, not after the way he'd spoken to her at the football field the other day. She watched as he looked down the street toward where a car had just pulled into a neighboring driveway.

It was almost nine o'clock, and while it was summer and Harbor Pointe was still very much awake, it did seem kind of late for an unannounced visit.

"Can I come in for a minute?" He looked almost pained to ask.

"Is something wrong?"

Cole met her eyes. "It'll only take a minute."

She held his gaze for *one-one-thousand, two-one-thousand*, then had to look away. The space between them sizzled in those two seconds, and it scared her. And he wanted to come in? Into a small space where it would just be the two of them?

How was she supposed to manage close proximity with Cole Turner without 1. Becoming the color of a summer-ripe tomato or 2. Fumbling all over herself in an effort to not look foolish, which she was bound to do?

Apparently, when it came to men, she had an awkward side. At least when it came to Cole. Her partner, Jameson, had been fine—but he was married. No chance of romantic feelings clouding her vision.

"Charlotte?"

She looked at him. Her vision was cloudy.

She'd been staring at him for far longer than was socially acceptable. She pushed the screen door open and moved out of the way so his much-larger-than-hers body could pass through, and as he did she stupidly inhaled the scent of him. She wasn't sure what she'd expected him to smell like. Maybe the inside of his truck? The turf on the football field? Dirt from working in the yard of that adorable cottage he lived in on the other side of town?

But he didn't smell like any of those things. And he didn't smell like any of the men who'd been her dance partners over the years. He smelled distinctly masculine, but subtly so. Like he'd washed his body that morning and then not given his scent an ounce of thought for the rest of the day. Unfussy. Delicious.

She closed the door and turned to face him. The entryway suddenly shrunk in size, like a room in Willy Wonka's chocolate factory.

He looked around. "It's dark."

"Oh." She moved into the living room and flipped the light on. "I was just starting dinner, so I was in the kitchen."

He shifted uncomfortably. "I didn't mean to interrupt your dinner."

"It's fine."

It's not like I had actual plans.

"Isn't it kind of late to be eating?"

"Yes."

He raised an eyebrow, as if he expected more of an explanation, but she didn't want to explain her eating habits to him. She didn't really want to explain anything to him. She wanted to hold a grudge against him, but that was considerably more difficult when he was looking at her *like that*.

"Actually, now that I think about it, I haven't eaten yet either." He looked away.

What now? Was she supposed to offer him some of the plain chicken and broccoli she was about to eat?

"I would offer to feed you, but I'm a terrible cook," she said.

He frowned. "I wouldn't have guessed that."

She angled her gaze in his direction. "Why?"

He lifted one shoulder in a half-hearted shrug, as if he'd made the comment without thinking.

"Are you here for a reason or . . . ?" Her nerves were distracting her as she mentally tried to sort out what it was that was causing them. Him or the anticipation of what he might say? Had the boys on the team changed their minds? What else could they possibly have to discuss?

"Kind of," he said. "Want me to make you dinner?"

Her eyes shot to his. "What?"

"You said you're not a good cook."

"I'm not."

Another shrug. "I am."

"Really?"

"Surprised?"

"I wouldn't have guessed that."

"Why not?" He almost smiled. *Almost.*

And it almost made her lose her breath. Now, she shrugged. Was he actually being nice to her?

"The kitchen's back here, right?" He turned.

She followed him into the mostly white room and stopped at the counter where she'd started preparing the plain dinner.

"What were you going to make?"

This was weird. Having him here, asking her questions, being nice to her—it was weird. Plus, she really didn't want to tell him what she was going to make. She glanced at the counter. "Chicken and broccoli."

"I see that," he said. "Were you going to stir-fry it?"

"I was going to toss it in oil, put it on a pan, and stick it in the oven." The same way she'd done a million times before.

He opened the refrigerator. "Think Lucy will mind if we use some of her food?"

"I bought most of that," Charlotte said.

"So I can use it?"

She shrugged. "I guess. But really, you don't have to do this."

"I don't mind," he said. "You brought breakfast the other day."

"Donuts are not breakfast." She sat on the stool on the opposite side of the island from where he had now set out the fresh asparagus and sugar snap peas she'd just bought earlier that day at the farmers' market. "Besides, you didn't seem all that impressed with that offering."

Without him moving his head, his eyes darted to hers. He stopped messing with the food. "I'm sorry about that."

She held her hands up. She hadn't meant to say it. She definitely didn't want to talk about it—especially not with him. "It's fine."

"It's not." He flicked on the faucet and ran water over the vegetables, then set them on a cutting board back on the island and started chopping. "I'm not great with people."

"That's surprising." She didn't hide the fake sarcasm in her tone.

This time, he actually laughed. It was short-lived and probably more like a chuckle, but it was a sign of amusement. And that was a win.

"Before you finish this meal, you should know I have a lot of dietary restrictions."

He found a mallet and started pounding the chicken breasts she'd taken out of the fridge. "Like what?"

"No dairy. No bread. No sugar."

"That's a lot of no's."

"I basically eat meat, fruit, and vegetables. Nuts, seeds."

"What do you do for dessert?" He'd stopped with the mallet now and stared at her. She found his eyes on her to be unsettling.

"Apples. Grapes. Strawberries."

"Sounds decadent."

She shifted. This wasn't a good topic for her. Her head spun back in time to the day Marcia caught her with a canister of peanut butter and a whole package of chocolate pudding Snack Packs. Her mom had been livid, launching into a heated diatribe about the perils of junk food and why ballerinas weren't ever allowed to eat it, and then she took Charlotte to the gym and made her run on the treadmill for an hour straight.

She hadn't had sugar since.

"It's always been my job to stay in shape." She didn't know what else to say—this was why she was considered an "elite" athlete. She didn't do things that made sense to other people. He probably thought she was a freak.

"Like Tom Brady," he said.

She frowned.

"I mean, he has a really strict regimen and look at him." Cole cut through four asparagus spears. "I can respect that."

"Are you comparing me to Tom Brady?"

He glanced at her, smirked, then looked away, moving around the kitchen like he knew what he was doing. She sat at the island, watching, finding this dance he did in front of her surprisingly relaxing. And hot. She couldn't deny it. Watching a solid, athletic, masculine man like Cole cook a dinner that was clearly designed for her—well, it did something to her on the inside.

She told herself to knock it off. Told herself Cole was not her type. Told herself she didn't even *like* the man.

So why did she find it impossible to stop looking at him?

Unlike most people, Cole seemed to only speak when he had a reason to. He didn't fill the space with chatter, and he seemed perfectly comfortable with the same silence that had her insides twisting in a knot.

She resisted the urge to ask him why he'd come in the first place, assuming at some point he'd tell her.

"Where are the plates?" he asked, pulling her from her unwanted thoughts.

She started to stand, but he quickly interrupted.

"Just point me in the right direction," he said kindly. "I'll get them."

She sat back down and pointed in the direction of a cabinet to the left of the sink. Who was this man? He was wholly different than the Cole she'd grown to expect.

He pulled out two plates, and that's when she realized they were about to have a meal together. Of course they were about to have a meal together—what did she think—he was making the food just for her?

He'd said he hadn't eaten. He was making dinner *for two*.

The thought of sitting across from him while they ate in awkward silence turned her palms cold and sweaty.

He plated the food, set the pans down, and took a step back.

"What's it called?" she asked.

"Chicken Scaloppine with sugar snap peas, asparagus, and lemon salad."

She frowned.

"What's wrong?"

"It just doesn't seem like something you'd eat," she said.

"Well, I made it for you." His face turned serious.

His words had an unexpected effect on her heart—one she wasn't prepared for. He had made it for her, she'd known this. But learning that he tailored what he made to what he thought she would like stirred something in her bones.

And that might've been the moment she knew that spending time with Cole Turner was dangerous. For her heart. If this kept up, the cranky football coach was likely to win her over.

Why did that make her nervous? Now that she had the time and was trying to change her life, should she at least consider romance?

What a ridiculous thought. Cole Turner was about as romantic as a lint roller. She had nothing in common with this man. And there was nothing appealing about him, aside from the way he looked. And the way he smelled. And, okay, the way he'd played football with those kids at Haven House. And the way he'd agreed to help Steve fix the fence. And his obvious concern for Asher and his nieces and nephew.

Darn it. There were a lot of appealing things about him. But—she was quick to remind herself—he was not kind or polite. She'd be smart to remember all the ways he'd made her feel stupid or small.

A broad chest and piercing eyes didn't change that.

"Thanks," she said. He picked up the plates and walked toward the table.

Charlotte grabbed silverware and napkins and took them to the table, where he was now sitting in a chair across from the one she was supposed to sit in.

Charlotte had never been on a proper date. Or any kind of date, come to think of it. She was the epitome of inexperienced.

But she did watch a lot of movies, and this whole setup felt a lot like a date. The very thought of it unnerved her.

"You okay?" he asked.

She sat. "Confused, I think."

"Why?"

She unfolded the napkin and laid it on her lap.

"I can't figure you out," she said. "To be honest, I thought I annoyed you."

He picked up the salt and generously shook it onto his food before even tasting it. "You don't."

She watched as he cut into his chicken and took a bite, finally meeting her eyes. When she realized he wasn't going to elaborate, she turned her attention to the plate he'd created for her. It not only smelled good, it looked beautiful. Maybe Cole had missed his calling as a chef.

"It almost looks too good to eat," she said.

He brought his eyes to hers.

"Thanks, but it's made to be eaten." He took another bite.

"Did you see the newspaper?" she asked.

He nodded. A man of very few words. Charlotte wasn't

sure she could hold up both ends of this conversation, but Cole seemed to be the king of one-word (or no word) answers.

"The first rehearsal is tomorrow," she said, working overtime to try and fill the gaps of silence left by her dinner companion. "For the tribute dances I'm choreographing, I mean. The students have been learning their recital pieces for a while now."

He nodded as he chewed.

"I didn't ask your team to be there because that's a big group, and I've already met with them once. You'll be shocked—some of them are actually decent dancers."

"Did you have any trouble with them?" he asked, his gaze fixed on her.

She shook her head. "No, they were very well behaved."

He nodded. "Good."

She glanced down at her plate.

"Is it okay?"

She'd hardly eaten for all the talking she'd been doing. His plate, on the other hand, was almost clean.

"It's really good." She took a bite, still surprised by how good it was. She'd been making chicken for years and it had never tasted like this. "Where'd you learn to cook like this?"

He set down his fork, picked up his napkin, and wiped his mouth. "Cooking class."

She nearly choked on her water. "You took a cooking class?"

"As a favor to—" He looked away. "I had my arm twisted."

She swallowed and took a drink of water. "Girlfriend? Bad break-up?"

"Wife. And yes."

Wife? He was married?

Something in the way he said it told her that topic was not up for discussion, much like almost every other topic she could imagine, since Cole Turner wasn't one to discuss anything.

Was this what everyone was always hinting about whenever his name came up? All the hushed, gossipy comments about "all he'd been through"—was that about some mysterious wife whose heart he'd broken? Or who had broken his heart?

Would she ever know?

"You?"

She glanced up. "Me what?"

"Ever married?"

Was that a thing people asked—like "have you ever had sushi?" When she got married, she was getting married for life.

"Um, no."

"Probably smart." He put his silverware and napkin on his plate.

"It's not a choice," she said. "Or at least not a conscious one." She took a bite. "I've never even had a boyfriend."

He stopped moving and stared at her. "Never?"

It wasn't a conscious choice to tell him that either. Her mouth seemed to have a mind of its own.

"Never." She shrugged, smiled, played it off like it was perfectly normal in her line of work even though she knew it absolutely was not.

She was the weirdo who'd never dated anyone. The head-down, get-it-done ballerina with something to prove, though she'd never quite figured out who she was proving it to. Her mother? Herself? There was a part of her that cried out, *Am I good enough yet?* but who was she hoping would answer that question?

"Was *that* a choice?"

She covered her plate with her napkin. "It was a choice to dance."

He eyed her like he was trying to make heads or tails of her, like he didn't know what to make of what she was saying. It made her feel even more like a weirdo. "So, this dance thing—it was a big deal."

"It was everything," she said.

"Yeah, it seems like you'd have to give up a lot to get to where you are." He took a drink of water.

She frowned. How did he know where she was? Before she could ask, he set his drink down and met her eyes.

"So, have you ever been on a date?" He watched her curiously, as if she were an animal behind glass at the zoo.

"I dated dance," she said with another shrug. "That was all I had time for."

And it's why I left. I'm looking to go out and get a life and friends and maybe even a boyfriend and I'm wondering a lot about you, Cole Turner. Would you make a good first boyfriend? And what would it be like to kiss you?

The thoughts sent heat to her cheeks.

She suddenly felt vulnerable, like she'd said too much. She wasn't hiding it, the fact that there was a whole long list of things she'd never done—but she didn't want to go around publicizing it either.

And she especially didn't want to talk about it with Cole. As if she needed another reason to feel foolish in his presence.

And as soon as he realized that never having dated meant a lot of other things she'd never done, she was going to feel even more ridiculous than she did right now.

She stood abruptly, piled her silverware onto her plate and her plate onto his, then walked into the kitchen. "That was really good," she called over her shoulder. "Like, one of the best meals I've had in a really long time."

She turned and found he'd followed her and now she was hollering for nothing.

"Sorry," she said.

He stood in the doorway, backlit by the light from the dining area. He was deliciously handsome. How she could think that of someone she truly disliked was one of life's great injustices. She shouldn't find him appealing for the sole reason that he wasn't a nice person.

In her mind, she saw him pick up Asher's little brother and prop him up on his shoulder for a victory lap after his remarkable touchdown.

Fine, maybe he was nice. But he wasn't nice to her.

She looked down at the plates. Making her dinner had been pretty nice. The thought kicked her nerves up like dust from a shaken blanket.

"I should probably get cleaned up and get to bed. I have an early run," she said.

"Let me help." He brushed past her as he walked toward the stove. "I made the mess."

"I think the rule is that if you cook, you don't have to clean." She opened the dishwasher and began rinsing off the plates. His nearness sent her insides swirling, like she was riding circles on a merry-go-round.

He handed her the pan he'd used to cook and looked at her like he had something to say.

I like you, Charlotte.

Maybe I could be your first date, Charlotte?

I really want to kiss you, Charlotte.

The possibilities raced through her mind, betraying her sense of logic. This was so silly. This man who liked nobody did not like her. And she did not like him.

You do not like him, Charlotte.

Her mind spun with questions.

If he didn't like her, then why had he shown up on her

doorstep? Why had he acted so nervous outside? Why had he made her dinner and why was he standing only inches away from her now?

"Charlotte?"

She looked up and found his dark eyes fixed on her. "Yes?" She wasn't sure if she'd said the word aloud or simply thought it.

"I need to ask you something," he said.

And her stomach flip-flopped the way she imagined teenage girls' stomachs did when the boy they liked asked them to the prom.

Whatever it was, she would say yes. She'd regret it later, but she'd say yes. Because there was no way in this room, looking at those eyes, she could ever deny this man anything he asked.

And knowing that made her equal parts excited and terrified.

Because changing the way she thought about this high school football coach seemed like a very, very bad idea.

24

What was he doing? He should've come in, asked Charlotte the question, and left. Instead, he made her dinner (dinner, for Pete's sake, who was he, Gordon Ramsay?) and was now standing in Lucy's kitchen trying to work up the nerve to ask Charlotte this ridiculous favor.

And she kept looking at him, which was messing with his cool demeanor.

He wasn't sure which part of this whole thing made him feel the stupidest—the idea itself or the fact that he needed Charlotte's help in the first place.

He didn't want to need help from anyone, but especially not Charlotte. Which he realized was a very old-fashioned and ridiculous thought. Women helped men all the time. He didn't have to be the one saving her.

Never mind that he wanted to be.

At dinner, she'd opened up a little about herself, about this solitary life she'd had—it made him want to introduce her to the world. She'd missed out on so much. Never mind that her life had been a wholly different kind of adventure. There were little things she'd never experienced.

And his lingering question about her love life had been answered. She'd never even been on a date. It seemed impossible, but he could see by the look on her face that it was true. That look seemed to want to own the truth and hide it at the same time.

Like maybe it embarrassed her to admit it.

"What did you want to ask?" She stood in front of him now, wearing black shorts and a tank top and looking slightly tanner than she had the last time he'd seen her. Her big, blue eyes were wide, and he realized he was dreading every single thing about this question.

But it's why he'd come here in the first place. He couldn't leave without asking.

"The dance thing—"

Her brow furrowed. "The recital . . . ?"

"Yeah." He chewed the inside of his lip. "I think I should do it."

"Like, perform?"

The look on her face confirmed his greatest fear—he was about to make a huge fool of himself, which was the last thing he needed, given the fact that his wife had managed to do a bang-up job of that.

"What changed your mind?"

He leaned against the counter and crossed his arms over his chest. "My niece."

She went still. "Amelia?"

He nodded. "What did Jules tell you about her?"

Charlotte closed the dishwasher and gave him her full attention. A soft smile played at her lips. "She told me that Amelia was like a younger version of her. They both had the same spunky personality. They both loved to dance."

"Right," he said. "And Jules loved watching her dance. I think Amelia's pretty good for her age."

"She is," Charlotte said. "Jules and I mostly wrote letters to each other, but every once in a while, she'd send me a video. Twice, she sent videos of Amelia dancing. It really was like watching a young Julianna."

Grief tugged at his heart. He hated that his sister was gone. He hated that her kids were going to grow up without her. It was unbelievable, really, even still. Most days, he expected her to show up at his door and force him to come over for dinner. He would never get used to the vacancy she'd left when she died.

"She's not dancing anymore," Cole said. "She's hardly even talking. It's like someone went in and yanked out everything that made her Amelia. Everything she loved is just gone."

Charlotte crossed her toned arms over her chest and leveled his gaze. Man, she was pretty. "You're worried about her."

He nodded. "Julianna was a great mom. I know there's no replacing her, but if I can do anything to help, I'm going to do it."

She squinted up at him. He wanted to hide under her scrutiny. "And dancing in the recital will do that?"

He groaned. "I made her a deal. If she dances, I'll dance."

Charlotte smiled. For a second, time stopped. That smile could stop traffic.

"You're making fun of me," he said.

She shook her head. "I promise I'm not."

"Then why the smile?"

"Because I just figured something out about you," she said, still smiling.

"Is that right?"

Her expression teased. "Yep. I figured out that you're nothing but a big softy."

He couldn't help it—he smiled too—and he felt a slight chink in the suit of armor he wore to keep him safe. "I'm really not."

"But you are," she said. "Why do you pretend to be so uncaring all the time?"

He didn't want to talk about all the reasons why. "Will you help me or not?"

Her smile skittered away, and just like that, he'd done it again. Ruined the moment.

Idiot.

She picked up a towel and wiped the counter. "Would you be standing in for her dad? I heard they usually dance at every recital."

"Yeah," he said. "I'm hoping I can talk him into it, but I'm not holding my breath."

"You saw how far I got when I asked him," she said.

He shrugged softly in reply.

"So, you need me to choreograph something for you and Amelia?"

"And keep me from making a complete fool of myself," he said.

She avoided his eyes. "That's why you came here tonight—to ask me to help you with this dance."

"Yeah," he said, as if it were obvious. "It just took me a little while because this is kind of embarrassing."

"Right." She looked away.

"Did I say something wrong?"

"No, of course not." She looked around at the dishes still littering the counter. "I figured it was something like that." She half-laughed. "I mean, why else would you come here and make dinner and spend time with me and help clean up the kitchen?" She ran a hand over her hair, which was neatly gathered at the back of her head in a high ponytail.

Why did he feel like he'd said the wrong thing?

She turned around and opened the refrigerator, pulled out a bottle of water, and took a drink—a long one.

"Are you okay?"

"Mm-hmm," she said.

"Look, I don't know anything about dancing, but I do know I have less of a chance of looking like a complete disaster if you help me."

"I don't know, Cole." She closed the refrigerator and walked into the living room.

"I'll work really hard, and I'll do whatever you tell me."

One of her eyebrows quirked. "Whatever I tell you?"

He nodded.

She ran her hands over her face. "This is a terrible idea."

"Why?"

"Because you're—" She shoved both hands toward him, moving them up, then down, as if to fill in the end of her sentence.

"I'm not completely uncoordinated," he said. "I used to have some serious moves on the football field."

"Well, you're . . ." Her voice trailed off, as if she'd thought better of whatever it was she was going to say.

"I'm what?"

Her shoulders stiffened, and she glared at him. "Not very nice."

That was fair. He hadn't been very nice to her. To anyone. There really was no excuse for that, though, was there? "I'm working on it."

She stared at him for too many seconds, leaving his mind to fill in the blanks as to what she was thinking.

"Never mind," he said. "It was probably a stupid idea. I'll

get out of your hair now." He made it all the way to the entryway before she called out for him to stop.

He wouldn't have—his humiliation level was sky-high by this point. But the truth was, he needed her. He owed it to Amelia. And he owed it to Jules. No matter how much he didn't want to do it. And he very much did not want to do it.

Cole wasn't a *life of the party* kind of guy. He didn't laugh easily, especially not at himself. And after what he'd been through with his parents and then Gemma, having the undivided attention of anyone in this town was just about the last thing he wanted.

"If I do this—" She stood in front of him now, looking up at him with a look so stern he had to tell himself not to laugh at her. "You will, in fact, do exactly what I tell you to do."

"Okay."

"You won't groan. You won't be late. You won't give me any guff."

"Guff?"

"Guff."

"People don't say 'guff.'"

"Well, I do." She stuck her hands on her hips. "If I do this, it's on my terms."

"You got it, boss."

"There's a meeting for everyone who'll be learning partner dances. It's tomorrow. We're going over some of the basics, assigning each couple a choreographer, that sort of thing. You'll come."

"Uh, sure," he said, though it wasn't a question. "Should I bring Amelia?"

"No," Charlotte said. "We'll fill her in later." She stuck her hand out in his direction and he allowed himself a slight, hopefully undetectable, smile as he took it and squeezed.

Charlotte barely allowed him a three-second handshake before she pulled her hand away.

"You should go," she said, opening the front door.

"Thanks for dinner."

"Thanks for doing this for me, Charlotte," he said.

"I'm not doing it for you," she said. "I'm doing it for Amelia. And for Julianna."

Point taken.

He watched her for a long moment before stepping out onto the porch. He turned back to thank her just as she closed the door in his face.

And he wondered if this was Charlotte giving him a taste of his own sour medicine.

25

About an hour before the first rehearsal for the would-be dancers, Charlotte arrived at Julianna's studio.

Walking in, she felt simultaneously close to Julianna and worlds away from her. Twice, she'd started letters to her old friend, just as a way to process all these changes in her life. No dance. No Marcia. No training. No pressure.

No Jules.

It required a lot of processing.

Brinley rounded the corner as Charlotte walked in. Her wide eyes seemed to plead for Charlotte's help.

"What's wrong?"

"Connor was supposed to be here an hour ago to pick up Amelia," Brinley whispered. "Hildy dropped her off, but she said he was picking her up."

She frowned. "Did she have a class?"

"She was supposed to," Brinley said. "But she's been sitting in the back studio refusing to do anything."

Charlotte's heart sank. She thought about the line of

worry etched in Cole's forehead the night before when he told her about his deal with Amelia. "Let me try?"

Brinley took a step back. "Be my guest."

Charlotte walked down the hallway and into the studio at the back of the building. There, on the floor, leaning against the wall, sat Amelia. And now, those same big eyes that had watched her from the second-story window on her first visit to see Connor were trained on her again.

Charlotte set her bag down on the floor and smiled at Amelia.

Amelia didn't smile back.

"Hi, Amelia." Charlotte approached her cautiously. It seemed like one wrong move could send the girl running for the door. "Brinley said you came here today to dance."

Still no response.

"It's funny, I'm here to dance too." Charlotte sat on the floor, took off her shoes, and pulled her pointe shoes from the bag.

Amelia's eyes widened so subtly Charlotte almost missed it. But she remembered the appeal of pointe shoes when she was Amelia's age. She wanted to learn to dance on pointe more than anything, mostly because Marcia said she wasn't ready and she knew she was.

Amelia likely had another year or two before she was old enough, but maybe watching Charlotte would help her remember how much she loved to dance.

Charlotte walked over to the Bluetooth speaker in the corner, pulled out her phone and connected it. "I'm a little rusty, but I need the workout." She found a classical piece that would be perfect for warming up, and she turned it on.

Amelia hugged her knees to her chest, as if to cement her position right there on the floor.

Charlotte decided not to push her. How many times did she wish she could ease in on her own terms? How many times had Marcia forced her? Charlotte didn't want to be that kind of teacher. She wanted to be the kind of teacher she imagined Jules was. Kind. Encouraging. Fun.

Did she even know where to begin?

She moved to the barre, faced the wall, and began treading up and over her shoes, warming up her ankles. She tossed a quick glance at Amelia, who still wore a vacant expression, but who, she noticed, was watching Charlotte's feet intently.

Charlotte continued to move through a warm-up she could do without thinking. She moved from plié, pushed up over the shoes, then straightened and came down.

She continued, then the song ended and the familiar music from *Romeo and Juliet* began to play.

Amelia sat up a little straighter.

"Do you know the story of Romeo and Juliet?" Charlotte asked.

Amelia hesitated, then nodded slowly.

"Did you know it was a ballet?"

The little girl shook her head.

Charlotte smiled. "Would you like to see a bit of it?"

Amelia nodded again.

Charlotte went to her phone, changed the music, and took her place on the floor. How many times had she danced this *pas de deux*?

But this time, it was different. This time, she had no partner. This time, she wasn't dancing for an audience of strangers. She was dancing for a little girl who'd lost her love of dance.

A little girl not wholly unlike herself.

She began to move through the familiar dance, as if her body had been made to perform the steps. It was a role she'd danced only a few months before—Juliet. She'd been born for that role, they'd said. The critics were blown away by her performance.

And every night, after the curtain closed, Charlotte realized she felt nothing. Technically, she nailed it every single time, but didn't any of them realize the emotion was all manufactured? Charlotte herself felt nothing. She had no connection to the movements or the role she was playing.

Was she even capable of connecting?

She wanted to find out, if only for herself. She zeroed in on how each move challenged her muscles. She paid attention to the way the music cued her how to feel, what emotion to portray. She knew the story, but now she wanted to feel the story. Not for an audience. Not for Marcia or her director.

She wanted to dance for Amelia. For Julianna. For herself. She wanted to let herself feel something, to use this gift she'd been given to help a little girl with a broken heart.

And as she danced, the memories of Julianna spilled out in front of her. Her laugh. Her smile. Her absolute love of dance, of life. All of it rolled out in front of her as she leapt, then landed perfectly, muscles tense and ready for whatever was next.

She danced the solo, which she'd performed over and over, night after night, a solo she could've done in her sleep —but she wasn't sleeping. She was wide awake and able to feel everything for the first time in ages.

Even her sorrow. Even the hollow space inside of her that had been carved away the day Julianna died. Emotions she preferred to ignore bubbled up from somewhere down deep, and she channeled them into her dance.

Another leap. Another turn. Another perfect landing.

Until finally, the music ended, leaving Charlotte breathless on the floor.

She glanced up and saw a small crowd had gathered in

the hallway, watching through windows meant for parents of tiny ballerinas. Some of them held their phones up, recording this impromptu performance that wasn't really meant for them at all.

Charlotte turned and found Amelia staring at her, tears streaming down her face. She moved over to the little girl and knelt down in front of her.

"Do you want to dance with me?" Charlotte asked.

Amelia stared up into her eyes, raw emotion painted on her face, and Charlotte's heart nearly broke at the sight of her.

"You know, your mom loved to watch you dance," Charlotte said. "She used to tell me about it all the time. She even sent me a couple of videos. She thought you were the most beautiful thing in the world when you danced—because you love it so much."

Amelia's bottom lip quivered.

"Sometimes I think it's the best way to feel close to her because she loved it so much too."

The little girl buried her head in her knees and her shoulders shook with soft sobs. Charlotte fought against the lump at the back of her throat, trying to stay strong for Amelia—for Jules. She reached over and took the girl's hand, squeezing gently.

"It might hurt a little," Charlotte said. "Dancing without her here. But I know for a fact she wouldn't want you to quit doing something that made you both so happy."

Amelia looked up, her cheeks wet, her eyes red.

"We'll start with something small. Warm-ups maybe. What do you think?"

Amelia nodded.

"Yeah?"

The nodding continued as Charlotte pulled the little girl to her feet.

"Miss Charlotte?" Amelia looked up at her now. "Do you love it too? Like my mom did?"

She smoothed Amelia's hair and smiled. "I'm trying to. Maybe you can help."

"Me?"

"Sure." Charlotte picked up her phone to change the music. "Maybe if you remember why you loved dance so much, you can help me remember too."

Amelia's face brightened ever so slightly. "Okay."

What followed was an impromptu dance class, in which Charlotte took Julianna's daughter through familiar warm-ups at the barre and then across the floor. As she watched Amelia slowly warm up to her and to ballet, she began to understand what it was that Julianna loved so much about watching the girl dance.

She shared Julianna's passion—Charlotte could see it in her eyes. She envied her that.

She watched Amelia take her corrections, then improve, a strong resolve lighting up her eyes. And seeing it stirred something inside Charlotte that had been dead a long time. Or maybe it had never been alive.

She didn't get much of a chance to explore the thought, though, because Brinley knocked on the door and poked her head in.

"Hey, girl, your dad's here," she said.

Amelia's shoulders slumped. "Do I have to go?"

"We can meet back here anytime," Charlotte said. "And I hear I'm choreographing a dance for you and your Uncle Cole?"

The girl smiled.

"Sneaky getting him to do this," Charlotte said. "I asked him twice, and he turned me down both times."

"Really?" Amelia's eyes widened.

"Really," Charlotte said.

Her face lit with a full smile. "Thank you, Miss Charlotte." She rushed over and threw her arms around Charlotte, who found herself unable to resist the urge to hug her back.

Amelia swiped her ballet bag off the hooks and raced out the door, leaving Brinley standing slack-jawed. "What did you do? Do you know how many times I've tried to get her to dance?"

Charlotte smiled. "She's talented."

"Don't downplay this, Charlotte," Brinley said, moving in front of her so she couldn't look away. "That's a big deal what you did for Amelia."

Charlotte shrugged. "I wish I could do more. I owe it to Jules."

Brinley took Charlotte by the arms and squeezed. "Is this why you're so successful? Because you're never satisfied?"

Charlotte laughed. "Don't we have a rehearsal to get ready for?"

Brinley grinned. "Yep. And don't be surprised if that video of you goes viral."

26

*D*ance rehearsal. Not a place Cole ever thought he'd go. At least not for anything other than to pick up his niece after class.

Well, that wasn't completely true. Gemma had insisted they take dance lessons before their wedding. They'd gone to a ballroom dance studio two towns over, and that's when Cole learned what he already knew—he was not a dancer.

She'd suggested asking Julianna to help, but that would've been even more horrifying. At least this way, he'd be embarrassing himself in front of someone he didn't know.

Cole had tried to get out of it, and had successfully postponed it twice, but Gemma wasn't having it anymore. Why couldn't they just stand and sway like most couples? Because he was marrying Gemma, that's why.

"Our wedding has to be perfect, Cole," she'd said. "And I really want to make our first dance one to remember."

What she wanted was the kind of first dance that was shared on social media. Cole couldn't have wanted that less.

But he loved her, and he wanted to make her happy, so he went along with it.

The drive to their first lesson gave Gemma the chance to grill him about the wedding.

"Did you get fitted for your tux yet?"

Cole took her hand. "Relax, it's all under control."

"Relax?" She pulled her hand away. "Cole, do you know how much work it is to put a wedding together this fast?"

Not really. Gemma wouldn't let him help with any part of it. So far, she'd picked out the cake, the flowers, the colors—she'd even vetoed two of the groomsmen he wanted because they weren't "tall enough to match my bridesmaids."

The way Cole saw it, though, was that he didn't care about the wedding as much as she did. He cared about their marriage, but the actual wedding? His take was—*whatever makes her happy.*

Didn't he owe it to her? Everything he did was for her, and he planned for it to be that way until the day he died.

Funny how some plans just don't work out.

The dance instructor was a man, which made the whole thing even more awkward and uncomfortable.

The lesson got off to a rocky start. Gemma had chosen Adele's version of "Make You Feel My Love" for their first dance. Cole asked her why she chose it and not "I Won't Give Up" by Jason Mraz, which was the song she'd claimed as "theirs." Gemma shrugged it off with a flippant, "This one is easier to dance to."

Apparently, she was less about sentiment and more about the way it all looked.

Cole listened to the teacher's instructions and tried to follow along, but he wasn't a natural, and by the end of the night, Gemma was dancing circles with the instructor while Cole sat in one of the chairs against the wall.

The whole experience had been a disaster, which was why Cole had no desire to attend a dance rehearsal now.

But he'd promised Amelia. And she was worth it.

Hildy and Steve met him on the sidewalk, where he stood staring at the door.

"You going in?" Steve asked.

Cole shot him a look.

"I get it, buddy, believe me," Steve said. "We're in this together."

Hildy elbowed his arm. "This is pretty great what you're doing, Cole. Julianna would be so proud."

Cole swatted the compliment away, same way he'd swatted away Charlotte's revelation that he was, in her words, "a big softy." He was also the kind of guy who drove people away, and whatever his strengths were, he had plenty of flaws to counteract them.

Through the glass, Cole spotted Charlotte behind the front desk, talking with Julianna's assistant, Brinely. Both wore the kind of clothes a person might dance in. He wore jeans and work boots.

"Let's get this over with," he mumbled as he pulled the door open and let the older couple pass through.

Charlotte looked up, made eye contact with him, then looked away. Maybe he'd imagined it.

"What was that about?" Hildy asked.

Or maybe not.

Cole shrugged.

"Did you make her mad?" Hildy pressed as they followed a few other people into a big dance studio and sat in the chairs set up around the perimeter of the room.

"I didn't do anything," Cole said, though he was pretty sure that wasn't true. He'd done something, he just didn't know what.

The three of them found their seats. Cole shifted, feeling

out of place. Not only because he was dancing with a nine-year-old, but because he was dancing at all.

Thankfully, everybody seemed preoccupied with their phones.

A woman he recognized as the wife of one of the athletic boosters made eye contact with him from across the room. "Coach, did you see this?"

Oh no. What now?

"What is it?"

She walked over, holding the phone out in his direction. On the small screen, Charlotte and Amelia moved in unison. The little girl looked up at Charlotte, clear admiration in her eyes.

Hildy leaned in closer. "She got Amelia to dance." There was awe in her voice. "Brinley called me this afternoon. She had no luck. I wonder when this was."

Cole watched for a minute, admiring the care Charlotte took with his niece. Amelia had been through more than any kid her age should, and seeing someone who wasn't even related to her treat her with such care turned his insides out.

Charlotte and Brinley walked in, each carrying a clipboard. Most of the chairs were filled, with only a few empty seats spread around the circle.

Cole met her eyes, the warmth of gratitude radiating through him. She'd done something nobody else had been able to do. And she really had nothing to gain by doing it.

She gave him a quizzical look, and he handed the phone back to the woman.

Did Charlotte know how amazing she was? Could he ever find a way to tell her?

Brinley clapped her hands together. "Ladies and gentlemen, thank you all so much for being here. We are so excited to move forward with our recital and turn it into a celebration of life for our dear Julianna. We all had a special connection to Jules, and—" A commotion in the hallway interrupted her.

Seconds later, a familiar face appeared in the doorway.

"Sorry we're late." Gemma strolled in—always making an entrance—with Max lolling behind like a lovesick puppy.

Cole felt pairs of eyes dart to him, and he wished he could swat them away like the annoying pests they were.

What was Gemma doing here?

"Oh, it's fine," Charlotte said. "We were just about to get started. Have a seat." She motioned toward two empty chairs just a few seats away from Cole. He steeled his jaw. His knuckles whitened as he fisted his hands.

Hildy straightened at his side, and Cole bit back words that would surely cause a scene.

"Where was I?" Brinley asked rhetorically. He didn't even know her, and even she seemed flustered by Gemma's presence in that room. Only Charlotte was unfazed by the presence of his ex-wife.

And only because Charlotte had no idea who Gemma was. Surely she would agree that Gemma's being here was inappropriate at best.

This was a celebration of life for *his* sister. Did Gemma's selfishness ever end?

"I want to turn the meeting over to a very special friend of Julianna's," Brinley said now. She ran down a list of Charlotte's awards and accolades before finally saying, "I'm excited to introduce Charlotte Page."

Charlotte took a step forward and scanned the circle. "I'm really excited by this turn out," she said. "You are the people Jules loved most, and for that reason, I think this is going to be really special."

Cole refrained from pointing out that Gemma and Max absolutely were *not* among the people Jules loved most.

Charlotte kept talking. Confidence came over her as she explained the plan to teach unique dances to each of the couples and groups.

"I'm obviously not an expert in all dance styles, but this is all in good fun, so we're going to do our best," she said. "Each couple or group will be assigned an instructor—me or one of the other teachers. We'll help teach, train, and choreograph your dances, and once we're done, we'll put on a show that would make Julianna smile."

At some point during Charlotte's speech, Gemma noticed Cole sitting there. He felt her eyes on him, and then he felt her surprise. It was possible he'd imagined it, but he knew her enough to know this was about the last place in the world she would expect to see him.

Because it was about the last place in the world he wanted to be.

And yet, he had far more right to be here than she did. Who decided it was a good idea for her and Max to participate in the event in the first place?

He'd take care of that, one way or another. Gemma was not going to take the stage at this event, no matter what.

"Now, can I get a volunteer to help demonstrate a few moves for the group?" Charlotte's question pulled his attention to her, and he shrunk under the weight of her gaze.

To his sheer horror, she seemed to expect him to stand and join her. And there was *no way* that was happening. He'd agreed to do whatever she said, but she'd asked a question—not issued a directive. He'd keep his seat, thank you very much.

Hildy raised her hand. "We'll volunteer."

Cole would thank her later. She and Steve joined Charlotte at the center of the circle. Charlotte shot Cole a raised brow that seemed to accuse, then turned her attention to the couple standing in front of her.

Charlotte had no idea what she was asking if she thought she was going to get him up in front of this group. It was bad enough he had to get up in front of anyone after weeks of practice—but now? Not a chance.

She began with a few moves that she called "basic," though Cole was pretty sure even those would've been hard for him, especially in his work boots, but Steve and Hildy picked up the steps quickly.

It soon became clear they'd done this before.

Charlotte took a step back. "You were holding out on me, Mrs. Hawthorne."

"Guilty." Hildy laughed. "We took ballroom dancing lessons a few years ago. I guess it's like riding a bike."

"I guess so," Charlotte said. "Let's see what you've got."

"Some music, please, Brinley?"

The blonde nodded, then pushed play on her phone. A familiar piano intro rang out over the speakers, and after a moment, Adele's haunting voice filled the space.

To his right, Max stood. "Babe, it's our song," he said.

Cole's eyes shot to him—gangly, smarmy, still-married Max—and he froze.

Their song?

"Max, sit down," Gemma hissed.

Charlotte beamed, as if it were the most romantic coincidence. "This is your song?"

Max spun around and faced Charlotte. Cole didn't want him looking at her, let alone talking to her—he had no right to feel that way and he knew it. But he couldn't help it—Max didn't deserve Charlotte's undivided attention.

"It was playing the night we met," Max said.

The night they met? Gemma had met Max before she met Cole, he'd discovered when the sordid details came out.

Max and Gemma, it turned out, had been carrying on for months before she even met Cole.

And while it may have stopped for a little while after the wedding, it didn't take long for Max and Gemma to find their way back to each other—and Cole was the last person to know.

His mind raced to try and make sense of what Max was saying. Had this been Max and Gemma's song when she chose it for the first dance the day she married Cole?

Had Max been at their wedding?

Cole couldn't help it, he scoffed, drawing Gemma's attention—and, to his dismay, everyone else's. Charlotte frowned at him.

"Max, let's not disrupt the class," Gemma said pointedly.

Slowly, Cole turned toward her, aware that she now wore the same expression she'd worn the night Max rushed in, pleading with her to take him back.

The night Cole learned the truth after three years of marriage.

And that expression said, *Caught.*

It was in that moment that Cole knew the truth. She'd chosen the song *for* Max. At their wedding.

"Can you turn that off?" Cole heard himself say.

The blonde's eyes widened. Charlotte's frown deepened. Steve and Hildy straightened.

"Turn it off," Cole said, this time more loudly.

"Dude, relax," Max said stupidly.

Cole stood, putting it all together. A year later, and he was still discovering new ways that Gemma had betrayed him.

The music came to an abrupt stop.

"Cole, calm down." Gemma moved between him and Max, holding a hand out as if she could protect her beloved from the man whose life she'd ruined.

"I can't believe you," he muttered under his breath. More to the point, he couldn't believe he ever thought he loved her.

"I told you, Cole." Her eyes turned innocent. "It's time to let me go."

He squeezed a fist, eyeing the two of them, replaying his public humiliation and realizing just how deep it went. There seemed to be no end to her betrayal.

"Is it time for Max to let his wife go?" Cole said.

A gasp raced around the circle, and Cole struggled to keep his mouth shut. He could air it all right there for everyone to hear. He could tell them all the truth about the woman he thought he loved.

How she'd started an affair with a married man months before she met Cole, that she dated Cole only to make that married man jealous, that she trapped him into marrying him by telling him she was pregnant with his baby, and that she invited her lover to their wedding and played "their song" as her first dance with her new husband—a man so smitten, so baffled how he got so lucky he would've hung the moon for her.

If he could go back, he'd tell that man what a fool he was to fall for someone so brazenly selfish and wicked.

It wasn't until they'd been married for two years that he learned the truth—that baby was never his. Gemma had a miscarriage, but if she hadn't, Cole would've loved that child until the day he died.

And finding out it wasn't his would've killed him.

He could spill all of that right here in front of all these people—make sure Max and Gemma shared in his humiliation.

But what was the point?

A hand on his arm startled him back to reality. He

glanced down and found Charlotte's wide eyes trained on him. "Can I talk to you in the hallway?"

He felt his jaw twitch as his eyes circled the room, a mix of pity and concern on the faces of everyone there. He followed Charlotte into the hallway and then into another studio at the back of the building.

"Look, I'm sorry," he said. "This was a mistake."

"What was? Trusting you not to start a fight in my rehearsal?" She crossed her arms and glared up at him.

"Agreeing to do this in the first place."

"If I remember right, you have a good reason to do this," she said.

He sighed. "I didn't know she was going to be here."

Charlotte frowned. "Cole, what is going on? Who is she?"

He didn't want Charlotte to know this story. It was humiliating enough that everyone in town had been audience to his personal pain, and he liked that she didn't know any of it. But she was going to find out—there was no sense pretending otherwise.

"That's Gemma," he finally said. "My ex-wife."

"Oh." Charlotte angled her gaze up toward him, and set something inside him off-kilter. She'd carried her confidence from the other studio into this one, and he couldn't help but be drawn in by it.

It was a different version of her, one he hadn't seen before. It was as if she'd taken a little time to find her footing here in Harbor Pointe, but now that she had, she was sure of herself. He envied her that.

At the moment, he felt like he'd been thrown into the deep end of the pool and his feet kept slipping off the ledge.

"Why is she here?" Charlotte asked.

Cole pushed a hand through his hair and sighed. "I don't know. To make herself look good? To get under my skin?

Her reasons for doing anything have never made sense to me."

Maybe one day he would tell her the whole story. Maybe one day he'd reveal all the reasons he was the way he was. But today was not that day.

She watched him—studied him, really. He didn't like it. He didn't like knowing he was a breath away from being seen.

"I'm sorry," she said. "That you had to go through any of that."

"Me too." He stood unmoving, locked up in her eyes. "Look, I don't blame you if you want to back out of this."

She lifted her chin. "I made a promise."

He saw her point. She made a promise, and so did he. He couldn't back out—she wasn't going to let him.

"What you did in there with Steve and Hildy, I can't do that."

She crossed her arms over her chest and the expression on her face changed. "Wanna bet?"

He looked away. He hadn't intended to challenge her.

She squared off in front of him. "I'll show you."

He tried not to groan.

She took his hand and positioned it on her waist, then lifted his other hand out to the side. "All you're going to do is move in a box. Left foot moves toward me, like this—" She moved back, forcing him to follow, then stopped. "Now we move to the side one step, like this—" Step by step, she led him in the tracing of an imaginary box on the floor with their feet. Once they returned to where they started, she glanced up at him. "See? Was that so bad?"

It wasn't, he realized. But not because the dancing had been easy—because his hand on her waist, his other hand wrapped around hers, it had been nice. Really nice.

They stood like that for a long moment, eyes locked,

hands touching, when the music in the studio next door began playing again. The same song. The same reminder. The same realization.

Cole took a step back, and Charlotte dropped her hands to her sides. He didn't want to let her down, but the reminder of his past pain was so vivid it nearly knocked the wind out of him. He couldn't go through that again, and he couldn't relive it—in spite of her watchful gaze.

"I saw a video of you dancing with Amelia," he said. "Maybe she doesn't need this deal after all."

Disappointment washed over Charlotte's face. Inevitable disappointment. Because that's what Cole did—he disappointed the women in his life, enough to make them leave. What was the point in pretending otherwise?

"Cole—"

"I need some air," he said. "I'll see you later."

And he walked out before she could say another word.

27

Charlotte stood in the empty studio for a beat. What was he saying? Was he dropping out after begging for her help?

She didn't know how to communicate with this man.

Brinley popped her head into the room. "Everything okay?"

She sighed. No. But yes. She was. She had to be. She was in charge. "Sorry about that."

"It's okay," Brinley said. "I finished up the meeting so I wanted to check in."

"Thanks for doing that." Charlotte followed Brinley into the hall and back to the first studio, where a handful of people milled around. Everyone else likely had a better understanding of Cole's history with Gemma than she did. It irked her that he refused to let her in. She felt like she was on the outside of an inside joke.

When they entered the room, Cole's ex-wife looked up and made a beeline for her.

"Charlotte," the woman said.

She stopped and gave Gemma her attention.

"I just wanted to apologize for what happened," she said. "I had no idea Cole was participating in this event." Her eyes practically sparkled, and she struck Charlotte as someone who was used to getting what she wanted.

"Julianna was his sister." Charlotte faced her now, aware that Hildy was only a few feet behind this woman, and she made no effort to hide the fact that she was eavesdropping.

The woman's laugh sounded nervous. "I've tried to get him to move on, but he's really stuck in the past," Gemma said. "He's not usually prone to outbursts like that, but the song—it was our first dance at our wedding."

Charlotte frowned. "But the man you're with said it was your song."

"Right," Gemma said, as if it were an acceptable explanation. "Maybe this is all too much for Cole. Maybe it's better if he removes himself from this part. To be honest, I'm not sure Max and I feel safe if he's in close proximity."

Charlotte stumbled over a response—was she serious?

"Or maybe you could remove yourselves?" Hildy said, taking a step toward them.

Gemma turned. "I beg your pardon?"

Hildy smiled sweetly. "I mean, if you're concerned Cole might actually do you harm, doesn't that make the most sense?"

Gemma half-laughed. "Max and I aren't the ones causing the problem."

"Aren't you?" Hildy still wore that same sweet smile. "You do know who this event is about, don't you?"

Gemma looked away, found Max standing off to the side holding her purse, then shrugged. "Whatever."

Charlotte watched the pair exit the studio before she turned to Hildy, wearing her best expression of disbelief. "So, that was Gemma."

"Yes." Hildy sighed. "That was Gemma. The woman who

stomped all over Cole's heart. I wish I could say I'm surprised she was doing this, but I'm not. It's like a game to her. I'm betting she weaseled her way on the roster specifically so she could get under his skin."

Charlotte frowned. "Why would she do that?"

Hildy shrugged. "She's the type of person who thrives on attention. She wants to make sure Cole is still in love with her."

"Is he?"

Hildy scoffed. "What do you think?"

"To be honest, I can't even see the two of them together."

"Not many people could," Hildy said. "But in true Cole Turner fashion, he did everything for that woman. He was far too good for her—and she repaid him in heartache and misery."

Charlotte crossed her arms over her chest and sighed. "I think he quit tonight."

"Don't give up on him so quickly, Charlotte," Hildy said. "Cole is one of the best men you'll ever know." She squeezed Charlotte's arm. "I'll be calling you to set up some time for you to teach us a dance."

Charlotte forced a smile, but mostly she felt an odd sadness for a man who didn't deserve her pity. Or maybe, he did. Maybe Cole was a completely different person before all this happened.

And even if not, nobody deserved to have their heart trampled like he had.

The following morning, Charlotte woke up late, but still went on her run. After all, she needed to clear her head. That was the plan anyway, but that was not what happened since she spent the entire forty-five minutes replaying the events of the previous night and thinking about Cole.

She came to a stop back in front of Lucy's cottage and groaned. Somewhere along the way, she'd concocted another one of her ideas, and though it was against her better judgment, she knew she was going to see it through.

She knew it because she was showering and dressing and driving to Hazel's Kitchen to pick up the pastries Betsy said were Cole's favorite.

And now, here she was mid-morning, standing outside his cottage.

What am I doing?

She could tell herself she was just checking in about the dance—they were supposed to start rehearsing that afternoon, after all. But the truth was, she couldn't get that look on his face out of her mind. She'd fallen asleep last night replaying the argument she'd witnessed and her brief conversation with Gemma. She'd tried to piece the story together, but she didn't have all the facts. Was Cole really still so hung up on his ex-wife that he couldn't be in the same room with her?

And maybe he was a combination of angry, bitter, and jealous—but the look on his face suggested he was something else too. Hurt.

Somehow, it made all of his shortcomings fall away. She understood he had a reason not to trust her. It made sense he was standoffish, even rude.

But how did she prove to him that not all women were like Gemma? How did she prove that he could trust her, that they could be friends?

She didn't know, but apparently a part of her thought it was a good idea to start with unannounced pastries.

More than likely another grand faux pas in the making.

She headed up the sidewalk and stopped just before she

stepped onto the front porch. She could still turn and run the other way. She could pretend the pastries were for Lucy. She could hurry off before he ever knew she was here.

She turned around, then heard the door open. "Is this payback?"

She stopped. She supposed she did look a lot like he had the other night standing on her porch. Caught.

Slowly, she turned on her heel and faced him, standing in the door with a toothbrush in his hand. He wore jeans and no shirt, and his hair was damp, but he looked clean-shaven and probably brimming with that *I'm not trying very hard* scent he wore so well.

"Hey," she said, trying not to look at his abs. They were impressive.

She wasn't doing a very good job of not looking.

He leaned on the doorjamb, his face void of expression. "Hey."

She held up the bag. "Breakfast?"

He looked at it, probably knew exactly what was inside, then turned around and walked back in the house, leaving the door open.

Was she supposed to follow?

She hesitated for a long moment before finally venturing up onto the porch and inside the cottage. She had to admit, she'd wondered what it looked like in here. With the lake in his backyard, she imagined this was prime Harbor Pointe real estate. It didn't have the same view as Lucy's house—no bright red lighthouse—but she imagined the sunsets were brilliant out the large windows that faced the lake at the back of the house.

"It's a work in progress," he said when he noticed her looking around.

"What a great place," she said.

The open floor plan made it feel bigger than it was. She would describe the space as "cozy," and while it could use some updating, she was pretty sure it had the potential to be stunning.

"Probably a lot different than your place in Chicago." He pulled on a worn gray T-shirt.

Shame.

"Bare walls, stuff in boxes, view of the lake—not that different," she said. And yet, completely different. This cottage had the potential to be a home. Not that she knew much of anything about homes—she'd never really had one of her own. She didn't count the apartment in Chicago as anything other than "the place where I sleep."

She'd considered framing some of her ballet photos and hanging them up, but it had never happened. She hadn't had time. Besides, it was slightly depressing not to have any other personal photos to display. So, she'd never really had a home—and she only realized in that moment how desperately she wanted one.

"Pity pastries?" He walked over to the sink, scrubbed his teeth for a few long seconds, spit out the toothpaste, and flipped on the faucet. He leaned into the stream, sucked in some water, spit it out, then wiped his mouth with a towel, tossing the toothbrush on the counter.

For some reason, she felt like she was watching something she shouldn't, which was ridiculous—he was brushing his teeth, not changing his clothes.

Heat rushed to her cheeks at the thought of it.

"Pity pastries?" she repeated.

"I used to get them a lot," he said. "Let me guess—cinnamon roll, apple tart, and a blueberry scone?"

"I honestly don't know. Betsy told me she'd give me a bag of your favorites."

His slow nod seemed to imply that his guess was correct.

"Okay, obviously I need to stop buying you gifts." She set the bag on the kitchen table and started for the door.

"Charlotte, wait," he said.

She should keep walking. She should've learned her lesson one of the other two times she'd tried to extend an olive branch. He had a habit of snapping them in half. But she didn't keep walking. For some inexplicable reason, she turned around.

"I'm sorry." He seemed to be forcing out the words. "It was nice of you."

She didn't respond.

"Really nice," he said. "I just kind of liked that there was someone in town who didn't pity me."

"I don't pity you," she said.

"You don't feel sorry for poor Coach Turner—got his heart trampled on, and now his ex is back to flaunt her puny boyfriend in his face."

She faced him now. "Sounds like you feel sorry for you."

He opened his mouth as if to reply but quickly snapped it shut.

"I just came to see if you were going to quit because if you are, I'm going to have to break it to Amelia." She stared him down, knowing it was slightly manipulative but also determined to make her point. This wasn't about Gemma and the skinny purse-holder. This was about a promise he made to a little girl.

Surely he remembered.

He seemed slightly gobsmacked by her comment, but he'd yet to respond.

"Well?"

He picked up the Hazel's Kitchen bag and opened it,

then moved over to the counter, opened the cupboard, and took out two plates.

"I don't eat—"

"Sugar or carbs, I know," he said. "But maybe today you do."

She frowned. No, today, like every other day, she didn't.

"I was thinking about redoing my kitchen, but I'm still working on the bathrooms. I actually hired Asher to help me. He'll be over in a bit." He pulled the pastries from the bag. He set one on each plate and carried them back to the table, set the plates down, and pulled out a chair. He motioned for her to sit down.

She hesitated for a moment, then obliged, and he sat across from her. "That's what you guys were talking about at practice the other day."

He looked at her, as if remembering. "Right, you were there."

"That was nice of you."

Cole shrugged. "He needed a job. I needed help."

She eyed him for a long moment. The words *big softy* popped into her head, but she didn't say anything. It was clear that Hildy was right. Despite his prickly façade, Cole cared about the people in his life. A lot.

"Do you want the cinnamon roll or the apple tart?" He looked at her now with an unexpected kindness behind his eyes.

She looked down at the plates, unsure what part of *I don't eat sugar* he didn't understand. But when her eyes darted back to his, her resolve crumbled. She would've eaten all three pastries by herself if he asked her too.

"Here, I'll cut them in half and you can try both." He did so, rearranging the pieces so each plate now had half of both pastries.

He was trying to distract her. It was working. She shook her foolishness aside and refocused.

"I just need an answer to my question," she said. "Are you still going to do this dance or what?"

He pushed the plate closer. "I need to know which of these you like better." He took a bite of the cinnamon roll. "These are homemade—Betsy's grandmother's recipe. She sells out of them almost every day. They're pretty hard to beat." He looked at her plate. "Go ahead—try it. It's not going to hurt you."

It did smell amazing. Really amazing. And as much as a mouth could water for something it had never tasted, hers was watering now.

She picked up the pastry and smelled it.

Cole laughed. "Go ahead, Muscles."

"Muscles?" She met his eyes.

"I saw your arms," he said.

"You noticed my arms?"

"Hard not to."

Her heartbeat thrummed, and she wished she had somewhere to hide. Instead, she found herself biting into the cinnamon roll. The taste of sweet cinnamon and sugar filled her mouth as she savored the bite.

He was eating his half of the pastry far too quickly, another bite swallowed in the time it took for her to swallow hers. "This is amazing."

"I told you," he said. "See what you've been missing out on."

The words were innocent enough. Simple really. She didn't eat sugar; she was missing out on cinnamon rolls. But for some reason, hearing someone else say it made her realize that she was missing out on so much more.

"You okay?"

Had her face given something away? She set what was

left of her cinnamon roll on the plate and regained her composure. "I'm fine. And if I remember right, we were here to talk about you."

He clapped his hands together, as if that would get the sticky frosting off, then found her eyes. "Listen, Charlotte, you really don't need to be in on this mess with my ex. It's an ugly situation."

"I gathered."

"So maybe it's better if I bow out."

"Better for who?"

He didn't respond.

"Better for Amelia?"

He held up his hands in surrender. "Fine, I get it. I made a promise."

"Right. You did. So, I think it's time to buck up and do the right thing."

He eyed her curiously. "Did you just say 'buck up'?"

She sighed. "Yes. Do you know what it means?"

He seemed amused. She was seconds away from being made fun of and she knew it. "Well? Are we doing this thing?"

"Are you going to make me tell you about me and Gemma?" A serious expression crossed his face.

"Did I ask?" She figured she could return his *guff* all day long.

"No, so I'm guessing somebody else filled you in," he said.

"Why, because I'm not pressuring you for information about your love life?" She laughed.

He looked away. "You'd be surprised how many people found it interesting."

"Well, I'm not most people," she said. "Besides, there seems to be some sort of code in this town whenever your name comes up."

He frowned.

"Nobody says anything. Just that you've been through a lot. It's strange, though, don't you think? That everyone seems to know the story, but nobody will share it. I wouldn't have even known who Gemma was if you didn't tell me."

"What are you saying?"

"I'm saying this community respects your privacy, Coach. For whatever reason, they want to protect you."

"I didn't ask anyone to protect me." He stood and walked over to the coffeemaker, filled two mugs, and returned to the table, sliding a mug in her direction.

"You're missing the point," she said. "Do you know what I would give to have people that watched out for me like that? Julianna was my only friend, Cole, and she's gone. You have an entire town that loves you, including that little girl."

"Seems like maybe she loves you too," he said.

Charlotte felt her cheeks turn pink.

"The video of the two of you dancing. Seems like she really admires you—enough to get back out there anyway." He took a swig of coffee and looked at her, his gaze so intense she had to look away. She didn't mean to tell him anything about herself. It was too personal, really, and not the kind of thing you shared with someone you hardly knew.

She stood. "I'll be at the studio this afternoon. If you decide to go through with it, you can join me."

"And if I don't?"

Charlotte forced herself to look at him. "Well, then you're not the man I thought you were."

28

Asher pulled up just as Charlotte was leaving. The kid got out of the Haven House work truck and shot Cole a surprised look.

"You and Miss Page?"

Cole groaned. "Not your business."

"I'm just saying, Coach, she's top rate."

Cole stood on the porch, blocking the entry to his house. "What is she, a cut of beef?"

Asher grinned. "Dang, you've got it bad."

Cole rolled his eyes and went inside, not bothering to hold the door open for his new employee.

"I fully support this relationship," Asher said, following him into the kitchen.

"There's no relationship," Cole said. "She's helping out with my niece. End of story. And if you want this job, I suggest you shut up about it. Got it?"

Asher's grin only partially faded, and he didn't respond.

"Got it?"

"Yes, Coach," Asher said.

"Great. So, are you ready to demo a bathroom?" He

turned and walked toward the first-floor bathroom. Cole had already removed the toilet and tub, but he'd left the real demo for Asher. "I'm going to get you started, and then I've got an errand to run."

"You're going to leave me alone?" Asher looked downright terrified. "You know I've never done this kind of work before, right?"

"That's why I'm going to show you what to do before I leave." Cole picked up a sledgehammer and handed it to Asher.

"What's this for?"

"Therapy," Cole said.

Asher frowned.

"I've already prepped the room," Cole said. "So all I need you to do is remove the old plaster and the tile."

The kid held the sledgehammer loose in his hands. "How do I do that?"

Cole took the hammer back, moved a few feet away, then hauled off and hit the wall as hard as he could.

Asher jumped at the sound. "Dang, Coach."

Cole handed over the hammer. "Your turn."

Asher took the tool but stared at it, unsure.

"You can't mess it up," Cole said. "And sometimes, I've found this is the best way to deal with your anger."

"You think I'm angry?"

Cole studied his quarterback silently until the kid looked away. "Got every right to be."

Asher refused his eyes.

"You think I don't get it, but I do," Cole said, really not wanting to get into any of this but certain he needed to—for Asher's sake. "My mom left us when I was about your age, and my dad dropped us off at Haven House in the middle of the night. Had no idea when he'd be back."

Asher's shoulders dropped, and he finally looked back at Cole. "Really?"

Cole nodded. "Hard not to be mad about all that."

Asher stilled. "Did she ever come back? Your mom?"

Cole shook his head. "My dad did, but he was different. He remarried a couple of years later. Has a new family now."

The kid's jaw quivered. "What if my mom doesn't come back?"

Cole remembered asking Steve that same question. Being on your own at sixteen was terrifying, especially when you felt responsible for a sibling.

"You know she didn't leave because of you, right?" Cole said, surprising himself.

"You don't know that," Asher said.

"Sometimes parents are working things out," he said. "They're supposed to have it all together, but they don't. They're just human, like you and me." He said the words without thinking, and only after they were out did he realize it was true. Asher's mom left because *she* had things to sort through—not because her kids were bad kids. Not because they drove her away.

That was her problem. Not Asher's.

Same way it was Cole's mom's problem. Not Cole's.

The realization smacked at him as he tried to unpack what that meant. He looked at Asher. "It wasn't your fault."

The kid's face fell.

"You know that, right?"

Asher shrugged.

Cole stood still, the words *not your fault* racing through his mind. Asher wasn't the only one who needed to hear it. To know it, in that deep place of knowing. "Parents sometimes suck, Ash." Cole grabbed the hammer, squared himself off, and slammed into the plaster with the full force of his strength. At his side, Asher jumped. Cole cracked into the wall for a third time, letting out a shout to accompany the crack. Adrenaline shot through his veins. He was both invigorated and out of breath.

"Your turn." He held the tool up to Asher again, and this time, the kid took it with a purpose behind his eyes.

He moved, squaring off the same way Cole had, then swung the hammer behind him and banged it into the wall. The plaster cracked, and Asher lined up and hit it again, each blow stronger and louder and harder than the one before.

After he'd put a decent hole in the wall, he stood back, out of breath. He wiped his face with the back of his arm, and Cole could see he was working to keep from crying.

He slapped a hand on Asher's shoulder. He wasn't good with emotions, but he understood Asher's better than most people. And he could stand here and belabor the point, or he could get out of the kid's way and let him beat up on the bathroom while he worked out his anger.

"I'm going to go," Cole said. "I won't be long, but everything in here needs to go. You can't mess it up. When you get to the wood inside the wall, stop."

Asher gave him one firm nod, and Cole turned to leave.

"Coach?"

He turned back and found Asher glassy-eyed and red-faced. "Thanks."

The word hung there between them, saying so much more than either of them had. Asher had an ally in Cole and now he knew it. And that was more important than any football game.

29

Cole pulled up in front of Connor's house and turned off the engine. What was his brother-in-law doing to distract himself? During Cole's divorce, staying busy had saved him. He imagined that went double for a man whose wife had died.

He knocked on Connor's door, waited a minute, then let himself inside. "Connor?" The house was eerily quiet.

It had been a few days since Cole had seen him, and now he was kicking himself for letting time pass. He should be checking in every day. "Connor?"

His mind raced back to the summer before his sophomore year. Maybe it was because he'd touched on the topic with Asher or because this moment, walking into an eerily quiet house, conjured familiar feelings. Whatever the reason, he was back there in a heartbeat.

He'd just finished football practice, and after waiting for a ride for half an hour, he concluded his mom had forgotten to pick him up, so he ended up walking all the way home. He was annoyed because he was a junior and he wanted his own car, but they couldn't afford it. Maybe this would prove to his parents it was time he got one. They lived on the outskirts of town, so it wasn't a quick walk, and halfway there, it had started raining.

When their small house came into view, he saw his dad's truck in the driveway, but his mom's Ford was not, which was strange because Dad should've been at work, and she should've been home.

Without thinking, he broke into a run, pushing open the front door just as the rain started slamming harder into the pavement, as if it were a warning of the storm that was about to ensue.

"Mom?" Cole called out as he closed the door behind him. He walked into the kitchen and found his father standing at the counter, staring at a piece of paper and holding an open bottle of beer.

"Cole," he said, almost as if he'd only just then remembered he had a kid at all.

"You guys forgot to pick me up," Cole said. "And I called, but no one answered so I had to walk home in the storm." Water dripped from his hair, running down his back and puddling on the floor.

"I'm sorry, son," his father said.

"What's going on?" Cole asked.

His dad's eyes drifted back down to the paper, but he didn't respond. Cole stepped forward, dropped his wet backpack onto the linoleum, and took the paper from his father.

"What's this?" His eyes scanned the page of his mom's familiar handwriting but words that made no sense. "I don't understand."

"She's gone," his dad said.

"What do you mean 'she's gone'?"

"You can read, right?" his dad snapped. He chugged from his bottle of beer. "She got a better offer."

Cole reread the letter. Phrases jumped out at him as he tried to piece it all together. *I'm sorry. I've got to see where this goes. I know you won't understand. I hope you can forgive me.*

"She's gone?" Cole looked at his dad. "Just like that?"

His father shrugged. "Just like that. This is why you should never trust a woman, Cole." His drink sloshed as he gestured with the hand holding the bottle. "They're all a bunch of liars."

He'd gone to Chicago that night to tell Julianna, but he remembered almost nothing about the trip. He'd never gone so far alone, on a bus, but Jules deserved to hear the truth from him, no matter how devasting it would be.

He'd made his sister promise to stay and finish out the dance program—she was better off there, not around their father, who'd always drank too much, even before their mom left.

Cole would take care of everything.

Looking back, it had been a lot for a sixteen-year-old kid. Too much, in fact, which was why he and Jules ended up at Haven House that fall.

How many times had he walked into the house, wondering if his mother might've returned? How many times had he instead walked in to find his father in a drunken stupor, his anger turning to bitterness the more time passed?

Eventually, his dad had gotten his act together. He moved to Florida, took a job in insurance, married a woman named Marnie, and now Cole talked to him about once a month. He came back for the funeral, and that was the first time Cole had seen him in two years. The man was more of a story from Cole's past than a father. Or maybe more of a cautionary tale. After all, he was the reason Cole stopped believing in love, marriage, women—all of it.

And Gemma was the sequel.

He'd fallen pretty hard for the perky blonde who picked him up at one of the many Harbor Pointe festivals a few summers ago. When she told him she was pregnant, Cole was full of shame. He knew better. He hadn't intended to sleep with her, but she was so persistent, he'd been unable to resist.

Doing the right thing by her wasn't the same as being in love, but he convinced himself they had a shot at the real thing.

For the first time, he challenged his dad's stance on the whole institution of marriage, and all Gemma had done was prove his father right.

She solidified what Cole already knew—women couldn't be trusted. Marriage was for fools.

And he vowed never to be a fool again.

Something about walking into Connor's dark house was reminiscent of those early days after his mom left, and he found himself whispering a quiet prayer that his brother-in-law was okay—that Cole wasn't about to find him drunk on the floor, or worse.

He walked through the entryway and into the living room. Particles of dust danced in the stream of light pouring in through a crack in the curtains, and there, on the couch, was Connor—asleep—surrounded by piles of clothes and cardboard boxes.

What the . . . ?

Connor stirred. Cole sat in the chair next to the couch but had to shift to remove a stuffed animal out from under him.

"Dude, what are you doing here?" Connor mumbled. He tried to sit upright amid the clothing and boxes that surrounded him.

"Came to check on you," Cole said. He stood and moved

toward the window. "You don't mind if I open these, do you?"

Connor started to protest, but Cole pulled the curtains open anyway. Light filled the room, and Connor covered his eyes, letting out a loud groan in the process. "Give a guy a break, would ya?"

Cole moved to the next window and did the same thing. "Where are the kids?"

"Josh and Carly took them for ice cream," he said.

Cole surveyed the room. "What is going on in here? Are you moving?"

Connor's head fell back onto the couch, and he still covered his face with his hands. In the light, Cole looked around and realized they were surrounded by women's clothing. Framed dance recital posters. Books. Photo albums. Boxes that had probably been packed away in a closet somewhere.

They were surrounded by Julianna's stuff.

"What is all this?" Cole asked.

"I have to get rid of it. The guy from the resale store is coming to pick it all up this afternoon." Connor rubbed his face with his hands, then sat up and looked at Cole.

"You can't do this, man," Cole said.

"I have to." Connor sighed. "She's everywhere. I can't function because everywhere I go—there she is."

"Yeah, but she hasn't even been gone two months. You're going to regret it if you get rid of everything." Cole scanned the room. "Is that her wedding dress?"

His brother-in-law's face crumpled and he nodded.

"Your kids might want this stuff," Cole said.

No response.

"Look, I'll tell you what—I'll take it. I've got a guest room at my place, and I'll just keep it for you until you're ready."

Connor wiped his face dry with the back of his hand. His lower lip trembled, but he nodded. "Thanks, man."

"Don't give it another thought," Cole said. "Go take a shower, and I'll load everything into my truck."

Connor stood, dazed, and walked toward the stairs. At the doorway, he stopped, then turned around. "She was the best thing that ever happened to me."

The words paralyzed Cole. He'd just been thinking about love—how it was a farce, how it didn't exist. He had proof—first his mother, then Gemma. Heck, he could even make a case that Asher's mom proved what he thought to be true.

But there was something in the way Connor said it, something behind his eyes that made Cole wonder if he was wrong.

Connor vanished up the stairs, and reality kicked back in. Maybe he and Julianna were the exception. Maybe they were the once-in-a-lifetime true love deal that people wrote stories about. But reality? That was much crueler.

Cole stood in the center of the living room, wondering what he'd gotten himself into. He was supposed to meet Charlotte and Amelia in just a few hours—if he intended to keep his end of the deal, that was. And now he had a whole room of boxes to clear out.

One at a time, he hauled them to the truck, neatly packing them in the bed, and saving the cab for the hanging clothes. He was on his seventh trip when he spotted a covered box in the corner. On the side, in bold black letters, were the words *Letters from Charlotte.*

He knelt down and pulled off the lid. The box nearly overflowed with stacks and stacks of stamped envelopes, all different colors, all with Julianna's name on the front and Charlotte's name in the upper left-hand corner.

And though something inside him told him it was wrong, he picked one up and opened it.

Dear Jules,

I know you don't want to hear this, but I feel like I have to say it. Don't leave the ballet. I know you really wanted the program in New York, but that's not a reason to leave the ballet for good. There are so many other opportunities. What will I do without you? It's not like I have a single other friend here. Truly—you're the only thing keeping me sane.

And I don't even want to go to New York if I have to come back here this fall and find out you're gone.

I know you're disappointed, and I know you said you wanted to go live your life—but is whatever you're going to find out there worth walking away from this dream?

I mean, yes, you're talking about things I've never done, so maybe there is something about it that I don't understand. I mean, you want to find true love and settle down and have kids, and I'm a girl who has never even gotten flowers from a guy. Plenty of bouquets have been delivered to my dressing rooms over the years, but none have ever been from anyone who didn't want something from me.

What would it be like to have a boy bring me flowers just because he wanted to make me smile?

I'll never know. And I guess a part of me gets it—why you'd trade ballet for the possibility of that excitement. But it feels so premature. So permanent.

And what if he's not out there? What if you leave and the things you're leaving for don't appear?

The sound of footsteps on the stairs pulled Cole's attention. He shoved the letter back in the envelope and the envelope back in the box. He picked it up and walked toward the front door just as Connor appeared at the bottom of the stairs.

"Thanks for doing this, Cole," he said. "You're a good friend."

"Anytime, man," Cole said. "I'm almost finished here, and then we'll grab some lunch. You look like you could use a meal."

"I have casseroles for days."

"Great. I'll heat one up. Be right back." Cole walked outside with the box under his arm. He reached the truck, opened the passenger side door, and set it on the front seat.

What other secrets about Charlotte Page were inside that box?

And how many ethical codes did he violate if he opened it to find out?

30

Charlotte propped her ankle on the ballet barre and leaned over it, stretching out muscles tight from neglect. While she had walked away from a life in professional ballet, the desire to push herself hadn't gone away, and that meant rehearsing and training.

That meant not letting her muscles get weak.

Thankfully, Brinley had agreed to let her in to the studio whenever she wanted, though she'd made no progress on convincing Connor to let her buy the studio. She'd left him two messages, but so far, no reply.

She had two hours before Cole and Amelia showed up (or not), and she planned to spend them the same way she would if she were in Chicago. She'd taken enough time off.

After she'd warmed up, she took her place on the floor and began to move. She was tentative at first, and then she remembered her moments with Amelia, her moments of recalling the way Julianna threw herself into every role she danced, whether she had a solo or was hidden in the back.

In her mind, she'd assigned sounds and words and numbers to the steps as her entire body moved to the music. An exhale here, a *zip-zip* there, then a *hah* on the button of music.

Julianna had a secret Charlotte had never uncovered. She didn't care for the spotlight—it wasn't what drove her. She simply loved to dance.

That wasn't why Charlotte danced. Not only did she not always love it, some days she actually hated it. So why? Why sacrifice everything for something she didn't love?

Shoo-turn-hah. Over and over, moving instinctively, her body taking on a mind of its own.

As she moved, realization struck her. It wasn't passion or even ambition that motivated her. It was an overwhelming desire to be worthy.

She was still, even now, trying to earn her place, as if she didn't have the same right to be here unless she had something to offer. She peppered Cole with gifts that all seemed to cry out, *Do you like me yet?* She'd tried so hard to be seen, to prove she had value.

And it had worn her out.

Earning her worth had exhausted her.

Was there another way? *God, is there another way?*

Is that what she was searching for? Permission to stop trying so hard? Permission to stop striving for more? To fill her soul with peace—elusive peace?

And would she find any of those things here?

She lifted onto her toes and turned, catching a glimpse of her technically perfect lines in the mirror. She still looked exquisite.

But what if she turned away from the mirror? What would happen to her body then?

She shifted her stance and faced the back wall, then picked up the choreography again. She moved through the familiar steps, but without her own body to assess, she simply felt the music and let it flow through her.

It was as if her body connected to the music in a way it never had before. The piece was haunting and dark, meant to pull emotion from the audience, to tie them to a deep sense of loss. The creators had been clear this was not a feel-good ballet.

And yet, Charlotte rarely felt anything when she danced it.

Until now.

As she circled the studio, her mind wandered, landing her back with Julianna, with all the deep regrets she had about their friendship. She was haunted by her poor choices, her inability to put anything or anyone above herself. She hadn't felt it before because she was still so consumed with her own wants and desires. She was still so consumed with proving she was the best.

Am I good enough yet?

But now? Now that she'd spent time in Julianna's space, now that she realized the days for making it up to her friend were gone—she was struck by profound, unmatched sadness.

The grief she'd been shoving aside assaulted her, demanding her attention. The pain of her betrayal mixed with years of regret, soured by poor choices, choices to put dance above friendship, to put her desire to be the best above everything else—it all tormented her now, and for the first time, she used the movement to let herself feel it.

And as it intensified, so did the deep grief she'd been carting around on her back since the day she found out Julianna had died. The one person in the world who loved her unconditionally was gone.

How could she just be gone?

How could she exist in a world without Julianna's love and acceptance? Because whether she succeeded or failed, Julianna's opinion of her never changed. Her love never wavered. She never stopped being Charlotte's biggest encourager, her best friend.

What would she have said if she knew Charlotte was the reason behind the event that drove her away from the ballet? Would that unconditional love still be hers?

She leapt wider, higher, farther than she ever had, and as she landed, something inside her snapped.

A heaviness settled on top of her, and for a moment, she couldn't breathe. She'd betrayed her only friend. And maybe it had all worked out—maybe Julianna had gone on to live exactly the life she was meant to live.

But what if she hadn't? What if there had been a different path—a path in the ballet, a path that could've kept her from driving on that country road at the exact moment another driver was preoccupied by his phone?

Would she still be here?

Had Charlotte stolen that from her?

She collapsed in a heap on the floor, the weight of her decisions, the secrets she'd kept, all too much to bear. The music played on as she struggled to catch her breath, tears streaming down her cheeks, pain welling up within her.

She'd yet to cry for Jules. She'd yet to cry for what she'd done. More than anything, she wanted to be absolved of her sin, but the one person who could've offered forgiveness was gone.

"Hey." The voice sliced through the now-silent room as the song ended and in its place, only the sound of her quiet sobs remained.

She looked up and found Cole, standing in the doorway, brows drawn like the curtains at night as confusion hung on his face.

She turned away, wiping her cheeks dry. Had it already been two hours? Had she been so caught up in whatever had just happened she'd completely lost track of time?

"Sorry, I'm early," he said. "I can go if . . ." He seemed unable to finish the sentence.

If you need more time to completely lose it.

She forced herself to stand. "No, I'm fine."

She couldn't think of anyone worse to have walked in at that precise moment. Surely he was thinking the same thing.

He took a step into the studio and she moved away, toward her phone, which had started playing a classical piece. She silenced it and turned to find him only a few feet away. And he was holding . . . flowers?

She frowned.

He followed her gaze to the brown-paper-wrapped bouquet of wildflowers, then met her eyes, an unexpected and uncharacteristic shyness coming over him.

"You brought flowers?" she asked.

He stuck them out toward her. "Seemed appropriate."

"Did it?" She took the bouquet but held on to his gaze.

"It's an apology," he said. "For being such a jerk."

Nobody had ever given her non-dance flowers. "Thank you." She drew them to her nose and inhaled their sweet aroma. "They're beautiful."

Oh gosh, was she going to start crying again?

His nod communicated finality, as if it was a topic they should stop discussing, then he found her eyes again. His head tilted as he regarded her for a fleeting moment.

Her skin tingled in awareness of his eyes. "What?" she finally asked, mostly to fill the awkward space.

He shook his head and looked away. "Nothing." But when he turned back, it was clearly not nothing. "Just wondering if you're okay."

It had been one thing to find him attractive yet crabby. But lately, her feelings where he was concerned were shifting. "I'm fine."

He nodded again, as if it were an acceptable answer, but then he squinted down at her, a question behind his blue eyes. "But you were crying."

She set the flowers down with a scoff. "It was nothing. Is Amelia on her way?"

"Yeah, my buddy Josh and his wife, Carly, have been hanging out with her today—they're going to drop her off."

"And Connor? Did you talk to him about doing this dance with her?"

Cole shook his head. "I think we can count him out."

Charlotte didn't press him for details about Julianna's husband. "We should get to work. Amelia will be easy to plug in. We have a lot to do if we're going to turn you into a dancer."

He groaned. "I can tell you right now you're not going to turn me into a dancer. The most we can hope for here is that I don't make a complete fool of myself."

She gave him a once-over, then smiled. "I'm not making any promises."

31

Charlotte smelled amazing. Not flowery or fruity, almost like fresh-baked cookies or a cake or something equally as delicious. Which was funny since she didn't even eat those things. He tried to stop thinking about it, but she'd ordered him to take her in his arms, and she was so close it was impossible not to notice.

She explained that partner dancing was different in ballet, so this was a bit of a learning curve for her too, but she'd done some research and had taken some classes over the years—plus, she was *Charlotte Page*, which more research had told him was a pretty big deal. To say she was far ahead of where he was, which was somewhere between "an epic disaster" and "a laughingstock in the making," was possibly the understatement of the century.

He willed Amelia to get there already, take some of the focus off of him.

He'd stopped by Forget-Me-Not on the way over, partly because of what he'd read in that letter and partly because he really did owe it to Charlotte to stop being a jerk. She'd been kind to him, and how had he repaid her?

By treating her like she'd been the one who injured him, not Gemma.

It wasn't fair and he knew it. As he pulled up in front of the dance studio, he considered telling Charlotte everything, the whole truth about Gemma. Maybe then she'd be more inclined to forgive him.

But then he saw her in a pile on the floor, and he couldn't bring himself to talk about it. She seemed to have her own demons to slay.

When he'd walked in to the studio, he heard the music filtering down the hallway, and as he reached the back room, he spotted her through the windows. He watched her dance for a solid five minutes, unable to move. She mesmerized him.

And he didn't even like ballet.

But with Charlotte, it was so much more than that. She was fierce.

And then she was crying. And that nearly wrecked him. That made him want to protect her, to go to battle with whatever or whoever had caused her this much pain.

Charlotte had more than proven she could take care of herself, but he couldn't deny his primal need to be the protector.

Or his primal attraction to Charlotte.

She was accomplished and beautiful, and completely out of his league. She was strong and independent and yet still had this sort of naïve, adorable quality about her.

How could all those things exist in the same person?

How could he be deluded enough to think that he—the person who couldn't even keep Gemma happy—could ever have a single thing to offer someone like Charlotte Page?

Standing there, with one hand at the small of her back and the other wrapped around hers and stretched out to the side, the only thing that needed protecting was his ego.

"You're really tense." She stepped out of his embrace.

He shook his hands at his sides. "I know. I'm sorry. I'm way out of my comfort zone here."

His phone dinged in his pocket. He pulled it out and found a text from Josh:

> *Dude! Totally forgot we were supposed to drop Amelia off for dance. We took the kids for ice cream and swimming and lost track of time. She's still in the pool—want me to get her out?*

Cole sighed.

"What is it?"

His eyes darted to hers. "Josh forgot about rehearsal. He's got the kids out at the pool—wants to know if he should bring her now."

"Is she having fun?"

Cole texted Charlotte's question.

Josh replied with a photo of Amelia and AJ in the pool, both wearing the same wide grin.

He turned the phone around and showed his response to Charlotte.

She smiled. "Let her stay. We'll reschedule."

"You sure?" Cole asked. "I hate that we wasted your time."

She smiled. "It wasn't a waste. I have a better idea of what I'm working with now."

"And you haven't given up yet?"

She shrugged. "You're not completely hopeless."

He took a step away. "I can't even believe I'm doing this."

"Just remember *why* you're doing it."

He texted Josh back to let him know that he didn't need to bring Amelia, then watched as Charlotte moved across the studio with a quiet elegance that he was sure had been ingrained in her from the start. He thought about her letter to Julianna, the box of letters that he'd unloaded into his spare room, and he wondered how many other things she'd never done. All the things that came with attending high school and college—dances and parties and high school football games. She'd apparently never had a cinnamon roll until he came along, and today was the first day she'd received flowers from a man.

He probably shouldn't be excited to have been that man, but he was.

After she mentioned at dinner that she'd never dated anybody, he'd spent more time thinking about that than he cared to admit. How did someone make it what had to be almost thirty years without a single date? Especially someone who looked like Charlotte. It seemed impossible.

And maybe that was the reason he wanted to protect her. Maybe he didn't want her to stumble on a guy like Max, someone who was married when he met Gemma and still started an affair. Someone who continued that affair long after Gemma got married, as if he couldn't pick between his wife and his girlfriend, as if he shouldn't have to.

But he wasn't the only guilty party in that scenario, was he? And Charlotte was nothing like Gemma.

"Okay, so, what? Practice again later this week?" Cole asked, shoving the thoughts aside. "I'll bring Amelia with me next time."

"Tomorrow." Charlotte took off her dance shoes and pulled a pair of sandals from a bag leaning against the wall.

"So, is this an everyday thing?"

"This recital is only a month away." She quirked a brow up at him, and he heard what she was too polite to say. If the goal was to keep him from making a fool of himself, then yes, they had to practice daily. He gave her a nod and stuffed his hands in his pockets.

"Does this time work? We can make it a standing date," she said.

"Yep."

She stood and slung the bag over her shoulder. "Great."

"Great."

They stared at each other for a long, awkward moment.

"I'll walk you out," he said.

"Thanks," she said quietly. She picked up the bouquet, and they walked out of the studio, then down the hallway to the lobby. She stopped in front of a framed photo of Julianna, surrounded by little girls dressed up as ballerinas. Jules's face was bright and happy, exactly the way Cole remembered her.

She'd loved being here, in this studio. She loved to dance, and sharing that love with her students gave her life meaning.

Her image looked back at him, eyes bright and kind, not a trace of inauthenticity anywhere. And even though Julianna's passion could sometimes get her in trouble—she was a bit of a hothead, after all—his sister loved with her whole heart. She did everything she could to make the world a better place.

Maybe God had taken the wrong sibling.

At his side, he felt Charlotte's eyes on him. "What are you thinking about?"

Normally, a question like that would've sent him running for the door, but he had a feeling Charlotte would understand.

"I was thinking about Jules," he said.

She shifted. "I think about her a lot."

Cole's mind wandered back to the day Julianna found out the truth about Gemma's affair. She showed up at the door, forced him to shower, and then dragged him to her house for dinner.

She fed him pot roast and made him help with the kids' bedtime duties while Connor cleaned up the kitchen.

She didn't treat him differently, didn't look at him like he was a failure. In fact, she made him feel normal. And for a minute, he almost believed there was joy to be had again, that just because he'd been unlucky in love, that didn't mean it didn't exist.

Of course, that feeling hadn't lasted long, but it had been there for a moment, because of her.

At his side, Charlotte touched the photo.

"You miss her," he said, aware that their collective grief could bond them together.

She nodded.

"I miss her too."

"You two were close," she said—a statement, not a question.

"We were," he said. "After our mom left, we kind of had to fend for ourselves. I told myself I needed to take care of Jules, but the truth is, we took care of each other."

"She had a way of doing that." Charlotte smiled. "Of taking care of people. It was kind of her thing."

He nodded. "She was special. Always put everyone else first. Sometimes I wonder if that's why she quit performing. That was the one thing she did for herself."

Charlotte looked away.

"But, in typical Julianna fashion, she turned it into something she could give back to other people. Nothing made her happier than teaching."

"You really think so?" Charlotte started toward the door. "I mean, you really think she was happy here?"

He followed her outside, and they stopped on the sidewalk in front of the studio.

"I do," he said. "I mean, not at first. She never told me

what happened with dance or why she decided to quit, but I know it wasn't an easy decision."

"How do you know?"

He shrugged. "She was devastated. There was a program she'd been working really hard to get into, and when they didn't take her, she took it as a sign. She came back here, broken heart and everything, and for a long time, I worried about her. She was so not herself. Sad. Mopey. Depressed."

Charlotte watched him intently.

"You probably already know this," he said.

"No," she said. "Not all of it. I mean, I remember when she told me she was quitting. I tried to talk her out of it."

His mind wandered back to the letter he'd read. Charlotte pleaded with his sister. It was clear Charlotte needed Julianna as much as the rest of them. Her death had to be weighing heavily on her. They had that in common.

Was that why she'd been crying earlier?

"I guess I wondered how she got from there to here," Charlotte said. "And I always wondered if she made the right decision."

"I don't know," he said. "But I do think she was really happy here. She met Connor a few months later, and they dreamed up this studio together. She had a great life, one I really don't think she would've traded."

"Really?" Charlotte's eyes sparkled with unshed tears, as if she needed the assurance for herself.

"Really."

She looked away, giving him ample time to study the curve of her shoulders, the slant of her nose, the smoothness of her skin.

She looked up at him.

Caught.

And yet, he couldn't look away. A tear slid down her cheek, and instinctively, he reached over and wiped it away with his thumb. Their eyes met and he pulled his hand away. "Sorry."

She gave her head a slight shake. "It's okay."

Neither of them moved for several seconds, held in place by an unnamed, invisible force. His gaze dipped to her lips, then back to her wide eyes, which seemed to be watching him a little too intently.

What would she do if he kissed her right now? Her lips were right there, full and so inviting. He pressed his own lips together, searching for common sense to talk him out of it, but his mind was empty.

"Well, I should go," she said after several seconds.

Her words snapped him back to reality, and he took a step back. "Tomorrow, then."

"Yep," she said.

He hurried off, simultaneously feeling like a first-class idiot and the luckiest man in the world.

After all, he had a standing date with a woman more interesting than anyone he'd met in a long time, and even though nothing could ever come of it, it gave him something to look forward to.

Seeing Charlotte would be the highlight of his day.

And that was as terrifying as it was exciting.

32

Charlotte drove home without checking her voicemail, without turning on any music, without making a sound.

Had she and Cole just had a moment?

Her heart had been beating so loud and so fast she could hardly breathe, and if that had been a scene in a movie, she would've been the girl on her couch chanting, "Kiss her! Kiss her!"

Something inside her had shifted toward Cole the instant he handed her those flowers. Why had he done that? Was he trying to get on her good side?

But that moment they'd shared only minutes ago had nearly done her in.

Dancing with him had been utterly unnerving. The way he smelled, the way he held her, the way he moved—all of it was new and different—and so was the effect it had on her.

She'd fall asleep replaying the moment on the sidewalk. Never mind that she'd ruined it. What would've happened if she hadn't said anything? If she hadn't backed away?

What she wouldn't give to find out.

She'd played a role the whole time, the role of an in-charge dance instructor, but truth be told, it was an act. Inside, her nerves seemed to be having a party.

Her skin tingled when he touched her. What was that about? And not just that either. Her heart raced when she tried to talk to him. Maybe because he wasn't quick to respond. Instead, he watched her with such intensity it set her completely off-kilter.

He was terribly handsome, unfairly so, and she got the impression that if he'd ever known that about himself, he'd forgotten it now.

Something about him was broken. Something inside, maybe deep inside, and she wondered if he had any idea what it was or how to fix it.

Listening to him talk about Julianna had comforted her somehow, giving her reassurances she desperately needed. She needed to believe that this life her friend had chosen had been the right life, the life she was meant to live.

And she especially needed to believe that she hadn't stolen her best friend's purpose from her. Because she had stolen her spot in the coveted dance program they'd both always dreamed of.

That program, the training Charlotte received there, it had catapulted her into the next tier of professional ballet. And it could've done the same for Jules if Charlotte hadn't let her jealousy get in the way.

But she couldn't change what she'd done. She could only do better from now on. If only she could keep regret from haunting her.

She pulled into Lucy's driveway, noticing there were two unfamiliar cars parked out front. She turned off the engine and made her way inside via the back door. She hung her bag on the hook in the mudroom and looked around on a nearby shelf for something suitable to put the flowers in. The sound of laughter mixed with the smell of Chinese food. That, she had sampled, but typically only the healthier dishes, usually prepared especially for her.

"Charlotte, is that you?" Lucy's voice rang out from the living room.

"Yeah, it's just me." Charlotte had to pass through the living room to go upstairs, but she thought she could do that without causing too much of a disruption.

Lucy appeared in the doorway. "Finally! We were waiting for you before we start."

Charlotte frowned. "Start what?"

"Girls' night." Haley pushed past Lucy, into the kitchen, followed by Quinn and Betsy.

"It's tradition," Lucy said.

Charlotte now realized the unopened Chinese food containers were sitting on the kitchen island next to a stack of plates. Five plates.

Was there a plate for her?

"Oh, I don't want to impose," Charlotte said.

All four of the other women stared back at her.

"Did you hear the part where we said we were waiting for you?" Lucy asked. "Grab a plate."

"Wait, can you eat Chinese?" Quinn asked. "Lucy said you have restrictions."

"I do," Charlotte said. "I'm sorry."

Lucy held up a hand. "Guys, give me a little credit. I ordered yours separate. Everything is steamed." She pushed two containers toward Charlotte. "But if you don't eat an eggroll, I'm not sure we can still be friends."

The other girls chatted and took plates, opening containers and dishing up the food, family-style. Everyone took what they wanted, sharing their dinners as if it were perfectly normal.

Charlotte only stared.

"You okay?" Quinn asked as she rounded the island to pour herself a glass of iced tea.

Charlotte nodded, unable to speak around the lump at the back of her throat. She'd never been invited to a girls' night. She didn't go out socially, and she'd certainly never been included in something that resembled a middle school slumber party.

Each of the women wore pajamas, had their hair up in buns, and looked like they were here for the duration. It set something off inside Charlotte, something like gratitude.

"Pretty flowers." Quinn faced her now, a tease of a smile playing at the corners of her mouth.

Charlotte looked at the bouquet, admired it, remembered the moment Cole handed it to her, and then, she was sure—blushed.

All at once, the four other women burst out in chatter. A chorus of "I told you they were for her!" and "You need to fill us in on what's going on" and "You've been holding out on me" rang out, filling the air with what Charlotte could only describe as obnoxious excitement.

"You should've seen him in the flower shop," Quinn said. "I don't think I've ever seen Coach like that."

"Like what?" Charlotte turned away, opening the cupboard in search of a vase, but really needing to escape four pairs of watchful eyes.

Stacks of bowls stared back at her.

Lucy appeared at her side, opened a different cupboard, and pulled out a tall glass vase, the perfect size, then handed it to Charlotte. "Here."

"Thanks."

"I don't know," Quinn went on. "He was unsure, I think. It seemed like it really mattered to him."

"Well, they're just flowers," Charlotte said, trying to wave off the idea that it was something more.

"I don't think that's how he saw it," Quinn said. "He made me put the roses back."

Charlotte filled the vase with water, found a pair of scissors, and began cutting the stems to the perfect length. "So, he chose *not* to get roses? Should I be offended?"

Quinn shrugged. "I wouldn't be. He said he wanted something sweeter. Less pretentious."

Verbal reactions from the peanut gallery—loud ones.

"I'm sure it was nothing," Charlotte said, setting the vase on the counter next to the sink.

"Judging by the way you're admiring them," Haley said, "I'd say they're not nothing."

They all laughed, and Charlotte picked up a plate. "Are you sure it's okay if I crash your girls' night?"

Lucy bumped her with her shoulder. "Are you kidding? We've been waiting all night for you to get home and give us the scoop about cranky Cole Turner. You're a part of this group now, whether you want to be or not."

Joy rose up inside her as she piled steamed vegetables and chicken onto her plate.

So this was how it felt to have friends.

The other girls made their way back into the living room, where they piled on to the sofas and chairs and put their plates in their laps. They talked over each other, teased each other, and just generally turned the air in the little cottage into something buoyant.

Charlotte watched from her place in the kitchen, where she poured a big glass of ice water from a pitcher Lucy had set on the counter.

"Charlotte, get in here!" Lucy hollered. "We need to dish about your hot football coach."

She set down the pitcher and picked up her plate. "He's not *my* hot football coach," she called back.

And then, before crossing the threshold into the other room, she glanced back at the colorful spray of flowers in the vase by the sink.

And she couldn't deny the feeling of hope that maybe one day . . . he would be.

33

The Harbor Pointe High School football team was comprised of very large, very loud, very sweet boys. And by their fourth rehearsal, it was clear that they were committed to making their number, which she'd choreographed to "Uptown Funk" by Bruno Mars, the most memorable one of the evening.

"All right," she said now, after they'd run through what they'd learned at their previous rehearsals. "We're going to finish this up today—are you guys even ready?"

The boys responded with cheers, and she had to wait for them to quiet down before she could speak again. She ran them through the last section slowly, answering their questions and trying not to giggle when one of them improvised. She wasn't sure how, but they all seemed to be having fun—even her.

Teaching the tribute dances for the recital had been a surprising source of joy.

"Let's run it!"

The boys groaned, chiming in a chorus of "We're not ready yet!"

She held up her hand. "Look, it doesn't have to be perfect. Just do what you can, and we'll practice it so many times it becomes second nature."

"Can we just watch you do it, Miss Page?" Hotchke asked, a gleam of inappropriate flirtation in his eye. "I think we'd get more out of that than tripping over our own feet."

She shot him a look. "You want me to tell your coach you just asked me that?"

Hotchke's hands went up. "Just joking."

"Don't joke with Coach's girl," Whitey said with a laugh.

"I'm not his girl." Charlotte rushed the words out so quickly they sounded defensive.

"Yeah, okay," Whitey said. "That's why you were leaving his house in the morning the other day."

Charlotte shot a look at Asher, whose face reddened. "Whitey!"

Clearly he'd spoken out of turn.

"Coach Turner and I are not a couple, boys," she said.

"Well, you should be," Asher said. "He's been way cooler since you came to town."

Charlotte frowned. "Well, we're barely even friends, so that has nothing to do with me. I'm helping him with his part in his sister's recital, end of story."

"So, it's just business," Dunbar said.

"Yes," Charlotte said. "Sorry to disappoint you guys, but there's nothing romantic going on between me and your coach." She scanned the room. "Now, can we get back to work?"

"Yes, ma'am," Asher said. He clapped his hands, signifying to the team it was time to buckle down, and she was glad he did. Charlotte was pretty sure if they continued down this line of questioning, one of the boys would find out that while there was nothing going on between her and

Cole, there was a part of her that couldn't stop wondering what it would be like if there was.

By the end of the rehearsal, most of the boys were doing the dance full-out, and they weren't half bad either.

"Okay, we're going to do this one more time, but you guys have to practice on your own, okay?" She spoke loudly, over their noise. "This time, give it everything you've got and leave it all out on that floor."

A chorus of cheers rang out in the studio.

At that moment, Cole strolled in the front door of the studio and caught her gaze through the studio window. Time stopped for a moment, and she couldn't look away. What was happening to her?

"Oh, yeah," Hotchke muttered under his breath. "Nothing going on there at all."

The other boys reacted—and not quietly—as Cole walked into the studio.

"You're early," she said.

"Yeah, I came to make sure these guys aren't giving you any grief." He eyed the group of kids, who grew oddly quiet.

She crossed her arms over her chest. "You didn't think I could handle a bunch of teenage boys?"

Cole looked flustered. "No, I didn't mean..."

"Boys, places, please." She commanded their attention, and they seemed to know she meant business. They took their spots for the beginning of the song. "You're going to do it like your life depends on it, and if you slack, I'll make you do it again. Got it?"

The boys nodded.

"Good." She shot Cole a look. "You might want to move."

His forehead scrunched. "Oh, right." He moved out of the center of the floor, off to the side, and she scanned the room of football players. "Make me proud."

They all put on their game faces and waited for her nod.

She pressed play on her phone and the low bass of the start of the song began.

The boys snapped straight into character, just like she'd taught them to do.

They each had their own parts to remember, and after all of their practicing, they mostly did well. She'd figured out which of the athletes moved best and featured them, and gave the others simpler moves.

"The most important thing," she'd told them, "is your attitude. I don't care if you get the steps right. If you sell it with your face and your swagger, nobody in that audience will care."

And look at that—they got it. They'd listened.

By the time they struck their final poses, Charlotte nearly burst with pride in these boys. They were going to be amazing. The audience would eat them up. And more importantly, Jules would be so proud.

The music ended and they held the moment for a beat. Then, after a pause, Cole started applauding, and the boys let out a cheer. High-fives wound their way around the group, and she dared a glance at their coach, to find him smiling. She really wished he'd do that more often.

"Wow," he said. "You guys killed it."

"We have a good teacher," Hotchke said. He draped an arm around Charlotte's shoulder and Charlotte slunk out from under it.

"You need a shower, Hotch," she said, eliciting laughs from the others.

"I can take a hint, Miss Page," he said.

"It wasn't exactly a hint," Asher said. "She came right out and told you you stink."

"All right," Charlotte said. "That was pretty good."

"Pretty good?" Dunbar's tone was incredulous. "Miss Page, we killed it."

"You did pretty good," she repeated. "But there's always room for improvement. Some of your moves were sloppy and, Greg, you were completely lost in section three."

"You saw that, huh?" Greg asked.

"I saw everything," she said. "That's my job. Remember, if you're on the stage, someone in the audience is always watching you. So, you can't slack off."

A quiet murmur worked its way through the room. "Promise me you'll practice this before our next rehearsal?"

"We're getting together tonight," Asher said. "In the parking lot of the high school."

"Okay, but don't let anyone else watch," Charlotte said. "We want it to be a surprise. You're dismissed. Good work today."

They congratulated themselves as they gathered their things and filtered out, saying goodbye to her and to Cole as they did.

Once the room had emptied, she found herself alone with Cole, and her nerves let her know exactly how they felt about that.

"Wow," he said. "How'd you do that?"

She picked up her water bottle. "Do what?"

"Get them to work together like that? That's the most cohesive I've ever seen them."

She shrugged. "I try to make it fun."

He held her gaze. "Fun."

She nodded. "It's taken me a long time to realize it, but fun is a great motivator."

"Obviously." He studied her for a beat. "Do you have fun when you dance?"

She shook her head. "I don't want it to feel like that for these boys. I want it to feel like it did for your sister. She always had the time of her life, every time she took the stage."

He half-smiled, but it was enough for her to spot a dimple in his left cheek. She hadn't noticed that before. It was nice.

She motioned for Cole to take a place on the floor. "We're going to pick up where we left off." Where they'd left off had been nowhere because once they learned Amelia wasn't coming to their last rehearsal, Charlotte had called it on account of her jittering nerves.

Would they betray her again today?

He slipped his hand around her waist.

Yep. The nerves were definitely little backstabbers.

"Let's just do a simple box step," she said. "The woman always leads with her right, which means—"

"I lead with my left."

She grinned. "You can be taught."

He rolled his eyes, then straightened, his grip on her hand firm. She counted him off and walked him through a 1-2-3 count, the most basic steps of a waltz.

And to her surprise, he caught on right away.

"I thought you said you were bad at this," she said.

He frowned. "Bad is an understatement."

She smiled. "Let's do it again." They'd worked their way up to moving around the floor when Amelia appeared in the doorway, Hildy at her side.

"You two look wonderful together," Hildy said, a sigh in her voice.

Charlotte stepped out of Cole's embrace. "Amelia, you're here."

The little girl turned shy.

"Are you ready to dance with your uncle?"

Amelia didn't respond. Brinley had told Charlotte that the week had been a productive one with Julianna's oldest. She'd danced in all of her classes, and she'd danced well. But maybe this dance, which she was supposed to do with her father, had a different sting.

"Why don't you two show her what you've done so far?" Hildy smiled softly at Charlotte. "We'll give her some time to warm into it."

"Good idea," Charlotte said. She returned to Cole, who still stood in the center of the floor while Hildy led Amelia off to the side.

Charlotte turned on some music—not their official song because she hadn't selected that yet—and led Cole in a circle around the room. When they returned to the place where they'd started, she lifted her chin to face him. "Okay, now you lead."

His arms went limp. "I'm not ready for that yet."

"Yes, you are," she said. She didn't give him time to think about it. Instead, she counted him off and waited for him before she moved. On her second "One-two-three" he nodded and off they went, the same way they'd done before, only this time, it was Cole who determined their direction.

It was his hand on her waist that guided her, and for the briefest moment, she let herself get lost in the most basic of moves.

They returned to the center of the room and came to a stop. She should step out of his arms. She should drag her gaze away. She should run for safety.

But she did none of those things.

Instead, she simply stared, memorizing the way it felt to be held.

Behind her, Hildy cleared her throat. "That was lovely. Cole, I had no idea you could dance."

"I can't," he said, still looking at Charlotte.

Finally, she took a step back. "Your turn, Amelia."

The little girl stood and stepped forward quietly and

stood in front of her uncle.

Cole smiled down at her. "Now the real test begins."

Amelia glanced up at him, a curious look in her eye.

"The real professional," he said. "I'm not sure I can keep up with you."

A shy smile crossed her lips, and something inside Charlotte's heart squeezed. "Are we ready?"

The pair nodded and Charlotte walked them through the first section of the dance. Cole wasn't as graceful as Amelia, but he never gave up, and after about forty-five minutes, they had a solid start.

They came to a stopping point, and Charlotte smiled. "I think we're going to have a winner on our hands."

Cole looked at Amelia, and the two of them smiled.

Amelia looked at Hildy, who'd parked herself off to the side. "What did you think, Miss Hildy?"

Hildy stood. "I think your uncle might need a little more rehearsal than you. You're kind of a pro." She looked at Charlotte and winked.

"Ouch," Cole said. "Hit a man while he's down, why don't ya?"

"I call it like I see it, kiddo." Hildy reached over and squeezed Cole's arm. "I'm sure Charlotte can get you up to Amelia's level. It's just going to take a little work."

There was a gleam in Hildy's eye that Charlotte didn't miss, though she pretended not to notice.

"Can we go back to the pool?" Amelia asked Hildy.

Hildy put a hand on the little girl's shoulder. "Sure, honey." She glanced at Charlotte, then at Cole. "We'll see you both later."

Amelia gathered her things into her dance bag, lifted her hand in a wave and walked out, Hildy close behind.

Charlotte slowly drew her eyes to Cole's.

"I'm a hopeless cause, aren't I?"

She laughed. "No. Not at all. But we can do some extra practicing if it makes you more comfortable. This really isn't easy if you've never done it before."

He groaned. "I'm going to make a complete fool of myself."

She stuck her hands on her hips. "Enough with the pity party. You have an excellent teacher."

At that, he smiled. "True. You've definitely made progress with my team. Gotta say, I was impressed."

"Really?"

He looked confused. "Yeah. I'm sure you've been told that before."

"Not so much," she said. "Mostly I perform. I've only done a little bit of teaching. Maybe that's why Connor hasn't gotten back to me about the studio." She walked toward the speaker and picked up her phone.

Cole frowned. "What about the studio?"

"I offered to buy it," she said.

His heavy sigh told her something was wrong.

"What is it?"

"It's just that he mentioned possibly selling to someone in Chicago." Cole looked genuinely pained to break the news, but once he did, she struggled to process it.

"He did?"

Cole shrugged. "Said he got an offer from someone wanting to buy the business. That's really all I know."

"Do you know if he took it?"

"I don't," Cole said.

"It was probably a longshot. I just got my hopes up," she said.

"Then convince him to sell it to you." The finality in his tone was unmistakable.

She scoffed. "How do I do that?"

He shrugged. "I don't know, but I bet you can think of something."

At the moment, she couldn't, but he was right, she didn't have to give up so quickly, especially since she didn't have any details about this possible sale. Besides, this was her second chance, her backup plan. And if it fell through, she wasn't sure what she'd do next.

34

The following day, Charlotte started her morning with a run that took her right past Julianna's house. She stopped in front of it and stared at the door. It was early. Connor probably wasn't even up yet.

She hadn't been able to sleep for fear of losing her chance of buying the dance studio, and honestly, it had tied a huge knot in her stomach.

She'd come here to take it over. She'd come because she wanted to be the one to carry on Julianna's dream. She'd come for absolution.

She marched toward the front door and knocked, aware that she might not be doing herself a favor showing up unannounced.

But when the door opened and Amelia stood on the other side of it, dressed and wearing a sparkly headband, she hoped she was in the clear.

"Miss Charlotte?" Amelia's big eyes stared at her.

"Hi, Amelia," she said. "How are you?"

"Fine." The little girl gave her a quizzical look. "You saw me yesterday."

"Right," she said. "Your turns are looking beautiful."

She smiled. "Thanks. Why are you here?"

"I'm here to see your dad," Charlotte said. "Is he here?"

Amelia turned. "Dad! Miss Charlotte is here to see you."

Connor emerged from another room, baby on his hip, looking slightly more alive than he had the last time she'd seen him. Charlotte smiled. Connor didn't.

"Charlotte?"

"Sorry to barge in on you," she said, stepping inside.

"I'm trying to get the kids ready for the babysitter," he said. "Can this wait?"

"Not really," she said. It wasn't true. It could wait. It wasn't life or death. And yet, it couldn't wait. Because if he sold the business to someone else and she missed her chance, she'd never forgive herself.

"Okay, well, here." He shoved the baby in her arms, and the little girl squirmed. "Follow me."

She did, straight through the house and into the sweetest nursery Charlotte could've imagined. The soft cream was accented by colors just slightly deeper than pastel and in the corner was a rocking chair. She could practically see Jules rocking her babies to sleep right there, singing a quiet lullaby.

"Charlotte?"

She turned to find Connor staring at her, holding a stack of diapers. "Sorry, what?"

"What's so important you showed up this early?"

She shifted the baby to her other hip and watched as he packed the diaper bag with all the necessities. He seemed better, but she wondered if he was just going through the motions.

"Don't sell the dance studio to that person from Chicago," she said.

He stopped packing and looked at her. "How'd you find out about that?"

"Doesn't matter," she said. "Sell it to me."

He shoved a small container of wipes and a change of clothes inside the bag and walked out of the room, Charlotte close on his heels.

"I know Julianna. I know what she wanted to do here," Charlotte said. "And I know I'm the person to carry on her legacy."

He was in the kitchen now, pouring coffee into a travel mug, and that's when she saw the threat of tears behind his eyes. The pain of thinking about Julianna was still so raw.

"I loved her, Connor," Charlotte said. "And I'm a good teacher."

"It's too late," he said. "I already sold it."

Charlotte's heart dropped straight to her feet. "You did?"

He shrugged. "I didn't have time to think about it. They made me a good offer."

"So, it's a done deal?"

He screwed the lid on his travel mug and took the baby from her. "I mean, there are papers to sign, but other than that, it's a done deal."

Amelia appeared in the doorway and took her sister from Connor. "We're going to be late."

Charlotte's eyes had filled with tears. She was so sure she knew what she was doing when she left the ballet. How could she be so wrong?

"I'll see you tonight, right, Miss Charlotte?" Amelia faced her now.

Charlotte nodded. "I'll be there to watch."

"What's tonight?" Connor asked.

"My dance class, Dad," Amelia said, her tone slightly exasperated. She walked out of the room. "We'll be in the car!"

Connor went still. "She's dancing again?"

Okay, so he definitely wasn't completely in the land of the living. Other people were still managing his life for him, and that was fine. But it meant that when it came to the studio, he didn't know yet what was best—not for the community or the students or for Julianna's memory.

"She's dancing," Charlotte said. "With me."

His face fell. "I didn't know."

She waited a moment before speaking. "Don't sign the papers."

"Charlotte—"

"Wait until after the recital," she said. "Come see how it goes, and if you still feel like you need to sell to this other buyer and turn her studio into something she would hate, so be it."

He paused at the door and smirked at her. "This is an interesting sales tactic."

She smiled. "I promise I will win you over. Please, Connor, let me at least try."

"I don't go back on my word," he said, pushing the door open.

She followed him outside. "I know, but you do have the right to change your mind." She grabbed his arm. "I know it might seem easier to just get this off your plate, but think about Amelia."

He frowned. "What about her?"

"Don't you want her dancing for someone who knew and loved her mother? That studio will radiate Jules if you sell it to me. If you sell it to someone who didn't know her, she just disappears."

His eyes flashed something terrible. "She already disappeared, Charlotte."

Her heart sputtered, her adrenaline coming to a complete halt. "No, I mean—"

"I'm late," he said. "I have to go."

And he left. Just like that. And Charlotte's new dream drove off with him.

35

Charlotte's days in Harbor Pointe unfolded with warmth and purpose. She'd found a way to fill her time quite nicely, and she'd settled into a new summer rhythm that made her heart thrum with happiness.

Her mornings started with a run by the lake. Coincidentally, she often ran by Cole's place at precisely the same time he was leaving for practice. She sometimes wondered (hoped) he waited until he saw her before exiting his house.

She worked with the football team and with Hildy and Steve. She checked in on the dance students. She met with the volunteers working on the recital. She ate breakfast daily with her new friends and repeatedly denied having a crush on Cole, a subject that seemed to come up frequently.

But it was getting harder and harder to deny that the part of her day she looked forward to most involved teaching the strong, handsome, unassuming football coach to waltz.

As discussed, she'd scheduled extra rehearsals with Cole, knowing that Amelia would pick up the steps much more quickly. Maybe she'd been overzealous in scheduling their rehearsals every other day, but she wanted the dance to be good. For Amelia. And maybe she'd been hypnotized by the way Cole looked at her when he thought she wasn't looking.

They'd been dancing together for two weeks now, and while normally that would lend itself to more comfort, Charlotte still found herself uneasy in his presence.

Cole made her nervous. Deliciously, excitedly nervous.

She arrived at the studio for that day's rehearsal and went inside just as Cole's truck stopped in the street. He skillfully maneuvered into a parking spot, turned off the engine, and got out. He made that look easy. Her still beat-up Jetta did not.

From just inside the door, she watched his every move, aware that she was holding her breath. Her insides turned a cartwheel as he met her eyes from the other side of the glass door.

Well, shoot. Her friends were right. She had a crush on Cole.

He pulled the door open and stepped inside, stopping on the opposite side of the counter, a hint of a smile on his face.

"Hey," he said.

She felt that smile all the way to her toes. She liked that he'd reserved it for her.

"Hey."

She led him to the back studio, the same way she had several times before. "I think we can put the finishing touches on the dance tonight."

"I practiced." He smiled. "I think I'm going to impress you."

"Is that right?" she asked. "I'm hard to impress."

"Believe me, I know."

Without another word, she turned on the song she'd

chosen—"Perfect" by Ed Sheeran. She turned around and found his eyes on her, and her pulse quickened. He watched as she moved toward him, then stepped in her place in front of him. His hand found her waist, and he pulled her closer, close enough that she drew in that familiar scent that hung faintly on her clothes after every rehearsal.

Cole wasn't a dancer, not the kind she was used to, but he was an excellent partner and took direction well. As they began to move, she realized that for the first time since they'd started working together, he was leading without her telling him to. His confidence seemed to be soaring.

They reached the end of what they knew and she stepped out of his embrace, the music still playing. "You have been practicing."

Shyness came over him, something that happened when he was complimented or recognized. His humility stunned her almost as much as his kindness. Her first impression of Cole Turner couldn't have been more wrong.

"Why the change?"

"I have Asher West to thank," he said.

"The quarterback."

"Yeah." He stuffed his hands in his pockets. "I've been trying to get him to play confidently for over a year, and today, in practice it dawned on me that everything I've been telling him about stepping up and being a leader, it's what I needed to do here."

"So you're a dancer now." She smirked.

His eyes widened. "Not even close. But hopefully my performance won't be humiliating."

She shook her head. "You're full of surprises, Coach."

His face turned serious for a moment, the way it sometimes did, in an unreadable expression she'd yet to crack. It was almost as if he had more to say, but every time they found themselves here, one of them pivoted.

"Let's go on, shall we?" She moved to the center of the floor, but he stood his ground, still watching her, eyes concentrating on her.

"Charlotte, has anyone ever kissed you?"

The words caught her so off-guard she couldn't find her voice.

He stood, unmoving, only a few feet away. "You said you've never dated anyone. I guess I just wondered."

Her face flushed. Why was she embarrassed to admit the truth? Because it made her feel unlovable? Or because it made her feel naïve? Or both?

"That's really personal," she said, mostly because she wasn't ready to admit this to him or anyone else.

"Sorry." He raked a hand through his hair, leaving it perfectly disheveled.

She found his eyes. "We should keep going."

"Right," he said.

She did her best to pull it together and teach him the end of the dance, but the only thing she could think about was what his lips might taste like and about a million different ways she could've answered his question.

Any one of them may have ended like a fantasy.

36

Cole spent the rest of the rehearsal kicking himself.

Never mind that he'd been wanting to ask her that question for days.

He wasn't proud of it, but he'd dipped back into the box of letters and found one from when Charlotte and Jules were in ninth grade. In it, Charlotte recapped Julianna's first kiss, peppering her with questions about what it was like *What did it feel like?* and *How did you know what you were doing?* and *Was it slobbery?*

He could only assume this was in response to whatever Julianna had shared in her previous letter.

And it was sweet and innocent, but if he hadn't already been wondering about her dating history, he certainly was now.

Because Charlotte Page had the kind of lips that needed to be kissed. Full and soft and the perfect shade of pink.

She made him think, for the first time since Gemma, that maybe it would be worth it to try again.

They finished the rehearsal and Charlotte gave him a

polite smile. He'd turned the air awkward between them, and he was desperate to change that.

"You hungry?" The words were out before he could properly consider them. She looked as startled by them as he was.

"Kind of," she said.

"I'm guessing you've never been to a fair," he said.

She frowned, but a smile played at the corners of her lips. "What makes you say that?"

"Just a hunch."

"Yeah, I've never been to a fair." She turned off the Bluetooth speaker and faced him. "Why?"

He shrugged. "They have corndogs and funnel cakes."

She laughed. "Two things I cannot imagine myself eating."

"Hey, don't knock it till you try it." He was trying to keep the tone light, but he feared he was failing. He didn't do "light." Heck, he didn't even do "friendly."

Apparently, he did do "forward" and, he feared, "creepy."

"Nobody told me there was a fair in town," Charlotte said.

"Just outside of town," he said. "Small towns love their fairs and festivals. Pretty much one every weekend in the summer somewhere around here." He watched her. "Wanna go?"

"Sure," she said quickly.

"Yeah?"

"Yeah." She smiled.

Why did he feel like he'd just won the lottery?

And why did something like a warning bell ring out at the back of his mind?

Time with Charlotte was dangerous, but he wouldn't do anything to risk his heart. Not again. He'd just take her out for fair food and make sure she had a good time.

Something she would've written about to Julianna if it had happened before his sister died.

Not a date. Just two friends hanging out.

Never mind that he couldn't get her vanilla scent out of his mind or that he was resisting the urge to put a hand on the small of her back and lead her out to his truck, as if she needed guiding. As if she were his to guide.

"Well, I guess I can cross 'going to the fair' off my bucket list," she said.

"Along with 'eat a cinnamon roll,'" he added, opening the passenger side door to the truck. "And get flowers from a good-looking man."

Her smile dazzled. Wow, she was pretty.

"And also 'take a hopeless cause and teach him to dance.'" She pulled herself up into the truck and he closed the door, unable to keep from smiling at her flirtation.

Maybe it was dangerous. Maybe all this could ever be was him taking a girl to the fair for her very first funnel cake.

Or maybe this time it would be different. More like Julianna and Connor and not at all like he and Gemma.

Was it too much to hope for?

He didn't know, but as he started the engine, he realized a very real part of him wanted to find out. He wanted to test the waters, to take a chance.

And while that excited him a little, mostly it scared him to death.

37

Charlotte and Cole maneuvered through the crowd of people, the smell of popcorn and something fried permeating the air. Twice she'd nearly been knocked over—once by a woman carrying not one, but two children (easily forgiven) and once by a guy on his phone who didn't even say he was sorry (not so easily forgiven).

"You okay?" Cole said after the second one nearly landed her in the dirt.

She nodded.

"I'm afraid the fair isn't making a good first impression." He held his hand out to her, and she stared at it like it was a foreign object.

"My crowd survival skills are excellent," he said.

Slowly, she slipped her hand in his. It was an altogether different experience than when her most recent dance partner, Jameson, took her hands. First of all, Jameson got regular manicures, so his skin was smoother than hers. Second of all, holding on to Jameson had never once elicited the kind of spark that her skin on Cole's had.

"Why did you ask if anyone had ever kissed me?" The

words were out before she could consider the ramifications of asking. "I'm sorry, I didn't mean to ask that."

He glanced over at her as he led her through the crowd. "I'm sorry about that."

"Don't be sorry," she said.

They cut through the throng of people and he stopped. "I was curious, I guess."

"Are you still?"

"Curious?" He eyed her. "Yeah."

She swallowed, then licked her lips, a horrifying reflex and the result of thinking about the fact that she most certainly had never been kissed.

Did that make her pathetic?

She looked up and realized they were in a line. "Have we reached our destination?"

He followed her eyes to a small white trailer that advertised an assortment of *delicious snacks*, all of which were certainly not on her diet.

"We have," he said.

They seemed to realize he was still holding her hand at the same moment, and he quickly dropped it as if he'd done something wrong.

"You know I can't eat here," she said.

"Yeah, yeah." He brushed her off.

"I'm serious," she said with a smile. "It would only take a few bad meals to undo years of discipline."

He dropped her hand and leveled her gaze. "Who told you that?"

She looked away. Marcia. Always Marcia.

"Someone filled your head with a lot of nonsense," he said. "You're at the fair for the first time ever. You're going to eat fair food."

The sound of a live band rang out in the warm night as fireflies danced on the breeze. She followed the sound to a large white tent, dimly lit inside with tables around the perimeter and a dance floor in the center.

"Have you ever done that?" She motioned to the tent with a nod.

"Sure," he said. "They have good bands in there."

"But the dancing," she said. "Have you ever done that?"

They moved forward in line. "Uh, no. I haven't."

She eyed him for a long, amusing moment.

"What?"

"I'll try this food that's probably going to make me throw up or gain fifteen pounds if you will give me one dance."

He stepped out of the line, hands up. "I'm out."

"Wow, I didn't peg you for a quitter." She grinned. She wasn't positive, but she thought maybe she was flirting. She'd never really tried it before—who was she going to flirt with when she was surrounded by gay or married men? Maybe she'd just discovered a new talent. Maybe she was an expert flirter.

He stepped back in line.

She did a poor job of stifling her smug smile.

When it was their turn, he stepped forward and ordered two corndogs, drinks, and one funnel cake, which she learned was large enough to share between two people.

To be perfectly honest, the thought of eating the corndog completely grossed her out, but a deal was a deal. They got their food (the corndog was ridiculously oversized), then made their way to a different tent, one lined with picnic tables, and sat across from each other. Every once in a while, Cole lifted a hand or tossed one of those very manly "guy nods" at someone by way of a greeting.

Two different parents she'd met at the dance studio stopped to say hello to Charlotte, which surprised her. She hadn't expected to recognize anyone at this fair. Was this what life in a small town was like?

"Okay." Cole interrupted her thoughts. "Are you ready for this?"

"Typically eating food on a stick is against my better judgment," she said, inhaling the doughy smell of the food between them.

"Going out in public is against my better judgment, but here we are." The expression on his face changed in such a way that it made her think perhaps he hadn't meant to say that out loud.

"Why is that?" she asked.

He waved her off and nodded toward the corndog. "Bottom's up."

She picked up the corndog and stared at it.

"You're looking at it like it's an alien baby," he said.

She laughed. "It might as well be."

He dunked his in the glob of ketchup he'd squeezed onto his wrapper, so she did the same. Then, he held it up as if it were a wine glass and he was giving a toast. She touched her corndog to his and he flashed her a dimpled smile. And wow—what a smile it was.

"Cheers," he said.

"Cheers." She took a bite, surprised by the mix of flavors that filled her mouth—the fried batter, the tangy ketchup, a hint of salty meat—it was good.

It was good?

She chewed, savoring the bite as if it were a delicacy.

"Well?" He swallowed, then wiped his mouth with a napkin he'd balled up in his fist.

She shook her head. "I can't believe I'm going to say this . . ."

He grinned. "Good, right?"

"So good." She felt her eyes widen as she took another bite. "Why have I never had one of these before?"

His smile faded, turning to a lopsided grin. "I don't know, why haven't you?"

"Why don't you go out in public?"

"Touché."

"The answer is no," she said.

He stopped chewing. "And what was the question?"

She watched as realization came over him. The kissing question. The one she'd avoided since he asked.

"Oh," he said. "Well, that's surprising."

"Is it?"

"Someone who looks like you—never been kissed? Very." He took another bite.

She shook her head. "Kind of embarrassing to admit it. I'm almost thirty."

He shrugged. "You were busy, you know, being amazing."

She waved him off with a smile. "Oh, how would you even know?"

"Google." He held back a smile.

"You Googled me?" She set her corndog down and leveled his gaze. "And?"

"And . . ." He gave her his undivided attention. "Blew me away."

She couldn't find words to respond. She was too amazed by the fact that he'd looked her up at all. Why had he done that?

And why had he told her? It would be a lot more difficult to ignore her little crush now, especially since that little crush wasn't so little anymore.

38

After the discussion about her lack of a love life, they ate in silence for a few minutes. Charlotte was shocked to realize that not only was she going to finish the entire corndog, she was going to have room to eat *at least* her share of that funnel cake.

The awkward silence that used to exist between them had vanished, and in its place was a comfortable familiarity. For the first time, Charlotte didn't feel the need to fill the space with chatter.

"We were out in public when I found out about Gemma," he said without looking at her.

She stopped mid-bite, set her food down, and gave him her full attention. Cole telling her this felt somewhat monumental—after all, he'd never opened up to her about himself.

"It was at a wedding, actually." He took a drink of his soda. "I hate weddings."

She looked away. "My partner Jameson got married two years ago. That's the only wedding I've ever been to."

"Your partner?"

"Dance partner."

"Ah." Cole took another bite. Chewed. Swallowed. "Gemma was seeing this guy, Max, well, you met him at the rehearsal."

She remembered. She'd been so relieved when Brinley told her the following day that Gemma and Max had withdrawn from the recital. That she'd ever tried to be a part of it at all still astounded Charlotte. It said a lot about the kind of woman Cole's ex was.

Her heart squeezed with empathy for him.

"So, they were a thing behind my back, but it turns out she wasn't very discreet. Pretty much everyone in town knew before me."

"And no one told you?"

He shrugged. "That bugged me for a long time. Most people said they hoped they'd heard wrong or they didn't want it to be true. It was small-town gossip. They thought they were protecting me, I guess."

She stilled. "I'm sorry."

"I'm over it," he said.

A lie if she'd ever heard one.

"I'm *trying* to get over it," he added, as if reading her mind. "I just felt so stupid. She made me feel so stupid. Just for trusting her."

"It shouldn't be like that," she said quietly. A man should be able to trust his wife.

"Anyway," he said, "it's a long story."

"I'm listening." She rolled what was left of her corndog in the ketchup, but her appetite was gone. Why did it bother her to think that not very long ago he'd had his heart broken? To think that perhaps there was a reason he was the way he was, like Lucy had said? Like everyone had said, come to think of it.

If there was a reason, somehow it excused his rudeness.

And if she excused that, he became nearly perfect. And that scared her to death.

"So, why would that one wedding make you not want to go out anymore?" she asked. "I'm sure you've been out lots of times where you didn't have terrible things happen."

"No, it wasn't the wedding. It was what came after," he said. "Everyone heard about what happened. Everyone knew that now I knew about Gemma and Max. My failed marriage became the talk of the town." He sucked more soda down through his straw, then looked at her. "People look at you differently, you know? Like, you walk in a room and everyone goes quiet. Or they try to mother you or bring you food."

"Pity pastries," she said knowingly.

He let out a light laugh. "Right. It just got easier to stay at home."

"I'm sorry that happened to you, Cole," she said.

"Yeah, me too." He looked down at the funnel cake and raised an eyebrow. "Are you even ready for this?"

The abrupt shift to light-hearted conversation took her off guard.

"I don't think you are." He smiled down at the plate.

The air between them shifted, and she told herself not to be greedy. He'd told her something personal, answering questions that had been on her mind for weeks. Never mind that his words only brought up more questions.

She tore off a bite of funnel cake and popped it in her mouth.

"So far, all you've done is introduce me to a lot of extra calories," she said with a laugh. She took a swig of water and told herself that was enough food for one night—but the sugary fried dough pulled her back again and again.

It was delicious. Marcia would blow a gasket if she saw her eating this way.

"I'm just showing you what you've been missing." He grinned. "And if you close your eyes, maybe you can pretend we're about to go to your senior prom or something." He nodded toward the tent where the music still rang out into the darkening night sky.

"I remember Julianna sent me a prom photo once, ages ago." She stood and met him on his side of the picnic table. "She went with a guy named—"

"Franklin Styles," he interrupted.

Charlotte laughed. "Yes! Franklin Styles. What kind of name is that?"

"I hated that guy," Cole said. Spoken like a true big brother.

"Jules thought he was *so cute*." She was sure to put proper emphasis on those last two words. "I remember being so jealous of that dress and that hair and that boy."

They followed the sound of the music toward the big white tent. As they reached the doorway, he stopped and offered her his arm. "Charlotte Page, will you be my date to the county fair barn dance?"

She laughed. "Of course." She laced her arm through his and he led her inside. The lights were dim, and there were people scattered all around the tent's interior. A bar had been set up on one side, and at the opposite end of the entrance, a band stood on a stage and played a rowdy song Charlotte had never heard. There were a lot of people out on the dance floor, but the way they were moving wasn't exactly what she'd call "dance."

Other people mingled, some sitting at the tables outlining the space, some moving through the crowd of people. Charlotte tried to stick close to Cole, but she wasn't great at pushing her way through a crowd. He reached back and grabbed her hand, keeping her close, until they reached a table with faces she recognized.

Lucy, Quinn, Quinn's husband, Haley, and Betsy, along with a few people she hadn't met, were gathered around a table.

When they walked up, everyone stopped talking to say hello, and Charlotte nearly cried, she felt so welcome. Having friends wasn't something she was used to. Walking up to a group of dancers usually elicited cold shoulders and a pointed side-eye.

The raucous music ended and the band began to play a slow song. Quinn and her husband disappeared onto the dance floor, and Charlotte turned to find Cole watching her.

"Should we get this over with?" she said with a smile.

He leaned in closer and whispered in her ear, "I'd rather take my time."

Charlotte's heart sped up as he took her hand and led her to the dance floor. The song was unfamiliar, but his arm around her waist was not. She'd grown accustomed to his nearness, but here Cole didn't hold her hand out to the side in a formal dance pose, he held it close and pressed it against his chest.

He held her differently now, his face dipped down toward hers, both of them enveloped by an intimate darkness. She clung to him more tightly, and as they moved, the rest of the world seemed to melt away.

"I wasn't completely honest with you." His voice in her ear tickled the skin on her neck.

She didn't move when she asked, "You weren't?"

He shook his head. "I didn't only ask if anyone ever kissed you because I was curious."

She looked up, her face so close to his they nearly touched. His eyes were squarely on her, sending a shock of nervous energy down her spine. "Why did you ask?"

She'd seen hundreds of movies with moments exactly

like this one, but standing there in his arms, unaware of anything else happening around them, she begged her knees not to buckle, her palms to stop sweating. How surreal that she found herself in this space at this moment with this man. Perhaps Cole was the biggest surprise that had come her way since quitting the ballet.

"Because I was too chicken to tell you what I was really thinking."

She found his eyes, leveled his gaze, stopped moving. "Which was?"

"Well." He slipped a hand up her arm, letting it rest on the back of her neck. "That I want to kiss you."

The air between them sparked, and she forced herself not to run away. She'd been putting up a wall between them every time they almost reached this point, and now, here it was, out in the open. There was no running away from what he'd just said.

"You do?" Her voice was thin and small.

He nodded. "But not here in front of everyone. Can we go?"

She nodded. He clung to her hand, but as they turned to go, Cole came to an abrupt halt. She peered out from behind him and saw they were standing face-to-face with Gemma, whose cheeks were streaked black with tears that had cut through her mascara.

"Cole, can we talk?" she asked.

His hand tightened around Charlotte's, but it felt more like an involuntary motion than a purposeful one. He glanced down at her, but she didn't say anything.

She had no right to tell him to ignore Gemma and leave with her, and if there was one thing she'd learned about Cole Turner, it was that if someone needed him—even someone who'd treated him as badly as Gemma had—he was going to bend over backward to help.

She loved that about him.

Except right now, knowing that he was about to leave her alone at a fair she hadn't exactly wanted to come to, she also hated it.

"Will you wait for me?" he asked. "I'll be right back."

Charlotte looked at Gemma, who wiped her cheeks dry with the back of her hand. "I'll just see you later," she said. "I'll go home with Lucy."

"Charlotte, no." He turned to her. "I'll be right back."

She looked him square in the face and forced herself to smile. "No, you won't."

And then she turned and walked away.

39

Cole followed Gemma out of the noisy tent and into the warm summer air, kicking himself for choosing her over Charlotte. It was so *Gemma* to show up at that exact moment.

A few yards away from the tent was a playground and, beyond that, a makeshift parking lot. They reached the swing set and Cole stopped. "What is this about, Gemma?"

She sat down on a swing, and Cole's mind wandered back to the day she told him she was pregnant. They'd only been dating three months, and sleeping with her had never been the plan. But Gemma could be very persuasive, and even though Cole tried to resist, his flesh was weak.

Somehow, her getting pregnant felt like a punishment he deserved. He'd never forget the moment she told him. His heart twisted into a ball of regret, followed by a healthy dose of fear. Because Cole was certain, that while he was a pretty great uncle, he wasn't ready to be a dad.

It had never occurred to him to ask if the baby was his. Of course it was. Gemma wasn't the type of girl to sleep around. So, he proposed. It was the right thing to do. They planned their wedding in record speed, as if that would stop people from talking, but three weeks after they got married, Gemma miscarried.

Cole got a call at work, and he rushed out without telling anyone where he was going. He arrived at the hospital in a matter of minutes, hurried in, and found her laying in a bed, covered with a sheet, staring off at the ceiling.

A nurse met him in the doorway. "Are you the husband?"

He nodded. "What's wrong? Is she okay?"

"I'm sorry, sir," she said quietly. "She lost the baby."

Cole's stomach sank.

The nurse squeezed his arm. "I think she's in a little bit of shock."

He nodded, holding back tears, then made his way to the side of Gemma's bed. He pulled up a chair and took her hand. A tear streamed down her cheek, and she closed her eyes.

"Are you relieved?" she asked.

He frowned. "Why would I be relieved?"

Her eyes fluttered open, and she looked at him. "Because you never wanted this baby in the first place."

"I wanted this baby," he said. "It might've taken some getting used to, but you know I was all in. I still am." It was true. He'd warmed to the idea, so much so that this miscarriage hurt.

They'd mourned together, promised each other they'd try again when the time was right, and that whole experience brought them closer. Maybe they wouldn't have gotten married if it hadn't been for her pregnancy, but Cole was committed to Gemma. He was convinced they could make it work.

Which was why her betrayal hurt so badly. He never

would've cheated on her. It never would've even occurred to him. He'd given up everything for her, and she repaid him with a knife in his back.

Now, she took hold of the empty swing beside her and shook it. "Sit?"

He let out a heavy sigh. "I can't stay."

She looked up at him through fresh tears that seemed to keep coming. "Do you need to get back to your girlfriend?"

Cole leaned against the metal pole of the swing set. "She's not my girlfriend."

Gemma eyed him for several seconds, as if deciding whether or not to believe him. "But you like her."

He wasn't having this conversation with her. "What do you want, Gemma?"

She looked away. She planted her feet on the ground but pushed herself back and forth. "Will you sit down for a minute?"

He hesitated. He didn't want to do anything she asked. He wanted to run and find Charlotte, apologize to her for leaving, then kiss her senseless the way he'd been thinking about doing for weeks now.

"Please, Cole?"

He sat, the sides of the swing digging into his thighs. "Can we make it quick?"

She looked up at him. "I'm sorry."

His stomach turned. "Okay."

"I need you to know that I know how wrong it was, what I did." She wiped away the tears as they fell. Gemma had always been great at emoting. She was a master manipulator—could he even believe a word she said?

"I was so wrong." She buried her face in her hands. "You were always so good and kind, and I was too stupid to see it."

He'd prayed for this day, the day she finally realized

what a terrible mistake she'd made—the day he got his revenge. He'd played it out in his mind, and it always ended with him spitting out some insult and walking away. Now that they were here, though, he couldn't think of a single word that would properly convey what he was thinking.

Gemma had torn his heart out and stomped on it, more than once. She'd ruined him for all future relationships. Why, then, was he resisting the urge to comfort her, to tell her it was okay?

"Once upon a time, I really loved you, Gemma," he said. "I thought we'd be together forever." He avoided her eyes.

"But now?"

He shrugged. "Now things are different. You're with Max, and I—" No. He wouldn't tell her anything about where he was. She hadn't earned that right.

"And if I wasn't?"

He leaned forward, elbows on his knees, and focused on the ground. "If you weren't what?"

"With Max." She'd stopped swaying and now turned all of her attention on him.

He drew in a breath. This was uncharted territory. He'd always believed that marriage vows were eternal. She'd never been faithful to those vows, but he had. He hadn't been with anyone else since the day he met Gemma, not even on a date.

But he'd spent the last several months trying to forget her—to forgive her even though she wasn't sorry—to move on.

That was the extent of his thoughts about Gemma. He didn't have capacity to consider anything else.

"You're not with Max?"

She buried her face in her hands and cried, shaking her head. "It happened again, Cole."

He frowned. "What happened?"

"I lost another one."

Cole stilled.

"I know it's not your job to console me, especially after everything I've done to hurt you—"

Cole stiffened, then forced a question. "What did Max say?"

Gemma scoffed. "He said it was better this way. Said a baby would complicate everything."

Cole didn't point out that for a married man, yes, a baby with his mistress would absolutely complicate things.

"He was just so flippant." She reached over and took Cole's hand. He didn't move. "I guess I took for granted how kind you were the first time I miscarried."

"You took a lot of things for granted, Gemma."

"I know, Cole," she said. "I'm sorry."

He pulled his hand away. They'd been here before. In fact, this was how they started. The only reason she'd ever come on to Cole in the first place was because she wanted to make Max jealous. It worked too. Max came running back, but Gemma failed to break things off with Cole.

And then she got pregnant, and Max reacted then exactly as he had reacted now, and Gemma got scared. So, she seduced Cole and told him the baby was his. She knew Cole would do the right thing. After she miscarried, Max returned, and the affair started up again, making Cole the biggest fool in the world.

He'd fallen in love with a wife and unborn baby that were never his.

"Gemma, you don't deserve this," Cole said. "I don't know why you're giving this guy the best of you when he's clearly not doing the same. You deserve better." He was surprised to discover he meant it. And while he knew Gemma didn't love him, not really, he did want to see her with someone other than Max.

Nobody deserved to be mistreated like this.

She dragged the back of her arm across her nose, still crying. "I really messed up with you."

He shrugged. "Yeah, you did."

She found his eyes. "Would you ever want to start over? Try again?"

The ill-timed question hung there, and while his heart knew the answer, his sense of duty seemed to be arguing.

Her phone buzzed in her pocket, and she pulled it out, looked at it, and then looked at Cole. "It's him."

He didn't say anything as she clicked a button, then held the phone to her ear.

"Gem, I'm so sorry." The volume was up loud enough that Cole could hear Max on the other end. "Where are you?"

Gemma looked at him. "I'm with Cole."

Just like that, he was plunged back into a world he'd tried to leave behind a thousand times. The world where he was the pawn in Gemma's game with Max. Their relationship was the unhealthiest thing he'd ever seen, and the fact that Cole had ever been in the middle of it would always remain one of his biggest regrets.

He stood.

She pulled the phone away and covered it with her hand. "Where are you going?"

"I forgive you, Gemma," he said. "But you need to get a little self-respect. That starts by dumping that guy."

"And what, be alone?"

And that's when he realized Gemma's insecurities made her do what she did. She believed she wasn't worthy of being loved. She believed that this—Max—was all she deserved. She sabotaged everything else. She thrived on the pain Max inflicted. She seemed to crave it.

"I heard someone say once that you'll accept the love

you think you deserve," he said. "I don't know why you don't think you're worth it, Gemma, but I hope someday someone comes along and you realize you deserve better than Max."

She stood.

"I'm sorry I wasn't the one to make you see it," Cole said. "But being alone is better than this."

40

The day after the fair, Charlotte woke up early and checked her phone.

Nothing. No calls or texts from Cole, leaving her with the memory of him and Gemma walking off into the darkness together. She'd returned to the table where Lucy and the rest of her new friends sat, and when her roommate asked what happened to Cole, it took everything in Charlotte's power not to cry.

"Um, Gemma showed up," she said, swallowing the lump at the back of her throat. "She was upset—crying."

"And he left?" Lucy practically spat the words.

She nodded, aware that her lower lip was trembling.

A collective concern wound its way around the table—not for Gemma and not for Charlotte, but for Cole.

"This is what she does," Betsy said. "She's a snake."

"She seemed genuinely upset," Charlotte said, though she wasn't sure why she was defending her. By now, even she was suspicious of Gemma's motives.

"I'm sure she was," Lucy said. "Max probably spent the weekend with his wife."

They sat in silence for several seconds, then Lucy turned to Charlotte. "Are you okay?"

"I kind of want to go home," she said. "But my car is at the studio."

Lucy nodded. "I'll take you."

They made their way out of the tent into the darkness, and Lucy sighed. "You really like him, huh?"

Charlotte kept her eyes ahead of her as they walked around the outskirts toward the fair entrance. "If there's a chance they can patch things up, they should. They were married."

Lucy shook her head. "They might've been married, but Gemma was never faithful. Cole deserves better."

Now, lying in bed, light streaming through the window, Charlotte tried to name the emotions bubbling up inside her. She'd let herself get too close to Cole, and that had been a mistake. He was clearly still sorting through his feelings for Gemma—and even she knew marriage vows meant something, even if they'd gotten divorced. Charlotte wasn't about to come in between a possible reconciliation.

A knock on the door drew her attention. "Come in."

The door opened, and she expected to see Lucy, but it was Cole standing on the other side.

She pulled the covers up to her neck. "Oh, hey."

"Hey," he said. "Can we talk? Downstairs, I mean?"

"How'd you get in here?"

"It's Harbor Pointe," he said. "No one locks their doors."

That was a fact. Charlotte always locked it on her way to bed, but Lucy must not have done the same when she left for work. "Why didn't you call?"

He watched her for a long moment. "I guess I wanted to see your face."

"I'm not even out of bed yet," she said.

He grinned. "Yeah, I timed it perfectly."

She threw a pillow as he closed the door. "I'll be downstairs," he called from the hallway.

She hurried to make herself presentable—brushed her teeth, brushed her hair, put on her bra—then made her way downstairs and found him sitting on the porch.

She braced herself for whatever he was about to say. After all, he could be here to tell her that he and Gemma were going to try again. And she'd have to pretend that it wasn't breaking her heart.

She pulled open the front door and found a cup of hot coffee from Hazel's Kitchen waiting for her.

"What, no pity pastries?" she asked as she sat down next to him.

He produced a small white bag. "Give me some credit."

She smiled, took the bag, opened it, and inhaled the aroma of a fresh cinnamon roll.

"I wanted to apologize in person for leaving so abruptly last night," he said.

She rolled the top of the bag closed and set it aside. "It's okay."

"No," he said, "it's not. But I think it was good I talked to Gemma."

"Yeah?" Charlotte dared a glance in his direction, bracing herself for whatever emotion she might find on his face, but she found this particular look unreadable.

He held his cup of coffee with both hands, leaning forward with his elbows on his knees. "I think I actually forgave her."

Charlotte stilled. "Wow, that's a big deal."

"You have no idea," he said. He took a drink.

She looked away as a car drove by. Down the block, a jogger rounded the corner and disappeared.

"Gemma kind of tricked me into marrying her," he said.

Charlotte remained still, not wanting to spook him. Was she finally going to get the rest of the story?

"I didn't know it, but when I started dating her, she and Max had already been an item for several months," he said. "She found me one night and struck up a conversation with the sole purpose of making Max jealous. He was at the same restaurant with his wife."

Cole talked and Charlotte listened, knowing without having to ask that Cole didn't share this story with many people. How lucky was she that he trusted her enough to share it with her? It didn't surprise her that he'd married Gemma when she turned up pregnant. It did surprise her to learn the baby wasn't his.

"The baby was Max's," he said now. "That's the bomb Max dropped at the wedding. He stormed in and started an argument with her that turned into a fight. Of course, I got in the middle of it—punched him, in fact—and Max . . ."

His voice trailed off, as if his pain had silenced him.

She reached over and put a hand on his arm, hoping it gave him the courage to continue.

"He was sitting there on the floor, holding his nose, and he looked up at Gemma and said, 'When are you going to tell him the truth about the baby?'"

She wanted to hug him. She may have never been in love, but it wasn't hard to imagine what that revelation had done to him. Was it wrong she wanted to hold him until that sadness drifted away?

"What's really awful is, when he heard about the miscarriage, Max came back," Cole said. "And they picked up right where they left off."

"That's why," she said.

"Why what?"

"Why you're so closed off."

"Because it just feels like everyone lies," he said. "And I hate lying more than anything."

Charlotte's heart twisted. There were things about her he didn't know. Old, childish, stupid mistakes—but they mattered. Hearing him talk like this, she knew they mattered. She should come clean, and she knew it, but she couldn't find the words. And while she knew that the closer she got to Cole the harder it would be to tell him the truth, she couldn't ruin this moment.

"I'm really sorry."

"Don't be," he said. "I think I finally got a clear picture of all of this last night. I realized that Gemma has spent all these years trying to make Max love her. For whatever reason, she thinks she can earn that love when really, she should be with someone who accepts her for who she is. That's what love is, right?"

Charlotte looked away. "I don't know. Is it?"

He stilled. "Yeah, it is."

She let herself meet his eyes—a mistake, probably, because she was fighting back tears. "I don't really know much about love."

A smile played at the corner of his mouth. "Me neither, but I do know it doesn't have to be earned," he said. "Not the real kind anyway—that kind is given. No strings. No conditions."

She scoffed. "I definitely don't know anything about that."

He took her hand. "You do now."

She stared at their intertwined fingers, and her pulse quickened as he hitched the thumb of his free hand under her chin and turned her face toward him. Charlotte's heart raced as he leaned in closer, closing the gap between them.

He's going to kiss me. Her mind repeated it over and over, and she shifted back.

"Sorry, I—" Cole looked away.

"No," she said, "I'm sorry. I'm just nervous."

He locked eyes with her. "About what?"

She didn't dare look away. "What if I'm terrible at this?"

"Not a chance."

"I might be," she said, feeling like a teenager.

His face lit into a bright smile, and he shook his head. "Then we'll keep practicing."

Charlotte had spent years imagining what it would feel like to kiss someone, but in all of her daydreaming, she couldn't have taken into account the deep emotions that would accompany this moment. Because it wasn't about the kiss.

It was about Cole. And about her. And about the way he made her feel, the words he'd just said.

If love was really unconditional, if it didn't need to be earned, she could stop striving so hard. She could simply be herself.

His hand wound up into her hair as he pulled her toward him. A shiver raced down her spine and straight back up again, anticipation bubbling through her body.

She knew it was customary to close your eyes when kissing, but she didn't. And neither did he. Instead, he watched her with such a fierce intensity it nearly melted her into a puddle of lava on the ground.

He took his free hand and slid her even closer, then placed a kiss so soft, so sweet on her lips that it stunned her. She closed her eyes and let his kiss fill her up, pressing her hand against his chest and imagining for a moment that the rest of the world had disappeared.

She was overcome by the very idea of him. How had he won her heart so completely in such a short period of time?

He took her face in his hands and kissed her so fully it took her breath away. Every one of her daydreams paled in comparison to the way his kiss made her feel, like maybe she'd finally found the something more she'd been searching for.

41

Kissing Charlotte could quite possibly rival football as his favorite pastime.

She was beautiful, of course, but that's not what he fell asleep thinking about. She had this *way* about her. Strong, yet elegant. And he adored the heck out of her. She was talented and hard-working, and she was going to make this recital happen for Julianna, her way of honoring his sister. The way she worked with Amelia only solidified what he knew—Charlotte loved his people.

He loved that about her.

If he didn't already know how much happier he was, Bilby and the guys on his team would've made sure to point it out. There had been more than one wisecrack at practice about "that goofy smile" on Cole's face.

What was he supposed to do—deny it? He was happy.

Cautiously, deliriously happy.

A few days after their first kiss, Cole called Charlotte in the morning and asked if she wanted to go out that night on a proper date.

"My first date," she said. "Where will we go?"

"It's a surprise," he said.

"Okay." He could practically hear her smile through the phone.

That night, he arrived to pick her up, and Lucy opened the door before he could knock. "You know this is her first date," she said.

"I know."

"Like, ever."

"Yeah, we talked about it," he said.

"So, where are you taking her? You're going to make it special, right?"

"I got it, Lucy," he said.

Charlotte appeared at the top of the stairs, and he felt like a teenager all over again, watching in awe as the light revealed her beauty. She reached the bottom of the stairs, and Lucy gave him a shove.

"You're in a trance, teddy bear," she said.

He couldn't take his eyes off of Charlotte, this gorgeous, unexpected, adorably sweet woman who, he feared, had stolen his heart so completely, it wasn't likely he'd ever get it back.

"You look beautiful," he said.

And she did. Her hair fell in long waves past her shoulders, and her lips shimmered with a glossy pink shine. Her eyes were so wide and stunning he knew it would be a matter of seconds before he was completely lost in them.

"So do you," she said. "Handsome, I mean." She glanced at Lucy, then back at Cole.

"Shall we?"

He'd put a lot of thought into this date. He didn't need Lucy to tell him the pressure he was under to make it special. He already knew.

He led her out to the truck, feeling a strange nervous energy he hadn't expected.

"Thanks for agreeing to go out with me," he said.

She smiled shyly. "Thanks for asking."

As they drove, she talked about working with his football players, about some of the other couples she'd met, about how she'd watched Amelia in dance class the other day and how much better she seemed to be doing.

"Her teacher thinks maybe she got over her hesitation," she said.

"Good," he said. "That was because of you, you know."

She stared out the window. "Or because of your bet."

He watched her for a few seconds, then smiled. "We'll share the credit."

Her eyes sparkled in recognition as he made the turn into the long driveway at Haven House.

He didn't explain. Instead, he drove straight past the farmhouse and behind the barn, where he parked the truck and turned off the engine.

"What are we doing here?" she asked.

"You'll see." He opened his door. "Stay there." He made his way around to the other side of the truck, opened her door, and helped her to the ground.

He took both of her hands and found her eyes. "I forgot to give you something."

Her brow furrowed with a question as he leaned in and kissed those lips he'd begun to crave.

When he pulled away, he found her smiling.

He took her hand and led her away from the house, away from the barn and down a trail he'd memorized a long time ago.

"I don't know if I'm dressed for this."

He did a once-over of her sundress and sandals. "We won't be walking long. And I like what you're wearing."

She squeezed his hand and soldiered on—only a few more minutes until they came through the trees and into a clearing, with a clear view of a hidden waterfall that used to bring him comfort every time he trekked out here.

Charlotte gasped when she saw it, the light of a setting sun glimmering off the water. "What is this place?"

"Pretty, right?" He let go of her hand and she stepped toward the water, awe on her face.

"Beautiful."

"I found it when I was living at Haven House," he said.

"You found it?"

Cole shoved his hands in his pockets. "Yeah, Steve and Hildy never told us about anything we might find on the grounds. They wanted us to explore for ourselves."

Charlotte glanced over at him.

"They thought it taught us to look beyond what was in plain sight. Said if we were willing to be curious, we never knew what we'd find."

She smiled. "I love that."

"Yeah," he said. "They're pretty smart people."

"And the picnic table? Did you just discover that too?" She turned and looked at it. He'd covered it with a tablecloth and placed a vase of wildflowers at its center. On it was a picnic basket filled with a selection of sandwiches, two with gluten-free bread, a cheese platter, a bottle of wine, and dessert.

Nerves swirled inside him as he watched her explore the space.

"Did you do all this?" she asked, pulling food from the basket.

He shrugged. "I might've."

"It's so perfect," she said.

"Just wait till the sun sets," he said. "You'll never find a better view of the stars."

They ate and kissed and danced under the light of the moon. Charlotte was so authentic, so genuine, it had taken meeting her to realize his life with Gemma had always been built on make-believe.

As the evening wound down, they lay on a blanket in the grass, her head on his chest, and he whispered a silent prayer of thanks to a God who'd likely given up on ever hearing from him again.

In Charlotte, he had everything he'd been praying for, and because of her, he'd even let go of his anger toward Gemma and Max. Truth be told, he felt sorry for his ex-wife, because she didn't have something real to hold on to, because she'd settled for less than she deserved because she believed it was all she was worth.

He kissed the top of Charlotte's head.

She turned on her stomach, resting her arms on his chest and her chin on her hands. "This was a better first date than I could've imagined." She inched upward and kissed him.

His hand stroked the back of her arm. "Even better than the drive-in movie theater and a shared box of popcorn?"

She frowned.

He glanced down at her. "Your dream first date."

Now she sat up. "What are you talking about?"

He reached in his back pocket and pulled out a teal envelope with fifteen-year-old Charlotte's handwriting on it.

She gasped. "Where did you get that?"

"I have a whole box for you," he said.

She crisscrossed her legs and opened the envelope, pulling the letter from inside. She read, one hand over her mouth, as if she couldn't believe this trip back in time.

"I read a couple of them," he confessed. "And I found this." He reached into his other pocket and pulled out a small photo—Charlotte and Julianna, wearing matching smiles and matching ballet costumes.

As she took the photo, tears filled her eyes. "Oh, my goodness."

"You meant the world to her," Cole said.

"She meant the world to me." Charlotte folded the letter and stuck it back in the envelope. "What do you think she'd say if she knew about the two of us?"

He propped himself up on his elbow and drank in the sight of her, lit from behind by a full moon. "I think she'd say, 'Finally, two of the most important people in my life are happy. All is right with the world.'"

She smiled. "I hope she would've approved."

He took her hand. "She would've. She does. She loved us both, why wouldn't she approve?"

Charlotte went completely still then, placing a kiss to the inside of his palm. "You're more than I could've hoped for."

He gave her a tug and she fell on him, their faces only inches apart, and as he kissed her, a familiar, unfamiliar phrase tossed around in his mind.

I love you, Charlotte.

Because as much as he'd fought against it, he couldn't deny it was how he felt. He'd been blindsided in the very best way, and now that he knew her, he was certain he wouldn't be able to spend a single day without her.

42

"I didn't tell you, but you gave me an idea the other day."

Charlotte smiled. They sat on the dock behind his house, staring across the water—a calming ritual she'd come to love.

They'd finished rehearsing with Amelia, who, as expected, had picked up her steps in very little time. She assured them both that she would be more than ready for this dance with her uncle, and Charlotte believed her. Amelia was a little pro.

"I did?"

He took her hand. "You're free tonight, right?"

She squinted at him. "I should say no. I don't want you taking for granted that I'll drop everything for you."

He kissed her hand. "But you would, right?"

She turned away, doing a poor job of hiding her smile.

"This particular outing will pull double duty."

"What do you mean?" She glanced over at him.

"Another first for you and a really important night for me." His eyebrows bounced adorably, piquing her interest.

"Give me a hint."

He took off his *Harbor Pointe Football* hat and put it on her head. "You'll need this." He stood and pulled her to her feet.

She frowned. "Isn't football season in the fall?"

He laughed as they walked down the dock toward the cottage, stopping when they reached the yard. "You know this place looks a lot better with you in it."

She felt her cheeks flush. Would she ever get used to being the object of his affection? She forced herself not to think about what might happen if she couldn't convince Connor to sell her the dance studio after all.

She couldn't stay in Harbor Pointe without a job—and her savings would only last so long. But the thought of giving this up—of giving *him* up—it nearly undid her.

They rode in silence to the high school, where the stadium lights had been turned on. Several cars were parked in the parking lot, and as soon as Cole pulled in, there was a cheer. But not from his team—from a bunch of older guys, about their age.

Cole grinned.

"I thought we were here to watch your team," she said.

"We are," he said. "You're going to watch my team against me."

"Wait. You're playing?"

"You gave me a great idea," he said. "An exhibition game—for charity. For Haven House."

How had he kept this from her? "For Haven House?"

Cole shrugged. "I mentioned it to the guys and they were all on board. Asher doesn't talk about it, but they know his situation. Any money we make goes directly to Ash and his brothers."

"So your team is playing a bunch of old guys?" She tried not to giggle.

"My team is playing the very distinguished Harbor Pointe alumni." He shook his head at her. "No respect."

"How did I not know about this?" She opened the door of the truck and got out.

"Wasn't hard," he said. "You're not on social media, and you've been so busy with the recital. All I had to do was ask Lucy not to say anything."

"So you wanted it to be a surprise?"

He leaned down and kissed her, as if it were a sufficient response to her question. And as his arms wound around her waist, she thought, in fact, maybe it was.

The sound of drums rang out in the distance. "Wait, is that a band?"

Cole met her at the front of the truck and took her hand. "Oh, everything about this is going to feel like a real game. I wanted to make sure you got the full effect."

She stopped walking. "What do you mean?"

He looked away. "Nothing. I'm just doing what you said —adding the fun back into football."

"Yeah, but that has nothing to do with the band. Or the lights. Or—" A group of cheerleaders warmed up on the track. "The cheerleaders."

He shrugged. "I made a list of things you'd never done. And I'm working my way through it."

Charlotte watched as something inexplicable passed between them. He seemed intent on making sure she experienced everything she'd missed out on. Nobody had ever cared about her with such detail before.

"I have to go get ready," he said. "And take some preemptive Advil."

She laughed and pulled away just as Lucy's car stopped in a nearby parking place.

"I'll cheer as loud as I can," she said.

He grinned, kissed her once more, and strolled off,

meeting up with a group of guys heading toward the locker room.

"Oh, Cee." Lucy had stopped at her side. "You've got it bad." She looped her arm through Charlotte's and pulled her toward the entrance of the stadium, but not before Cole looked back at her and smiled.

"Oh, wow," Lucy said. "He's got it bad too."

She looked around, doing her best to take in the sights and sounds of her first football game. The smell of popcorn filled the air, and people filled the seats. Everyone was decked out in royal blue and gold, the Harbor Pointe Hawks' colors.

Quinn and her sister, Carly, arrived a few minutes later, followed by Haley and Betsy. The girls all sat together, watching as the teams took the field.

And Cole was right—it was fun.

The team had fun. The older guys had fun. The crowd had fun. *Charlotte* had fun.

The entire town seemed to be crammed in those seats, and Charlotte fit right in. She loved watching Cole show off on the field, wholly aware that he showed off for her. She loved the way he moved, the way he took off his helmet and grinned up at her when he scored a touchdown. The way he had one foot on each team, still coaching his guys even though he was technically their opponent.

And while Charlotte didn't understand football, it didn't matter. She understood that Cole's plan had worked—his guys were working together and loving the game again. She understood that he'd turned this event into a really good fundraiser for a place that meant a lot to him. And she understood that here—in this place with these people—was where she belonged.

She only hoped she could find a way to make it last.

43

After making their public debut, Charlotte and Cole became an official couple. And she quickly found she liked being half of an official couple.

When they weren't working, they were together. Renovating his bathrooms with Asher. Eating dinner at Haven House. Taking Amelia and AJ for ice cream and stealing kisses whenever they found themselves alone.

She loved kissing him most of all.

Cole continued to check things off his list, taking her to her first concert in the park, her first swim in the lake, and her first unicorn birthday party when Alaina, Julianna's baby, turned one. That was the day Cole gave her a box overflowing with letters she'd written to Jules over the years, and that box had quite possibly become her most prized possession.

Today, the day before the recital, Charlotte arrived at the studio for her final rehearsal with the football team. She stood behind the counter as the boys began to arrive, surprised when Cole walked in in the midst of them.

She couldn't help it—she smiled as soon as he met her

eyes. Maybe she was remembering the toe-curling trail of kisses he'd placed on her neck when they were supposed to be watching a movie at his house the night before.

"I didn't know you were coming to this," she said.

He leaned closer. "You kidding? I don't trust these boys with you. I need to make sure they're behaving around my girlfriend." He squeezed her hand.

My first boyfriend.

The boys filtered through the door. Several of them waved at her or said hello as they passed by. She knew them all by name now, and while she didn't let on, she really liked them.

She narrowed her gaze. "I've been handling these boys for weeks by myself, Coach."

"Fine," he said. "I'm making up reasons to come see you. Sue me."

She started down the hallway. "All right, but I can't promise I'm not going to make you get up and dance."

He stopped, and his expression turned.

She laughed. "I'm kidding. I'll save that for later."

They walked into the noisy studio, a bit more chaotic than normal. She drew in a deep breath, shot Cole a *wish me luck* look, and called their rehearsal to order. Cole might've seen the team dance a few weeks ago, but now, after hours of rehearsals, they'd nearly perfected their number. She couldn't lie—she was proud of them.

"Why don't we show your coach what you've been working on?" she said above the din of their laughter.

"Why don't you and Coach show us what *you've* been working on?" Dunbar called out.

The other guys responded a lot like her friends might've—with obnoxious teasing, and she felt her cheeks turn pink.

"Or are those dances private?" Hotchke added.

Cole's pointed look shut him right up, and Charlotte tried to compose herself. Was it obvious she was flustered?

"All right," she said. "Let's take it from the top. The performance is tomorrow, so give it all you've got."

"If we do it without any mistakes, will you and Coach show us your dance?" Whitey called out.

"Coach and I aren't dancing," she said. "He's dancing with his niece, and I'm dancing a solo."

"But you know the dance," Asher said. "You made it up."

That was true. And while normally she wouldn't turn down a chance to be in Cole's arms, she couldn't imagine he'd agree to these terms.

She glanced at him and he crossed his arms over his chest. "Coach?"

"What are the odds they'll win this bet?" he asked.

"Slim," she said. "Whitey has two left feet."

The boys reacted loudly at her joke, and she winked at Whitey, who shook his head.

"It's on, Miss Page." He removed his hat, then put it back on backward.

She grinned. "Show us what you've got."

She started the music and the boys turned serious. They'd amped up the personality, and two of them had even inserted some breakdancing moves she had not approved.

The song ended, and they hit their final pose.

Whitey slammed his hands on the floor and shouted, "Take that, Coach."

The whole group erupted in laughter, but before Charlotte could tell them if they'd won the bet or not, Brinley stormed in from the hallway. The beautiful, young blonde had everyone's attention.

"Sorry to interrupt," she said. "But Charlotte, you have to see this." She handed her phone to Charlotte. On the screen was an article by a critic named Maude Delancey, a woman who'd always been kind to Charlotte.

Until now.

The headline read "Prima Ballerina Abandons the Company That Made Her a Star." Charlotte skimmed the article, enough to get the gist. Maude, and apparently many others, were upset with the way Charlotte had left the ballet. She'd been too abrupt, and her departure was like a slap in the face to all the people who'd supported her throughout her long career. It sent the message that she was ungrateful, spoiled even, and nobody at the ballet had come to her defense.

Now we learn from a small-town newspaper's website that the former principal dancer of the Chicago City Ballet will don her pointe shoes once again. But this performance is only a step higher than an elementary school talent show, the kind thrown together by the math teacher.

"Ouch," Charlotte said, handing the phone back to Brinley. "I guess Maude isn't a fan anymore."

Brinley only stared. "Isn't this the equivalent of a burned bridge?"

She shrugged. "I mean, I wasn't planning on going back so, I guess it doesn't matter."

"But, Charlotte, you didn't *really* think you were going to stay here forever, did you?"

The words landed squarely on Charlotte's shoulders, and something that could only be described as panic settled inside her. That feeling only worsened when she remembered that her plan to buy the studio had been a faulty one.

Had she simply been prolonging the inevitable?

Seconds later, Cole was at her side. "Is everything okay?"

She forced herself to nod, but the fear that had found her wasn't going away. She'd been confident in her decision to leave, but that was when she thought she had a plan. If she'd burned her bridge at the ballet *and* she wasn't going to be able to buy the dance studio—what was she doing here?

She scanned the room and realized the entire Harbor Pointe High School football team was staring at her, waiting for her to get back to their rehearsal.

From the corner, her phone rang. "Brinley, could you supervise while they run through this a few more times?" Charlotte asked.

Brinley nodded and moved to the front of the room while Charlotte grabbed her phone and slipped out into the hallway. Her hands were sweaty and her mouth had gone dry.

Her mother's face stared back at her from the screen of her phone. She declined the call.

She found the article on her own device and read a little more closely this time.

Quotes from her mother, from the other dancers, from Martin—all expressing surprise and hurt that she'd left the way she had.

"We really had no warning," Artistic Director Martin DuBois said. "She was here one day and gone the next."

"She really let us all down," one of the dancers in the company said. "It was a selfish thing to do."

Anger rose up inside her. Selfish? She'd given everything to that ballet—everything! And they were calling *her* selfish?

And then Maude mentioned Julianna.

The recital in which Page will perform honors Julianna Ford, a former ballerina who left the professional dance world as abruptly as Ms. Page appears to have done. Ford was killed in a car accident in May, and Page's mother, renowned dance instructor Marcia Page, speculates that her death may have contributed to her daughter's rash decision.

"I can see no other logical explanation," Marcia Page said. "I *only hope that when she comes to her senses, there's still a place for her in ballet."*

Charlotte had been ignoring these kinds of comments from her mother since the day she drove out of Chicago—why were they hitting her so wrong now? Because text messages were personal and this was out there on the internet for everybody to read?

She didn't like people commenting on her personal life. Especially people who didn't really know her. To Martin and the other dancers and Maude and even her mother, Charlotte was a dancer, nothing more. What gave them the right to say anything about what she was doing now?

What gave them the right to make her fear her choice was the wrong one? Or rather, to confirm the fear that had been niggling at her for weeks now.

"You okay?"

She turned and found Cole standing in the hallway behind her.

Her phone buzzed, and Marcia's face lit up the screen again.

Her mother had more quotes in the article.

"I really thought my daughter was smarter than this—throwing away her career after she worked so hard to get where she was—well, maybe I've been giving her too much credit."

"Charlotte?"

Maybe this was what she deserved. Maybe after what she'd done—the mistake she still kept from Cole—ending up alone with nothing was unavoidable.

What was she doing here? She didn't deserve any of this.

Did she think she could just waltz in here and steal everything her friend had? Her business? Her friends? Her brother?

Hadn't she stolen enough from Julianna? Where did she get off grabbing more?

Cole stood beside her now, close enough to touch. His expression was laced with worry and kindness, focused on her in a way that comforted and unnerved her at the same time.

"Do you want to take a walk?" he asked.

She glanced to the half-opened studio door behind him. "The rehearsal..."

"Can wait," he said. "The guys will be fine. They really did do that perfectly."

She shook her head, wishing she could just as easily shake away this consuming doubt that had curled up inside her. She'd been living in a dream world. Connor had sold this place to someone else. She'd been a horrible friend to his wife—why would he have trusted Charlotte with the dance studio?

And Cole—once he knew the truth, would he ever be able to forgive her? He'd made it clear how he felt about lying.

And a lie by omission was still a lie.

"Tell the guys I'll see them tomorrow."

Cole looked at her, confused.

"I think I need to be alone."

44

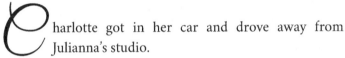harlotte got in her car and drove away from Julianna's studio.

She felt like a fraud. Maybe coming here had been a huge mistake. Maybe she was trying to atone for sins that were too old to be forgiven. Maybe she was still trying to steal what was rightfully Julianna's.

And maybe walking away from the ballet really had been a terrible mistake.

She parked her car behind the barn at Haven House, hoping Hildy and Steve wouldn't mind that she was there. She got out and walked the path she'd first discovered with Cole on their first date. He was the single best thing that had ever happened to her, but were they fooling themselves to think it could ever work?

Was it foolish to believe she could be happy here? Was it foolish to believe that she and Cole were meant to be together? That their love could withstand mismatched backgrounds and a truth she'd yet to confess?

The article had suggested that Charlotte had something to "get out of her system." Marcia explained that her daughter had never really explored a world outside of dance. Several people speculated that Charlotte was simply rebelling, and that she would realize, probably soon, that the ballet was where she belonged.

"Ballet isn't simply what Charlotte does, it's who she is. This company made her, and I have to believe she'll be back when she realizes she has nothing without it. I only hope there's an open door for her when she does."

Marcia's words haunted her now. What if her mother was right? What if she woke up one day, full of funnel cakes and cinnamon rolls, and realized she'd made a terrible mistake? What if it was too late?

"I thought that was you."

Charlotte turned toward Hildy's voice and saw the woman emerge from the trees into the clearing where she sat on the picnic table.

"Sorry I'm trespassing," Charlotte said.

"My waterfall is your waterfall." Hildy sat down next to her. "You look like you're working something out. This is a good place to do it."

Charlotte stared out at the water. "Is it that obvious?"

Hildy wrapped an arm around her and squeezed. "It is to me."

Charlotte hesitated a long moment, then finally told Hildy about the article. She pulled it up on her phone and let the woman read it, even though it was humiliating.

"It got under your skin." Hildy handed the phone back to Charlotte. "Why?"

She shrugged. "I'm not sure. I guess maybe because Marcia has been controlling my life for as long as I can remember. And this was the first real decision I made on my own."

"The decision to come to Harbor Pointe," Hildy said.

"Yes. And the decision to walk away from ballet."

Hildy paused thoughtfully. "Does it feel like a mistake?"

"It feels like I finally have everything I've been missing," Charlotte said, aware that her eyes had clouded over with fresh tears. "But dance is who I am."

"Dance isn't who you are, Charlotte," Hildy said. "It's what you do. There's a difference."

"Is there?" Charlotte wasn't so sure. People always told her she'd been born to dance. If she stopped doing what she was born to do, what was left?

"Of course there is." Hildy went quiet, then regarded Charlotte with new curiosity. "It was you, wasn't it?"

Charlotte frowned. "What was me?"

"The friend Julianna left to protect," she said. "The one she took the fall for."

Charlotte shrank under the question. "You know about that?"

"Not all the details," Hildy said. "But enough."

Charlotte's head spun. "You've known this whole time, and you still let me come here?"

Hildy looked out over the water, thoughtfulness on her face. "She did what she did because she loved you."

A tear slid down Charlotte's cheek. "But it was wrong. My bad judgment cost her everything."

Hildy drew in a deep breath. "Oh, I don't know, Charlotte, I think it depends on how you look at it. Did it cost her everything, or did she gain everything?"

Charlotte swiped a tear from her cheek and willed herself to stay strong. She'd never told anyone what she did, not even Julianna. They never discussed it—Julianna just knew. She knew and she fell on her sword, all so Charlotte could go on dancing.

"Cole told me once he thought Julianna wouldn't have traded her life for anything," Charlotte said.

"I agree with him." Hildy glanced at her. "You aren't so sure?"

Charlotte shrugged. "How can we really know? How can we know that she wouldn't have gone on to be something great?"

"Oh, honey, she did," Hildy said. "I know you didn't get to see her with her family or with those kids she taught, but Jules was born for this life."

Charlotte stilled. "Do you think she would've forgiven me?"

"I think she did forgive you," Hildy said. "Don't get me wrong, she was devastated when she came home. She told everyone else she decided ballet wasn't for her, but I knew there was more to the story."

"Yeah, there was me," Charlotte said sadly. "Me and my horrible mistake."

"You can't change it," Hildy said. "Though it seems like you're trying awfully hard to make up for it."

Was that what she was doing? She didn't even know anymore.

"I'm the worst kind of friend," Charlotte said. "I did something terrible because I wanted this certain kind of life, and Julianna sacrificed her own dreams so I could have it. And the day she died, I decided what I really wanted was the life she'd stepped into. How selfish is that?"

"It's not selfish," Hildy said. "It's human. You're discovering what Julianna discovered—that there's more to life than just one thing."

"Why couldn't I see that then?"

Hildy shrugged. "You're seeing it now."

Charlotte sighed. "But if she'd stayed—if I'd been the one to walk away—she'd still be alive today."

"Don't do that," Hildy said. "Julianna loved her life. She

loved her family and her dance studio. She loved teaching, and she loved Harbor Pointe."

Charlotte knew it was true. Julianna's letters had said so. "And you loved ballet."

"I loved applause," Charlotte said. "I loved being the best."

"And now?"

Charlotte shrugged. The only thing she could think of was Cole. She loved Cole. He'd proven to her that there was so much more to life than being the best. He'd proven that there was more to strive for than the approval of everyone else. But would he also prove that what he said was true—that love was unconditional? Would he still feel the same once he knew what Hildy knew?

"You seem to be searching for something, Charlotte," Hildy said. "What is it?"

Charlotte couldn't have put it into words if she tried. She didn't know. She just knew that the day Julianna died, the day they laid her to rest, something inside her shifted. Suddenly, everything she'd been working for seemed meaningless.

But if she hadn't been born to dance, then why *had* she been born? She was trying to find out.

"Can I tell you what I think?" Hildy asked, as if Charlotte could've stopped her. "I think you're looking for forgiveness."

The knot at the back of Charlotte's throat loosened.

"You're trying to *earn* forgiveness the same way you're trying to earn love."

Charlotte dared a glance at the older, wiser woman. "I think you're right." Her voice cracked as she spoke. "This is all new to me."

"What if I told you that you've got nothing to prove?" Hildy reached over and took her hand. "Love and forgiveness aren't earned. They're freely given. Like a gift. God created you—not only to be a dancer, but to be His child. He loves you for who you are. No strings attached."

Like Cole.

The words came to her without warning.

Gifts Charlotte received usually came with conditions. They were usually a result of her performing well or getting a good review or going to a fundraiser and schmoozing the right people.

But that was true about nothing Cole had given her. He expected nothing in return. He'd painted her a picture of a love like she'd never known.

He didn't care if she ever danced professionally again—to him, she was just Charlotte. And that was enough.

"I don't deserve it," she said aloud, though she hadn't intended to.

"That's the point," Hildy said. "None of us do."

Maybe she'd been led here so she could learn this exact thing. Maybe it wasn't Julianna's family or her dance studio or even her passion that Charlotte envied most. Maybe what she really wanted, what Julianna had always possessed, was a deep understanding that she was worthy—and she always had been—of love.

The realization settled inside her like a warm and welcome friend.

She was loved.

Maybe now she could finally forgive herself. Maybe she could stop striving, stop trying to prove herself worthy. Maybe she could rest in the fact that God had already accepted her the way she was, whether or not she ever stepped foot on a stage again.

She'd been so convinced that she'd destroyed Julianna's life, when clearly her friend had gone on to do beautiful and important things right here in Harbor Pointe.

For Jules, bigger wasn't best. Some people didn't need an audience to make a difference.

And Charlotte wanted to be one of those people.

Hildy stood. "I'll leave you. Stay as long as you want. And have faith in Cole, enough to be honest with him."

Charlotte nodded. "Thanks, Hildy."

Once she was alone, Charlotte inhaled the warm summer air, thinking how fortunate she was to be here in this moment. Her life had grown infinitely richer because of Julianna's fingerprint on it, and she wanted to honor her friend by living free of the burdens that had always held her down.

It was time to let go of the past. She'd come here, she realized now, to make peace with Julianna, when what she really needed was to make peace with herself.

She gazed at the waterfall and prayed. It was clunky and stilted, but it was honest. She asked God to forgive her for the mistakes she'd made and to give her courage to tell the truth. Even if it meant losing the one person she loved most.

It wouldn't be easy, and she knew it. But the idea of having nothing to prove left her feeling lighter and freer than a balloon being carried away on the wind.

There was just one more thing she needed to do to be completely rid of her shame—and while it would be hard, she owed it to Cole to be honest. The recital was tomorrow, and she didn't want to do anything to ruin it. Immediately afterward, she'd tell him everything.

She only prayed he would find it in his heart to forgive her.

45

Saturday morning, the day of the recital, Cole woke up nervous. Not only because he had to go on stage that night, but also because it had been hours since Charlotte walked out of rehearsal and the only word he'd gotten from her was a text late last night that said:

Hey, I'll be tied up with last-minute details all day tomorrow, but I'll see you at the theatre later.

He was worried about her.

That worry, mixed with his nervous energy, turned Cole into a giant mess—and he had a whole day on his own.

A knock on the front door pulled his attention.

Maybe Charlotte had some time for him after all. He pulled the door open, and it was Gemma—not Charlotte—who stood there.

"Hey," she said.

"Hey."

"You look good," she said. "You always look great fresh out of the shower."

He didn't respond.

"Look, I came to thank you for what you said the night of the fair. You didn't have to be nice to me, but you were, and I appreciate it. A lot."

"'Course," he said.

She clung to the bag hanging off her shoulder, as if she needed it to stand upright. "I wanted to also tell you that I took your advice."

He frowned. "About what?"

"About Max. I ended it. For real this time."

Cole didn't respond.

"I know what I did to you was wrong, and I hope you meant it when you said you forgave me. I'm going to try to spend some time alone for a while. Get myself right. Maybe we could even be friends again someday."

"That'd be good," he said, shocked to discover that his animosity toward her had melted away. It wasn't an act. He'd forgiven her. Out of her own brokenness, she'd hurt him, but he'd finally gotten to the place where he could put it behind him.

Once and for all.

"I'm going back home," Gemma said. "To Ohio. I'll stay in touch if that's okay."

"Yeah," he said. "I hope you do."

She stood on her tiptoes and kissed him on the cheek. "She's a lucky girl, Cole Turner."

He smiled. "I'm the lucky one."

"Well, I wish you guys the best," Gemma said. "I mean it."

"Thanks, Gemma."

He closed the door, surprised by the strange turn of events that this summer had brought. He'd not only rid himself of his anger toward his ex-wife, he'd let go of his inherited feelings about women. In looking at Asher's situation and now this ordeal with Gemma, he finally understood. People are broken. And when they're broken, they hurt the ones they love. He'd made peace with that. All he could do now was put the hurt behind him.

Charlotte made him want to be the best version of himself, and he was pretty sure he'd love her till the day he died.

Which, if nerves could kill, might be that very night.

The backstage area of the theatre bustled with excitement and energy. Tiny ballerinas wearing white tutus ran around as if they were playing tag at recess.

Cole wore a tux that threatened to choke off his oxygen supply, and as he watched the audience filter in, he backed into the shadows, afraid he might be sick.

And then he saw her.

Beautiful, graceful, elegant Charlotte Page. She stepped onto the opposite side of the stage, wearing the red dance costume he'd seen in one of her videos. She'd had this costume and two others sent to her from Chicago, but he hadn't been prepared to see her like this, in her element.

Her lips were bright red, her hair pulled back in a bun reminiscent of the one she'd worn the day he met her on the street. And her eyes shone bright and full of promise.

He loved her. More than he'd ever loved anyone before.

He'd tell her tonight, after his dance with Amelia, assuming he was still breathing.

Charlotte had been scarce all day. He'd only seen her briefly when he arrived and not since he'd gotten dressed in his tuxedo. He missed her.

How pathetic had he become that he couldn't go a handful of hours without missing this woman?

Her solo would kick off the whole recital. They'd had

two rehearsals in the theatre earlier that week, but she'd never performed her pieces in front of anybody, and thankfully she'd ensured that he and Amelia didn't have to either.

But standing here now, watching her get her "game face" on, he was taken with her beauty, her strength, her talent. And he wondered if she regretted giving up her spot in the ballet.

Maybe that's why the article upset her so much. It made her unsure of her choice.

As the lights dimmed and the stage went black, he caught her eye from the opposite wing. What if she was going to tell him she was leaving? What if that's why she'd stayed away from him all day?

She took the stage and the music began, and Cole, like everyone else in the theatre, watched in awe as she used her body, her face, her movement to tell a story. She captivated the entire audience. She captivated him.

She moved with such power, such authority. She made it look easy, but he knew defying gravity the way she did was the result of years of training, of sacrifice, of focus. All things she would be throwing away if she stayed here.

A small crowd of crew members gathered around him, each one held prisoner by her beauty.

Charlotte was the best of the best, even he could see that. He couldn't let her give that up.

Not for him. Not for anything.

The song ended and Charlotte struck her final pose. The audience erupted. Even his football players, lining the back wall and waiting for their entrance down the aisles, burst out in cheers.

In the darkness, she exited the stage.

He raced out into the hallway that connected stage right from stage left and found her standing there, thanking the many, many dancers clamoring for her attention.

She turned and their eyes met over the crowd of tiny humans. She smiled and made her way over to him. He pulled her close, hugged her, and prayed it wasn't the last time.

"Wow," he said. "You're amazing."

"Thanks," she said. "It was fun." She pulled from his embrace. "You look incredible."

He smiled. "I clean up okay?"

She waggled her eyebrows. "You clean up hot."

He laughed. "I love you, you know."

Her eyes widened.

"Sorry," he said. "I didn't mean to blurt that out. It was supposed to be a lot more romantic than that."

"Do you mean that?" The stunned expression hadn't left her face.

He nodded.

Her eyes glassed over, and a single tear slid down her cheek.

"Hey, don't cry." He wiped it away, then took her face in his hands.

She wrapped her hands around his wrists and closed her eyes, inhaling a deep breath. "Nobody has ever loved me before," she whispered.

He leaned down and kissed her forehead. "Then nobody has ever known you."

She found his eyes. "You're right. You're the first."

He smiled. "But I'm not the last. People seem to keep discovering how amazing you are."

"Cole, there's something I need to tell you." Her face fell.

His stomach went hollow for fear he knew what that might be. "You're going back, aren't you?"

"What? No."

"But you belong on the stage, Charlotte," he said. "You're incredible."

She looked at him thoughtfully. "I belong with you."

A woman dressed in black, wearing a headset and carrying a clipboard, appeared from the side of the stage. "Cole, you've got one tiny tappers class, the football team, and then you and Amelia are on."

A look of worry washed across her face as she brought her eyes to his.

"Go," he said. "We'll talk afterward."

"Okay." She squeezed his hand, then inched up to place a gentle kiss on his lips. "And Cole? I love you too."

Her words lingered as she dashed off to the quick-change room to prepare for her next dance. He wasn't even nervous anymore. Because Charlotte loved him.

And foolish though it may be, he was pretty sure that was the only thing he needed. Everything else was just detail.

46

Cole stood backstage with Amelia as the tap class banged their feet to an upbeat song he didn't recognize. He turned and found Connor standing in the doorway.

"Have you already gone on?" he asked.

Cole frowned. "No. What are you doing back here?"

Connor knelt down in front of his little girl and took her by the shoulders, pulling her into a tight hug. "I'm so sorry."

Amelia squeezed his neck and Cole saw a lone tear slide down her cheek. "It's okay, Daddy."

Connor pulled away and looked at her. "I told the sound guy that you and I are dancing together."

"But you don't know the steps," Cole said.

Connor didn't look up. Instead, he focused on his little girl. "I know the steps for the last number her mom ever choreographed for us." He smiled. "Do you remember?"

Amelia nodded. "I remember."

"I gave them our music," Connor said.

The tiny tappers exited the stage—and not quietly. Cole

glanced up and saw his football players taking their places. "So, wait. I'm off the hook?"

Amelia crossed her arms over her chest and glared at him. "Not a chance."

"Well, I'm down a partner," he said. "Doesn't make much sense for me to stand in when your dad is here."

"The deal was that if I danced, you would dance," Amelia said. She should be a lawyer when she grew up. She sure liked to argue. "You can dance with Miss Charlotte."

At that moment, Charlotte walked up. "Connor, hey. What are you doing back here?"

"He's dancing with me," Amelia said. "And you're dancing with Uncle Cole."

Charlotte looked at Cole as the familiar intro to "Uptown Funk" came through the speakers.

One of the stagehands moved toward them. "Just heard about the change. Coach, you and Miss Page will go next. Then we'll slide in Connor and Amelia later. Sound good?"

They all nodded, and Cole tried to ignore the knot of nerves in his stomach.

"Come on, Dad," Amelia said. "We need to be on stage right."

Connor smiled down at her, then looked at Charlotte. "Thanks for doing this."

Charlotte's expression changed. He knew she was hoping to buy the dance studio. He knew it meant more to her than just about anything else. And while Connor was putting on a brave face at the moment, it was pretty clear to Cole that it was an act.

Being here had to be killing him.

"It was my pleasure," Charlotte said.

Amelia tugged on her dad's hand and pulled him out the door, leaving him and Charlotte standing in the wings.

"So, you and me," Cole said. "You okay with that?"

She smiled up at him. "More than okay."

They moved closer to the stage for a better view of the football team, and Cole marveled at how far the boys had come. Not only in preparing this number, but as a team. They were friends now, and thanks to Charlotte, he'd found ways to make practices more fun.

The boys had responded. Asher had stepped up. They wouldn't win state, but Cole was pretty sure they'd have an impressive season.

He took Charlotte's hand and they watched the boys, who were met with whistles and applause from a thoroughly entertained audience. Of course, the boys ate up the attention, going more full-out than he'd ever seen them go in practice.

When the song was over, the crowd sprang to their feet and the boys strutted off the stage. He slapped shoulders and backs and gave high-fives all around, almost forgetting it was nearly his turn to take the stage.

"Finally we get to see your moves, Coach," Asher said.

Cole turned back toward Charlotte, who stared at him with wide, full eyes.

"You ready?" she asked.

He nodded. "Ready as I'll ever be."

In the darkness, the two of them took the stage. They'd given Amelia a seat of honor in the wings to watch her uncle, and the little girl beamed so brightly he could see her smile in the dark.

Behind him, one of the football players whistled, followed by the low murmur of the crowd.

He reached a hand toward Charlotte, their opening pose, and she took it, then smiled up at him. "Just pretend we're alone."

He grinned. "But there are children watching."

She stifled a giggle, confirming what he already knew—

this was the woman he wanted to spend the rest of his life with.

The lights slowly came up as the music for "Perfect" began, and Cole glanced at his niece and winked.

All for you, Amelia.

He should probably thank her, actually. Without this little deal he'd made with his niece, would he have ever gotten past himself long enough to discover what a treasure Charlotte was?

A cheer from the back pulled him to reality, and Charlotte stepped into his arms. They moved exactly the way they'd practiced, gliding around the stage in perfect unison. He watched as she became someone else but still remained uniquely Charlotte, turning herself over to the music, to his leading, to the performance, in a way he would never master.

That simple box step she'd taught him during their first rehearsal had been transformed into so much more, and now, as he spun her, a strong hand on her waist, he almost didn't have to think about the moves.

She circled around him, her blue dress flowing behind her as she did. Then, she was back in his arms, and they swayed in perfect unison. The dance gave him a moment to hold her body to his, then she backed away as the music swelled, and he lifted her with such ease that it was as if he'd been made to help her soar.

The audience cheered.

He set her down and the dance ended, and without thinking he leaned in and kissed her so fully the cheers turned rowdy. *Hotchke.*

He'd forgotten where they were.

He pulled away to find her face lit in a bright smile. "That wasn't what we rehearsed."

He laughed as they left the stage. "Sorry. I got carried away."

She threw herself in his arms and he caught her, held her, inhaled her.

"I have another dance," she said. "I'll talk to you after."

She raced off, leaving him standing dumbly as another dance class lined up for their entrance.

After a few more numbers, it was time for Connor and Amelia's dance.

Now it was his turn to watch.

The pair took the stage, and Cole found a spot in the wings where he could watch without disturbing anyone. Before the lights came up, Amelia glanced at him and winked.

He smiled back at her.

He knew he couldn't take all the credit for getting her out there, but it made him feel good to think he'd done a little something to help.

Michael Bublé's smooth voice rang out through the auditorium as a song called "Daddy's Little Girl" began.

This town knew Connor, and they knew what he and Amelia had been through. Cole was pretty sure that as the dance went on there wasn't a dry eye in the place. Even he had trouble keeping it together. What the audience didn't know, however, was that this was most likely the first moment of connection Amelia had had with her dad since her mother died.

And that made the whole thing more than special—it made it powerful.

Cole never knew a dance could do that.

Connor moved well, but the number was meant to highlight his daughter—and that he did flawlessly.

The little girl shone up there, beaming as she performed

her little heart out, and Cole knew that both of them were doing this for Julianna.

She would be so proud of them.

The song ended and the stage went dark. Cole watched as Connor picked up Amelia and hugged her, his shoulders moving as soft sobs overtook him. Amelia clung to him like she was afraid to let go, like this moment would disappear and she would lose her dad all over again.

When they didn't exit the stage, Cole walked out in the darkness and ushered them into the wings on the opposite side, where Charlotte stood, her brow laced with concern.

"You okay?" Cole asked.

Connor glanced at Amelia. "Thanks, Bug. For letting me dance with you." His voice broke and Cole had to look away.

Amelia squeezed her dad's hand. "I love you, Daddy."

Connor nodded, then looked at Cole. "I'm gonna . . ." His voice trailed off, his sentence unfinished, as he walked out the door.

"Should we make sure he's okay?" Charlotte whispered.

"I think he might need some time on his own," Cole said. "I'll check on him in a little bit." He put a hand on Amelia's head. "You were sensational."

Her smile looked forced. "Thanks."

"You've still got one more dance," Charlotte said. "You okay?"

Amelia nodded. "I'll go change." She rushed off, and Cole looked at Charlotte, who wore pointe shoes and a light pink costume.

"I'm going to watch your final dance from the audience." He leaned down and kissed her cheek. "Just another one of your adoring fans."

And he meant it. He'd adore her for the rest of his days.

As he walked out into the dark lobby, his stomach

wobbled when he remembered that she was holding on to something she wanted to tell him.

Aware that whatever it was might end up splitting them apart.

And Cole was pretty sure he wouldn't withstand losing her now that he'd let himself fall in love.

47

Cole was about to pull open the door into the theatre when a woman's voice stopped him.

"That was some performance."

He turned and found a tall, pale-faced woman with dark hair and bright red lips staring at him. She wore thick eye makeup and her cheeks had been blushed pink.

"Thanks," he said.

"And some kiss."

A nervous laugh escaped. "That wasn't part of the plan."

"Caught up in the moment, perhaps?" She moved toward him like a lioness stalking its prey. Cole's guard went up. Who was this woman? "You saw her dance, yes? You can't possibly think that kind of talent should go to waste."

"I don't think it's going to waste," he said.

She laughed. "Here? What could she possibly do *here*? That girl needs to be on the world's biggest stages. She's one of the best in the country—we certainly wouldn't want to deprive audiences of her talent. Or Charlotte from her potential."

He took a step back. "I think that's for Charlotte to decide." Never mind that he'd worried about that exact thing. "Now, if you'll excuse me—"

"You're the brother, right?" She stood directly in front of him now, and though she was several inches shorter than he was, her presence dwarfed him. "Julianna's brother."

"Did you know my sister?"

"I taught her for a time," the woman said. "Very promising young dancer."

"She was," he said. "What did you say your name was?"

"I didn't." The woman eyed him. "I'm surprised you're so willing to be a part of my daughter's penance."

He frowned. "What do you mean?"

The woman tilted her head and sized him up. "Charlotte has always had such a guilty conscience about what she did to Julianna."

His frown deepened. "You're Charlotte's mother?"

"Marcia Page."

He ignored her extended hand.

"I never understood why she was so ashamed," Marcia said with an elegant wave. "In our business, you do what you need to do to survive. I was proud of her, if I'm honest. I really didn't think she had it in her."

"I don't know what you're talking about," Cole said.

"No, I don't suppose you would," Marcia said. "The girls were young. I think we can blame it on that. There were three of them up for a big apprenticeship in New York. The dancer who won that honor would have the world at her fingertips. Her pick of companies. The best instructors, the best future. It meant everything to Charlotte. There were two other dancers standing in her way. One was your sister, and the other, a beautiful ballerina named Irena Pomchenko."

Nausea rolled through his body as Marcia continued, her tone clipped and staccato and yet mildly lyrical.

"Technically, Charlotte couldn't be beat, but she's always had trouble connecting to her emotions. She didn't display her passion as well as some of the others. Still, we knew she had to come out on top. Her future—our future—depended on it."

"I really should get in there," he said, wanting to get away, to ignore whatever it was this woman was about to say.

"Of course," she said.

Cole turned to go.

"I'm just glad she's found someone so willing to forgive her for destroying his sister's life."

He stopped short and faced her. "What are you talking about?"

"It certainly wasn't premeditated, more of a spur-of-the moment crime." She laughed.

Cole didn't.

"Irena's costume was sabotaged. The beads were cut right off the front, leaving a gaping hole. She had to hurry to find another costume, but it threw her off. Badly. She fell twice and left the stage in tears."

He frowned. "That's terrible."

Marcia gave a soft shrug. "That's ballet. Only the strong survive."

"Who sabotaged her costume?"

Marcia nodded toward the stage.

"Charlotte?"

"Yes, but she wasn't the one who took the fall."

Cole didn't understand what Marcia was trying to tell him, and his face must've said so, because she was all too happy to explain it to him.

"Your sister won that apprenticeship, Mr. Turner," she

said. "But when the faculty found out about the sabotage, they demanded somebody own up to it. Julianna came forward and she was immediately dismissed. Charlotte went to New York, and your sister went home. The rest, as they say, is history."

"So, Charlotte let Julianna take the blame—"

"She did what she had to, to get ahead," Marcia said. "In this life, we have to take what we want."

"Julianna was devasted when she left the ballet." Cole had never seen her like that. She'd been working so hard, and she loved dance more than anything. Never mind that it wasn't many weeks later that she met Connor and her new life began—she'd never had another choice. And Charlotte had been the one to steal that from her.

"If you'll excuse me," Cole said.

"Of course."

He rushed past Marcia and out the front door. He'd been fooled again. Charlotte was just like the rest of them. A liar.

Her moving back to the city, he could've handled. But this? This, he hadn't seen coming. And maybe being blindsided all over again was the wake-up call he needed to remember why he'd sworn off women in the first place.

48

After the recital, everyone who'd performed took a bow. Charlotte had looked for Cole backstage, but he was nowhere to be found.

The curtain closed and everyone cheered.

Charlotte was making her way through the crowd of performers when she felt a tug on her dress. She turned and found Amelia standing at her side, tears in her eyes.

"Thank you, Miss Charlotte." The little girl flung her arms around Charlotte's waist and squeezed her so hard she thought she might explode.

Charlotte clung to Amelia, feeling the grief, the pain, the sorrow seep out of the little girl by way of that hug.

"I know your mom is so proud of you," Charlotte whispered as Amelia drew back.

The little girl opened her hand to reveal a small, folded piece of paper.

"What's this?"

Amelia shrugged. "My dad told me to give it to you."

"Amelia, come on!" one of the other girls shouted. "My mom is taking us for ice cream."

"I love you, Miss Charlotte."

She ran off, leaving Charlotte standing under the dim lights of the stage. The words were like a cozy pair of pajamas on a cold and rainy day. Two people loved her. Two people she loved back. How had she gotten so lucky?

She opened the small piece of paper and saw the words scrawled on it.

It's yours. Make her proud.

Tears sprang to Charlotte's eyes. The studio was hers. She could stay. She and Cole could have a real shot at a real life and who knew? Maybe she would be loved until the day she died.

"Are you done with this charade now?"

She'd been so lost in thought, she hadn't realized someone had come up beside her. She turned and found her mother, all hard angles and coldness, glaring at her.

"What are you doing here?" Charlotte asked.

"You wouldn't respond to my calls or my texts, so I figured I'd drive up here and talk some sense into you."

Charlotte started off the stage, aware that Marcia followed. "I have to go, I'm meeting someone."

"If you mean that good-looking football coach, he left."

Charlotte spun on her heel and faced her mother. "What did you do?"

"I never should've let you go to that funeral," Marcia said. "I should've known it would bring everything back up again. How many times did I tell you to let it go? You did what you had to do."

"You don't know what you're talking about," Charlotte said. "What did you say to Cole?"

Marcia shrugged. "I told him the truth. That you didn't belong here anymore than he belongs in your world."

"That's not your call." Heat rushed to her face.

"And, of course, we had a conversation about how much you really owe to Julianna."

Panic washed over her. "You didn't."

She waved her hand, feigning innocence. "Of course, I thought you would've told him. The two of you looked pretty close when you were dancing up here."

Charlotte's mind spun. This couldn't be happening. This was not how he was supposed to find out.

"I spoke with Martin," Marcia went on. "Now that you've gotten this out of your system, it's time to get back to reality."

"Do you have any idea what you've done?" Charlotte drew in a taut breath, as if that would calm her nerves.

"I've saved you from making a giant mistake," Marcia said. "From throwing everything away. Let's not forget what Julianna gave up so you could have this dream."

Charlotte was so angry, the only thing she could do was walk away.

But Marcia followed her. "So, you'll be back on Monday. You'll have to rehearse for a few weeks before they let you perform. Looks like you might've put on a few pounds during this little sabbatical, so we'll hit the gym right away."

"It's not a sabbatical." She smoothed her hair back and drew in a breath. "This is my life. I'm staying. I'm buying Julianna's dance studio, and I'm staying. That man is the best thing that's ever happened to me."

Marcia inched back and studied Charlotte a little too intently. "You can't be serious. You and the high school football coach? In what world is there a happy ending for the two of you? Especially now that he knows what kind of person you really are?"

"No, Mother, what kind of person I *was*. Before Julianna showed me what sacrifice looks like. Some people learn that from their mothers, but I learned it from her."

"Fine, but you'd still be an idiot to waste everything you've accomplished," Marcia said. "If you stop dancing, what do you have left? You're nothing without the ballet."

The words hung between them, confirming every fear Charlotte kept bottled up, every motivation for living the way she did.

And she thought about what Hildy had said. Real love didn't have strings. She might not have earned it, but she'd found it just the same.

She'd found it in Cole, in her friends, in Hildy, in Amelia.

But she'd never found that in her mother.

"If I give up dance, I'll just be Charlotte," she said. "And I would hope that that would be enough for you."

Her mother started to say something, but Charlotte held up a hand to silence her. "I'm done living the life you want me to live."

Charlotte walked away, toward the stage door, and didn't turn to look back. Not even when her mother called out, "I'll tell Martin to expect you on Monday morning."

It was pointless to try and make her understand.

After all, Marcia didn't know her at all.

49

Cole yanked the tie loose and raced to his truck. He got in and drove around, replaying the events of the night over and over in his mind.

How could his feelings change so swiftly? Only an hour ago, he'd been so smitten with Charlotte he couldn't have imagined a day without her in his life.

Now he wondered if he knew her at all.

What kind of person would sabotage someone else? Was that how she'd gotten to the top? By stepping on anyone who got in her way?

It sickened him to think that Julianna had taken the fall for Charlotte's wrongdoing, that Charlotte had let her. Worse, Charlotte showed up here, invading Julianna's world—as if she could step in where his sister had left off.

He parked the truck, got out, and walked toward the one place he might find a bit of peace. But when he neared Julianna's grave, he discovered he wasn't alone.

A nearby streetlamp illuminated Connor's silhouette sitting on the ground beside her headstone.

So this was where he'd gone when he rushed off after his dance with Amelia.

Cole took a step toward his brother-in-law, and a twig cracked underneath his foot, drawing Connor's attention.

Cole froze. "Hey, man," he said.

"What are you doing here?" Connor asked.

"What are you doing here?"

Connor lifted a bottle of beer. "Drinking."

Cole frowned. "You don't even drink."

His brother-in-law held up the six-pack. "Want one?"

"I don't drink either."

"But maybe we should," Connor said. "Maybe it'll help us forget."

Cole sat down next to him in the grass. "Do you really want to forget?"

Connor shrugged. "It'd be easier, right?"

"Maybe," he said. "But life isn't supposed to be easy."

Listen to him throwing out platitudes that even he didn't want to hear. He was nauseating himself.

They sat in silence for what felt like an eternity. Cole wasn't good at consoling anyone—he'd yet to work through his own grief, and frankly, he'd come here to talk to his sister. And maybe to wallow a little.

"That was hard," Connor said, his voice tight. "Getting up there again."

"I would've stepped in for you," Cole said. "Everyone would've understood."

Connor took a swig from his bottle. "I needed to do it for Amelia."

Cole stilled. "It was good you did. I'm glad she's dancing again."

"Thanks to you," Connor said. "And Charlotte. She's been amazing."

"Yeah, amazing." Cole didn't hide the sarcasm.

"I was hard on her when she first got here," Connor said. "Think she'll forgive me?"

Cole shrugged. "Maybe she's the one who should be asking for forgiveness."

"No," Connor said. "Without her, I never would've married Jules in the first place."

Cole frowned. "How do you figure?"

"She's the reason Jules left ballet," Connor said.

"You know about that?"

He shrugged. "Sure, Jules told me."

"Was she upset?"

Connor shifted. "I mean, yeah, but it didn't take long for her attitude about it to change. I think she was relieved. A part of her was, anyway. She was tired of all that cutthroat pressure. She danced because she loved it. I told her she could do that here—that I'd help her. That's when she started the dance studio."

"So, she was okay with everything?"

Connor took another drink. "She was grateful, I think. Said that dream meant more to Charlotte than it had ever meant to her. She never had that same drive, you know? Jules just wanted to be happy. And I think she hoped it would turn something in Charlotte—make her a better person, knowing that someone had sacrificed so much for her."

"Do you think it did?"

Connor shrugged. "No idea. She didn't show up for Jules like she should've, but she seems different now. You'd know better than me, lover boy."

Cole pulled a handful of grass and tossed it aside. "She didn't tell me what she did to Jules. I just found out."

"She's probably embarrassed," Connor said. "You guys are good together. I haven't seen you this happy in a long time."

Cole stared at the headstone. Jules would've certainly had an opinion about all of this. He wished she were here now to tell him what to do. "She knows how I feel about lying. Maybe she and I are a mistake."

"Why, because she has a past? Do I need to remind you that you do too?"

Cole sighed. It was more than that, wasn't it? Or maybe it wasn't. Maybe he'd put Charlotte on a pedestal, and this revelation made her human again. He'd told her real love didn't have strings, but was he just blowing smoke? When it came down to it, did he actually believe women could make mistakes and still be trusted?

"Was it worth it?" Cole asked.

"Was what worth it?"

"If you'd known you were going to go through this—that it would end this way—would you still have built a life with my sister?"

Connor tossed the bottle aside. "You kidding? You know I would. Julianna was the best thing that ever happened to me. She loved me no matter what. And as much as it hurts right now, I wouldn't trade the time we had together for anything."

"I think she felt that way too."

"I hope so," Connor said. "I mean, look, man, there are no guarantees in life or in love. You know that as well as I do. All we can do is the best we can do. We can give ourselves completely to another person and they can stomp all over us or break our heart or die. But we learn from it and we move on. I mean, what's the alternative?"

Cole had lived the alternative. It was lonely.

Connor stood.

"What are you doing?" Cole got up too.

"Walking home," Connor said. "Jules may not be there anymore, but she's not here either. And at least I can still see her in our kids' faces. I owe it to them to pull myself together, and I owe it to her to make sure they never forget how remarkable their mother was."

"Jules loved you more than anything." Cole clapped a hand on his brother-in-law's shoulder, realizing in that moment that what Charlotte had done had been a huge lapse in judgment, but it hadn't ruined his sister's life, not the way Marcia wanted him to believe it had.

He owed it to Charlotte to hear her out.

Lie or no lie, he wouldn't run away just because life was messy.

Charlotte left the theatre and went straight to Cole's house, but his truck wasn't there and all the lights were off. She called him twice, but it went straight to voicemail, so she sent him a short text:

Let me explain.

But what was she going to say that would possibly justify not only her actions but her misrepresentation of herself?

Her stomach roiled. She'd brought this on herself. She should've been straightforward right from the start.

Knowing how Cole felt about honesty, she had a better chance of being eaten by a pack of wolves than she did of convincing him to forgive her, no matter what Hildy said. Maybe if she'd been the one to tell him it would be different, but Marcia had swooped in and ruined everything.

It would be easier on everyone if she left—but where would she go? Connor had agreed to sell her the studio. It was the whole reason she'd come. She didn't want to throw that away.

Marcia's words rushed back—*"I'll tell Martin to expect you on Monday morning."*

Did she dare?

How could she return to the ballet after all she'd been through? How could she pretend it was enough for her, that she'd happily marry her career, that she didn't want anything else out of this life?

She'd gone searching for more—for something she didn't deserve—and she'd found it in spades. She would never be able to pretend she hadn't.

And she'd never be able to pretend she didn't need Cole in her life.

But as much as she didn't deserve his goodness, he didn't deserve the pain she'd likely caused him by withholding the truth.

She had to at least try and explain.

She drove around town in a Honda Civic—her replacement rental car she'd picked up two weeks ago, looking for Cole's truck, praying for some clue of where he might've gone, and praying that he'd give her a chance to tell the truth.

Too little, too late.

The words turned to fear as they raced through her mind.

The night was dark, and it started to rain. She rounded a corner and stopped in front of the cemetery. Cole's truck was parked at the entrance.

She parked next to him, and the rain kicked up. She fished around in her back seat until she found her umbrella, a city-living staple.

Outside, the sky flashed like a strobe light and a low rumble of thunder rolled in the distance.

She hurried into the cemetery, eyes searching the darkness for any sign of Cole. Another flash of lightning and she spotted him up ahead, sitting on the grass, getting soaked straight through.

"Cole?" she called out as she reached him.

He turned. "What are you doing here?"

She stopped at Julianna's grave, the sight of her name on a headstone pulling every last bit of sadness to the surface. The last time she'd been here, it hadn't felt so final. There was fresh dirt and flowers and a tent set up for the crowd to stand under. But now—this was where her friend had been laid to rest.

"I came to find you," she said.

He stood.

"You're soaked." She tried to hand him the umbrella, but he refused it. He stood there, still in his tux, rain streaming down his face.

"I'm fine," he said. His cold shoulder had returned, reminiscent of the Cole she'd met her first day in town.

What did she expect? Did she really think he'd take one look at her and forget everything Marcia had told him? Did she think she could skate by forever without any consequences? She deserved his coldness.

"I'm sorry," she said. "I was going to tell you."

He scoffed, shaking his head. "When were you going to tell me?"

"Tonight," she said. "It's what I wanted to talk to you about. I didn't want anything to come between us."

"Like your shady past?"

Her eyes found the ground between them. "I'm not that person anymore, Cole."

He'd probably heard that a million times from Gemma. She knew convincing him to trust her wouldn't be easy with a past like his. But it was worth it to her to try.

"I didn't ask her to do it," Charlotte said.

"No, but you let her."

"And I've regretted it every day since. She deserved the best of everything, and I stole her chance."

He took off his jacket and slipped it around her shoulders, his white shirt turning transparent in the rain.

"Yeah," he said. "You did."

Charlotte realized in that moment she would've done anything to make him forgive her. Their future hung in the balance between them, and she was desperate to win his approval, to win back his love.

"Tell me what to do to make it up to you," Charlotte said. "I'll do anything."

He shook his head. "You don't get it, do you?"

She frowned. "I'm sorry, Cole. I wish I could take it back, but I can't."

He stood just on the other side of her umbrella, rain trickling through his hair and down his neck.

"I understand if you never forgive me," she said. "I deserve that."

He shook his head. "I already forgave you."

Her heart must've stopped beating. She must've heard him wrong. "What?"

"We all mess up, Charlotte. I've messed up—heck, even Julianna, perfect as she was, messed up. But I have to believe that everything happened just as it was supposed to, because what I said before was true. Jules wouldn't have traded this life for any other life—not for all the fame or money in the world."

A sob caught at the back of her throat.

"We don't have any guarantees in life that we won't get hurt." His tone turned husky. "But the risk is worth it to me. For the chance at being with you, I'll risk it all."

She tried to find her voice, but it was so small, so weak. Still, she managed to say a quiet, "You forgive me?"

As the seconds ticked by, Charlotte felt like she was waiting for him to decide her fate. His jaw twitched, and the rain fell, and somewhere in the distance a car horn honked.

Then, all at once, Cole grabbed the umbrella, threw it in the grass, pulled her body to his, and kissed her with the kind of passion she'd been searching for her entire life. His hands wound up through her wet hair, and he held her so tightly, it was as if he couldn't get close enough to her. He cupped her face in his strong hands, his kisses growing deeper and more intense until finally, she drew back, breathless and overwhelmed.

She found his eyes. "You forgive me."

"Of course I do, Charlotte." He pressed his forehead to hers. "You taught me to love again."

And as the rain fell, it washed away the past, making everything between them new.

And Charlotte whispered a silent prayer of thanks to her dearest friend, Julianna, who'd given up so much so Charlotte could live the life she thought she wanted. A friend whose sacrifice had led them both here, to a place of realizing that life isn't only about one thing. That you don't have to stay in the place where you are. That there is so much more to be discovered, and if you're willing to put your heart on the line, you can live full and rich and in the sweet embrace of unconditional love.

And that was something she'd cling to for the rest of her days.

His arms were familiar around her body, one hand on her waist, the other holding hers close to his chest the way he had so many times in rehearsal. They stood like that, a nearby streetlamp scattering light over them in a golden hue, and she realized they were dancing in the rain.

She lifted her chin and smiled up at him. "We're dancing."

He smiled. "All because of you."

She leaned into him. "I'll spend the rest of my life loving you, Cole Turner."

He kissed her so sweetly it almost made her cry. "I wouldn't have it any other way."

THE END

A NOTE FROM THE AUTHOR

Dear Reader,

When a pandemic interrupts your writing plans, there's a very good chance a book is never going to get finished. I confess, our very long quarantine of uncertainty did a number of my creativity. I spent a solid four weeks in *woe-is-me* world and wasn't sure I would ever come out of it.

And then somehow, I remembered that it's within the storyworld that I find the most comfort. Somehow, I found the energy to reopen *Just Like Home* on my computer, and what I found there were two characters who deserved a happily ever after.

And boy, was I craving one myself.

So, I wrote. And Charlotte and Cole and the good people of Harbor Pointe saw me through what has been one of the most challenging seasons of my life. And now, I get to share that with you.

It is my prayer that this story does the same for you— that it transports you away from your troubles and envelopes you in the charm, romance and wistfulness we all need a little more of these days.

I have loved creating this world, these characters and this adventure in Harbor Pointe—now four books long—and I'm so very thankful to each and every one of you who has journeyed with me.

Of course, I'm incredibly grateful anytime one of you leaves a review, shares my book with your friends or online or requests it from your local library. These little things really DO mean the world.

One of the things that makes me happiest is connecting with my readers. There's something extra wonderful about being able to picture you when I'm writing, and it truly makes me feel like the luckiest author on earth! I hope you'll find me online at one of the places listed below, and drop me a note via email at courtney@courtneywalshwrites.com

It would brighten my day!

With gratitude,

Courtney Walsh

    www.courtneywalshwrites.com
Join my Reader Room: https://www.facebook.com/groups/431426064247750

ABOUT THE AUTHOR

Courtney Walsh is the author of *Just Look Up, Just Let Go, Just One Kiss, If For Any Reason, Things Left Unsaid, Hometown Girl, Paper Hearts, Change of Heart,* and the Sweethaven series. Her debut novel, A Sweethaven Summer, was a New York Times and USA Today e-book best-seller and a Carol Award finalist in the debut author category. In addition, she has written two craft books and several full-length musicals. Courtney lives with her husband and three children in Illinois, where she co-owns a performing arts studio and youth theatre with the best business partner she could imagine—her husband. Visit her online at www.courtneywalshwrites.com.

facebook.com/courtneywalshwrites
instagram.com/courtneywalsh

ACKNOWLEDGMENTS

To Adam. Always and forever. Me + You. Thanks for not letting me give up.

For my kids. I'm so thankful you're mine. I don't consider being your mom a job, but if I did, it would be the best one ever.

My Parents, Bob & Cindy Fassler. So grateful for your love and wisdom in my life.

Charlene Patterson. Thank you for helping me make this book stronger. I'm so grateful for your wisdom.

Stephanie Broene, Danika King & the Tyndale team. For being amazing humans who just happen to be incredible at their jobs. I'm grateful for every day I get to work with you both.

Carrie Erikson. For always, always making me laugh.

To Natasha Kern, my agent. Thank you for challenging me to be better and write stronger. I am so thankful for your wisdom on this journey.

To Deb Raney. Always my mentor and always my friend. For all you've done to help me understand story—I am grateful.

To my writing friends, especially Katie Ganshert, Becky Wade and Melissa Tagg who tolerate my rambling voxes all day every day.

To Jenny at Seedlings Design for taking my vision and turning it into a beautiful cover for this book!

To the Readers in my Facebook Reader Room who helped brainstorm a title for this book (and who help me with research more often than they realize!)

To Chelsea Gallivan, for being the most inspirational dancer I've ever met. So thankful for your friendship.

To my Studio kids and families. For the support and joy you bring into my life. You are such a gift to me.

And especially to you, my readers. I hope you know how special you are. I hope you know that your kind words (either directly to me or via a review or social media) are so greatly appreciated. I hope you know that these stories are my way of sharing my heart with you, and I am so grateful to have that opportunity. You mean the world to me.

Sign up for Courtney's Newsletter

Don't miss the latest book news, freebies & more. Sign up for Courtney's email list at: courtneywalshwrites.com.

Return to Harbor Pointe...
AND FALL IN LOVE

Available now at bookstores and online.

Made in the USA
Coppell, TX
21 August 2020